The Walk

of the

Wandering Man

Ric Szabo

ISBN: 9781973467687 (paperback)

A catalogue record for this book is available from the National Library of Australia.

First published by Pytheus Press, 2017
This paperback edition published 2020

www.ricszabo.com

Central Europe, 5000BC

Prologue

The Ancestors, the boy had been taught, passed their memories on. Their joy could be so rich, their pain so deep, that traces carried through the generations. The feeling of having been somewhere before, or having events relived, bore clues. Take heed and they would let him know his calling in life, show him his true home. Heed not and there may always be a longing in the heart.

The more tedious the work, the more the boy thought of these things. Sickles and adzes had never felt comfortable in his grip, nothing like the bow or spears he practiced with. There was no stirring in his blood, no desire to put them to use.

It was mid-harvest, his sixth autumn and second away from home, and now he missed it more than ever. He had toiled in the fields since sunup, dragging his feet behind the woman, tying the stalks she gave him into bundles before carrying them to the girls on the threshing floors.

Sweat stung his eyes and the sticky heat made him itch all over. A gust of wind shook the crop and he straightened to let it cool his baked skin. Patterns flashed and swirled around him, like wind over water, reminding him of fishing the lakes back home with his father.

'Not long now, and we shall rest and eat,' the woman said behind him. He glanced over his shoulder and saw her smiling. The boy liked her because she chose simple words and spoke slowly.

She bent over, clutched another handful of stalks and sliced it cleanly with her flint-bladed sickle. As she held it out for him raised voices turned his head.

In the village the girls were bobbing up and down as normal, flinging grain into the air to let the wind take the lighter chaff, catching it on the way down in large, circular baskets. To their side, some men had gathered around a visitor.

'Ah!' the woman said, straightening. 'A friend has come.'

The visitor was doubled over with his hands on his knees, panting deeply and gasping out his words. He saw the boy and stopped talking. Voices stopped as head after head followed his gaze.

The woman's face turned grave. She dropped her sickle and hurried off over the freshly cut stubble toward the group of men. The boys around him stared after her, then an older boy shrugged and resumed reaping. One by one the rest followed his lead.

The boy had barely tied another sheaf when he heard his name called: 'Konli!'

He looked up and saw the woman waving her hands frantically. Again, everyone stopped working.

'Konli, here!' she cried again, but the boy froze, worried he'd done something wrong.

The woman broke into a run, fat breasts bouncing beneath her tunic. She reached him, grabbed his hand and hauled him tripping back to the village.

They hurried past men talking in low voices and entered a longhouse through a large doorway. They passed quickly through the stables and went into the main room where she grabbed a pack and began plucking dried meat and fruit from the shelves. Several men followed them in.

'Where am I going?' he asked, taking care to get the words right.

'This man will take you,' she answered, pointing to the visitor without looking.

'Why am I leaving?'

She turned around, laid a hand on each of his shoulders and looked him in the eye. 'You remember what I said about your father,' she said, 'and how strong men are prone to make enemies. Something has happened. Your father has – '

'Men are coming,' the visitor cut her off and glared at Konli with dark, unblinking eyes. 'If they find you, they will open your neck.'

Three days later the man arrived with his charge at the small, far-flung village of an old friend who offered his roof. Task complete, he left the boy there and then headed home, cautious in his choice of *villages he stopped at along the way. A day's walk from his own, he chose the wrong one.*

As his hosts bade him safe passage, men with darker intentions waited in the forest. They surrounded him quickly and a scuffle ensued, the man tried to flee and a recklessly fired arrow pieced his throat. As they crouched over him demanding the boy's whereabouts, he smiled with his last breath and spat blood at their faces.

There was one person on earth who could have answered them now. And that man was a simple farmer with a name seldom heard outside his own village, far from the wretched troubles of men.

Ric Szabo

Part 1

The Ancients

One

A young man ran alone through the forest, a spear in one hand and a spearthrower in the other. A braided headband, light running shoes and a loinskin draped over a thin belt were all he wore. A flint knife in a grass scabbard bounced on his waist.

It had been a rich summer; no longer could he pinch the skin of his belly and feel his fingertips connect. Long hunts and return marches weighed down by dripping carcasses had his fitness at a peak. He ran as if he floated on his feet, arms tucked neatly against his sides, his breathing timed to the rhythm of his legs. Light struggling through the tattered canopy cast confusing shadows over the tracks he followed, and yet his eyes missed nothing. Beneath a scatter of paw prints the press of his quarry's hooves was shallow now, the stride length shorter.

You are growing tired, yes? he thought. *Have you run from me before? Perhaps in your younger days, when it was you who was strong, and me who was weak.*

At length he heard faint yipping, much higher pitched than earlier. As he slowed to fit the spearthrower in place a clearing opened up before him.

Backed up against a blackberry thicket, the stag was making a stand. His thick mane was streaky and wet, and his muzzle swung low, bubbling froth and flinging strands of saliva. Outside the reach of his antlers several wolf-dogs held him at bay, snapping at the air with their backs bristling.

The stag wheeled on his feet. For a brief moment hunter and hunted locked eyes, and they saw each other clearly, perfectly, but the stag felt his years now, and he was heavy in the legs as the hunter drew his spear. A wolf-dog rushed in and snapped at the stag's hooves, the beast turned broadside and the hunter threw.

The spear found its mark with a dull thud. The stag reared up on his hind legs, clawing at empty air with his hooves. He came down off-balance and his eyes rolled white in their sockets as he roared in panic. A wolf-dog latched onto his hindquarters and forced him to his knees, and then, as if on signal, the rest of the pack fell on him, snarling through jaws clamped tight on his flesh and shaking their heads viciously. The hunter came in from behind, grabbed the antlers and wrestled his quarry down clear of the thrashing hooves.

'This is your last fight,' he said calmly, throwing a leg over the stag's shoulders and pinning him tightly, 'and it will be over soon. I will sit with you because you are scared. I am Vratu, take heart knowing that I am your friend.'

The beast stopped struggling. The heaving of his chest slowed and his frightened eyes stopped blinking.

One by one more hunters burst into the clearing. Exhausted faces broke into smiles as each man lowered his weapon and slowed to a walk, sucking in deep breaths. A man pulled the spear from the stag's chest, blood bubbled from the hole and the stag bleated sadly. A wolf-dog sniffed at the wound and was kicked away. Vratu rested his hand on the battle-scarred snout and waited for the dark eyes to cloud over.

'I saw when you missed,' a tall, finely proportioned man humoured him. 'Close your eyes next time, you will find it easier to hit something.' His name was Banan and he was their *Uru* – the clan's headman.

It was true. Earlier on Vratu had missed a doe by an embarrassing distance and had hoped it went unwitnessed. He stood and addressed a young man standing behind the small party.

'Where were you, Ilan?'

His best friend replied, 'You run too fast.'

Vratu slit the stag's belly open with his knife, pushed the brightly coloured entrails aside and cut open the diaphragm. He reached inside up to his elbows, made a cut here and there and pulled out the blood-warm, dripping heart. After biting off a generous chunk he handed the remains to his Uru and gave him a cheeky grin.

'So,' he beamed through a mouthful of meat. 'I see your spears,

7

and all are clean. Did no one else make a kill?'

'Why would we do that?' Banan replied as he took a bite. 'We knew you would.'

Stopping only to collect clothing and sleeping gear from their overnight camp on their way home, they followed trails said to have been made by behemoths long gone; through woods of oak, age-bent and bloated and covered in moss; through transitional admixtures of lime and ash and maple with grappling limbs and squeaking boughs, shaded by an unbroken golden canopy that swayed and sparkled in the wind.

The sun was strong on their faces when the first of their thirteen beehive-shaped dwellings appeared through the trees. The surrounding valley slopes glowed in the sun's rays and darkened the camp in its shadows. Wolf-dogs stretched out over the dust lifted their heads, raised their ears and pointed their snouts at the approaching party as it weaved its way past spits and tripods laden with drying meat.

The children met them first, surrounding the hunters in a tight mass and bustling for the best positions to poke at the body parts being carried. Vratu let the stag's head drop from his shoulders.

'Ah!' he cried. 'Who will clean my kill? Who will do my hard work?'

Behind the children came a band of women. Excited young mothers led, behind them marched the older and wiser, just happy to see their men return alive and well once more. Vratu's mother sat in front of her dwelling with a quern at her feet, pounding seeds into flour with a rounded pestle.

'Tell me of the hunt,' she invited as he passed.

'Have we had visitors?'

'No. Tell me of the hunt.'

'You saw how it went.' He reached the dwelling he shared with Ilan, opened the fur door-flap and ducked his head as he entered. Trophy horns and antlers hanging on the wall decorated what was little more than a pragmatic assemblage of twisted hazel and dried clay. The roof rose toward a smoke-hole above the hearth where he could stand at full height. He dumped his weapons and backpack onto a frayed reed mat, then stripped off his patchwork shirt and leggings and kicked them over to the wall. Wearing only his loinskin he returned outside and sat down on a log beside his mother.

'Where is Voi?' he asked.

'Where he always sits before dark.'

A little girl jumped on his back. 'What's that?' he asked, craning his head. 'I have a squirrel on my back.'

The daughter of Banan squealed in delight and hung on tightly. He disentangled her arms and sat her on his lap. Men sat down for a rest while women and children dragged the stag parts away for butchering beyond the camp perimeter in order to keep vermin from sniffing about at night.

Vratu turned toward a steep hill looming over camp and screwed his brows. 'What does your grandfather do up there, little one?' he asked. The girl said nothing, just put a finger in her mouth and sucked it.

Darkness always came quickly here in this valley of long shadows. Vratu settled the infant on her feet and gently prodded her on her way, then went to find his old friend.

Amongst their kind, few people lived long enough to see age wrinkle their skin. Old man Voi, however, had always been one of a kind. Health, shrewdness and luck had put him in good stead for longevity, an abundance of friends and a gift for softening his enemies had seen to the rest. Though his hunting days were over someone always put meat on his plate, though his body housed many ills someone always found the right herbs to add to his medicine. Yet even these were small charities for what he gave in return. It might be identifying unknown plants for the women, pointing hunters in the direction of clever game, or making simple words out of issues no one else could make sense of. Little in life was new to him anymore.

But when they had arrived at their winter camp, Voi did something he had not done in a long time. He took up a new habit.

9

And a new habit was a welcome thing for an old man. Every evening he dragged his ageing shell up the hill to this quiet spot overlooking camp to reflect on his long and wholesome life.

It had been a good life, one he was proud of. More and more lately he found himself dwelling on it. Sights that stirred his memory were getting more frequent, the melancholia that followed stronger. Old memories seemed clearer than new ones. Tracks at his feet might pass unnoticed, but not some unremarkable tree he had bent into a snare as a sapling when he was a boy. For a while he might wonder if it meant anything, then a stone would burst in the fires below, or a child's laugh would drift faintly to his ears, and he would ease himself back to the present and see treetops dancing in the wind, a sky painted by gods, and remind himself there was still much to enjoy in life. Sounds here were kind on his old ears, and he could hear Vratu coming long before he got there.

'What are you thinking, old man, when you sit up here all the time?' Vratu asked, settling down beside him.

'Old men's thoughts.'

'Tell me an old man's thoughts.'

'Look toward the camp of Iyanah,' Voi gestured with his chin, 'and tell me what you see.'

Vratu shaded his eyes. Beyond the fading hues of their autumn forest, the river that passed alongside their campground snaked out of sight. Far ahead along its banks lay the winter camp of their closest neighbour. On still days it might be revealed by a tinge of lazy smoke in the sky, at night a campfire might be strong enough to pulse like a star.

'I see an empty forest,' he replied after some time.

'Is that all?'

'Are you telling me the Clan of Iyanah is there?'

'They are there. Look again.'

After straining his eyes a bit longer, Vratu gave up. 'Now I am worried. If an old man has better eyes than me I will stop hunting and weave baskets.'

'You cannot see them?'

'No.'

'Ah, this makes me feel better. Before you came I was thinking my eyes are getting weaker still.'

Vratu looked at him puzzled. 'You cannot see them either?'

'No.'

'My mother said we had no visitors.'

'We have had no visitors.'

'Then how do you know they are there?'

'When I woke this morning my legs felt fresh, so I went for a walk.' Voi lifted his chin again. 'Over there. It was a good walk, a long walk. As it happened I arrived there not long after they did.'

'Could you not have just told me that?'

'And spoil an old man's fun?'

Vratu's frown faded as he eased back slightly. 'Did you see Nura?'

'I saw your girl.'

'She is not my girl,' Vratu corrected.

'No, not yet.'

'How is she?'

'You will see. Now that everyone is here they will have the Arrival-feast tomorrow night.'

'So soon?'

'There are signs of aurochs nearby,' Voi answered. 'Iyanah sent a runner to his brother's camp for more men. There should be meat by tomorrow evening.'

Vratu smiled with secret thoughts. 'There and back in one day?' he teased. 'You do well with your old legs, old man.'

Voi tore his eyes from the dimming scenery. 'How was the hunt?'

'Good. We have stag meat.'

'By whose hand?'

Vratu looked away, as if embarrassed. 'Mine. Are you coming down?'

Voi grinned, impressed by how humble the young man could be at times. 'Not yet.'

'Are you hungry?'

'It can wait.'

11

There was a pause as Vratu thought about this. 'Are you well?' he asked, not for the first time. 'Do you need medicine? I can look tomorrow.'

'Leave herbal lore to the women, that way I will not be poisoned,' the old man joked. 'But you can retrieve one of my fishnets in the morning, if you wish. It snagged again, and someone has to swim out to free it.'

They sat on in silence, enjoying the splendour of sunset. After a while Vratu asked, 'What are you *really* thinking, old man, when you sit up here all the time?'

Voi took his time to answer. 'This is my season.'

Vratu gave him an odd look and opened his mouth to say something, then changed his mind. Together they sat quietly, watching the last of the light fade into the horizon.

For dinner Vratu ate heartily of venison, berries, and some jam-coated biscuits his mother had baked from the seeds. He sat in the middle of camp with several others on a long log smoothed by generations of backsides, talking trivia. Children fell asleep on their mothers' laps while their older siblings chased each other around camp. After everyone had eaten they commenced discussion on their options for the morrow.

If they left around midday they would arrive at Iyanah's camp for the feast well before dark, which gave them the whole morning to attend to their own affairs. Autumn was a busy time for all and their stores were still short for what thirty-six hungry mouths needed over winter.

A woman complained that the fruit-bearing trees close to camp had been picked clean and they had to forage much further away now. Banan let them know that earlier on the hunters had passed a large stand of bilberries and blackberries close by that were overdue for picking. Perhaps some of the younger men could show them where.

An older woman then reminded them that most of their homes were in a state of disrepair. Making them warm for winter was more important than taking leisurely strolls through the forest. An elder then said that the levee bank they used as a platform for fishing could do with an extension. Both requests for assistance were returned with a transparent lack of enthusiasm. Having only recently arrived at their winter camp, the younger men pointed out, they needed to check where food trees may be ripening or where game habitually frequented. They could leave earlier than everyone else and assess the status of some reliable land pockets en route to the camp of Iyanah.

Vratu listened to their suggestions with sinking spirits. His preference was for hunting with friends or spending time courting his woman. Although there was nothing *really* stopping him from doing either, in his position he knew it was wise to be given approval first. And it sounded like he wouldn't get it tomorrow.

Two

The camp of Iyanah was overcrowded when Vratu's group arrived late in the afternoon. Everywhere he looked he saw slabs of meat being worked and cut, sinews detached, fat trimmed and spits prepared. He negotiated his way through the crowd, politely acknowledging each greeting or pat on his shoulder with a nod and a smile, until he came to a man sitting on a log with an infant girl on his lap.

'Too soon for you, brother,' the man quipped, 'to clutter up my home and steal food from the mouths of my children. Is Mother Ulke well?'

'Yes – she comes in the group behind.'

Sired by the same man, the half-brothers had little else in common. Vratu was sinewy and streamlined; Kihad was top-heavy and trunk-legged. Both had the broad faces and swollen brows typical of their kind, but Vratu's eyes were deeper set, giving his gaze a more thoughtful and intense quality. Wrinkles of mirth, friendly eyes and lips curled into a permanent grin always made his older brother the more sought after company.

They exchanged witticisms and updated news for a while. Vratu waited for the correct moment to ask, 'Where is Nura?'

'Hiding,' Kihad answered predictably. 'She heard you were coming and ran off with Iswahl.' He chuckled at his little joke as Vratu rotated his head in various directions. A little girl sprinted forward and threw herself into his open arms.

'*Buno*, little Nukul,' he greeted her. 'Where is your sister?'

'Over there,' she squeaked, bucking out of his arms and running off in the direction of the river.

Vratu sat down to wait. Occasionally he caught a stern look from tribal elders, reminding him that his behaviour was being monitored.

Nura's head appeared as she ascended the riverbank carrying gourds of water, and he stood to greet her.

Growing up, he never thought that the girl he had teased to the point of tears would have her day of reckoning. Each time he saw her some new curve or swelling had appeared on her figure to tease his imagination. Now she wore a short leather skirt cut in a way that exposed her thighs brilliantly, and her legs moved with perfect symmetrical balance. A necklace of clay beads hung over a short vest threatening to burst its laces should she draw too hard a breath, while a flat navel winked at him from her rippling, creamy white belly. Just as the flash of her eyes signalled she had seen him a light-footed young man stepped into view behind her.

Vratu tensed his shoulders when he saw them engage in talk clearly enjoyable to both. His lips curled into a snarl and he had to fight the urge to charge his adversary like a bull. She laughed out loud and he lurched forward.

'Vratu!' Nura greeted him happily. 'There you are!'

Head erect and body taut he closed the distance briskly, his face contorted into a grimace that was supposed to be a smile.

'Iswahl!' he greeted the young man with cool courtesy. 'What brings you here? Trying to make friends or following the smell of food?'

'Uh! Funny!' Iswahl smirked. 'Those were going to be my words to you.' He made a lazy gesture at the meat being worked around them. 'See what we brought back? If you behave we might give you some.'

'Are you not eating already? I thought you liked your meat raw.'

Iswahl guffawed. 'Ah, I longed for your company all summer, Vratu. It matters not to me what they say about you. My heart sings when you are here.'

'*Uh*, your voices are like the squawk of ravens,' Nura moaned. 'If this is all I have to listen to I am leaving.'

'Wait,' Iswahl reassured her through another chuckle. 'I think we are finished. Yes, my friend?'

Vratu ended the exchange with a grunt and let them resume their meaningless chatter without protest, confident she listened more out

15

of politeness than interest. His attention diverted to the newcomers, several of whom he recognised as coming from afar. One, in particular, always stood out. The man's face looked sculptured from stone, with a bony ridge overhanging deep, cavernous eyes. Muscle tone leapt into definition with the slightest movement, giving him an air of physical superiority few would care to test.

'Your uncle's face is unhappy as ever,' Vratu interrupted.

'Which one?' Nura asked.

'Uru Ukmaar.'

Iswahl said, 'Perhaps he has seen that you are here.'

Talking to her uncle was another man named Krul, an Ubren headman of the east who only ever bore grim tidings. An intuitive distrust had always kept him from fraternising with either man, an attitude that seemed mutual. Standing around them were several strangers.

'Who are those men with him?' he asked.

'Ubren of the east,' Nura answered. 'They came to see my father.'

'What do they want?'

'Go and ask,' Iswahl suggested. 'They will be happy to see you.'

Vratu sighed. 'You bore me.' He turned his back on their laughing and rejoined his brother.

The higher-ranking men were summonsed into Iyanah's dwelling for council, and some younger men started up an archery contest. Nura was called away to help prepare for the feast and Vratu took the opportunity to spend time with her family, doing his best to appear a worthy prospect.

By nightfall the smell of the feast hung thick in the air. The men emerged from Iyanah's dwelling with their noses lifted like wolves and headed toward fires that spat and flared beneath dripping chunks of meat. After dinner the girls disappeared into dwellings, followed by the older women who would see they looked their best.

Vratu joined Banan and Voi by their fire. 'You sat in council a long time,' he remarked. Neither man answered, just sat staring at the flames. 'What was the talk?'

Banan said, 'Council talk stays with council, Vratu.'

Vratu gave an offended grunt.

'Some Ubren are here,' Voi offered. 'They ask our permission to travel through. They spoke of troubles in the east that concern the People-of-the-Longhomes and some strong words were said. Krul and his cousins of the east are quarrelling again, which makes it hard to know the truth. That is all you need know for now.'

'There is always talk of the People-of-the-Longhomes,' Vratu reminded. 'Have we reason to concern ourselves now?'

There was another long pause. Around them people laughed and children squealed and wolf-dogs sniffed for titbits. 'We may,' Banan replied. 'Not you.'

Vratu felt patronised. 'I see. It would have made me yawn anyway.'

Roaring fires cast long shadows over the centre arena where several men were already seated and testing their drums, thumping the tightly stretched deer hides intermittently, a signal which served to hasten proceedings and draw the women back outside. The balance of the tribe came armed with an assortment of tapping sticks, bone flutes, pipes, rattles and bracelets, forming into an expanding ring and waving encouragement to the girls assembling in the shadows.

'Start the dancing, start the dancing!' children shouted.

'Not yet, not yet,' the girls called back.

As Vratu headed over he observed at the edge of camp the strangers he'd seen earlier, fidgeting with their packs as they prepared to depart. They moved quietly, and he could see their demeanour was heavy. He walked over and a tall, brawny man noticed him approach. In the glow of the firelight the man looked tired; his cheeks sagged and his eyes hid some lingering hurt.

Vratu nodded in friendly fashion. 'Where are you from, friend?'

'Uryak,' the man answered tonelessly.

The name made Vratu instantly wary. He spared a moment to ponder the appropriateness of probing him further. 'You are leaving early,' he said.

'We have a long walk ahead and our families wait in the dark.'

17

'Our women are fine dancers.'

'It will be some time before we will enjoy dancing again.'

Vratu watched each man closely. *These men mourn,* he thought. They shouldered their belongings unenthusiastically and their backs bowed under a weight far greater than what they carried.

'Where do you go?' he asked.

'Your leaders tell us of lands to the north where we will not be unwelcome,' the man answered. 'We will begin again there.'

'You do not return home?'

The man stopped fidgeting. 'They keep our story from you, yes? This is wise. I would do the same.' He turned his back and began walking away with his men, into the waiting darkness.

'Friend!' Vratu called after him. 'Do you run from something?'

'Talk to your headmen,' the man replied over his shoulder.

Vratu held up his hands appealingly. 'They tell me less than you.'

The man stopped and turned around. He looked past Vratu to where everyone else had gathered for the dancing and something he saw seemed to make a difference. He bowed his head and spoke in a wounded voice.

'There are no words for what we run from. It is a curse that covers the skin like something that lives and plays games to see who will live and who will not. It cannot be fought with weapons or medicine. People-of-the-Longhomes bring it with them, then they finish what it does not. So we go with what is left of us. Their gods are stronger than ours, Illawann man. Pray they are more merciful to you than they were to us.'

They could have been ghosts disappearing into the dark. No one but Vratu watched them go. Everyone either stood or sat in the centre of camp and not one head was turned any other way. *So be it,* he thought. His own leader had advised him such things were not his concern.

He found a free space in the ring and sat down. A howl went up and the girls surged into the circle. Melted fat shone like honey on their skin, covered where needs be by tightly laced skirts and vests stripped at the fringes to make them shimmer and come alive.

Necklaces of teeth, shells, bones and beads bounced in rhythm to painted tassels, quills, downy feathers and rabbit tails sewn onto their vests.

They formed into two equal lines and synchronised to the beat of drums and sticks. Their feet pattered the earth and their legs lifted in unison, some older women began to sing and the volume increased threefold when spectators joined in the chorus. The song was popular and a favourite for dances; the story of a girl with magical powers of seduction.

Vratu slid to the front and glued his eyes on Nura, and as he sat tapping his sticks he compared the beauty of the dancers with his gruff company of men, with their hair unkempt and stubble growing like moss over their cheeks, and felt his smile broaden. Not another thought was given to spiritless men fleeing the troubles of their homeland. All that mattered to him was when he would have his woman, and how happy they would be.

The father of Nura slept with one eye open that night. He knew his eldest daughter well. And sure enough, in the feeble light of dawn, that one eye caught a glimpse of her fingertips on the door-flap as it closed soundlessly back into position. He rose quickly and nudged it open in time to see her duck into the dwelling of his good friend Kihad.

Iyanah accepted this begrudgingly. She would snuggle into Vratu's bed and lie in his arms harmlessly until morning. This was permissible. They might not sleep, but they needed privacy for anything else.

But it served as a timely reminder that he needed to give serious thought to Vratu of the Clan of Banan. And he was troubled. The young man's behaviour was too presumptuous, completely lacking in humility. He was still a long way from ready. Today, Iyanah decided, he would speak to higher authorities.

The family head slipped back into bed and relaxed his guard. The next thing he knew his wife was standing over him, prodding his ribs with her toes. 'Enough with your laziness. Even the sun is up.'

He dressed and went outside. People were up and about, seated before fires, picking their teeth after breakfasts. The family of Kihad were quickly accounted for but to his disappointment neither Nura nor Vratu could be seen. He saw Kihad talking to a group of men and reminded himself that it was not someone else's responsibility to keep watch over his daughter. He walked briskly over to Kihad's dwelling and put an ear to the door-flap. Nothing.

'Nura!' he called.

He heard faint rustling from inside, followed by: 'Father?'

'Come outside and help your mother.'

'All right.'

'Now!'

'*Yes.*'

Nura emerged with her tunic ruffled and loose. Iyanah shot her a look of disapproval and walked off, missing the tongue she poked out at him.

He walked over to Banan eating breakfast nearby and sat down beside him. Vratu emerged from Kihad's dwelling and gave the two headmen a cheeky grin as he headed over to where Nura sat with a group of girls. He sat down amongst them and launched into a speech that seemed to require a raised voice and the wild waving of his arms.

'Look at him,' Iyanah grumbled. 'Does he think they will kneel at his feet?' Banan smiled and stayed quiet.

For a while Iyanah tolerated the spectacle, but the sound of the girls suddenly bursting into laughter was too much. 'Come,' he said. 'It is time we had words with Marhala Wunn.'

They went over to the dwelling of their tribal shaman and Iyanah called from outside. On receiving the invitation to enter he pulled back the door-flap and followed Banan inside, where dried hides and stuffed animals bore evidence of its tenant's rich animistic religion.

Their medicine man was hunched over a bowl of berries, picking at the better ones. He lifted his brow-heavy face slowly and brushed a wisp of grey hair from his eyes. Seeing who it was, he sent his wife away with a short wave of his hand.

The two adolescents had been a regular topic of discussion lately and only an update was necessary. Marhala Wunn listened

20

respectfully to everything Iyanah said before asking, 'Does he trouble you?'

Iyanah searched his thoughts. 'At times I am uneasy with him. Too often no one knows where he is or what he is doing. He seems to prefer hunting alone, and though he might return with a kill he leaves the place bare for anyone that follows. His smile does not come easy and his laugh never lasts long. This boy I find hard to see into.'

'He is a fine hunter,' Banan said. 'He would provide well for your family when you are old and feeble.'

'My family needs more than a fine hunter.'

'My father speaks highly of him,' Banan added.

'True. And for this reason alone I have made allowances.'

Marhala Wunn asked, 'Have they obeyed the Waiting?'

'I think so,' Iyanah replied. 'She is not in seed.'

'Is your daughter happy with him?'

'She speaks little of anything else.'

Marhala Wunn scratched the grey stubble on his chin. 'They have been behaving like this since last winter, yes?'

'I suspect earlier,' Banan answered, 'but I have seen nothing to make me believe Vratu has been without respect.'

'I agree with what Iyanah says,' Marhala Wunn summed up his thoughts. 'There is still much we need to see of Vratu and we will do our part, lest we are all made fools of. But for now,' he said, fingering his berries, 'I will talk to Nura.'

Iyanah left to find his daughter and returned with her shortly after. He sat down and left her standing by the door with a frightened look on her face.

'Nura,' Marhala Wunn said, 'you are drawing attention to yourself.'

The colour of her cheeks deepened as her gaze flitted about.

'How is it between you and Vratu?'

'Good . . . I think,' she stammered.

'Is that all?' He saw her blank look and elaborated: 'Have you joined with him?'

A frown appeared on her face. 'No.'

21

'Have there been others?'

'No,' she answered with dignity.

'What do you want of him?'

Nura sought help from her father with a silent look.

'Could you be happy with him?' Iyanah asked.

'Yes . . . but what – '

'You can go,' the shaman excused her. She relaxed and exited quickly. 'When do you want to go back?' he asked Banan, stuffing a handful of berries into his mouth.

'Tomorrow,' Banan replied. 'Today we hunt south.'

'Take Vratu with you,' the shaman said through a full mouth. 'When you come back, bring him to me and we will have a Sit. Then we shall see.'

All morning Vratu sensed something in the offing. Elders talking in hushed tones cut their voices short when they noticed him watching. The discussion between Iyanah and Banan about hunting strategies and which wolf-dogs they should take was without its usual flair of disagreement, as if it hardly mattered. With this congenially sorted, Banan came over and told Vratu his participation in the hunt was required.

Given the scant attention to detail, not surprisingly the hunt failed. The wolf-dogs picked up a spoor late in the afternoon and the younger, inexperienced of the pack outran every other leg in pursuit and vanished far ahead. Vratu was too preoccupied to devote his full attention to the task and lagged alongside the next slowest hunter.

Leaving the wolf-dogs to find their own way home, Banan and Iyanah terminated the hunt, for which Vratu was grateful. They arrived back at camp at dusk and he watched Banan speak briefly with Marhala Wunn. Vratu dropped his weapons next to his brother's dwelling and nodded loosely at his sister-in-law in greeting. Then he sat down, pulled a burin from his belt pouch and passed the time retouching some arrowheads that needed an edge.

Elders disappeared into the forest in small groups while Banan stayed in sight watching him, playing the role of conspirator perfectly, building up the effect. Anxious for support Vratu looked out for Voi, but it appeared the old man had headed home already.

The wait was short. Banan came over to him, thoroughly enjoying himself. 'Come,' he beckoned with a finger. 'Your shaman is waiting.'

A well-trodden path guided them through the fading light. Spider webs stuck to their faces and bugs orbited about their heads. Vratu felt both excited and nervous. Without knowing what he was in for he assumed it could only be a shamanic ritual, which usually meant some form of pain and humiliation for its subject.

In near dark he spied the twinkle of an orange beacon which led them to a rocky overhang. The elders were sitting in a semi-circle around a small fire beneath it. Banan put a hand on his shoulder and steered him over to the fire. 'Sit down here,' he said pleasantly.

Vratu complied and all was quiet. He looked over the elders with their thought-creased faces and patient eyes, and felt himself shrink. Banan grinned and disappeared into the darkening forest.

A fat beetle hummed into the cavern, made a slow circle and smacked into a wall. Marhala Wunn followed it in, amulets and holy bone necklace rattling against his chest.

'Let me tell you about a man you might know, Vratu of the Clan of Banan.' His voice sounded amplified within the cavern walls. 'When he goes hunting his quarry hears him coming. The river is murky when he looks for fish. His arrows never fly as straight as they should, his spearheads are brittle and his bowstring snaps when he takes aim. The weather turns foul when he is a long way from home. He hears what he wants to hear, sees what he wants to see and blames his misfortunes on everything but himself.' He paused for effect and raised his eyebrows. 'Is this man you, Vratu?'

'No.'

'No?' Marhala Wunn began pacing back and forth. 'This man. . . would he be what he was, if he could see what he was?' He let it sink in before resuming. 'Let me tell you a secret. Unless you can show me a man who never misses with his arrows, or finds beasts whenever he steps into the forest, this man is all of us. We all struggle – some more, some less. How must we look to gods with all the answers?'

23

Vratu sat there dumbly. This, he thought, could only be the leadup to punishment.

Marhala Wunn stopped in front of him. 'So where does that leave you, young friend?' he asked, drilling him with his winter-grey eyes. He kneeled down close enough for Vratu to smell his breath.

'Listen carefully to me, Vratu. We have been where you are now. We have made the same mistakes, blundered down the same path. Look closely at these men around you, men of the same beginnings. Tired and old, sitting on a mountaintop, seeing every place and every person they have ever known below; where they have been and where they are going. Seeing people like you and wondering how to reach them. But it is a big mountain, a high mountain, and our voices are not always listened to, even if they can be heard. Young men are the worst,' he sighed. 'They waste their ears.'

Vratu wondered what the elders were thinking. Was this treatment standard, or unique to him?

'Are you a man that listens, Vratu?'

'Yes.'

The shaman looked confused. 'Oh? How can this be so? You – who cannot obey a simple instruction to leave our daughters alone?'

Vratu slouched submissively and dipped his head to avert the shaman's glare. 'This is not so easy,' he mumbled.

'This is because you are not ready.'

Vratu glanced at Iyanah. Until then he had given little thought to him as a father-in-law, certainly less than he had given to Nura as a possible wife. But now, moved by the occasion and his auspicious role within it, he found himself willingly accepting both. 'I am ready,' he said boldly.

'What makes you think you are ready?'

'My being here.'

A snigger rippled along the row of elders. Marhala Wunn rose with a scowl, and yet there was the twinkle of mischief in his eyes, as if this was all part of a setup.

'I will tell you the story of two young men,' he said. 'Equal in all ways, the best of their clans – good men, fine hunters, loved by everyone. Their people argued who was the better man, and who would make the better leader, but they could not decide, so they had the two men brought before a wise and respected elder. And the elder asked them, "Are you true to our laws?"

"Yes," they both replied.

"Do you honour our gods?"

"Yes," they said again.

"Do you respect your elders, obey their words? Do you trust them, put your faith in them?"

"Yes, yes, yes . . ."

"As you would put your faith in me?"

"Yes."

"Come," the elder said, and he took them into the forest. They came to a large pond and the elder pointed to it and said, "In this pond swims a fish, and you must catch this fish. But you cannot use your nets or hooks or spears or arrows." Then he held up a hood. "Even more, you must go into the water with this hood over your head and catch this fish with your bare hands."

And the first man said, "But this is some kind of trick, yes?" And the elder assured them it was no trick. "What madness is this?" the first man cried. "It cannot be done! How are we supposed to catch a fish with bare hands and no eyes?"

"Nevertheless, it must be done."

The first man said, "Then this is a test for fools, and only a fool wastes his time on such nonsense," and he strode away in anger.

But the second man said, "I do not understand the purpose of this task. I fail to see how it can be done. But you are our teacher, and I will do as you say."

'So he put down his weapons and placed the hood over his head and waded into the pond. He reached out with his hands and felt nothing but water. He splashed about everywhere, he thrashed with his arms and grabbed at emptiness. He became disheartened and sad, but he did not stop. Day and night he splashed to each end of the pond, throwing himself everywhere, and yes, once or twice he felt the swish of a tail, yet never did he put a hand on it. He kept going

25

and going until he became so weak he thought he would drown, and he waded out of the water and lay down on the bank where he began to sob.

'But then he thought he could hear something – a flutter like the wings of a bird. He followed the sound until it was at his feet, and he kneeled down and felt with his hands and *yes* – there was the fish, flapping on shore. Quickly he threw himself over it and grabbed it with both hands, and he danced and wept with glee until he thought he would burst with happiness. Then he heard the elder, who had been there with him the whole time, speak. "Take off your hood."

'The young man obeyed and saw how dark was the water in the pond, so stirred up that no fish could possibly breathe in it.'

Marhala Wunn squatted down in front of Vratu, so close that their faces almost touched. The ancient eyes buried into his and Vratu leaned backwards. '*This man,* is ready,' the shaman whispered. Then he stood up. 'Which of these men are you?'

Vratu found his voice. 'I . . . don't know . . . what you – '

'Want?' the shaman finished for him. 'What you are really asking is why you are here. A fair question. To answer that, let me tell you why these men are here.'

The shaman's voice went soft and Vratu thought he heard sadness in it. 'If the gods are just we will pass from this earth long before you, Vratu,' he said, raising his arms toward the elders. 'When a man has spent his life protecting his people from the perils of today he wants to know they will be protected from the perils of tomorrow. We want to know our grandchildren will fish the same streams of our youth. We want to know the songs we sing by our campfires will be sung by our people generations from now, in the same places, with the same smiles on their faces. Our greatest fear is that we might fail, that we entrust this task to those incapable of delivering it. Our greatest happiness comes in knowing there are men ready to take our place.' He sighed. 'We live through our sons.'

Vratu nodded dutifully.

'I hope my words do not make you yawn, Vratu of the Clan of Banan.'

26

The words felt like a slap in the face. Vratu watched nervously as the old man reached inside his vest and pulled out a piece of folded leather.

'Take this.'

Vratu took it from his outstretched hand.

'Put it over your head.'

Vratu's heart sank as he unfolded a hood. He slipped it over his head and braced himself for pain.

'Wait here,' Marhala Wunn ordered. 'Do not take the hood from your head. Do not sleep. Do not move. Do nothing.'

He heard feet shuffling away and had to fight the urge to ask where they were going. Soon he was left with nothing but a crackling fire and a silly hood over his head.

Surely, he thought, the fun must now begin. From somewhere came the soft chirr of a nightjar. This bird should have left these parts by now. Perhaps it was part of the conspiracy.

'Am I to catch a fish now?' he enquired aloud. He tilted his head this way and that, like a bug using its antennae. All was quiet. He shifted his backside in anticipation of a long wait and yawned idly, consoled by the thought that some initiation rituals could be far worse than this.

There was still time for that. He had no doubt he was in for much more before they granted him the right to marry.

The night passed slowly, the men never returned. His toes tingled, the ache in his back swelled with every breath and his backside turned into one large bruise. Every muscle protested at its configuration and it became harder to resist the temptation to unfold himself, or stand and stretch his legs, or at least take the hood from his head. Occasionally he extended a leg or raised a buttock but for the most he sat as directed.

The fire died and the autumn chill crept into his bones. Perhaps this was to test if he would freeze to death, he thought. And there were other perils. Every snap or rustle sent icy panic through his veins and nervous moments would pass before he could attach the sound to something other than a wolf or bear or monster of myth.

As the night wore on he became sleepy with exhaustion. His head started pitching forward, further and further each time until it became too heavy to hold upright. To make his weight less punishing he shifted his centre of gravity, his backside went mercifully numb and he let his head fall to his chest and stay there.

Much later, more delirious than asleep, he thought he heard the sound of approaching footsteps. He shook himself wide-awake and raised his head. He felt a hand on his scalp and the hood lifted away. A faint glow in the sky flushed the darkness from the forest. Banan appeared in front of him, grinning broadly.

'*Buno,*' he said.

'Now my eyes hurt as well,' Vratu complained, squinting repeatedly. Everything looked blurred.

'How was your night?'

'Cold. Can I go now?'

Banan chuckled, 'Yes.'

'Where are the others?'

'They left some time ago. You go back and rest.'

Vratu stood and stretched, howling as his muscles uncoiled and the kinks in his spine cracked free. 'What did I do wrong?' he asked, massaging the small of his back.

'Nothing,' Banan reassured him. 'You did well.'

'What did he want?'

'Uh! I don't have the mind of a shaman.'

'Is this what happens with everyone?'

'Not always. For everyone it is different.'

'What do I have to do now?'

Banan shrugged. 'There will be more things, but don't ask me what. I wouldn't tell you even if I did know.'

They walked along the trail and Vratu felt better with each stride. 'Ah, that feels good!' he said happily, shaking the soreness from his limbs and joints.

'Were you scared?'

'Why would I have been scared?'

Banan smiled. 'Speak the truth.'

Vratu gave him a depressed look. 'I only hoped the wolves would finish me before the cold did.'

'You were safe,' Banan said. 'We were watching you.'

On returning to Iyanah's camp, Vratu went straight to his brother's dwelling and collapsed into a dreamless sleep inside.

He rose around midday and learned that a hunting party had slain a woodland bison, and a group of women and boys had gone to help butcher the carcass into transportable pieces and bring everything home. Nura and the shaman were amongst them and so he thought to wait. He wanted to see them both before returning to his own camp, particularly the shaman.

He was worried about Voi. Worried that his old friend's spirit was abandoning him long before his health deemed it should. It was a common condition amongst his people, particularly the elderly. Grieved by a traumatic event, like the loss of a loved one or ones, a person would slip into a comatose sleep from which they never woke. The recent loss of his lifelong and only wife had made Voi a changed man, more reclusive than ever, ambling about with head down and with little appetite for food or laughter. Those who had successfully willed themselves to death displayed identical symptoms.

Later that afternoon the hunters and porters returned, bloodied and bent beneath chunks of dripping flesh carried on their backs, or dangling from poles between pairs of shoulders. Another joyful reception followed and Vratu thought this might mean another feast and them staying another night, but those left in Banan's group voted to head back and take their share with them. The shaman disappeared into his dwelling with a few men and Vratu was again denied his opportunity. When Nura approached he greeted her with modest restraint, mindful of those watching.

By the time the shaman's meeting broke up the shadows were lengthening and Banan's group was keen to go. They made their farewells and Nura gave him a strong hug. 'I will come again soon,' he promised her. Then he went to get it over with.

He saw Marhala Wunn talking with a visitor named Imruk. The man's wife sat closeby with a small boy on her lap, a little further away their two little girls chased a feather the wind had caught. The lines of anxiety on the woman's face had Vratu instantly curious. He wasn't alone; several women were also watching them, he noticed.

'Vratu,' one of his companions called from behind. 'We're leaving.'

Vratu acknowledged him with a hand signal and walked close enough to hear the men's voices.

'He cannot run with the other boys?' Marhala Wunn asked in his brusque voice.

'No,' Imruk replied.

'When was he born?'

'Two winters ago.'

'You had to carry him here?' Marhala Wunn asked. Up to a certain size a child could be transported in grass-woven baby-carriers slung over the shoulders; a boy this big was expected to walk.

'Sometimes he walks, sometimes we carry him,' Imruk answered.

'Stand him up,' Marhala Wunn instructed, and kneeled before the boy. Imruk's wife did as she was told. 'I have forgotten his name,' he added.

'Nusol,' she answered.

The shaman clicked his fingers. The boy blinked but the lustreless eyes remained unresponsive. 'See how his eyes are like small stones. And here – ' Marhala Wunn touched the boy's forehead ' – the shape is wrong.'

Both parents watched quietly. Marhala Wunn made a 'V' with two fingers. 'Nusol, how many fingers is this?'

'No,' Imruk replied. 'He does not understand.'

Marhala Wunn stood and tousled the boy's hair. Imruk flicked a finger at his wife, who had gone completely still and was staring into space. 'She wanted to hear it from you,' he said in a sombre tone.

'It will get harder the longer you leave it,' Marhala Wunn advised her. 'It should have been done already.' He looked up at the sky, grey as smoke. 'Winter comes.'

Imruk took his son by the hand. Without a word his wife began pounding hazelnuts with a stone, not realising she missed her mark every other time. The faces of people watching turned sympathetic when they saw Imruk leading his boy into the forest; others politely looked away.

Marhala Wunn saw Vratu watching and his face flashed with annoyance. 'What do you want, Vratu?'

Vratu thought for a moment. 'Never mind.'

He joined his group as they made to leave. 'Wait,' he said, stopping them with a hand gesture toward Imruk and his son. No words needed to be said; at a glance every one of them knew what was happening.

After waiting respectfully for a short period they followed them into the forest single file along the same path. The trees closed around them and Vratu saw Imruk and his son appear briefly a short distance away, heading in another direction.

They returned home in the early evening. Vratu did a round of his snares closest to camp and found a stoat necked in one. The meat wasn't the best, but meat was meat.

He took it to Voi's dwelling and invited himself inside. The old man was seated at the hearth, carving a pattern into a bison horn. His craftwork was legend. It was said it had turned the hearts of their hardest enemies soft.

'I talked with the Ubren that were at your council,' Vratu said as he sat down and offered up the stoat.

Voi took it and turned it over in his hands, feeling its weight, smoothing its fur. 'He is old,' he said. 'Winter comes, food is scarce. He took chances, new trails . . .'

'And poked his head where it should not have been poked.'

Voi picked up a knife and made a slice around the heel. 'Only to eat what he could.' The lines deepened on his forehead as he focussed on his work.

Vratu picked up where he left off. 'They came from Uryak.'

31

His mentor said nothing. Vratu sighed. This was going to be a struggle, again. Voi had rare knowledge of Uryak, having grown up in the area as a boy. But every time someone tried to ask him about those early years, his words dried up.

'Why did they leave their homeland?' Vratu pressed.

Voi made several more cuts before answering, 'Things are happening there we do not understand.'

'Was it for the same reason you left Uryak all those years ago?'

'I was only a boy when I left with my father,' Voi skirted the subject. 'I was too young to understand what was happening.'

'What happened to those you left behind?'

'We do not know.'

But Vratu knew this was more an incomplete truth. A long history of reliable rumours suggested that the People-of-the-Longhomes had eliminated them. 'Who are these people that can so easily force men from their homeland?' he asked. 'All I hear are whispers. Where do they come from?'

'East,' Voi answered, attacking the stoat a little more vigorously. 'How was it?'

'How was what?'

'Your Sit with Marhala Wunn.'

Vratu shot him a frustrated look but let it rest, resolved to continue the elusive topic another day. 'It would have pleased me to see you there,' he said instead, adding mood to his tone.

'You weren't there to be pleased. You were there for the elders to see inside you, to learn what they do not know. I have no need of this.'

A moment of silence passed as Vratu looked him over warmly.

'What did he get you to do?' his old companion asked.

'Sit with a hood over my head all night,' Vratu grumbled. 'I don't know what he wants.' He waited until it was clear Voi wasn't going to respond. 'So?'

'So?'

'What does he want?'

'Ah!' Voi grinned lopsidedly. 'That's not fair.'

'You are as bad as them.'

'That's not fair either.' Voi sliced a stubborn piece of fur from a tendon. 'Vratu is not fair tonight.'

'Are you going to help me with this?'

'With what – a wife?' Voi chuckled softly. 'It is you who should know who is right.'

Vratu sighed miserably. 'What happens now?'

'Wait and see. A shaman's words you can follow, even if his purpose you cannot.'

'Now you sound like him.'

The muscles of Voi's forearm bunched tight as he gripped the fur and pulled. It ripped away from the carcass with a sucking sound and caught at the head. He picked up a hand-axe, hacked it free and tossed the mess to one side. 'You will do the Walk soon.'

'I know I will Walk soon; that's not what I'm asking.'

'What are you asking, then?'

'Nura and I are good for each other. What more do people need to know?'

Voi brushed away a piece of fluff that had stuck to the naked pink carcass. 'To take a wife is always a sensitive matter, and you've made it harder by choosing the niece of Uru Ukmaar. This man has powerful connections amongst the Ubren and the man she marries will come to their attention. Nura is highly valued and your interest in her is not taken lightly, especially when your blood is Illawann and hers is Ubren thick.'

'My dwelling is ready for her.'

'But can the same be said for Vratu of the Clan of Banan?' Voi asked with a chuckle.

'Not you, too,' Vratu lamented. 'Why do you laugh at me?'

'You never had much patience, and now you have no choice. You squirm like a chick in its nest, begging for its mother,' Voi responded with amusement. 'We will see the dance of Vratu and his woman. But first you must go through what every young man goes through. Just do your best.'

Vratu decided to ask him something that had been on his mind

33

for a long time. 'You're not fond of her, no?'

The creases in Voi's face lengthened. 'That is an odd thing to say,' he replied. 'I was right. Vratu is not fair tonight.'

'Everyone tells me what a fine choice I made. Everyone but you.'

Voi gave the carcass a final brush over. 'The fondest memories of mine, are those left by my Lupu. You deserve the same.'

His hands paused, his eyes glazed over and Vratu knew it was time to leave. Voi's darker moods had a habit of being contagious.

Vratu stood. 'I will go now.'

The old Uru blinked and he was back, but the sad vacancy left by the woman he had spent his life with remained in his eyes and voice.

'You deserve the same,' he repeated, and tossed the meat into a basket.

Three

The sun grew lazy. Plants wilted and shrank, gold turned brown. Leaf by leaf the forest roof fluttered down, unharvested nuts and fruits bounced over the fresh spread. Vegetation untangled, distance showed through the trees and the sky grew overhead. Birdsong went quiet, replaced by bitter winds that moaned through empty crowns and hanging limbs and gnarled branches clutching at wet air. Clouds fattened and sank, unloading rain and drizzle that swelled their streams into unfordable nuisances. An array of brightly speckled fungi burst from logs that crumbled to the touch.

The forest shut down, but its people did not. Vratu spent his days chipping stone into axe and arrowheads, or twisting bast into nets, or whittling dogwood and wayfaring shoots into arrows, or binding wicker into fish and eel traps until his vision swam and calluses grew on his fingers. He pierced holes in bivalve shells and fish vertebrae and made a necklace for Nura, he decorated his weapons and artefacts with naturalistic engravings, carvings, or schematic patterns. For respite he took to the forest, sometimes hunting, sometimes prospecting for flint, slates, or the rare piece of obsidian, sometimes for no other reason than to escape the bickering endemic of people living side by side for months on end. Careful not to make it too regular a habit, he visited the camp of Iyanah. With remarkable restraint he successfully fought the urge to sneak Nura out of sight; in any case whenever the opportunity presented itself there was the inhibiting thought of her mother and father, and their uncanny presence of mind, alert to the occasion.

A visit from another clan saw him happily change his routine. There was laughing and haggling and trading, and now and then some girls found an excuse to do a bit of dancing. There was celebration in the form of games and pranks and fathers dancing around camp holding their tightly wrapped newborn aloft, there was grief in the form of parents staring water-eyed at the funeral pyres of children wasted away by infection and mystery horrors.

The temperature dropped and the snows came, first in delightfully short bursts that inspired frolic and games, then in more serious falls that drove people into their homes. For long days and nights, in front of a burning hearth, they turned their hands to craftwork and waited for it to pass.

Marhala Wunn woke to the sound of children squabbling outside. He rose from his warm bed and warmer wife and dressed. By the time he had flung the door open, primed to unleash his temper, Nura was there to make the peace. In one hand she gripped the wrist of a small boy, her other hand was raised threateningly above a boy of similar proportions cowering beneath her.

'Give it back!' she ordered. A small boar figurine appeared magically in the offender's hand. 'Did he have it first?'

'Mine!' was his brazen reply.

'Did you bite him?' The youngster glared at her with eyes like a bear cub. 'Did you bite him?' she repeated, sterner this time.

'Mine!'

Marhala Wunn grinned and returned to bed. As he listened in amusement to the muffled efforts of Iyanah's daughter, his thoughts began to twist and turn in the manner of his profession.

He had been monitoring Nura of late, and was impressed. She would make a good mother, but like Vratu, was she *ready?* It was time to move ahead on the matter. Soon Nura's father would ask for him to do just that. Signs in people were easy to read; those of gods were a different matter. He would have to go looking.

The two boys responsible for waking him up, best of friends again, flung snowballs at him courageously as he left camp. The shaman ignored them. Already he was deep in thought. The snow was receding and no longer sucked at his foot, gaps in the clouds showed a deep blue sky behind. These were good signs.

A few steps beyond the last dwelling the wilderness opened up at his feet. A few steps further and he found what he was looking for.

There in the snow he could see the prints of a mouse followed by some sort of cat, probably a small lynx. He had seen many prints about the camp – mostly small mammals topping up their winter fat – but it had been a long time since he had seen active engagement. He crouched down to inspect the find. Where another man might see a cat after a mouse, a shaman saw much more.

The simplest sign of animal carried a message. If he debated a decision the wink of an owl might mean approval, the inverted climb of a nuthatch disapproval. A raptor heckled by a mob of smaller birds might be a warning. A carnivore might eat a certain grass or fungi to let him know it had medicinal value. Even the plant spirits helped. A plant might bend in a manner to show him it was medicinal.

Their friends of the forest, of course, were purer than men, more intimately tuned to the rhythms of nature. People were too impulsive and prone to mistake.

Small creatures running around after each other were a sign things were getting back to normal. The bad weather had broken. The signs he had seen of Nura lately had been good. The signs he had seen of Vratu had also been good.

A few more days and it would be his time.

It came on a typically freezing midwinter morning.

Vratu sat warming himself by the fire. As he poked at the embers contemplating what to do on this miserable day, he saw the medicine man walk into camp ahead of a party that included Kihad and Iyanah. It was their first visit since the bad weather had broken and Vratu assumed it to be nothing more than that.

Then he saw how serious they were. They approached with the deportment of a party in mourning, a secret bearing down on him. Children backed away and people stopped talking. Vratu stood. Marhala Wunn stopped in front of him and aimed a crooked finger at his face.

'It is time for you to walk with the Earth Spirit,' he said.

Everything went quiet. Vratu turned toward his mother and saw a flutter of a smile appear on her face and a look he sensed was part pride, part fear. Water dripped from her gourds and landed with an audible splat at her feet.

Vratu walked over to his dwelling. Inside he found his thick body belt with pouch attachment and double-checked that the pouch contained his essential travelling gear – a retoucher for giving his flint blades and arrowheads their edge, extra microliths for his arrows, a blade scraper, flint drill and chisel, a sliver of bone for punching holes in hides and picking his teeth, a spare bowstring of twisted bast, several pieces of twine and sinew to mend the seams of his clothing and bind arrowheads. To these he added his fire lighting equipment – a lump of iron pyrite, a flint core and a supply of dried tree fungus in an airtight mollusc shell.

He replaced his everyday belt with the body belt and pouch, and tied the gathers of his leggings. He tucked in his loincloth and tied his dagger and scabbard to his waist. Into his backpack went an empty birch-bark container, a scarf, his split-hafted hand-axe, an arrow-shaft smoother, and a generous piece of dried venison.

Next, he put on his thigh-length winter pullover with hood. A bison blanket compressed neatly with a length of sinew, which he tied to the bottom of his backpack. To one side of his kit he secured his quiver tight enough to not bounce and checked the open end was drawn tight. Satisfied all was in order, he hefted the load onto his back, put on his mittens, picked up his trusted bow and returned outside.

Marhala Wunn gave him a lazy nod. Vratu reassured his mother with a carefree smile, then scanned the camp for Ilan and Kihad and saw both grinning ear to ear. No one said a word as he left the camp.

Young men reacted differently to the command. Some despaired, some took it as a matter of course. Vratu had actually looked forward to it. For years he had rehearsed it over in his mind. A little over a two-day walk was his chosen destination. Many times had he hunted there and he knew the lay of the land intimately.

At a short distance downstream he crossed the weir of a beaver dam and from there entered the winter forest, damp with moss and lingering mist. By midmorning the woods opened up and he shuffled onto patches of steppe with drab-coloured herbs poking through the snow, then he was back into various oak complexes and towering beech woods with their open vistas of tall, straight trunks that made passage between wonderfully brisk.

In creeks tufts of snow bobbed along with the current, icicles dripped from the underside of the banks, and rushes and sedges swayed under a chilly breeze. Each crossing required him to strip off his footwear and leggings and lunge through the icy waters with his bundle held high, his legs turned numb and his manhood clenched tight as a fist.

By late afternoon the low-lying cloud hung bloated and the air had a snow-making edge to its chill. He arrived at a gully named Birdsong and located a cosy fissure in the sedimentary rock. In a corner of the small cave he found several bundles of dry wood, thoughtfully left by the last person who stayed there.

In the fading light, he searched a while for browse marks on trees and found nothing. On returning to his cave he lit a fire and silenced the growl of his stomach by nibbling on a few morsels of dried meat and some edible fungi he had gathered. He felt good. The first day was over, there were many more to go. Consistent with tradition, he had his mind set on being gone for a full lunar cycle. This would be long enough to impress them all.

Silence draped over the forest as he watched it dissolve into blackness. The air thickened with chill and he tightened the blanket around his shoulders, wondering what manner of beasts lay behind the eyes that were surely watching him.

'I have come for your secrets,' he whispered.

For all his presumed connections, the shaman was only human. He made as many mistakes as any mortal, although his were more often conveniently overlooked. His weather forecasts were no better than anyone else's.

Late in the night the wind picked up, the fire flared and Vratu was torn from sleep by grit and sparks stinging his face. Muttering profanities, he crawled forward until his head popped out in the open. Snowflakes settled onto his upturned face.

'Oh, go away.'

All night he drifted in and out of sleep, waking constantly to spasms of shivering and icy gusts that sent snow and ash around the cave in a mad swirl. Around dawn it all stopped and a heavy, tired silence settled outside. He gave up on sleep and sat sulking until light thinned the darkness, revealing a bloom of lumpy snow within the roofless mist.

The path he wanted to take that day would lead through open woodland and steppe, exposing him to the full force of the elements. But, he reminded himself, the Walk was always going to be a test of mind and muscle. The rules were few and simple. He could not seek assistance. He had to be gone a respectable period of time. And, most importantly, he was not to be seen. Failure to comply with any of these conditions rendered him liable to doing it all over again, which would delay his coming of age and his right to take a wife. The Winter Grounds were still too close for his liking.

So he collected a few coals from the fire, wrapped them in a cradle of damp moss and placed them in his birch-bark container. He wrapped the scarf around his neck, gathered all his gear and what remained of the wood, and crawled out of his cave.

A bitter wind started blowing and heavy flakes sifted through the empty crowns above, swelling the path until it disappeared. Hidden obstacles stubbed his toes, turning numb from the cold despite the insulating layer of grass padding inside each boot. A steady plod kept his blood warm until finally, in the afternoon, the oak and ash became stunted and more spread out. He had reached the edge of the Grasslands.

This leg would take him the rest of the day. Though visibility was poor Vratu's path was ahead, would always be ahead, and turning back was not an option. He tightened his cape, tucked his chin into his neck and pushed on.

Out on the steppe the temperature plummeted. Strengthening wind whipped loose snow from his path and into his face, relenting just long enough for him to take hasty bearings before starting over again, hiding landmarks and turning his walk into a blind stumble.

The blizzard intensified. His face felt bruised and numb and he had to keep rearranging his scarf in order to keep only the thinnest of slits for his eyes. No markers aided his sense of direction now; all he had to steer by were his last footprints and instinct. If not for the odd shrub thrashing wildly in the snow he would have lost all sense of perspective.

'The weather turns foul when he is a long way from home,' he recalled the prophetic words. A tickle of panic urged him to move faster. Frostbite rode the wings of this blizzard, and he feared it might already be nibbling away at his numbed extremities.

At one point the ground dipped and levelled off, offering an easier march. He tucked his head down and had only taken a few more steps when there was a crack beneath his feet and a heartbeat later he was thrashing about in freezing water up to his waist. By the time he had hauled himself out of the marsh and back onto firm ground his garments were stiff with ice and freezing water trickled down the inside of his leggings and sloshed at his feet. When he removed a mitten to drain the water inside all that fell out were a few feeble drops that cast solid and flew away with the wind. His bare fingers tightened so hard with cold that he feared the bones inside might crack.

But he knew these marshes. He was way off course.

His leathers scrunched at the elbows and knees as he resumed his march. His feet turned so numb he couldn't feel his footing, his teeth shivered so violently they felt like they were working loose in his gums. Cramps clutched his neck and the ice congealing on his clothing refused to brush free. Whichever way he turned seemed to point him into the full force of the blizzard.

Exhaustion and cold and pain narrowed his consciousness. His world had been reduced to a dimensionless white oblivion, kept that way by his mind's suffering. And now the numbness was moving up his legs, confusing the effort he put into each stride. Perhaps he relied on some inherent sense of direction, but for the most he simply put one foot in front of the other and let his weight drag him wherever the blizzard offered its least resistance.

– *Do you see me, Illawann Man?* –

He stopped and raised his head. Grains of ice hit his face like a lashing of thorns and he had to clamp his eyelids closed. He bowed his head and staggered forward. 'How can I see anything in this mess you put before me?'

– *Then you are not looking properly* –

'What would you have me do?'

– *Make a snow break, dig yourself in. Curl within your warmth as the creatures do. Nothing walks here now* –

It was tempting. He had been taught such tricks of survival and even tried them once or twice. But not under conditions as appalling as these, with his clothing this stiff and heavy, or as damp and cold on the inside, or his fingers, toes and nose so frozen he thought they might snap and break away.

He lifted his head to the heavens. 'Why do you fight me? Am I not friend to the beasts and the forest?'

– *But I am friend to all of you. I make the fur thick, the nose keen. I destroy the weak, spare the strong. I made your forefathers what they were; I make you what you are. With each generation I better your kind* –

'I know what you are doing.' His foot slid and he stumbled to his knees, his hands shot forward and his arms sank into the snow up to his elbows. 'You think I am weak, but I am prepared for you. I have climbed as many hills as would reach to the sun, run so far as to take me to the ends of the earth, with my legs turned to stone and my lungs on fire.' He stood wearily and stumbled ahead. 'Though my skin is soft I wear the hides of friends at home in the cold. See how they walk with me now.'

– *Put less faith in your furs. I slay beasts now with fur thicker than yours* –

'This is true. But I have other help.' He gritted his teeth as he spoke. 'Do you see? I *have* been here before. Not in this lifetime, perhaps. My forefathers walk with me too; you know who they were. They live inside me.' And with these words came a burst of renewed energy that made every muscle, fibre and tendon strain beyond its potential. His legs steadied and he walked straighter now.

'I think we will talk again when this is over.'

And so he clung to his abandoning reason by rambling nonsense into the wind and concentrating on the mechanical movement of his weary legs – foot forward, still, next foot forward, still – driven more by stubbornness than any preconditioned constitution.

As if in a dream, he saw woodland appear from the depths of the white haze, like the blurred resolution of logs beneath the surface of a lake. The sight rallied the last of his reserves and he picked up his pace, feeling the gradient rise beneath and trees press in around him.

Still he lost his way and had to backtrack several times, and then at last, guided by blind luck as much as memory, he found what he was looking for. The chasm yawned out of nowhere and he let it suck him inside, into its violent vortex of snow and ice, and now his strength left him and a great weight brought him down, and he had to crawl the final distance on his hands and knees. Had the snow blocking the mouth of the cave he sought been a finger width higher he would have missed it altogether.

Like a mole he burrowed his way inside and collapsed. A breath or two later he forced himself upright and shored up the hole he had slithered through with snow, leaving only a small space to let the light in. He stripped off his wet clothing, wrapped himself in his blanket and somehow directed the energy of his violently shaking blue hands to the business of assembling a fire and landing a spark from his pyrites into a tuft of tinder. Before the cave filled with smoke completely he opened a hole in the windbreak just large enough for fresh air to clean his lungs.

Darkness settled as he curled like an unborn child in the warm womb of the earth, shivering and gagging on smoke, his fingers and toes feeling as if they'd been crushed under a rock. The wind howled and prised its icy claws through the gap, but safe and warm now he fell into an exhausted sleep.

Four

Day and night were lashings of wind and snow intent on wearing down the rock protecting him. Each morning he stumbled into the blinding maelstrom to renew his supply of soggy firewood, or look for hazel he twisted into a pair of snowshoes and bound up with strips of bast. Finally the blizzard gave way to solid sheets of sleet. The heavens were mocking him, he imagined, spilling ice-tears of mirth.

'You see? We talk again,' he mused. 'I am still here and soon the sun will smile on me.'

By the time he woke to patches of glorious blue beckoning him from afar, he was truly hungry. Prey had had the good sense to stay hid, he had eaten all his dried meat, and scrounging through snow for wisps of edible herbs was poor foraging strategy. It was time to leave.

'You are trying to send me home early, yes?' he addressed the clouds as he strapped his new snowshoes on tightly. 'You want me to appear unworthy in front of my people, yes?' He stomped on the ground a few times to test his new footwear. 'But I am not going home, not yet. I think you have tried too hard. I will show you.'

The frigid air kept the snow hard and his feet moving swiftly until midmorning when the haze thinned and the sun broke through the smear of high cloud, making the snow shine so brightly it hurt his eyes. Tendrils of rising steam danced about his feet as they sank deeper into the softening snow, so powdery in places that he sank to his hips. Anything with an edge snagged his feet, the bindings on his snowshoes loosened and one or two hazel rods actually sprung loose. Each clumsy step convinced him that there was no way he could get to his original destination now. It didn't matter. He had a new one.

Early in the afternoon, with the sky stretched blue from end to end, he arrived at the eastern margin of his tribal lands: the River-of-Heavy-Fish. As he'd predicted, it had completely frozen over. This was as far east his people usually ventured. The other side was a troubled place, a land of evil origins and evil spirits, where one felt that every thicket or meadow of tall grass hid rogue bands of Ubren warriors obsessive about border protection.

But this did not deter him now. The deplorable conditions would keep them close to their camps, he reasoned.

'See what you have done?' he spoke to the sky. 'See this bridge you have made for me? Now I do not have to walk so far.'

He kneeled and scraped aside the crusty surface snow, then hacked at the glazed ice beneath a few times with his hand-axe to check its thickness. Satisfied it would take his weight, he distributed himself evenly on all fours and began crawling across, thumping the ice beneath him with his hand-axe as he went, the words of his shaman following him all the way: *'Are you a man that listens, Vratu?'*

On the far bank he stood, straightened his aching spine and brushed himself down. Lands of the Illawann were behind him, lands of the Ubren were in front. He set off for his new destination at an eager pace.

Upon reaching the first fork he turned upstream and followed the tributary through a lightly wooded plain until a series of hills named Crumbling Rock rose on both sides. The snow here was not as thick and the protection offered by the sheltered ravines should be attractive to game seeking refuge from the abysmal conditions.

As dusk fell he picked the most accommodating of the overhangs that pocketed the base of the shaly hills and lay down hungry and tired beneath his furs without lighting a fire. It was his sixth night away, he had eaten only a few mouthfuls of dried meat and fungi, and he wanted no living thing to know he was there.

The light had gone out of the buck's eyes by the time Vratu caught up. The feathered end of his arrow stuck out two hand spans from its chest, dark blood spilled from its mouth and melted the snow.

It was late afternoon of the following day and he had won. He savoured the moment, letting the thrill build up inside him. It had tasked him to get this far, it was true, but now it was done and here

45

was enough meat to last his entire stay. Nothing would be wasted from this animal. The pre-digested mash of the stomach was rich in vitamins. The bladder was a water gourd. Antlers and bone could be turned into weapon heads, fur made into clothing. Stomach and intestines could be dried and used as bindings and cordage, hooves boiled down could be glue for his arrowheads. He might even make a comb for Nura out of the shoulder-blade, or tassels out of the whiskers and hair.

His whole body felt lighter now, his limbs nimbler. Giddy with success he clenched both hands, lifted his arms high and began hopping around on his feet.

'Haha!' he howled to the heavens as his dancing intensified. 'Do you see me now? Look what I have done! This is not so hard! This is not so hard!'

He kneeled and made a series of precise cuts with his knife, reached inside the belly up to his elbow and pulled out the steaming heart. It was a good heart, a strong heart, and he devoured it quickly, feeling stronger with each mouthful. When he shouldered the carcass after wiping his bloodstained hands in the snow, he thought he could feel a difference in the weight.

'See what I have now?' he addressed the heavens. 'Send me your snow and ice, I am here, I am not going anywhere. This time it will be me laughing!'

Looking forward to his first proper meal in days, the buck a welcome weight on his shoulders, Vratu was halfway back to his camp when the first of the wolves found him.

He caught it at the corner of his eye. The hideous black brute regarded him with an eerie expression of calm as it hunched in the snow, its tangled winter hide ruffling in a light breeze. He let the carcass drop and looked for others.

'There is nothing for you here,' he said. 'Go back to your friends and leave me alone.'

He gathered up the buck and resumed his walk. The wolf followed, pink tongue flapping. Though not entirely alarmed there was an edge to Vratu's walk that moved him slightly quicker now.

Once or twice he dropped the carcass and rushed the wolf, which loped away a few steps and waited until he turned his back before resuming pursuit.

In this stop and start manner he arrived at the overhang and assembled a fire. The wolf settled down patiently a stone's throw away. Once the fire was crackling Vratu picked up a rock and stood. The wolf took to its feet as he threw, the rock smacked into its hide and it sprinted away with its tail tucked between its legs.

'Next time it will be an arrow!' he yelled. He skewered a few chunks of venison and set them up over the coals. His mouth watered at the smell of cooking meat and he had to fight the temptation to pick at it while raw.

Night settled in, the chill seeped through his leathers and a light screen of cloud hid the face of a gibbous moon, three nights from full. When his meat was almost ready he leaned forward to adjust the skewers and saw just beyond the rim of firelight a ghostly shape glide past.

It disappeared before he had really seen it. He stood and stoked the fire, sending a plume of sparks into the roof. Light stretched out a bit further and yes, there it was again – a different wolf to the one he had seen earlier. Then there was another, and another. He picked up a skewer and took a bite.

'Mmm,' he cooed cheekily.

At the edge of the light the wolves squatted down on their haunches. One by one their company trotted out of the darkness, weighted down by shaggy fur and yet light on their feet. Their frames were poor, shadows within shadows, but hunger spilled from their eyes with frightening menace. Hoping to extinguish the mouth-watering smell he buried the skewers into the snow, but still more of them came, eyes gleaming and mouths drooling, dipping and raising their noses.

He picked up a flaming branch. 'Go, before you feel the tip of my arrows!' he shouted, swinging the branch and leaving a trail of sparks. The wolves gnarled and retreated, then crept forward as soon as his back was turned.

The night laboured on. A stiff breeze blew up, the screen of cloud scattered and light from the brightly waxed moon gave the prowling wolves an ethereal silhouette. Closer and closer they crept, darting side-to-side and poking forward to test his reflexes. Each time he shouted and bore down on them with his torch they merely backed away and new wolves took their turn. Hunger no longer clawed his stomach, only sick, lumpy waves of fear.

Deep in the night the huge black brute reappeared.

In the waning firelight Vratu could see every detail; upper lip raised and quivering, froth dripping from polished fangs and a tongue swinging like dead weight beneath. It paced back and forth, swivelling at each turn without taking its wicked eyes off him. From somewhere came a blood-curdling howl, followed by the rest of the pack pointing their snouts skywards and uniting in chorus. The sheer volume agitated the air; blood sped through his veins and charged his muscles with the high of adrenalin.

The wailing rose to a crescendo. The fire was much weaker now; dying flames licked over the coals and its reach of light over the paw-trampled snow was shortening. There was no alternative. Cursing loudly, Vratu picked up the carcass with both hands and slung it over the advancing pack.

They caught it mid-air; a hoof or two at most touched the ground. There was an explosion of screeching and howling and clashing teeth, and a bristling swarm grew in front of him like a single organism, ripping into itself and flaying particles of snow and fur at his feet. Slowly it swirled away into the blackness like mist, taking the yelping din away with it.

But there were too many wolves. It looked like the pack had gone nowhere. The big black brute flicked its head toward the carcass being fought over, as if in contempt, then turned its attention back to Vratu and resumed its calculated gait.

Vratu grabbed a branch from the fire. Yellow flame sputtered weakly from the tip as he thrust it in front of him. 'Do you think I am weak and puny?' he shouted. 'Do you think I would be here if I had nothing to match your teeth? Have none of you ever felt our spears or arrows?'

Still the black wolf did not yield. Side-to-side it went, faster now and coming closer with each pass. Vratu snarled and shadowed its mechanical pacing.

Enough was enough, he decided. Before the fire died completely he would teach these wolves a lesson on the authority of men. He dropped the branch, quickly fitted an arrow to his bow and pulled back until the microlith rested alongside his forward grip. Under the strain of full draw he held his breath and tried to maintain the correct poise, but his nerves were so much on edge he could hardly hold the weapon steady. The arrow tip danced lightly as it followed the ghostly impression of his target.

The wolf did not respond. It glared at him with a face akin to human expression, and in that short space of time Vratu felt their minds fuse.

He lowered the bow. 'I know you, brother hunter. Leave me be, the meat on me is as foul as on you.'

The wolf stopped and faced him. The head dipped and both ears flattened against its skull, there were a few hesitant steps, a coiled hunch, and then it sprang.

Vratu dropped to one knee and quickly drew his bow. Everything slowed in his eyes as he chose his mark in the fleshy part of the neck, away from the thick bone of the lowered cranium.

The wolf was only a leap away when he released. The arrow stuck fast in the furry throat, the wolf yelped and contracted inwards, neck twisted as it snapped at the protruding arrow. Vratu sidestepped, grabbed the glowing branch and stabbed the beast as it ran around the cave.

The wolf fled yelping and Vratu kicked snow after it. 'You see now!' he screamed. 'I have a bow, arrows and fire!'

The wounded wolf disappeared from sight, shaking its head violently. At the limit of Vratu's vision a wolf nosed the fresh blood. One by one they all vanished, leaving him poised with his smouldering branch crackling in the silence.

The breeze flung another patch of cloud across the moon. The

49

silvery edge of the trees disappeared, beyond the fire-glow the shadowed dimples of countless paw prints merged into darkness. He returned to his cavern, stabbed the stick into the coals and stood to attention with bow and arrow in hand.

From out in the blackness there suddenly came a vicious yipping and tortured screaming. The sound was unlike anything of earthly flesh; an ear-piercing shrieking that rose and fell with the agony of life bursting from its lungs. As Vratu felt the hairs rise on his skin he wondered if the sound might have been his own had things gone differently.

The screaming died and all that filled his ears now was the crackle of embers, the thumping of his heart and the heaving of his lungs. The fire went out and left a scanty base of embers. Vratu left it at that. The cold wind didn't bother him; the last thing his senses allowed was feeling for the chill. Armed with his bow and arrows he stood vigilant all night, his muscles twitching ready for action.

The wolves never returned. At the first glow of dawn he took the opportunity to snatch a bit of sleep.

The tinge of the sun was strong in the trees when he woke. He stepped from his cavern into a paralysed stillness and followed the trail of dark red droplets through the snow. A short distance from the overhang he found what he was after. A head, some vertebrae and a few pieces of scattered fur were all that remained of the black wolf. He hacked the head from the tattered remains and returned to his cavern.

In deep thought he sat chewing on a strip of venison he retrieved from the snow, staring at the face before him. And the wolf stared back, opaque eyes half-closed and tongue poking out in a macabre gesture of mockery.

With his meagre meal in his belly he extracted the wolf's canines with his knife and packed them away. He gathered his gear, kicked the fire dead and ascended the far side of the gully to its highest point. There he gazed southeast waiting for the haze to lift, but the hills he tried to see stayed shrouded in mystery.

'Uryak,' he said out loud.

Was there a light breeze on his back, an invisible hand nudging him that way? Did a strange, top-heavy sensation tilt him forward?

'Do you beckon me?'

The foothills and lower reaches of those far-away hills should be teeming with quarry driven down from the colder highlands, he reasoned. There were numerous caves offering shelter, he had been told. He looked behind and down, into this haven for deranged wolves. Something was not right here. What he had witnessed the night previous was a bad omen.

Down the hill he went, headed to a place he had heard so much about, but never been to.

Five

All day he walked, surrounded by ghostly trunks and drooping limbs and mist that crept through the forest in waves. Not once did the sun break through. For direction he relied on an inborn compass, imprinting subtle rises and dips of the land into a cognitive map he would call upon on his return. In front of a small fire that night he ate what precious little remained of his venison without further cooking, having decided not to push his luck two nights in a row.

At first light he was on his way. Around midmorning the ground tilted beneath his feet and he could see fir-freckled hills disappearing into the cloud above. He followed a frozen creek until the first of the slopes bowed into each other, and there began his climb.

By midafternoon he had scaled the foothills and reached the first of the intervalley slopes protected from the biting northerly wind where he found a passage that led him past a series of collapsed boulders to a cavern roughly three man-lengths deep and shoulder height. Other than scaling a near vertical rock face the only way to get there required a deftness of foot that wolves and bears seemed reluctant to test. A majestic view settled the matter. The uppermost reach of the firs stopped only a footstep or so from the edge of the rock face, over which he could see the mantle of forest stretching ever-onwards.

He built a healthy fire and placed a generous supply of damp wood to dry beside it. Protected from beasts and the elements, and with a strong fire to keep him warm, he had his best night's sleep since leaving his people.

Then the drizzle came down. For days it fell, turning pathways into depressing quagmires. For the better part of each day he stumbled and slipped through the slush setting traps and snares, turning over fallen logs and breaking into hollows, grovelling on his hands and knees to scratch and dig at any cavity that might hide some slim picking, with incessant pangs of hunger reminding him how desperate his predicament had become. All he ate during this time were a few pieces of fungi, some bracken and silverweed, and a sleeping hedgehog plucked from the roots of an old oak.

He fashioned a windbreak from brushwood and branches big enough to shield him from wayward winds and keep his fire secret. He polished the wolf's teeth until the enamel shone like snow, drilled a hole through each and added them to his necklace to sit proudly amongst his deer teeth and mussel shells. Each night he checked his weapons, retouching arrowheads or straightening shafts that had begun to warp.

But he saw nothing to use them on. Hunger had shrunk his stomach and a vitamin deficit expressed itself in a craving for herbs nowhere to be found. Short climbs left his head feeling dizzy and his lungs labouring for air, bones had risen beneath his skin and his garments felt like they had grown. Every joint ached, his nose dripped continuously and his lungs felt tighter than ever.

Rarely had he stayed at so unfriendly a location. It was little more than a snow-drowned gully of shifting mists, a starving silence where anything that moved cowered in air pockets hidden from the eye. This was a no-man's land. The only hint people ever passed through came in the form of an abandoned campfire littered with microliths and bone fragments. Campfires of the Ubren he suspected, several months old. They knew better. Never would they seek refuge here in the depths of winter.

On a bleak morning several days after his arrival, he emerged from his cavern and examined the sky. Light from a lifting sun paled the thick cloud. He coughed and spat into the snow. Today, he was going to hunt elsewhere. Keeping the hills tall on his left he would follow the creek he had come in on and head south, all the way if needs be to a mighty river Voi had once taken him to a long time ago, far upriver. His people called it the Great River. Others called it Blue Waters. In later times they would call it the Danube.

As the morning progressed a breeze blew up. One moment he was walking in sunlight, then mist floated in from nowhere and he was enveloped in a clammy drizzle.

By midmorning his pace had halved and his wheezing over what should have been easy ground had him worried. He diverted from his path and climbed a hill to get his bearings. At the summit he sat his weary body down on a rocky outcrop for a welcome rest and looked below. A snow-coated forest stretched out over the plain as far as the eye could see, broken here and there by folds of low hills. Hidden behind one of those hills, he hoped, was the Great River.

A patch of drizzle descended, thin drops swirled in the gathering breeze and pattered against his hides and cape. A rainbow appeared and he let the spectacle take his thoughts away from his aching limbs and groaning stomach.

All at once he became aware of a soft tapping sound.

It was so faint he may have been listening to it for some time without knowing. He angled his head and heard it drifting weakly through the muffled silence, a steady rhythm that changed volume according to the strength of the breeze on which it rode: the sharp report of stone on stone.

His sharp eyes quickly homed in on an unnatural break in the forest canopy; the sort of break that bore the mark of human hands. He stood and descended the slope.

Now he was the hunter again, navigating by sound and moving in bursts, hastening when the sound was clear and far away, easing off and softening his footfall whenever it went weak. A peculiar marking in a tree trunk drew his attention. A deep groove encircled the trunk and dead branches lay around the base. Above, sagging limbs and boughs thinned into bone-like fingers that seemed to claw at the air in agony. Now he could see around him several more patriarchs of the forest treated in similar fashion, and as many mossy stumps poking from the earth nearby.

The ringing came back to him, louder and clearer. He resumed his course.

Soon he could hear the sound of wood chopping. It was strange to hear this familiar sound again, to be returned to the world of men. He edged closer, keeping to the shadows until movement caught his eye.

Two men passed before him hauling a tree trunk. He waited for them to pass before following at a safe distance. The tapping became louder and he heard human voices. Smoke found his nose. Something large and symmetrical appeared ahead and he quickly diverted to a tree and peered around the trunk.

Three men stood in front of a fire. Thickly set in garments, they looked little different to his kind. But Vratu knew what he was looking at. These could be none other than the People-of-the-Longhomes. Strange people from distant lands, talked about behind closed doors. People he suspected he might come across.

Behind them stood the huge rectangular frame of what could only be a place of living in the making. Even incomplete it had a scale unlike any man-made thing Vratu had seen before.

'Their homes are as long as a tree is tall,' he recalled the accounts, *'with walls straighter than arrows. Many trees make one house, and it takes many hands to put them together. Men and beasts share the space within; of both there are many.'*

A pair of men with large hammers stood on each side of a tree trunk taking turns hammering a stone wedge into a split running lengthwise down its middle. Blow by blow the wedge disappeared into the crack, splitting the trunk further. After several strikes they stopped and moved further down, leaving the wedge in position. Another wedge was inserted into the crack and the process repeated.

It was a confronting sight. Well did he appreciate the skill required to work trunks and limbs into these precise proportions, the hands and muscle needed to raise it and fix it all into position. Glimmers of wonder flashed in his mind and he weighed the benefit of making contact against a passionate urge to set the whole thing on fire at first opportunity.

Compelled to see his mission through, he slipped back into the forest and resumed his southerly course. A path trampled bare by countless feet led him past an escarpment. He climbed to its highest point to see what he could see.

The last time Vratu had seen the Great River he had felt a deep reverence. A howling wind had turned the surface into rolling whitecaps, waterfowl had been so densely huddled in the shallows that the river there had disappeared. The image contrasted so strongly to what he saw now that he feared magic might be toying with his senses. Not once had he heard of the Great River freezing over, nor had he expected it to be now.

And there on the far side, well above the riverbank to protect it from flooding, was the village. From where he stood he counted at least five longhouses lined up parallel to one another in a northwest-southeast orientation. Smoke trailed lazily from escape holes in the rooves.

He walked down the hill and stopped at the river's edge. A small skin-hide canoe sat nearby with a rope attached to the prow piled beside. Freshly heaped snow lay against the hull and drag marks showed straight as an arrow over the ice toward the village. Several animal tracks meandered across, daring him.

The far bank was one he had never put foot upon. He stood there for a long time, gazing at it as if seeking inspiration for his next move. Once or twice he put his foot on the ice, but never did he leave the bank.

The sky greyed over as he headed back.

'They do not live with the forest as we do. They fail to feel its fortunes or its sufferings; fail to nurse it when it is sick. They change it to serve their needs, take from it without giving back. They break it into pieces, leaving sores that do not heal. The wounds they make stretch far beyond their villages, and their smell comes not from the world we know. And so the forest retreats around these people like night around a flame.'

Sitting on the ledge of his cavern with his blanket wrapped tightly around him, Vratu stared into darkness, turning suspicion into fact. On returning to the Hills he had checked his snares and traps and found nothing, but this did not bother him as much as his newly acquired reasoning for the absence of game here where it should have been. Under normal circumstances he might blame it on natural phenomena, after all it had been a harsh winter – the worst he could recall – which would have scattered his quarry or sent it into hiding. A divinely inspired imagination might attribute it all to the whim of gods. But not this time.

These people were to blame. He kept going over what he knew of the People-of-the-Longhomes, regretting now how little this was. Stories that filtered through to him over the years served more to demonstrate his people's ignorance than relay reliable information. As yet they were no hindrance to his way of life and interest was sparked only when passing bands stopped by bearing hearsay.

He looked up at the stars. 'Why have you led me here, to a place made sad and empty by the People-of-the-Longhomes?' he asked aloud. 'This is their work; they leave me nothing. What would you have me do? This was our land and I have the right to be here. I am listening but your voice is not clear to me.'

His voice seized up and a coughing fit rattled his lungs. 'I know I am bound to forsake what belongs to men,' he rasped once his breathing was restored. 'So I will be fair, if you will be fair. I will wait another day or so. If my stomach is still empty then, I will fill it with what I can find over there.'

A tremble ran through his body and he tightened the blanket over his shoulders. 'This will be to your liking anyway. Perhaps you can punish me some more.'

Briefly he wondered if something else was at work here. That a spiritual charter had brought him to this river, at the only time he knew of it freezing over, was suspiciously coincidental.

The following day brought no respite. Nor the next. His course of action was decided. Gone were his honourable intentions of complying with tradition. This was a matter of survival, and he was starving to death.

Six

Not a drop fell from the long spears of ice hanging from the branches above. The silence was as deep as it was cold; all that stirred the frigid air were the frosted plumes of his breathing. Before him, the work-site lay abandoned.

He had woken with the feeling that this day would be different. Whatever its outcome, he knew he would not return to his cavern in the same state as he left it. Now he felt the day was about to take a turn already.

An opening at the front of the house showed him into a large section open to the sky beyond a partial ceiling that covered the front end only. The walls were a double layer of interwoven hazel plastered with clay and straw, with insulating material in the way of straw and dried reeds stuffed between. Roof ribs joined at the apex like pairs of splayed fingertips and five columns of large, evenly spaced support posts took the weight of the upper assemblage. Bundles of thatching lay piled against the protected end.

Woodcuttings littered the snow-covered floor, shaped timber and partly assembled frames leaned against walls. An assortment of wooden stocks and stoneheads were piled into a corner, as if left there for some future purpose.

Vratu crouched and picked up a shoe-last stonehead. Unlike those his people chipped, this one had been smoothed by extraordinary patience and somehow a hole had been bored clean through the middle. It might have suited his needs had it not, like every other discarded piece he saw, been blunted beyond any craft of his to repair.

The workmanship intrigued him. Their carpentry and tools evidenced a people far advanced in ideas and technology. Even to his inexperienced eye he could see the far-reaching implications of their skills. And they were coming, so it was said. To bear witness to it left

58

him with an uneasy feeling, one that deepened which each new discovery.

He went back outside. Now he noticed a pit running alongside the wall where they must have dug for plaster. Tree trunks lay stacked about the clearing, along with planks and finely cut sleepers of wood piled according to length.

He left the site and followed a well-trodden path toward the river. Not far from the shoreline he left his bulky backpack beside a tree, then proceeded upriver until the village disappeared around a bend. After giving the far side a careful scan he began his crossing over the awesome white emptiness, anxiously checking the sky every few steps for arrows.

'Who can say he has walked on the Great River before?' he encouraged himself with a chuckle.

On the far side he increased his pace, using the stunted alder and birch that edged the frozen swamp as cover until he noticed a number of coppiced stumps amongst some felled trees. There he slowed and moved with greater caution.

An organised jumble of architecture appeared through the trees. The longhouses were at least twice the length of the one he had inspected. Fifteen or more men laid head to foot would be less than the length of the largest, four or five men on top of each other might reach the highest point of a roof.

A strange, foreign scent wafted to his nose. He took a deep sniff, unable to match it with anything familiar. As he moved along the periphery the full extent of cleared ground surrounding the village came into view.

'They pull the forest from the earth, fill it with seed,' he recalled.

People moved about everywhere. Some carried identifiable objects like tools or baskets but the loads in other people's arms were mysteries. Occasionally the silence was broken by the thump of stone on wood, or the crack of stone on stone. Pigs wandered about aimlessly and he could see to one side several wattled enclosures and the curve of bovine spines rising above.

'Their beasts are of softer flesh and mind, like them. Their

medicine makes their beasts easy of heart, and they live amongst men as fearless as they live amongst themselves.'

A number of dogs sat about lazily, stockier and higher standing than the canine breed of his people. It was all so terribly fascinating it took a force of will to pull away.

He found a dry creek not far from the village where he lit a fire and waited for darkness. Set to a pattern of sleep that was rarely adjusted, he would have found himself dozing if not for the chill and the nature of his assignment to keep him on edge. His plan was not without flaws. All he could come up with was to shoot something like a small pig with an arrow and hope it died peacefully. This last part was new to him. Creeping up to his prey undetected may have been an accomplished skill, rendering it quiet after it had taken a mortal wound was something he had never needed to do before.

As dusk settled he decided to get moving. By habit he took a coal from the fire, wrapped it in a piece of moist leather and put it into his belt pouch. Then he gathered his weapons and negotiated his way out of the gully.

The fat trunk of a maple provided good cover for him to spy on the village. A few people still moved about but work appeared to have stopped for the day. To his complete disappointment not a beast was in sight. Mooing and muffled grunts coming from inside the longhouses told him they must have been brought in for the night. Now and then a door opened and someone would appear and walk off somewhere. On one occasion a woman holding a lamp and a basket walked over to a small building. Three dogs converged on her, hopping around on their hind legs with their muzzles reaching for the basket she carried. She did something at the door, swung it open and went inside. A short time later she emerged empty-handed and headed back. She opened the door of the house and the dogs followed her inside.

Vratu's hopes lifted. A silent barn was a much safer option than a squealing pig.

The noises gradually quietened and he sensed a settling down behind the sturdy walls. He fitted an arrow to his bow and crept forward, stopping here and there to crouch and listen, stepping off again as light as a lynx. A longhouse materialised ahead. As he passed by a distinctive pungency confirmed the presence of livestock within.

He reached the barn and pushed on the door. It gave a little but then held fast. The cause, he discovered quickly, was a wooden bar that sat on brackets fixed into the door and adjacent frame. He lifted the bar clear of the door-bracket and it swung inwards with a light creak from its leather hinges. He stepped inside and closed the door, but without a catch it settled slightly ajar.

Once inside, he couldn't see his hand in front of his face. His heart thumped against his ribcage and his breathing tightened, but the darkness put an edge to his smell; there was a foody whiff in the musty air that could not be mistaken. He took the coal from his belt pouch, chipped the crust away and blew on the core a few times. Using its feeble light he found a dry stalk on the earthen floor and set it aflame against the ember. The darkness retreated and shadowy objects glowed around him. A small clay lamp hung from the roof on a string. He transferred the dying flame to its wick and the entire room was revealed.

The woman's basket was sitting on a neat row of large clay pots with incised linear patterns. He took the basket down and looked inside it. Bones, offal and food scraps; reasonably fresh. He put it aside, lifted the lid off one of the clay pots and held his lamp above it.

'They grow fat on the seed of grass.'

He sank his hand into the grain and his mind reeled at the enormity of labour required to fill only one of these vessels with any type of seed, and there were five of them. He checked the contents of the others and confirmed they were full.

An assortment of wooden handles and stocks rested against the walls. Scattered over a shelf skilfully worked into the far wall were various stone tools and pieces of flint and bone. A small leather pouch caught his eye. He looked inside. Empty. Further searching revealed a few baskets of acorns, and that was it.

He emptied a large basket of acorns over the floor and filled it full with seed. On top went the food scraps. Vratu's kind could not afford a refined sense of taste.

With the basket cradled in his arms he carried more weight than he'd anticipated. He knew he should lighten the load but relished the thought of gorging himself for the first time since setting off on his miserable Walk. He blew out the lamp, bumped the door open and stepped blindly outside.

A low, menacing growl sounded ahead.

Vratu froze. The growl sounded again, louder this time. Yes, focussing now, he saw a dark shape only a leap or two away. He fumbled for the hand-axe at his belt and backed away. Then a better idea occurred to him. Before the watchdog could move he stepped back inside and nudged the door closed with his foot.

Working fast, he set everything down and relit the lamp. He selected a wooden stock and took the pouch from the workbench and tore it into strips. He wrapped the strips tightly around one end of the stock and poured burning fat from the lamp over it. Armed with a flaming torch, he scooped up his possessions and kicked the door open.

His greeting from this culture came in the form of an angry dog.

Ivory teeth shone sharp and ready, formidable strength showed in stocky, well-fed muscle. Deep scars circling its muzzle and tattered ears let him know what it thought of running from a fight. The shaggy coat typical of the wolf was missing but not the instinct; it knew the difference between friend and foe.

'Come to me,' he dared, lifting his torch.

Slowly he made for the river. The dog sucked its tongue in and followed him a few steps behind, lips curled and growling. As Vratu passed by the front of the longhouse he heard a grunt inside, followed by a minor commotion. Encouraged, the dog snarled louder.

The squeak of muffled paws in the snow behind made him turn. Three dark shapes rushed toward him, legs at full stretch. He lowered the basket to the ground and stood fast with his torch in both hands as a familiar scene of holding wolves at bay flashed in his mind.

The dogs skidded to a halt, Vratu swung his torch viciously and they backed out of reach yipping excitedly, giving him time to regather the basket. With the village guardians snapping at his heels he half-ran, half-kicked his way down to the riverbank, turning regularly to give an awkward one-armed sweep with his torch.

The flame was dying when he reached the river. He turned for one last sweep and saw the door of the closest longhouse open and a man emerge with a lamp in one hand and what looked like an oversized axe in the other. Two more dogs shot out of the door. The words the man hollered into the night were not of a tongue Vratu had heard before.

Then he remembered the food scraps. Quickly he set the basket down, grabbed a bone and tossed it at the dogs. Three sets of jaws set upon it furiously and engaged in a tug of war as the two new dogs charged up from behind and pulled up short. Piece by piece he flung what remained of the leftovers over their heads and they turned their teeth onto each other. Dropping his spent torch, he gathered his basket and ran.

Over the ice he went. He checked behind and saw lamps on shore and vague shapes trying to round up the miserable brutes. The chorus of whimpering and whining faded behind him until all he could hear were his feet crunching through the snow.

Out on the river the darkness became consuming. He kept running but the far bank seemed to keep its distance. The load in his arms threatened to topple him over and his stride became unsteady. By the time the shoreline gained clarity he could barely lift his legs.

He didn't hear the crack underfoot, but he felt it. It passed through the leather sole of his shoe, travelled up his leg and sent slivers of panic through his veins.

A few steps further he felt another crack. He tried to change direction but his foot skidded out sidewards, his knee came down hard and he thrust an arm out to break his fall.

There was a loud, sickening crunch, a bolt of blinding pain on his forehead and then the river clamped its icy jaws on him with heart-stopping force, sucking the air out his lungs and plugging his nose and ears. He shut his airways reflexively and rolled into a vertical position, and his hands and then head bumped onto solid roof. The current had dragged him beneath the ice.

He opened his eyes wide and his eyeballs froze, sightless in the black. In blind panic he scraped wildly with both hands against the rippled ice-roof above, his lungs convulsing with the need for air. He kicked madly into the push of water, against where it wanted to send him, but his leggings and pullover were water-traps. By sheer fluke his fingertips found the sharp edge of the break and managed to take hold. Lifted almost horizontally by the current, he hauled himself forward and up and his head burst into empty space. His lungs heaved in the life-saving air but the river still wanted him, inhaling him with equal determination. He rested a while to collect his wits, kicking against the current as his chest contracted in spasms. He felt for his bow and discovered it gone.

With supreme effort he found he could propel himself high enough to slide his stomach onto the ice, but as soon as he lifted his knee the edge crumbled and he slid helplessly back into the water. After several futile attempts he had to rest.

– *You were right Illawann man, we talk again* –

Sparing no thought to technique he lashed out wildly with fists and elbows and legs and knees and smashed his way forward, sucking fragments of ice and water into his lungs, coughing it all out in pain-racking gags; then it was another mad effort and choking spasm, and another, followed by a short, lung-heaving rest before starting over again.

The bank came tantalisingly closer. Safety was only a few body lengths way when he paused, too numb and exhausted to go on. Only for a moment, he thought. The icy water closed over his scalp and he raised both arms as he sank in a gesture of capitulation.

His feet touched the bottom. Everything he had left in him went into his legs as he kicked off, rose to the surface and fought his way forward until he could stand. A few steps further put him at waist height where he was able to slide his entire torso over the ice.

This time it held his weight. For a while he lay spread-eagled sucking in air, shaking and groaning with exhaustion and cold, then slithered to the bank like an eel. He turned his weary head behind to check for signs of pursuit and saw nothing.

The cold was insufferable. It reached into the marrow of his bones and made him shudder so violently his limbs would not respond to command. Water dripping into his eyes was warm and sticky. He wiped his hand across his forehead and felt mangled skin.

With water streaming from his heavily soaked garments he hurried back along the bank to retrieve his discarded items. He shouldered his bundle awkwardly and set off for the only place he could think of.

The formless, half-made house made a welcome sight this time. Once inside he quickly stripped off his clothes, untied his blanket and wrapped it tightly around him. The contents of his belt pouch were saturated and he needed dry implements to light a fire. It was useless. When he had more energy he might try to light some thatching, but right now he needed to seriously warm up and rest.

He lay down and curled into a flex position, like a corpse in a grave. The shaking subsided but then something more sinister than the river's freeze took hold. Each time he coughed he heard it – a vile sound he had never heard himself make – and he knew then that evil spirits had entered his body, bringing his blood to the boil and hastening him toward their dark world.

Seven

Barak Hrad-Uik closed the door to the barn, satisfied there was nothing more to learn. They had lost a bit of grain, hardly comparable to what they lost to mould and mice. It was the manner of the break-in that interested him now. A long time had passed since this sort of thing had happened.

Icicles on the eaves sparkled from the first sunlight in days. He cracked off a length and chewed on one end as he headed toward the river. At the lip of the bank he stopped and saw his brother-in-law Ivnisi standing at the shoreline, looking out over the ice.

'Should have let the dogs run him down,' Ivnisi commented when he saw him. 'Looks like the ice held him up.'

Hrad-Uik didn't reply. Out on the river his eldest son Borchek was about halfway back, pulling a canoe by the bow while one of Ivnisi's boys pushed from behind. Even at that distance Hrad-Uik could see his son had taken most of the weight and still moved with ease. Ivnisi's son, supporting himself on the rim of the canoe, looked ready to collapse.

They moved quickly and so Hrad-Uik decided to wait. The two young men reached the bank and slid the canoe up a short distance. Borchek disentangled himself from the rope attached to his waist and walked over.

'Find anything?' Ivnisi asked.

'No,' Borchek informed, panting slightly. 'He fell in the river.'

Hrad-Uik turned his head sharply. 'What?'

'There's a break near the far side.'

'Did it swallow him?'

'No. We could see where it went all the way to the bank.'

'How thin is she over there?'

'Thin. We had to turn around.'

'He is dead then,' Ivnisi commented. 'If the river didn't kill him, the cold did.'

Hrad-Uik eyed the brother of his wife quietly a moment, then turned to his son. 'Take Yanukz and check around the new house.'

'Can I go too?' Behind him within earshot his youngest son Nuridj, feeding breakfast leftovers to the swine, appealed enthusiastically.

'Do you know how to use the canoes?'

'Yes pa,' Nuridj answered drolly.

'Enough with that. Keep it close to you, all the way over. Tie rope around you and listen to your brothers. Stop scaring your mother sick.'

'Will you come too?'

'No.'

Ivnisi regarded Hrad-Uik with a quizzical frown. 'Won't be long before she breaks up,' he reminded. Hrad-Uik stayed quiet as he looked out over the river.

'I will never understand you,' Ivnisi said. 'This could only be one of them. Why do you risk sending your boys over there to help him after what they have done to us?'

Hrad-Uik said nothing. He marched off to his house, where the hearth was warm and his breakfast waited.

Time had no bearing where he was, nor did sound penetrate. For what could have been a morning or a thousand years Vratu hovered helplessly in a dark void, drawn toward some fearful destination the poisons of his sickness conspired to send him.

When dreams came he was in the river again, fighting against its current and trying to haul himself onto the ice. Horrifying images plagued him and he called for his friends whenever their faces flashed in his mind's eye, but they always disappeared.

Every so often he felt tender hands at work, punching into the abyss like shafts of light and hauling him up from the depths. One time he found himself lying naked on the bed with the ceiling glowing orange and smoke being blown over him by a masked man intoning a chant similar to the song of a bird. Other times he woke groggily to hands lifting him from beneath, and he would stiffen at the sight of women smiling from above, but their whispers took the resistance out of his limbs, and by the time they had removed his soiled furs and lowered him onto clean ones he was drifting off again.

Sometimes a wooden bowl was lifted to his lips and he tasted boiled willow bark, or meadowsweet, or valerian, or some other foul mystery, and he would feel the magic of medicine until the fever struck again, prying for weakness like a scorpion aiming for a soft spot on its victim.

On one occasion, during the familiar exercise of having his bedding changed, he caught sight of a girl in the semi-darkness. Her face was so impossibly pure he suspected it was just another figment of his delirium. Desires of old stirred in his sluggish mind and he tried to fight the drag of sleep, but the feel of the warm leather rag she brushed against his forehead was too powerful a sedative.

Slowly the crisis passed. The mess of confusing images untangled and he woke to a sense of order, although the periods of remission blurred into the next and gave him no perspective on the time lag between each. Bit by bit he was able to distinguish the real from the unreal until finally the sights he opened his eyes to started making sense again.

Logic told him he was in a house of the farmers. The first thing he noticed were crude feather bracelets attached to his wrists. He checked himself over and found similar attachments circling his ankles. Faint impressions of red ochre showed on his chest.

A small pedestal burner lay next to his bed, the convex lid filled with a pool of speckled liquid responsible for the fragrance of foxglove. His bed of straw and furs lay inside a wattle and daub cubicle that appeared to serve as a private bedroom. His clothes were draped neatly over a rail fixing and his backpack lay against a wall. A wooden toilet pot sat near his bed. From beyond came the occasional voice or thump or clatter, and fainter still, the lamentations of pigs and cattle.

As soon as they saw his turn of health they fed him thin soups with strange green and brown vegetables floating within, sweet tasting drinks and herbal teas. His appetite returned and with each mouthful he felt his strength return. When he slept now a calming presence descended on him like a warm blanket, and the demons left his dreams, replaced by angels of unbelievable beauty that swirled over his bed, calling his name and whispering strange words into his ear.

There were loud noises, the sound of an argument. A woman's voice, smothered under the authority of a man's. Vratu tried to shut it out by covering his ears with the blanket. A short time later he heard the shriek of a woman in full vent, followed by an exclamation of disgust. Then all fell silent.

For the first time since falling ill he had difficulty going back to sleep. Familiar pain had returned; his joints ached and the tightness in his lungs made breathing painful. To lift an arm or leg required ridiculous effort. A child could beat him to death if it tried.

His first attempt to rise from bed was met with giddiness and an icy spasm that sent his body into a shiver. He collapsed back onto the bed and waited for the tingling sensation to pass.

With his head swaying and knees protesting stiffly, he managed to stand and fasten his loinskin. Panting with even these exertions, he draped the blanket over his shoulders and slowly, like a child taking his first steps, hobbled out through the narrow opening of his room.

It appeared he was in the sleeping quarters. A woman sat on a bed against the wall opposite, breast-feeding an infant. She looked up with a startled expression. Regularly spaced on both sides of the wall were several more beds, and an arrangement of walls at the far end of the quarters suggested more private cubicles. Familiar trophies decorated the walls – boar, deer, bison, aurochs. A rectangular opening through a wall running floor to ceiling showed into the next section. Swaying slightly, he plodded through.

A large table with two benches of equal length featured prominently in the middle of a large room. At the far end a pot simmered above an open hearth, on each side of which were large beehive-shaped clay ovens. Wooden and earthenware utensils sat on shelves running along the walls; bundles of dried herbs and meats, bladder-gourds, and the odd rabbit and grouse hung from crossbeams above. A neat assembly of large clay pots, vases and flasks, complete with elaborate spiral and meander twists from base to funnel, sat against the wall. A smoke-hole was open in the roof. For all their inventiveness, it appeared these people were still unable to completely rid an interior of smoke. A ladder ran to a ceiling loft extending half the length of the room.

No one was present. He walked ahead and reached the far door, held closed by a solid beam in the same manner as the door on the barn. He lifted the beam from its rest and swung the door open.

The roof pitched forward into an ante-room. Nestled on each side were several stables, all empty. The after-smell of cattle was rich in his nostrils, slightly different to what he caught downwind of wild herds. Daylight twinkled invitingly through a wattle door at the far end. He walked ahead and pushed it open.

The sun and the crisp clean air were like the return of old friends. Many people moved about but no one noticed him. He tilted his head backwards, closed his eyes and bathed his face in the warmth of the sun. He inhaled as deep as his sore lungs allowed, dropped his head down and opened his eyes.

Every head had now turned his way.

He pulled the blanket tighter. For the first time in his life he felt like an intruder, at least amongst humans. It was like stumbling upon a herd of bison. They watched him with the confidence that came with numbers and strength, but with a wary poise, as if their feeble minds feared some unlikely danger. He looked for the river but it was obscured from view by longhouses and the drop of the bank.

No one moved. They ogled him expressionlessly. A few women looked familiar, perhaps they had treated him. His hunter's eyes registered cattle in the pens, dogs sitting quietly and pigs straying about. A fat boar snuffled the earth close enough for him to kick. The tusks were gone and a ringlet of bone pierced his nose. He was too round for a boar and too heavy, with legs too scraggy for the weight they supported. He paid attention to no one, made so soft a target that Vratu's fingers twitched reflexively for a weapon.

The snow cover had diminished. The empty fields that stretched beyond the village retained only meagre patches of snow and he marvelled at how long he must have been in the world of no sense. He turned to retreat inside and saw the breast-feeding woman standing at the door. Reacting on an impulse more animal than human, he headed for the forest.

His bare feet squelched in the mud. Planked walkways ran in various directions, none leading to where he wanted to go. No one stopped him, no one said anything. The eyes on his back felt as strong as the sun.

After only a few steps the strength left his legs and he stumbled onto his knees. The blanket fell from his body, he thrust out his hands to steady himself and mud slipped between his fingers and dizziness flooded his head. Slowly it cleared and he saw that still no one had moved. He wobbled slowly to his feet and took one, two steps forward, his will greater than his strength.

'Epnuk du na sekros!'

He turned and saw an old woman hurrying toward him. Immediately he recognised the face. Many times this woman had forced foul liquid down his throat.

She jabbered loudly and a girl answered in a sheepish fashion and came forward. The old woman lifted his arm and thrust her shoulder under his armpit. Vratu tried to disengage but the woman mumbled more gibberish and fought away his attempt. The girl fastened onto his other arm and they led him inside.

They lay him down on his bed and fretted over him. Soon they were gone and he was left wondering what the foreign babble going on outside his partition was all about.

The old woman returned and gave him a bowl of soup, presumably by its ghastly smell more medicinal than culinary. She poked her chest with a finger.

'Nankyi . . . Nankyi . . .'

Vratu tilted his head curiously.

'Nankyi.'

'Oh, Vratu,' he muttered, surprised at how weak his voice

71

sounded.

'Vra . . . tu?'

'Vratu.'

She patted him on the shoulder and pointed to the bowl. 'Urhgos, Vratu.' Sincerity was in her tone and he decided he liked the old woman. She smiled and walked out.

He had drunk about half the soup when five men filed in. As he went to sit up an old man with deeply furrowed brows and intense eyes put a hand on his shoulder to keep him there. Vratu flicked his gaze nervously over the men standing around. One or two of them looked familiar; he couldn't be certain. They studied him with cold faces.

The old man moved forward. 'Kos ni usu?'

Vratu shook his head feebly.

The words the old man spoke next were so thick with accent that Vratu barely understood them. 'Do you hear me now?'

Vratu answered hesitantly, 'I hear you.'

A shade like smoke passed behind the old man's eyes and his features froze, a reaction akin to someone pulling back a blanket and discovering a snake. He turned to the others and they spoke amongst themselves in low voices.

Throughout the gibberish Vratu heard one word repeated clearly. The word itself did not concern him as much as the way they reacted; it brought no smiles, no gasps of surprise. They stopped talking and pored over him intently. Then they were gone.

Vratu despaired. He wanted his strength back, wanted to flee back over the river to his cavern in the Hills of Uryak. The word he had heard was *Ubren*. They thought he was one of them.

Surrendering to weakness he closed his eyes and fell asleep.

A noise like a grunt woke him.

A man stood next to his bed. He was tall and bulky and his eyes were dark and unfriendly. Vratu gathered his senses quickly and raised himself on his elbows. The man's face tightened and when he spoke his voice sounded like a snarl.

'Us nu duna, Ubren tus.'

There were no noises in the house. It appeared they were alone.

The man looked down at Vratu's half-empty bowl. He inflated his lungs, hawked loudly and tilted his head forward. A long, stringy glob of spit dripped from his lips and plopped into the bowl.

He wiped a hand across his lips and walked out. Vratu closed his eyes and let the warmth of his bed drag him back to sleep.

A gentle prod woke him. Nankyi stood over his bed, chattering and gesturing with her hands. The light was weak and he guessed he must have slept most of the day. Faint voices sounded from somewhere.

The old woman went to lift his shoulders off the bed but he sat up quickly on his own. He felt strength in his legs and arms that hadn't been there earlier, a little less stiffness.

'Etnu?' she asked, and Vratu reassured her with a nod. She walked off, motioning for him to follow.

He gathered his clothes and dressed. At first he thought they belonged to someone else. They felt heavier than ever and his limbs found too much space inside.

A blast of warmth met him as he passed through the walkway into the main room. A large group of people sat around the table eating. Oven smoke hung in the air, along with the appetising smell of cooked food. They lifted their heads as one when he appeared and the talk stopped. The old man who had spoken to him that morning came forward with his arms outstretched, and then Vratu spied the girl. The lamplight gave her a golden complexion, and he saw that her beauty was no figment of his delirium. Her cheekbones were slightly raised and her eyes nestled beneath a forehead noticeably flatter than his people. Her hair was the colour of dark honey, wavy with a natural neatness. And yet there was a quality about her that went beyond her looks, a quiet manner that implied careful observation.

'Vratu?' the old man's voice interrupted his thoughts, and Vratu dragged his eyes off the girl. 'Barak Hrad-Uik,' he said, poking his chest. Then he waved his hands at the people seated. 'Prihos vi per genhes Uik.'

73

Hrad-Uik put a hand on Vratu's shoulder and led him to the table. Nankyi thrust a plate of lukewarm vegetable and meat broth under his nose, dusted it over with a few herbs, and gave him a mug of mint-smelling tea. A mouth-watering smell wafted up his nostrils and he took to his dish with revived appetite.

They resumed their idle chatter. They laughed as all people laughed, erupting in chorus and making his silence all the more out of place. Children gaped at him, whispering and giggling. The young native possessed a natural affinity for politeness and did not lower himself to eat as he might have amongst his own, instead he watched every move they made and the order in which they ate. Only after Hrad-Uik had taken the food on offer did others take their serve.

After dinner the girls stacked the kitchen utensils into a corner. They scraped the leftovers into a large bowl and flung a few scraps at the dogs seated patiently nearby. A little girl walked over to Nankyi and held up something small and fluffy. The woman mumbled and pointed at Vratu, the girl walked over to him and held up a tassel made of feathers. He took it from her outstretched hand.

'Nice,' he said, and his hosts tittered.

The little girl started chattering away with gay nonsense. She poked at his clothes and giggled.

'Ah, you laugh at me too,' he croaked. 'This makes me feel at home.'

There were all manner of protocols amongst his kind directed toward the treatment of guests. Whatever else this family might have been, he was grateful they employed a comparable standard. He was equally grateful they left him to himself. Tonight he preferred not to labour over attempts to communicate.

When a boy left the room bound for the sleeping quarters, Vratu took the opportunity to follow. He nodded shyly to his hosts on his way out.

The boy was sitting on a bed untying his shoes when he passed. 'Unad du ginos?'

Vratu let his expression show he hadn't understood.

The boy folded his arms and rubbed his hands over each

shoulder, as if miming the act of washing himself. 'Ginos?'

Vratu shrugged and kept walking. At the entrance to his quarters he stopped to contemplate his bed of straw and furs. Cold as this night may have been, he thought only to take a blanket and find peace under the stars in accordance with his design.

He ignored the puzzled expressions on the faces of Hrad-Uik's family as he headed out. He passed through the stables, the raw stink of livestock thick in his nostrils, and gave the formless beasts either side only a sideward glance, resolved to satisfy that curiosity at a better time.

The cold tightened the skin of his face and hands as he stepped outside. He headed to a cluster of trees and found a place to his liking beneath a large maple. As he knelt to scrape away the snow he saw a light coming toward him. The boy emerged from the dark with a tallow-lamp in one hand and a thick blanket in the other.

'Ginos?' he asked, offering up the blanket. Vratu felt a smile crack his face. The boy handed him the blanket and left.

Vratu lay down and pulled both blankets over him. A few breaths later he was lost in an impenetrable slumber.

Eight

He woke to a deep sense of something wrong.

His memory was as murky as the fog around him, through which he could see strange shapes and figures moving about like apparitions. For a few alarming moments he could not recall how he came to be there. A bull snorted and it all came back.

When he sat up he found strength where it hadn't been the night before, and he decided then to leave this place of strange tongues and men who spat in his soup. With a small donation of meat and grain from his hosts he could return to his home in the Hills of Uryak to sit out his recovery; perhaps he could explain this affably to the man with the difficult name and gentle voice. He rolled up his blankets and returned to the house.

Going through the stables he passed two cows. It was his first close look at domestic cattle and they differed slightly to the beasts he hunted. Their bodies swelled in the wrong places; smoothness and padding showed in place of hard, sinewy muscle.

Nankyi greeted him in the main room. 'Vratu! Sa ni suerg?'

Hrad-Uik sat at the table, along with the boy who had given him the blanket the night before, and next to him, a man several years older with a brotherly likeness.

'Vratu,' Hrad-Uik said, pointing to the two young men. 'Toru szunner hunyos . . . this Borchek son, this Nuridj son.'

Vratu returned the borrowed blanket to Nuridj. A wordless communication passed between Hrad-Uik and his sons, and the two boys stood and departed.

The old woman brought him a plate of milky porridge. A dog appeared from nowhere and flopped down at Hrad-Uik's feet. Vratu saw the scarred muzzle and yellow eyes and knew at once it was the same beast that had given him grief the night of his abortive pillage.

'This Vek,' Hrad-Uik said, smiling. The dog yawned and exposed a monstrous set of teeth.

Vratu lifted a spoonful of porridge and took a sniff. He took a small mouthful, then a larger one. It contained nothing to alarm his tastebuds and he emptied the bowl without giving it another thought. Nankyi took it away and Hrad-Uik looked at him meaningfully.

'Here, Vratu,' he said. 'We talk.'

They tried. Failing in words, the old man drew lines on the earthen floor. He pointed this way and that and made shapes with his hand. He mentioned names that meant nothing to Vratu other than one – the Ubren headman Krul who had made an appearance at the Arrival-Feast. Hrad-Uik sounded keen to know more about him, particularly his recent movements, but the more specific he tried to be the more he erred and became unclear. Vratu didn't care much for Krul and his clan anyway. They hunted east of Heavy-fish and were the primary reason the Illawann were reluctant to cross over it. After a period of quiet chin scratching, Hrad-Uik patted Vratu on the shoulder and stood.

'Come,' he said, motioning for him to follow.

Vratu stood, wondering how long his legs would hold him up. Vek picked herself up from the floor and trotted out after them.

In the stables two girls were milking the cows. Vratu saw the milk squirt into a ceramic pail and frowned in distaste. The milk of a cow belonged in the stomach of a calf. Where was it? Why do such a thing? Astonished at the bizarre sight he kept glancing behind as he followed Hrad-Uik out.

The earth steamed beneath a kind sun. Vratu paused to get his bearings and looked for the river, out of sight from where they stood.

'River?' Hrad-Uik anticipated his thoughts. 'You see.'

They walked a bit further, the river came into view and Vratu discovered he was going nowhere.

The ice-sheet had broken up. Riding the slurry were ice floes of all shapes and sizes, packed in places so tightly they had slid on top of each other. Water flowed in channels between the largest, some so long they seemed part of a single mass, moving downriver without end, like clouds across the sky. And yet everything moved at such a calm pace that he played with the idea of crossing over. Down on the bank several robust looking canoes and dugouts beckoned. Then he thought of all the mistakes he had already made on his Walk and decided not to add to them.

'Yi yi yi . . .' Hrad-Uik commented. 'Bad, yes?'

Hrad-Uik led him away to some rectangular enclosures that held several large bulls. As his host rambled away Vratu stood fascinated. Like the cows they lacked girth in the shoulder and neck, the muscle needed for clashing heads and maiming opponents. Their eyes bulged with boredom, their curiosity killed.

Where is your fire? he wondered. *How did they take it from you?*

He counted seven beasts in this one enclosure alone, more stood in others. There was a snuffle at his feet and he started when he saw a large hog nuzzling his ankles with a moist pink snout. A soft kick sent it scurrying away, then it blithely poked its nose into the dirt.

During his tour of the village Vratu saw men and women patching rooves, fixing fences, tending animals. But why did a woman pulverise small rocks with a stone hammer? Why did men walk out into the fields, paw at the sodden earth and return with looks of misery? The more he was shown the more disorientated he became.

Occasionally someone joined them and Hrad-Uik went through the motions of introduction. A few people showed genuine curiosity, others eyed him with undisguised condescension. Hrad-Uik tactfully diverted away from the sourest faces, including the spitting-man, but it was clear the old man commanded influence, and despite being poorly received at times, Vratu felt he had the right to be there.

He was being shown the contents of a barn when his stomach began to churn and groan. Before long it had worsened beyond a mild upset, and by the time they'd wandered over to some stalls the sharp sensation had descended into his bowels. Vratu pointed to his stomach and made the appropriate sign to Hrad-Uik. The old man nodded and Vratu hurried away to the forest.

Screened by the trees he attended to nature and sat down afterwards on the twisted root of a friendly oak. It felt good to be back in the forest. The air was easier to breathe and he rested there a long while savouring the smells of fresh earth and mulch.

Recharged, he wobbled to his feet and returned to the village. Several people had gathered in a cluster around Hrad-Uik. They saw Vratu and stopped talking, and as he came closer they dispersed in the same manner as the pigs scrounging around the village had done.

For the rest of the day he lay in bed groaning, wondering what he had done wrong this time. His stomach felt bloated, bursting with air. It rumbled like distant thunder and Vratu held it with both hands moaning softly, one eye on the wooden toilet pot at the foot of his bed. He desperately wanted to take his sickness out of there but had no energy to spare for tramping about the cold forest. He had thought he had beaten his sickness, had recovered for good, and now this.

Around dinnertime Nankyi came in with another steaming decoction. His stomach cramps had weakened and he reassured her as best he could that whatever afflicted him wasn't life threatening. She poked at his stomach briefly, then left.

Later in the night, with the house completely silent, he sat up on his bed. He felt much better now. He dressed and fingertipped his way past obstacles until he was out of the house, then walked down to the river's edge and squatted on his haunches.

Somewhere out there in the dark his cavern in the Hills of Uryak awaited his return. And beyond that, far away in the cold wilderness, his home at the Winter Grounds. Above him was nothing but blackness, no way to tell how long he had been there.

'Why do you keep me here?' he asked the heavens. 'When do I go home?'

He heard soft panting behind him and turned his head. A dark shape padded closer and he caught the blur of a wagging tail. He held his hand out and felt over a scar-ridged muzzle.

'Vek, yes?' Her ears pricked up and a wet snout nuzzled him in friendly fashion. 'It is your fault I am here.'

Much later, as he returned through the stables, he stopped to

79

consider the amount of body heat trapped in there. He waited for a gesture of protest from the sleeping beasts on either side, but nothing happened.

He collected his belongings and blanket and returned to the stables. In a corner was a large pile of dried plant matter that smelled like elm. Quietly now, he arranged it into a crude bed and lay down to sleep.

The sound of someone chuckling woke him. He opened his eyes and saw Nankyi standing above him. She was still chuckling when she opened the door to the main room and closed it behind her.

He sat up slowly, wincing with infirmity as the cattle stirred around him. The door opened and Nankyi reappeared, flanked by Nuridj and Borchek who laughed heartily at Vratu's choice of evening bed. Nankyi beckoned him in for breakfast.

This time they gave him a plate of watery porridge. It lacked the murky white colour of his dish the day before, and then he made the connection with the milk squirted from the calf. He sniffed at his dish as a fox might sniff at a snare, feeling his stomach curdle. Had this caused his cramps? Not wanting to appear rude he took his chances on this variation of dish and ate heartily.

Nankyi set about cleaning up, and the others left. Vratu sat at the table wondering what he was supposed to do with himself. Get up and go? Perhaps this was not such a bad idea.

'Di na so buksom sevrut?' Nankyi looked him over with raised eyebrows, then smiled and dropped some bowls into a tub of water.

Vratu stood and went to gather his belongings from the stable. This was not his place. It would be better to find a campsite nearby and wait until the river calmed enough for him to cross over. Later perhaps, in command of his situation, he could come back and pay his respects. This is what he would do.

Without giving it another thought he walked out into daylight. No one challenged him as he left the village and took a muddy path into the forest. Now he was back where he belonged his pace took on the sprightliness that had deserted him. It felt odd without his bow and arrows. They were so much a part of his attire he felt naked without them.

He had not gone far when the forest thinned, the land dipped away and he stopped in his tracks at the sight of another village way off in the distance.

In that instant his enthusiasm for exploring the area and setting up camp was quashed. The forest here suddenly felt less pristine. Around every corner and over every hill some unwelcome surprise awaited. He scowled at the village a long time, noting how the tiny figures within it moved with purpose, had some place to go.

He put the sight behind him and spent the better part of the day wandering aimlessly through the forest, going around in circles. Several times he passed potential campsites tucked into ravines with a growing sense of homelessness. A patch of dogwood buoyed his spirits and he took to the task of plucking the straightest stems from the ground for arrow shafts, and whittling away the excess.

The distraction freed his mind to think. There was, he knew now, only one option. In Hrad-Uik and Nankyi he sensed hearts as warm as their beds. He could afford to rest in their village at least another day or so. This would also give him time to make a new bow and set of arrows, a prerequisite for any man who walked the forest.

But when he arrived at the outskirts of the village late in the afternoon he could not find the nerve to take those final steps. The day was losing its colours, beasts were being led inside and he had almost succeeded in talking himself back into the forest when the door to Hrad-Uik's house opened and the girl with the magical face appeared. She threw a handful of food scraps at the pigs and went back inside.

Vratu aimed himself forward and kept his eyes fixed ahead as he passed people by, wondering if they saw him as he saw himself – going the wrong way, running home like a lost child to its mother. He reached the door, yanked it open and stepped inside.

In the main room he found three young girls seated at the table pounding strips of dried meat. The focus of his attention had her back to him, unhooking wooden utensils from an overhead beam. Vratu unslung his pack and dropped it onto the floor. The girl turned around at the sound.

'I saw you in my dreams,' he said in his most manly voice. The three young girls giggled, but not the one he was speaking to. 'How are you called?'

The girl shook her head.

'Your name. Vratu.' He demonstrated by thumping his chest.

Her quick comprehension showed with a smile. 'Abinyor.'

'Ub . . . un . . .'

'Abinyor.'

'Abin . . . *yor*.' It sounded right the second time. 'You stir men's blood, I can see.' Then he pointed to her necklace. 'Show me.'

She fingered it hesitantly. 'Mie monoi?'

'Yes that,' he persuaded. 'I'll give it back.'

She lifted the necklace over her pretty head and gave it to him. He sat down at the table to examine it, watching her from the corner of his eye. Yes, she moved closer.

A cord of plaited vegetable fibres threaded through deer's teeth and painted clay-beads – a fairly common piece. 'I could make you a necklace better than this,' he boasted.

She pointed to his neck. He removed his own necklace and handed it over.

Without understanding a word that followed he enjoyed the following exchange of sign language and hand gestures. His interest in the items she presented was more feigned than genuine, a ploy to keep her communicating. For the first time since arriving he felt comfortable in someone's company. As they took turns swapping words, constantly interrupted by the other girls keen to participate, he wondered how so beautiful a woman could not be married already.

They were joined by Nankyi, who took immediate interest in proceedings, but with her involvement he quickly tired of the pursuit. A little later Hrad-Uik entered with members of his family and made words Vratu assumed related to his absence. He answered by holding up his dogwood stems and mimed the act of pulling back on a bow.

Interest showed on the old man's face.

'Neh, di na toksom!'

Everyone was ushered to the table to eat. This time the food given him was a pottage of grain, beans and strings of meat disguised by a thick seasoning of herbs, a plate of unleavened bread with a syrup spread, and warm tea.

Before going to bed Vratu took Vek outside and sat with her by the water's edge, listening to the ice heave and creak in the dark. He felt much more at ease with these people now. Better still, he had spoken to the girl and learned her name was Abinyor.

That night he did not sleep under the stars or in the stables. He returned to Hrad-Uik's house after everyone had gone to sleep and lay down in the bed provided for him.

There was a gentle tug on one of his braids. He opened his eyes and saw a small girl standing before him, smiling from ear to ear with the tip of her tongue poking through a gap in her snow-white teeth. She squealed and ran away giggling.

When he sat up he noticed someone had placed the pedestal burner at the foot of his bed again. Traces of wick-soot floated in the lid. The tempting thought that it might have been Abinyor sneaking into his room to see to his wellbeing made him grin. Now he knew he was truly on the mend.

Domestic noise let him know the day had begun but it wasn't until Nankyi came in with another steaming remedy that he felt compelled to rise. 'Uhrgos, Vratu. Etnu, su nah pitos.'

Vratu responded with a gracious grunt and the old woman left smiling.

After a light breakfast, he went to check on the state of the river, now more of an ice-slurry. The water level had dropped a fraction and the floe cover was thinner and less threatening than before. With a bit of diligence he might be able reach the far side in a canoe without being crushed between floes or flipped. For now though he would return to the forest and search for yew for his bow.

He was heading for the trees when a voice called from behind:

'Vratu!'

He turned around and saw Hrad-Uik and Nuridj standing by a table and bench beneath a large roof that appeared to serve as their communal centre. They upturned two bags over the table and an array of small objects fell out and bounced to rest. Hrad-Uik beckoned him over.

Vratu approached and saw everything needed for making arrows: microliths, feathers, sinew and birch-bark for pitch, along with flint and bone saws, burins, scrapers, arrow straighteners and other tools. Hrad-Uik mumbled words to the effect that they were keen for him to stay in the village that day, and without a reason not to Vratu nodded his consent and the old man left.

The villagers gawked at him constantly as they went about their business. A few children chased each other nearby, screaming happily. Pigs and dogs sniffed about in their ceaseless quest for food. Abinyor wandered around the village replenishing feed for the animals and chatting with friends. The spit-man was tying bundles of thatching over by a longhouse. Every so often he looked Vratu's way, singling him out with hostile eyes.

Vratu ignored him and focussed on his own work. When his backside became sore he stood for a stretch and noticed Abinyor with a group of girls over by the pens. He was working up the courage to join them when he saw Borchek swagger toward them. The eldest son of Hrad-Uik was a big man, heavy in the shoulders but narrow in the waist, with powerful legs and a face that seemed set on provoking trouble. But when he reached the group of girls his posture of combative virility vanished so abruptly it was comical.

As Vratu turned back to his work he noticed the spit-man staring at him again. Vratu had had enough. They openly glared at each other until Nuridj noticed and nudged him in a friendly manner.

Vratu was just about to let it pass when he saw the man drop his bundle and stride toward him. Halfway over, his nostrils flaring like an angry bull, he scooped up a boy with barely a falter in his step. With the child bouncing in his arms he stomped the rest of the way over and stopped an arm's length from where Vratu stood stiff and ready to receive him. The man thrust the boy's face at him side on, shaking him with forced restraint.

'Epnu tul vostok buszno, ke!' he shouted.

Vratu saw the shockingly melted skin that stretched all the way down one side of the boy's face, and felt a sharp twinge travel up his spine. The man shook him again, eyes brimming with hate, and raised his voice. '*Tul vostok, neh?*'

The size of the man took on a frightening significance, reminding Vratu of his own fragile state. A great weakness soaked into his muscles and made his limbs shake. The man put the boy down and pulled the vest off the boy's shoulder roughly. Every piece of exposed skin Vratu could see had the same cobwebbed scarring.

'*Se vun Ubren tus?*' the man roared. '*Neh vostok! Bah!*'

'Bregnos, nuh!'

Vratu turned quickly. Borchek was coming over, speaking in a tone of such persuasive calm that the redness faded from the spit-man's face. His eyes lost their wild shine and watered over.

There were lively voices behind and Vratu spun around, still tickling with an adrenalin hit. Three strangers were walking toward them. Thick furs inflated their size and travel kits hung from their backs.

'Yehu Bregnos, Borchek, vun detok?' the leading man said on approach. The spit-man walked away mumbling, leading his boy by the hand. A few more words were exchanged, there was a bit of laughter, and then the leading man addressed the native.

'You are Vratu, yes?' Apart from a strong accent his words were clear.

Vratu nodded warily.

'I am Kulej, this is Varsi, this is Variknud,' he said, indicating his two companions with a mittened hand. 'You are better, yes?' He held a steady gaze, and notwithstanding his thick clothing his shoulders were broader than most.

Vratu found his voice. 'Yes.'

'Come,' Kulej beckoned. 'We talk.'

They followed Kulej into Hrad-Uik's house and main room. Hrad-

Uik barked an order to those inside and they exited obediently.

'Sit,' Kulej repeated. Vratu seated himself at the table. Hrad-Uik and Borchek sat down beside him, the visitors settled in opposite.

'No one here speak your words,' Kulej said, 'so I come. I try to be here more soon but had work north. Friend Variknud come before, make medicine for you when you sleep with the spirits.'

'How do you speak my words?'

'You are Ubren, yes?'

'No.'

'No?' Kulej looked genuinely surprised. 'Not Ubren? Who then?'

Vratu preferred to hold his tongue. If they thought he was Ubren and let him be, he wanted to leave it at that.

Kulej waited until it was clear he wasn't going to get a reply. 'Where is your home?'

Even if he'd wanted to, this was too difficult for Vratu to explain.

'You are of the Wandering Tribes, yes?' Kulej led gently. Still he received no answer. 'Vratu, you are not in trouble here. Free to go. But we need to know things. You meet these people before?'

'Who are they?'

'They are Oronuk, live all along river here. You say no?'

'No.'

'You come from other side of river, yes?' Kulej asked, pointing in the direction.

'Yes.'

'From far?'

Vratu said nothing.

Kulej eyed him quizzically. 'Your people camp there now, close perhaps?'

'No.'

'Ah! Why did you come here?'

Vratu feared he was about to be reprimanded for stealing the food. 'I was hunting.'

'Hunting? Alone? In this bad winter, worst we ever see. How you hunting?'

Vratu dropped his gaze. 'How do you speak my words?' he asked

86

again.

'I am Henghai. All my life I learn your words.'

'Where are the Henghai?'

Kulej smiled. 'Henghai not a tribe,' he explained. 'A name . . . like your *Uru,* yes?'

Nankyi brought in a flask of ale made from germinated barley that had been dried and mixed in water with a few herbs. After pouring their mugs full she placed a hand on Vratu's shoulder and spoke sternly to the others, pointing her finger as she did. Vratu was touched; it appeared she was warning them to go easy. Then she left.

They quizzed him for a long time but his answers were short and noncommittal. Communication became more difficult when certain concepts and terms could not be translated literally or expressed in an equivalent. Kulej's dialect also included corrupted Ubren cognates Vratu could only guess at, so they kept it simple.

Vratu let them do most of the talking. Every time they tried to come back to his people and their whereabouts they were thwarted by his reticence. They learned that he hunted northwest of Heavy-Fish and had travelled for a number of days on his own to get here. Yes, it had been a very bad winter. He felt much better. That was it.

Every so often Kulej translated for the others. During one of these translations Hrad-Uik mentioned the name of Krul, to which Kulej responded with a lift of his eyebrows. 'You know Krul, yes?' he asked.

Vratu fidgeted with his fingers and stayed quiet.

'You know Ubren east of Heavy-Fish?' Kulej probed.

'Kulej,' Hrad-Uik interrupted, and the two men spoke briefly.

Kulej nodded reluctantly. 'All right,' he said, switching back to the native dialect. 'You go. We talk later.'

Vratu decided to ask a question that had stuck in the back of his mind throughout the entire discussion. 'Who was the boy with the face of burns?'

Kulej's forehead creased in confusion. He spoke to the others and Borchek answered in an austere voice: 'Bregnos du szunner.'

Kulej rubbed his chin thoughtfully. 'Not for you to worry,' he said to Vratu. 'We talk later.'

Nine

There was one amongst them who took little comfort in the arrival of the visitors. Abinyor of Hrad-Uik, the youngest, prettiest, and brightest of her father's daughters, had a habit of forming hunches and fears that proved prescient. More often than not the coming of these men set them into action. Their names were synonymous with the troubles of the east. They planned lives that were not theirs to plan. Their presence instigated change. And for the time being, Abinyor liked things the way they were.

There were several reasons the Henghai might have come, she knew. Livestock mortality this winter was worse than ever before, and their dormant winter crop had everyone worried. Traders were ignoring her village because influential tribes to the east and north were quarrelling, again, and safe passage through disputed territories was no longer guaranteed. Enter a native of unknown origin to make them suspect a band was close, settling in perhaps, and there was another reason to draw important men to their village. They may not be there for the reason she feared most.

Abinyor of Hrad-Uik had come of age.

But the most asked about girl of the village showed an interest in no one. For an ordinary girl this might have been cause for concern, but Abinyor was no ordinary girl. She was their prize asset, favoured by gods as much as mortals and treated accordingly, from the very day she entered the world – delivered onto her birth-bed stillborn and drawing her first lungful of air just as her mother breathed her last. It had been a miracle, everyone agreed. And so it could also be argued that being her father's favourite was amongst her charms. The spirit of her mother lived on.

Perhaps it was this spirit that made denial so poor an option for her sharp young mind. When Borchek found her in the main room that afternoon dressing a pig for dinner, she didn't look up. Almost to the word she knew what would follow.

'Abinyor, they want to talk to you,' he said.

She put her flint-blade down and washed her hands in a bowl of scented water. Without another word she followed her oldest brother out.

Borchek led her into Ivnisi's house where she found Varsi and Kulej seated with her father at the main table. Her father greeted her with a weak smile. Varsi's was much more inviting, giving her greater cause for concern.

'Abinyor, it is time to talk. Come and sit with us,' Varsi instructed politely.

She sat down nervously. Women seldom went before the Henghai, even less was a meeting convened for their benefit.

'I understand your heart is still empty,' he said.

She sat still, a meek expression in her eyes.

'Speak openly girl,' her father persuaded.

'I don't understand,' she replied, not entirely truthfully.

'Listen to me now,' Varsi instructed. 'You have been gifted with beauty that cannot be ignored, and I think you know this. It is a fine gift and you are right to take your time, for you do your people proud.'

Abinyor forced a smile.

'Your father and I have been talking,' Varsi resumed. 'It is time you had a man. Do you know the Clan of Attuaal?'

'Yes.'

'Have you heard we are having problems with them?'

Abinyor nodded.

'We have been trying to honour relations with Attuaal but they are being difficult. You have an opportunity to do your people proud. Attuaal's son Segros has been asking about you. Do you know this?'

'Yes.'

'What do you think of this man?'

'I don't.'

'It appears he thinks highly of you.'

She looked to her father for support, and saw in his face a helpless look. 'I don't know much about him.'

'He is the son of a very powerful headman who shares blood with the Ubren clans of the north. His wife's passing came last year and now he is alone. Many girls would be proud to take her place, and you have been chosen above them all. He is still young and has many qualities.'

'What if I don't like him?'

'You cannot say that yet,' Varsi replied flatly. 'We propose you meet him over winter. There are several gatherings coming up, including some weddings he will be attending.'

She sat motionless, averting his stare. 'I would like to think about it.'

'You can discuss it with your father. But remember Abinyor,' Varsi emphasised with a pointed finger, 'your own people cannot provide you with a man to be happy with. Now you can benefit yourself as well as them. You would do well to think about that. Thank you, Abinyor.'

She left the room. Hrad-Uik sat with his head bowed. 'It is for the best,' Varsi reassured him, 'and you are fortunate she will be so close. Two days of travel, no more.'

But this was not what troubled Hrad-Uik. He knew his daughter, he knew Segros. A marriage between them was supposed to ease tensions between the two tribes, create an enduring alliance.

They couldn't have picked a worse match.

After his talk with the visitors, Vratu resumed his search for yew. He had made enough arrows now, and all he needed was the right wood for a bow. As he walked through the forest he came across a small antler. A use came to mind and he hooked it into his belt.

Late in the afternoon, having failed to find a suitable tree, he was heading back to the village when he saw Abinyor hurrying toward him on the same path. Her head hung low and strands of hair fell about her face. A step or two away from colliding into him she looked up and he saw tears streaming down her cheeks. She hastened past and

90

disappeared around a bend. Vratu followed.

The track led to a glade where a pond spilled into a series of riffles. Abinyor was sitting on a log with her back to him. The sound of rushing water drowned his approach, and not wanting to startle her, he stopped a short distance away and called her name.

She turned her head. For an instant her face showed surprise, then she turned it away again, though not enough to put him beyond the edge of her sight. Vratu stood there not knowing what to do. A weeping girl usually annoyed him, but not this time.

It was a pretty place, with willows draping their thin branches over the stream, patches of clean snow gleaming from the shadows. He felt her stare follow him to the edge of the pond where he picked up a stone and skipped it across the surface. When he turned around he saw her watching him through hooded eyes.

'I could make you laugh,' he said, walking closer. 'People are always laughing at me. But my words are like the chatter of squirrels to you, yes?'

She wiped a hand over her cheeks.

'Your face is prettier when you smile.'

She mumbled something in a voice that sounded spent and sad. He reached out a hand and laid it gently on her shoulder. She sniffled and didn't pull away from his touch, so he sat down beside her. Then, to his complete bewilderment, she draped an arm around his neck and buried her head in his shoulder.

He almost fell backwards in fright. It was the last thing he'd expected. Smack his hand away, push him back and hurl foreign insults perhaps, but not this. He glanced around nervously but the woods remained empty and quiet.

He put an arm around her shoulders and drew her closer, feeling in his fingertips the delightfully warm fullness of her body through the leather. She talked softly, letting it out, and though he couldn't offer a word of comfort he felt puffed with virtue just by being there for her.

They sat that way until he noticed that the light had dimmed. He gave her a nudge and they set off along the path. Not a sound came from her mouth the whole time. At the village perimeter she stopped and motioned for him to wait, then after checking that no one was in sight, she gave her eyes a final wipe clean with the back of her hand and walked briskly ahead.

Vratu gave her sufficient time to settle in before following. He found Hrad-Uik's family seated at the main table eating but Hrad-Uik and the visitors were absent. The smell of roast pork hung in the air. Abinyor kept her head down when he entered. Borchek stood next to her doing all the talking but when he saw Vratu he cut his voice short and his eyes darkened with suspicion. He held Vratu's gaze long enough to press home some sort of message, then resumed his chatter.

After dinner Vratu sat on his bed carving an impressive figurine of an aurochs out of a section of the antler he'd found, made soft by a soaking in water. When this was complete he went for his usual walk down to the river where he could feel as much as see the ice surging past. Vek strolled over and he sat scratching her head. The clouds parted and there amongst the familiar constellations appeared the blank face of a new moon. Vratu couldn't believe it. In three days a full lunar cycle would have passed since he set off on his Walk.

Again he returned to his bed after everyone had retired, and fell asleep easily. But he was mended now, alert to the sound of feet padding over the floor, the swirl of air about his face. He opened his eyes and saw Abinyor kneeling beside his bed, setting the wick of the pedestal burner alight.

She stiffened slightly, like a rabbit suddenly aware of being spotted. She withdrew her hand and he saw her eyes; liquid amber and dancing with flame, and before he knew what was happening she leaned forward and blew out the lamp. He felt the blanket lift away and cold clothing against his skin as she slid into bed and pulled herself close.

At first, he couldn't move. By nature he was an assertive young man, always the one to initiate. To find himself on the receiving end of such brazen behaviour from a woman left him as defenceless as a baby. Now she began grinding her hips into his slowly, breathing deeply and rubbing her face against his cheek. 'Plehk, plehk, kal bhosus, kal bhosus hner,' she crooned. A wild and aggressive energy was at work in the dark beside him, something he had never experienced, and now he felt something of his own respond, gathering thrust in a manner he was powerless to prevent. A delightful womanly scent filled his nostrils, urging him on.

She was moaning softly now, almost frantic. It was his invitation to rise from his state of helplessness, nice as it was, and take command like the man required of him. His muscles tightened, bursting with anticipation as he moved into position above. She moved her hands somewhere and he felt her tunic creep higher and warm thighs against his.

The hunter in him took over, weapon raised, his prize all but won. She would be his. To submit would be a sweet memory and a fitting finale to an extraordinary phase of his life. No need to worry about reprisals from medicine men, headmen or relatives; no need to ponder her motive. Perhaps this was how things worked here, this is how guests were treated. Why should he not oblige?

'. . . because you are not ready . . .'

It was as if his shaman had spoken over his shoulder. His hand, eagerly sliding her tunic upwards, froze. Another presence was with them now, hovering in the dark like an unwelcome ghost. The gyrating beneath him ceased abruptly and in that instant he knew the opportunity was lost. Whatever she offered had hung in a delicate balance, and his hesitation – even that brief – had tipped it the other way. His prize had fled.

But as the flame dwindled inside him, his better judgment returned. Something hadn't felt right. It was as if some affliction had possessed her, and she needed him for medicine. And then he thought of Nura, awaiting his return. The occasion was rightly his and hers.

She pulled him down, firmly but gently, without the urgency that had so greatly inspired him moments before. He lay peacefully beside her and felt the stroke of her fingers on the back of his head.

Too soon the hand slowed and stopped, her head turned to one side and her body went slack. When her breathing became deep and drawn out he nudged her awake. She sighed in the dark, stood from the bed and was gone.

For some time he lay on his back, staring up at nothing, thinking. When he finally fell asleep she came to him in his dreams, sweet-faced and pure as snow.

As the first light of dawn crept through the eaves he woke and dressed. Quietly he gathered his belongings and walked out of the room. As he passed Abinyor's bed he stooped to insert the aurochs figurine into one of her shoes.

He opened the door to the stables. Inside, Vek lifted her head and pricked up her ears. He walked on through, one or two pigs grunted sleepily and the dog gathered herself up and followed him out.

The morning was still and his breath came out in vapour plumes. Vek watched him longingly.

'Do you never sleep?'

He walked down to the riverbank where the canoes sat in a neat row, and placed his gear inside the smallest. A narrow shoulder of ice still clung to shore, beyond it the river was choked with moving ice floes. He pushed the canoe onto the ice and was about to step inside when he noticed Vek pacing side to side behind him.

'Stay.'

Carefully he put a foot inside the canoe, the ice crunching and cracking as it took the weight. Using the paddle for leverage he hauled himself forward, groaning with effort as he parted the ice with the hull until he was into free-flowing water. The canoe became part of a moving mass; only by watching the shore could he see how fast the current sent it downriver. Ice floes glided along with him, nudging his craft threateningly. Delicately he steered between them, pushing the smaller ones out of the way with his paddle until he drifted into the ice packed loosely in the shallows of the far side. By the time he reached the bank the inner lining of his garments was wet with sweat.

He stepped out of the canoe and dragged it upriver along the bank to a point opposite the village. Just before leaving he glanced back one last time and saw Vek still pacing the far shore.

Before the day lost its light, Kulej crossed over with Varsi and Borchek. Like Vratu, they were carried downstream a good distance and had to drag their canoe back upriver. They found the canoe Vratu had used and commended his gesture of leaving it where it could easily be found.

Varsi and Borchek set about tying the vessels together for the return journey while Kulej stood off to one side scratching his chin, glancing back and forth between the tracks at his feet and the canoe Vratu had used. The same words kept repeating themselves in his mind: 'You are Ubren, yes?'

And Vratu's answer intrigued him. 'No.'

Natives did not make a habit of speaking untruths. And this one had not spoken in an Ubren tongue. Close, but not the same. Somewhere out there were people they had yet to meet, an entire new tribe perhaps. People they had yet to come to terms with, negotiate with, begin with. A task as elusive as the destination of the footprints he studied.

'Where did he come from, do you think?' Borchek asked the question consuming Kulej's thoughts.

'Not from here,' Kulej concluded.

'Do you want to look for him?'

'No. Fed and rested he's probably well on his way back to his people.' Kulej sighed regretfully. 'Whoever they may be.'

They returned to the village and a few people made passing enquires as to the whereabouts of the native. There was not a lot of interest. They had work to do and mouths to feed. Now they had one less.

Ten

The Henghai had been wrong. Vratu had not returned home but to his cavern in the Hills of Uryak, for his Walk was not over.

It was as if he found a different place. All that remained of the snow were patches hiding in the shadows; everywhere else the ground steamed, rocks sparkled and trees glistened. Snowmelt trickled down hills like the veins of a giant beast, funnelling into a network of creeks and streams running loud and clear through gullies afresh with activity and noise. With every shift of breeze or turn of his head a new scent or mark caught his attention.

Now he could return to his task. Though he had been on his Walk long enough there was still something he needed to prove, as much to himself as any higher power. In any case it would be foolhardy to take the long trek home just yet: a mild climb left him short of breath, his limbs lacked their former lift and he found himself relying on frequent rests to accomplish fairly simple tasks. His lungs felt like they were filled with sand and ached with every exertion.

The pressing issue of a bow stock he resolved first by hacking a limb from a yew tree he remembered seeing. The rest of the day he devoted to checking and resetting his traps and snares. That night he sat chipping away at the yew until the stock was complete, and the next morning he put the final touches on it with his burins and knife before hardening it over a fire. A day later, a mud-caked sow digging her snout into the earth delivered him success.

'You have made me a hunter again,' he praised the fallen swine as he manoeuvred the arrow out of her ribs, careful not to detach the arrowhead. 'For this I will carve you into my hand-axe.'

Inside the sow he found a bonus delicacy – several foetuses, each about the size of a fist. Quickly he returned to his cavern and started a fire, soon afterwards sweet, wonderful pork was melting in his mouth. After that it was a leisurely affair of butchering the carcass, removing sinew from the muscle, laying out strips of meat to air-dry in his cavern and filling his shrunken stomach with small portions at a time.

Protein rich, he directed his efforts over the following days to foraging for plant matter a full recovery required: vestiges of corn salad, wintergreen and wintercress leaves, sorrel and dandelion stems, bracken rhizomes and nettle shoots. From the soft earth down by the creeks he plucked the starchy roots and tubers of cattail, arrowhead, bulrush, marsh roundwort, silverweed and brooklime, stuffing what he could into his mouth raw, taking whatever required cooking back to camp. His stomach never went empty and with each passing day he grew back more into his garments.

A change came over him. He found an unexpected fulfilment in being his own master, knowing that his survival rested entirely with himself. With no need to conform to rules or behave in a certain way, no need hunt or steal about in a state of virtual non-existence, he freed himself of his weapons and became one more harmless citizen of the wilds. The slap of the beaver's tail, the bark of the stoat, the hoot of the owl that had formerly let every ear know exactly what he was doing, took on a slightly different note now, a lesser urgency. Vratu enjoyed the distinction. It made him think they had a name for him.

Each day bared new wonders, new creatures emerging from hiding to scamper and scratch at uncertainties in the dirt and snow. He came to know them individually, their habits, their moods, their secrets. They shamed him with their superior senses, their imperviousness to the cold. They showed him how tight the margins for error were here; how something as simple as swallowing a minnow tail first could mean a choking death for a kingfisher, how the untimely twitch of a rabbit's ear could send a fox leaping into the thickets where it huddled. Every tragedy he witnessed, no matter how small, reminded him how his surviving the odds was cause enough to consider each day thenceforth a celebration of life.

But most of all they showed him the true value of his clan. They revealed in him a weakness that had no place here, a weakness that set him apart from all others. He missed the company of his own kind.

He wandered the Hills of Uryak in those final days with a gnawing guilt at having deserted the people he owed his life to. The thought nagged him long enough to send him back to the worksite one morning, only to find it deserted. From there he continued on to the Great River and with mild relief found no way of transport to the other side.

The snap of twigs or rustle of leaves during the night were so common he had learned to ignore them. Taking full advantage of his relaxed guard some badgers plundered his cache of dried meat, fungi and herbs from under his nose one night. Caught in the act, the cheeky thieves waddled off into the darkness grunting with the better portion of his carefully rationed supplies already in their stomachs. The following morning he tracked them to their sett and wasted daylight throwing all manner of insults into their tunnels until it occurred to him how foolish a sight he must have made. He stopped and laughed out loud. Then he realised he had laughed for the first time since beginning his Walk, which made him laugh louder still, and it felt so good that he gave it the full power of his lungs, and when he heard the Hills echoing he knew he was truly recovered. It was the sign he had been waiting for. It was time to head home.

That night, sitting in front of his cavern beneath a bison-head moon, the plaintive wail of a vixen sounding from the darkness below, he found himself in an introspective mood. The Walk he had entered into had taken on a new meaning. To treat it as a test of one's mettle, or a lesson in advanced survival skills, or a cull of the weak, was to overlook a deeper purpose.

Some things were plain enough. He had learned an indispensable lesson in humility. Never again would he underestimate divine potential, never again would he overestimate his own.

But some things were far from plain. He had never imagined, nor thought possible, the experiences he had had. Now he harboured the suspicion that something unique had happened to him, or been *done* to him. Something that would have consequences. Try as he might he could not put it into words.

But he knew it had something to do with *them.*

He lifted his head and spoke to the heavens. 'Your voice may be only a whisper, but I hear it all the same. I heard you in the blizzard, I heard you in the cry of the wolves. I heard you in the river and again when I was sick. You had to make me small in order to make me grow, I understand.'

The vixen stopped wailing, the silence grew heavy on his ears. The night held its breath, waiting.

'I am *ready.*'

He smiled contentedly. For now he could turn his thoughts to seeing his friends and clan again. He could look forward to the dance he was due, for a dance there would surely be: not everyone returned from a Walk with the Earth Spirit. And he looked forward to seeing his Nura again. He felt no shame about his attraction to Abinyor; on the contrary he was proud of his exemplary restraint.

He stayed up later than usual that night, admiring the stars and absorbing for one last time the essence of the Hills of Uryak. A chill air gripped his bones but he was not uncomfortable. He had been wrong about this place. Like his forest friends, it had shown him a new perspective.

The following morning, after eating a hearty meal, he gathered his belongings and stood with a melancholic ache on the ridge overlooking the gully that had greeted him every morning. The sky was a cloudless blue, a fitting day for a walk. And so with the sun rising over his shoulder he took his first steps home, tucked into some faraway hills where his people waited.

Eleven

With food in his belly and firm ground at his feet he had an easy march home. Creatures of weaker means scurried from his path, wolves loped by in attitudes of play, and grumpy old bison snorted and brandished their horns, warning him to keep walking. He paddled naked through the freezing waters of Heavy-Fish on a makeshift raft and emerged feeling home soil beneath his feet for the first time in almost two months. It took the bite out of the cold and made him stand taller, straighter. There were fewer surprises here.

The final night of his Walk he spent at Birdsong. The following morning he stacked a corner of the cave with a generous supply of firewood for its next occupant, and set off on his final leg with a bounce in each step.

The light was fading when he strolled into camp. First to see him was Ilan's infant sister, about to be smacked on the buttocks by her mother. The child's mouth had opened wide for a wail and then frozen when she spotted Vratu. Immediately she tried to wrestle out of her mother's grasp, pointing urgently with her finger. Ilan's mother looked up, her jaw dropped and the little girl wriggled out of her hands.

As Vratu crouched to pick her up he heard his name shouted from all corners of camp. Hands stopped, tools dropped, and giggling children charged at him as if in a race. Everyone came forward, some running, some walking, all smiling. The children showed no respect, pushing everyone out of the way and surrounding him in a pack so tight no one could move.

Banan parted the mass and held up his arms jubilantly. 'Vratu!' he cried. 'Back with the living!'

Hands gentle and rough were all over him, smothering and patting and shaking him. He saw his mother stopped at the edge of the crowd and had to fight through the wall of limbs and torsos to get to her.

'You came back,' she murmured.

'I came back,' he agreed.

'But why were you gone so long?'

'Ah!'

Laughter erupted at his reply, and nothing more would be asked of his time in the wilderness. Ulke used the distraction to gather her son in her arms in a manner they had long abandoned.

Voi ambled over with a smile, but it was a smile that only deepened the wrinkles on his face, and no lustre shone in his eyes. His walk looked more hunched, his stride shorter. He put a hand on Vratu's shoulder and joked, 'Next time we send you out there we will not make it so easy for you, yes?'

Vratu looked them over one by one, this family of friends, and saw how their eyes peered out of dark, sunken sockets, and how gaunt was the skin on their faces, and his heart went out to every one of them. It was clear that conditions here had been just as gruelling as his. Several women had their hair cut short in mourning-style. And still they found within themselves the heart and energy to rejoice at his return. Vratu could have wept.

They sat him down and food came to him from everywhere, but when he tried to turn away their precious offerings he was defeated by vehement protest. He felt even guiltier upon learning there had been unusually high mortality amongst his people, mostly infants and sick. As he listened to their woes he realised there would be no celebration for him that night. Voi summed it up.

'They cannot give you the greeting you deserve, so take what they offer. It is all they can do for you.'

Vratu took the confirmation without disappointment and Voi added, 'A dance when everyone is hungry and in mourning is a dance without laughter.'

'I understand,' Vratu replied.

'But they are happy you are back. It is the only thing worth rejoicing of late.'

'How are the other clans?'

'No better, no worse.' Voi sounded tired. 'Marhala Wunn has been very busy.'

'He needs to know I have returned.'

'Our hunters will pass through there tomorrow. They will tell him.'

'What then?' Vratu asked morosely. 'More tests?'

'No,' Voi answered solemnly. 'There has been too much of that already.'

Early the next morning, as Vratu sat watching the hunting party prepare to leave, Banan joined him. 'You are staying?' he asked.

'With my mother,' Vratu mumbled through a mouthful of dried pork he brought back from Uryak, by then as tasteless and tough as leather.

'That is good. She suffered greatly while you were gone.' Banan opened his mouth to say more, then thought better.

Vratu asked between chews, 'Will you pass through the camp of Iyanah?'

'Yes. We will take their hunters with us, and head north. There is nothing near here.'

'I would go if you waited another day.'

'You have seen how hungry everyone is.'

Vratu knew the hunting over winter had been exceptionally poor and they needed to make use of every day. 'I thought to see Nura tomorrow,' he said. 'If you tell me where you will be I will try to meet up with you afterwards.'

'Stay here with your mother. We will bring Nura back with us, and your brother. You have walked far enough, let them come to you.'

Vratu gave up on the piece his molars were wrestling with and spat it out. 'Bring me fresh meat,' he called after him.

In the dim light of evening a runner entered camp, sweating and smiling. Vratu recognised the grandson of Marhala Wunn himself. The runner made a beeline for Voi and conferred with him in private. Something was going on, again, and Vratu felt his insides curdle. After much chin scratching and furtive glances, Voi beckoned him over.

The runner raised a hand in greeting. 'It is good that you are here, Vratu. My grandfather asks that you wait for him tomorrow.'

'What does he want?' Vratu asked warily.

'You will see.'

Vratu appealed to Voi with a worried look, only to see a smile escape his lips. 'Oh no,' he winced. 'What is it this time?'

His old friend just smiled and walked away.

And so Vratu spent an uneasy night tossing and turning. The next morning he sat before a fire sharpening tools that needed no sharpening, and waited. Around midday a group of men arrived, including Marhala Wunn, Kihad, and those of Banan's clan who went hunting the day before.

'Are you back *already*?' his brother humoured.

Vratu staggered under a round of heavy backslaps, and then Marhala Wunn stepped forward and surprised him with a rare smile. An atmosphere of solemnity settled over the group as he perused the young man he had sent to a near death.

'How strange,' he said, 'is the manner of the gods.'

Vratu felt a lump grow in his stomach.

'Your people have done what they can to honour your return,' Marhala Wunn went on. 'What do you say to them?'

'I think they are too generous,' Vratu replied cautiously. 'I am just happy to be back. I want to help make us strong again.'

Marhala Wunn turned to Banan. 'Has he grown, do you think?'

'He has grown,' Banan replied firmly.

'Come then,' Marhala Wunn said to Vratu.

As they left camp Vratu glanced behind and saw the men wander off nonchalantly in various directions, and the lump in his stomach grew heavier when he realised he was on his own with the shaman this time. What would it be? he wondered. Another night blindfolded in a cavern? A beating?

They walked to a grove in the forest where a small creek sparkled. Marhala Wunn untied the knot on his belt pouch and pulled out a cold ember wrapped in leather.

'Make me a fire,' he directed, handing the package over. Then he pulled from his belt pouch a sliver of bone with a tiny inverted hook at one end, a burin, a bone tube with plug, and a small clay dish with lid.

Without a word passing between them Vratu gathered some wood and used the core of the ember to start a small fire. Marhala Wunn placed the clay dish on some coals to melt the fat within, then poured fine charcoal dust from the bone tube into the dish and mixed it into a paste with his burin. When this was complete he motioned for Vratu to sit on a log and began gouging a series of small, closely spaced holes into the flesh of his shoulder.

Vratu endured each little prick and sting feeling half proud, half deflated. Is that what all this is about? he wondered. Couldn't he have done this back at camp?

'This marks your ascendency among men,' Marhala Wunn said, punching another hole. 'You did well.'

Vratu almost fell off the log. Long ago he'd concluded he was more likely to hear a song from a fish than a compliment from his shaman. He was a strange man.

They sat in silence. Each time Marhala Wunn wiped the blood away he smeared a mixture of charcoal dust and fat over the skin and pressed the grit into the wound with the hook of the sliver. Every so often Vratu craned his head and saw a pattern of dark lines taking shape. The man's fingers intrigued him – cracked like baked mud and stained from wear and tear – yet still able to move with the dexterity of a spider spinning a web.

'I sent Iswahl on the Walk not long after you,' Marhala Wunn said.

Vratu's ears pricked up. 'Yes?'

'He came back early, long before you. This was a bad omen for me. I sent no one else.'

Vratu had to fight hard to stop a smile from breaking out on his face.

'It is well you missed the suffering while you were gone,' the shaman added.

Vratu was tempted to enlighten the man on *his* suffering.

The shaman took on an absent look. 'It was not my intention to send you into a blizzard. But there is a purpose to this we cannot see, as there is a purpose to everything. We are all mercy to the plans of the gods, yes?'

Vratu had little hope of thinking up a reply to this sort of talk.

The heaviness in the shaman's face lifted and a smile gathered on his lips. 'Voi had words with me when the blizzard hit,' he said. 'He wanted to look for you.'

'Oh?'

'I told him that if the weather improved it was unnecessary. If it did not, it was a sign no man should try.'

Vratu thought quietly. 'I fear for Voi,' he mumbled at last.

'Why do you fear?'

'He is losing his spirit.'

Marhala Wunn nodded. 'His time is coming,' he said in a solemn tone, causing Vratu to eye him closer. Not a wrinkle stirred on the old man's face. 'What would you have me do?'

'Talk to him,' Vratu suggested.

'For what reason?'

'Your words are stronger than mine.'

'Even if it was proper, what could be said? Your friend has had more time than anyone to prepare himself.'

'What do we do, then?'

'We give him what we have always given him. No more, no less. Do you think he wants it any other way?'

Vratu rubbed his forehead. 'How can he believe his time is coming? Surely he can see his heart is strong and his mind is still with us.'

'Tell me Vratu, do you need your eyes or ears to make you believe in something?'

'No.'

'So what makes you believe it, then?'

Vratu felt frustrated; he hadn't brought this up to receive another lesson. 'How do we know he hasn't many years left?'

'Who will ever know how many years he has left? Voi has had

105

more than most of us will. Perhaps he does not wish to be remembered as an old man shrivelling away like a leaf in the sun.'

'Is there no medicine you can work on him?'

The shaman's upper cheek twitched, as if answering was becoming an effort. 'Medicine needs a will to live.'

Vratu gave up. He sat silently and waited for him to finish.

There came a pause in the pricking and Vratu felt his shoulder wiped. 'It is done,' Marhala Wunn said, packing his tools back into his pouch. 'Go and wash it in the creek.'

As Vratu kneeled to clean his wound he considered his new tattoo, surprisingly small for the amount of effort that went into it, both Marhala Wunn's and his. This I carry for life, he thought, disappointed he didn't feel more enthusiastic about it.

He walked back and kicked the fire dead. 'It will sting for a while,' Marhala Wunn said merrily. Nothing more was said thereafter as they made their way back.

The scent of cooking meat came to him long before they sighted camp, followed by the excited shouts of children, harsh and high-pitched against the forest-quiet. Marhala Wunn picked up his pace. Vratu saw the blaze of several large fires through the trees and had his guess confirmed.

'They wanted to surprise you,' Marhala Wunn said, 'and they needed time to prepare.'

They walked into camp and a shrill cry went up, louder and louder it became until Vratu had to put his hands over his ears. Laughing faces filled his sight, children came running and girls studied him with fresh interest. Several members of Ukmaar's clan surprised him with their presence amongst the hundred-strong crowd. Everywhere thick slabs of meat hung from spits, dripping fat into sizzling fires, the smell so thick he could taste it. The crowd of children parted and there was Voi and his mother beaming proudly.

'Show me,' Voi asked as he came up. Vratu presented his shoulder and Voi looked over it approvingly.

'There are others still coming, Vratu,' Marhala Wunn promised. 'They will not miss this night. Come and sit, you have nothing to do but watch.'

Vratu's head swelled with pride. 'Is this what I think it is?'

Marhala Wunn lifted his hands to embrace the scene. 'Look what our hunters returned with, the very day after you returned.' He turned to Vratu and regarded him with frosty eyes. 'I am your shaman and this is clear to me. Your return is a good sign.'

Everyone sat down in a ring in the centre of camp and Vratu took his place proudly at its head next to Voi and Banan. Two girls carried freshly cooked bison ribs over to them on bark plates. 'Fresh meat,' his Uru said with a smile. 'As you wished.'

The celebrations were particularly meaningful; the curse that had stretched skin over bones was broken. They had slain two woodland bison and were in no mind to ration or preserve their windfall now.

Predictably, he had not seen Nura. He was the man of the moment, and she the woman, and he knew they were preparing her.

The music and dancing commenced. The women set the mood with a few traditional dances, and then a unique variation took place. The girls turned their backs and drew into a tight, circular huddle with their arms around each other's waists, then swayed side to side, tossing their heads back and forth. The huddle spun slowly, bouncing off sections of the audience time and again, until finally they returned to the middle of the ring. A piercing cry rang out, the huddle broke up and the girls scattered, and there in centre stage Nura appeared like magic.

Though the night was cold she had not covered up. Like everyone she had lost what little body fat she had carried into winter and her ribs shone from a sunken midriff heaving with each breath. Bony curves defined her hips, smooth enough around the edges to retain their fullness. Her legs, kicking urgently to the beat of the drums, were slender and lean. A complement of fine bead necklaces, bracelets and anklets added to her splendour, and even these compared poorly to the gifts given to her by nature.

She held the crowd captivated until her solo dance ended. They applauded her performance with howls of appreciation and a line of girls danced back into the circle to relieve her. Nura skipped away on feet that made her appear as light as a feather and disappeared beyond the rim of light.

Vratu could have been the happiest person alive at that moment. Everyone was paying tribute, and if he felt pride it was tempered by the thought that were it not for the sort of help he was supposed to avoid, his soul would be wandering restlessly far from his ancestral homelands that very moment.

A short time later Nura joined him. She had changed into plain warm clothes and looked no less spectacular. By then the men were dancing; a typically masculine display full of violent revolutions, but Vratu preferred to stay seated where he was with his woman resting her head on his shoulder.

At one stage Iswahl approached with a drooping face and sat down beside him. 'You are their favourite tonight, Vratu,' he said. 'I am happy for you, even if it makes me look poor.'

Vratu was in too good a mood for hostilities. 'You do not look poor.'

'Where I went I never saw a land so bleak, so empty of life. Was it the same with you?'

Vratu averted his eyes. 'Yes.'

'Aside of your faithful following most people thought you had perished. None more so than me, for I saw what it was like out there.'

Vratu shifted uncomfortably.

'Perhaps, if it pleases you, you can tell me how you did it. I may need to know for next time,' Iswahl said, demoralisation strong in his voice. 'But there is no hurry. I fear it will be a long time before our shaman sends me on a Walk again.'

The dancing finished, voices drew quiet and the gathering broke up. Before retiring, Vratu diverted to where Marhala Wunn was seated with a group of men. The talk respectfully stopped as he approached.

'Tonight I am honoured,' he said, 'but now I am tired. With your permission I will rest my head.' There were nods of approval and he turned to leave.

'It is a sign of providence,' Marhala Wunn's voice stopped him, 'that you have returned from your Walk with the Earth Spirit after the skies tried so hard to fall on you. It tells me He has grand intentions for Vratu of the Illawann.'

The men nodded reverently, but Vratu was not as easily swayed. The shaman had made similar predictions about other young men many times before.

The next morning he stepped out of his dwelling and found Nura waiting for him. They hugged each other and she leaned back in his arms and viewed him proudly, hair freshly combed and everyday jewellery smartening her appearance.

'Come for a walk,' she invited.

Vratu observed no one paying them any mind. Even her father was respectfully ignoring them.

Nura read his thoughts. 'Just you and me,' she said. 'Come.'

She grabbed his hand. He pondered the grounds for guilt and decided they were needless. Nura's father muttered from the side of his mouth as they went past, 'Don't go too far Nura,' and Vratu smirked at the double meaning.

They had to turn several bends in the river before he felt comfortable. They sat down on the bank and she told him how heavy her heart had been while he was gone, and he did the same, and with the river running quietly beside they spent many joyful moments proving it. At an interlude in their petting she sat up suddenly.

'What is it?' Vratu asked.

'I heard something.'

They waited innocently for a while and nothing happened. She brushed a strand of hair from her eyes. 'Where did you go on your Walk?'

Vratu frowned at her. 'The Walk is sacred. Not even our shaman dare ask me where I went. Why do you?'

She smiled cheekily. 'I am a woman.'

Vratu could have kicked himself. What a stupid question.

'What was it like?' she persisted.

109

'Cold.'

'Did you go south?'

'Perhaps.'

'We might be going south for spring.'

'What?' He sat up straight. 'Why?'

'My uncle and father want to go back to the Sleeping Grounds. They are worried the People-of-the-Longhomes are there.'

'They should tell me these things.' He slouched forward, thinking. This complicated things. The Sleeping Grounds were far from the Clan of Banan's spring hunting grounds, which would make it a lot harder to visit her. Worse, the move would take her closer to Iswahl, his proud antagonist of the Clan of Uru Ukmaar.

'They talked about you while you were gone,' Nura offered.

'Oh?' he asked, trying not to sound interested. 'What did they say?'

'Good things.'

'Yes?'

'No!' she laughed. 'Your head will swell and look like the moon.'

'Then let it look like the moon. The only talk I hear of me makes my head feel heavy.'

'You worry too much.'

'They give me reason to.'

'Oh, stop!' she groaned.

'I thought about you out there.'

Her eyes lit up eagerly. 'Oh?'

Vratu struggled with his jealousy; he wasn't making this up. 'I imagined how hard I would kick Iswahl in his shy parts if he tried anything with you while I was gone.'

She broke into a giggle. Vratu watched without sharing in her amusement. 'Did he?' he demanded.

'No,' she assured, and gave him a hug.

They picked up where they left off, but before his enthusiasm could get the better of him the reeds rustled behind them and this time it was obvious. Nura stood quickly. Her youngest brother and two children rose from the reeds and ran away laughing.

'Yah!' Vratu yelled after them, waving his hands angrily. Nura swore after them, not the least bit amused.

'Spies of your father,' he said irritably. 'Do you think they learned anything?'

She took his hand. 'Perhaps we should go back.'

Vratu kept his face sour and his feet firmly planted. Nura took a step away and jerked like a wolf-dog on a lead when she took up the slack.

'Come,' she persisted, pulling harder. It took a powerful surge of effort for him to comply.

Marhala Wunn sat staring into the hearth, a troubled frown darkening his face. Seated on the other side were Iyanah and Banan, waiting patiently.

They had not talked long. They had not needed to. The subject the Urus were there to discuss had been a regular topic over winter, and they had requested an audience with their medicine man only to see if he was closer to a decision. It seemed he was not.

And as they waited, his face perked up. Out of nowhere a lark had occurred to him. It was perfect. It might not solve the immediate problem, but it would help in an unrelated matter.

'Bring Vratu to me,' he said.

The headmen gave him a puzzled look, but said nothing. They were used to odd requests from their medicine man.

Banan left to get Vratu and returned with him shortly after. Marhala Wunn slid his backside and made a space. 'Sit Vratu,' he invited. 'Did you have a good night?'

'Very much, yes,' Vratu answered, sitting down with Banan.

'Show me your mark.'

Vratu unslung one side of his vest. 'It will look truer with time,' Marhala Wunn promised. 'I have a small task for you.'

Vratu felt the blood drain from his face.

'An easy task this time,' Marhala Wunn reassured him, and grinned when he saw Vratu relax. 'You know the lands of Oyub-ka have been Sleeping Grounds for two years now. No clan has been

111

there since I forbade them entry. Word from Krul is that People-of-the-Longhomes have crossed Heavy-Fish and moved onto the plains there. There is talk that we need to go back and see into this intrusion, proclaim what is ours. What are your thoughts?'

Vratu's initial flush of pride mellowed when he realised the true purpose of his being there. This was far too important a decision for him to have a bearing on. He thought hard, knowing they were only interested in how well he could make his answer sound, and mindful of where each man's opinion lay.

'I remember when we used to go hunting there how hard it was to find anything,' he said. 'Our friends of the forest knew us too well. They knew our scent and the sound of our feet. If we go back now they will scare easily. They will not have forgotten the smell of our traps and snares. I think they might not be ready for our return, and would move away.'

'Surely, not all our friends would remember us,' Marhala Wunn contended. 'And there will be those that came after we left, and those born since.'

'When I walked through Oyub-ka those years ago I found many bird nests filled with empty shells, yet I saw few chicks. I saw bears with only one newborn, wolves with only three or four. The fawns and calves took longer to learn to run and were slower than they should have been. Our friends were always weak and hungry; they had no meat on them. I do not pretend to think like a holy man but to me these are signs the land is in sickness. Even the song of the birds and frogs sounded sad. I think we should leave these lands to heal.'

Marhala Wunn's face beamed approvingly, in contrast to the grim faces of his Urus.

'These things may have been so; they may not have been so,' Iyanah answered. 'How many eggs a bird should lay . . . how fat the fawn should be. These are things we may differ on; it matters not. The intruders that have come into our lands are real. They can be seen, they can be heard. It might serve us well to walk away from our land when it is in sickness, but now it needs our return . . . ' his voice deepened, 'to see to this. I am in agreement with my brother. It is because we left these lands empty for so long that this has happened. These people are blind to all signs – signs that we will live there again, signs that the land is not well. This is because they have no respect. What damage have they done? Have the fish left our rivers? Have they scared the deer and the bison away forever? Let these people be scared away – forever. This will serve our purpose.'

And so the talk went on. Despite him knowing that his opinion had no influence either way, Vratu took heart that he was being listened to. This young man, so seldom taken seriously, was making a valid argument in front of his leaders, and he spoke freely knowing that he had no better ally than the shaman himself.

Each man exhausted his viewpoint, all but Marhala Wunn who sat staring with disquiet into the fire. After a break of heavy silence, after all that could be said had been said, Iyanah spoke.

'Of course, it would be a long walk for you to see my daughter,' he mused, 'should I take my people south.'

Vratu thought desperately for a response to suggest this had nothing to do with his reasoning. When nothing came to mind he looked down.

They waited for Marhala Wunn to speak. By then his head had tilted forward and his eyes were closed. They thought he had dozed off, which was also not unusual.

'There is much to think about,' he said abruptly, eyes shut. 'Last winter was a bad sign and I am troubled. Things are taking place in our lands to the south that require looking into, but until we heard these rumours it was not my intention to head back there so soon. We court ill-tidings if we do the wrong thing.'

He opened his eyes and they shone in the firelight. 'We will wait until spring. It will be clearer to me then.'

The visitors to the Clan of Banan trickled away in family groups with smiles on their faces, the women tilted forward with small children strapped into baby-carriers, men with backpacks and overnight gear. After they had gone Vratu kept an eye on Voi's dwelling, intending to pay a visit. The talk with Marhala Wunn the day before about his old

113

friend's health and state of mind had left him unsettled.

As dusk descended he saw Voi emerge and head up the hill for his evening sitting. He gave him a bit of time before following.

'Vratu of the Illawann,' the old man said when Vratu found him at his usual spot. 'Back from his lonely wanderings and here now to intrude on mine.'

'Yes, back from the Walk,' Vratu said as he sat down. 'And I am ready. When will I have my woman?'

'When *they* think you are ready.'

'Ah! I shall be as old as you.'

They watched the horizon shimmer and melt beneath the fiery ball above. 'I wanted to ask you something,' Vratu broke the quiet. 'What is happening in the lands of the east where Krul and his cousins hunt?'

'All we hear of them is ill. It reaches here and darkens the minds of men like Iyanah and Ukmaar. I fear a trouble coming.'

On saying this, Voi turned his head toward him, eyes still searching. Vratu knew that look; it made him think the old man was reading his thoughts. To block the sixth sense probing him he looked away and gestured at the forest with a lift of his chin. 'It goes on and on, yes?'

'Yes.'

'You didn't think I could do it, no?'

The old man chuckled; the sort of chuckle that suggested he knew something. Vratu frowned, at a loss as to how. 'Am I being funny?'

'You came home,' Voi replied. 'That is all that matters.'

Vratu opened his mouth to speak, but no words would come.

'Whatever happened to you out there is yours,' Voi added reassuringly. 'There is no need to talk about it.'

Vratu fidgeted with the wolf's teeth on his necklace. There was nothing he could ever hide from this man, wittingly or not. 'Are the signs so strong?' he mumbled faintly.

Voi kept staring ahead as he answered. 'You've been sick. Very sick. I hear it in your voice, see it in your eyes. You're filling out again but a shadow still hangs over you. Winter made us so weak we could barely lift those who passed, and yet you managed to stay away in it longer than anyone before you, with the means to carve a new bow and arrows. Now you come to me asking questions about the People-of-the-Longhomes and troubles in the east.'

Vratu could see the logic in this, but even this wasn't enough to convince him the old man wasn't psychic. 'I found them,' he confessed.

Voi nodded. He turned an ear slightly more toward Vratu and waited.

'South of the Hills of Uryak on the far side of the Great River. It had frozen over and I was able to cross. I fell in on my way back and they found me at the edge of the spirit world.'

The rim of the sun was sitting on the horizon when Vratu started his story, and by its end had long sunk and stars were pricking the sky. He had told Voi everything, all but the finer details of his involvement with Abinyor, and throughout his old friend had listened quietly. Vratu was enthused. It took a lot to impress the old man these days.

Afterwards, Voi sat in deep thought. He rubbed his temple and said, 'You left them without saying anything?'

'Yes.'

'What made you leave?'

'I needed to be back in the forest.'

'Where things are more easily understood, yes?'

'Yes.'

'For you saw much that you did not understand.'

Vratu nodded.

'Were you afraid?'

Vratu opened his mouth to refute the suggestion, then remembered who he was talking to. 'Perhaps.'

'And fear makes a man weak, while it makes the man or beast that stands before him taller, stronger.' The old man's eyes went soft as they turned toward Vratu. 'You have asked me many times why my father took us away from Uryak all those years ago.'

Vratu nodded cautiously.

'Now you understand.'

Vratu thought carefully about how to proceed. He desperately wanted to keep the subject going but feared the wrong question would make the old man evasive. 'Are these the same people you knew as a boy?'

'That is hard to say.' Voi's brows contracted as he thought. 'We hunted the lands surrounding Uryak, but more to the north. The last time I heard the name of the Oronuk was long ago.' His voice became weaker as he reminisced. 'I remember the dancing and feasts we had with these people; for so long it was like this. Then without warning it all stopped, and in the days that followed I heard strong words between my father and grandfather. Soon after this came a night when I heard crying and the names of many people sung in mourning. The next day we left, but my grandfather and others stayed. The last I saw of him there were tears in his eyes.'

Vratu sat spellbound. It was as if he had been told something sacred. He waited respectfully for more but it seemed his old friend had said enough.

'Is it true what the clans say?' he prompted. 'Did they make war on our people?'

Voi shrugged. 'My grandfather Ubnakar was a good man. I was only young when I last saw him, but what I did not know of him then I have come to know since. Such men do not let their people perish. He promised to return to us one day and it is only because he never did that people say they no longer walk in this world. But I think not. There must have been a good reason he could not keep his promise, the only one he never kept. And those who stayed would never have left him. The truth is that none of us know what happened to them. I always thought to return east to find out, but I know now it will never happen.'

Vratu thought about the kindness shown to him by the People-of-the-Longhomes. 'It is hard for me to believe they can be the cause of so much suffering.'

'Do not be fooled. They mourn their dead as we do and their vengeance is just as merciless. They have medicine we do not, medicine powerful enough to turn people from their ways. They hunger less and grow stronger. You will learn what you need to know of these people in your own way, in your own time. I will never see them again. But you,' Voi nodded, 'I think you will.'

From the distance came the far-carrying whistle of a roding woodcock. Voi waited until the sky was silent again. 'You should keep what you told me to yourself,' he advised. 'Talk of these people fills our minds with worry. We are not ready for them yet.'

Vratu had already decided to keep the details of his Walk secret. People would think he had cheated.

His old companion smiled and pointed at the twilit sky. 'See the stars?' he said. 'Some say the spirit of our Passed reside within, watching over us. If you look closely you can see their hearts beating.'

'Who will teach me when you are gone?' Vratu blurted out at last.

Voi gave no reaction other than a slight shift in posture. When he answered his voice sounded more tired than ever. 'You said you were ready.'

'How does someone know?' Vratu asked. 'Are you?'

The ghost of a smile flitted on Voi's lips. Vratu watched him closely, this man already part of folklore, revered by his peers and loved by all. He looked more aged than ever, weather-beaten like the scaly rock around them, so far removed from his proud seat at banquets where men had paid him homage and fine women had danced. And now those days were like old friends, passed away long ago, and everything about him seemed spent, and Vratu knew his spirit was preparing him, and there was nothing he could do except respect his will.

'This is my season,' Voi said softly.

Vratu stood with a sigh, then left the old man to himself.

Twelve

Winter faded, life pulsed with the coming of spring.

As he often did when he had to make a difficult decision, Marhala Wunn withdrew into the forest. Strange forces had been at play the winter past and he needed the sort of guidance only nature could give. Here energy flowed about him, and through him, like wind through the crown of a tree.

How he loved the colours that burst from each level of the forest. How he loved the song of the warblers – the first to return home from their warmer climes. Following in faithful procession were swifts and swallows and martins and flycatchers, dipping and slanting at speed through the greening canopies. There at his feet dormant seeds sprouted from their beds, while all around him defunct, wisp-like plants shrunken over winter fattened and flowered and unfurled with urgency. Shaggy nests appeared on every conceivable perch and small shapes darted along the tangle of aerial walkways. Here and there he saw clearly where heavy paws had flattened the undergrowth, or where snouts had turned the soil. He smiled at catching a glimpse of cubs or pups or kittens emerging from winter dens bright-eyed and hungry for the outside world, tripping after their lean mothers. Peeling back the bark of trees or inspecting the upturned blade of a leaf revealed a profusion of joint-legged miniatures emerging from cocoon and egg. A steady hum of wing beats vibrated the air, dancing with a menagerie of iridescent purple wanderers and fritillary butterflies.

He arrived at the overhang of Vratu's Sit and stood over the ashes of the abandoned fire, thinking about the young man. He had been doing a lot of this lately, thinking about Vratu and how his coming of age coincided with some extraordinary developments over winter. Sometimes these thoughts made him uneasy. Not that he thought ill of Vratu, or held him to account. If things went well he would happily marry him to Nura before long.

But this was not what he came here to think about. He shook the distraction from his head and set about rebuilding the fire. Once it was alight he sat down cross-legged and opened his belt pouch. He pulled out several small chunks of dried fly-agaric toadstool, balled his hand into a fist and turned his thoughts to the subject he had struggled with these past months.

The Sleeping Grounds. Bound by marshes in the south, a series of hills to the north, and with a plain of thin woodland and steppe between. Well did he understand the logic of those who wanted to go back there. Why then, his hesitation? What made him so uncomfortable with what the leadership of the clans wanted to do?

There was much to the logic of giving the land time to recoup its losses, to allow their forest friends time to develop a sense of security ripe for their hunters to pick. Yet there was also much to a graver logic, one he would not talk openly about. It was there in the back of his mind, shadowing all other considerations. His greatest responsibility was to protect his people, and he knew that if they returned to the Sleeping Grounds there was the strong possibility of conflict.

Rarely did he resort to what he was about to do now. He opened his palms and contemplated the dried toadstool. This needed to be done correctly. Take too little and he would fail to hover between temporal orders of existence, take too much and it would feed him false messages. Worse, it could seriously harm him. For this reason he carried an amount that he knew from previous experience was safe.

He placed a small piece in his mouth and chewed. A bitter taste flooded his mouth and he swallowed quickly. Bit by bit he downed the fungi, waiting after each swallow, feeling the floating sensations come to him in waves. After finishing it all he closed his eyes.

Slowly the sensations intensified. His head became light and tingly and his thoughts turned hazy and surreal, prising into dimensions closed to normal consciousness.

Hallucinogenic images began to bombard him. He thrust his

119

hands out in front repeatedly, as if clutching at something in murky water, and he would grab it and pull it closer to see what it was, but each time it slipped between his fingers and kicked away. It was hard to focus with all the strange patterns and colours glowing around him, with pieces of the wall swaying and eerie humming in his ears. Several times he stood to dance and chant in the language of the spirits, then he would drop to his knees sweating and wait until the energy built up again, pulling him to his feet to send him dancing back over the floor with his limbs moving to a volition not his own.

This went on for some time. In due course he dropped onto his back exhausted. The roof revolved above him. He closed his eyes and let sleep overpower him.

A whiff of smoke brought him back. He opened his eyes and saw thin grey curls rising from the ashes. It made him think again of the poor young man he had made sit here a whole night, equally frustrated and without answers.

'Vratu . . . Vratu,' he groaned. 'Why do you keep coming to me? I am here to decide on a matter of great importance for all of us. Go away, I am making talk with spirits that know far more than you or me.'

His head felt squeezed and his fingertips were numb and tingly, like pins and needles. There were cramps in his stomach and his mouth was as dry as sand.

The cavern was a darker shade when he sat up and massaged his forehead. As he gazed at the dying embers he could feel Vratu's spirit lingering. Strange that when asked for his opinion on Oyub-ka, Vratu had mentioned drops in litter and clutch sizes and the poor health of the young. Hunters far more experienced than Vratu often missed these subtle observations. Voi had mentored him well. Was Vratu's opinion indeed worth listening to?

No, he decided. A young man's ulterior motives should not interfere with such an important decision. He frowned, irritated with himself. It was time to go.

He stood and stretched, reeling slightly. There had been nothing in the experience that qualified as a vision and he was as much in the dark as before. But he knew what to do now. The consensus of his men was that they should go south and nothing from the spirit world had warned him otherwise.

This would make Vratu unhappy. He would think it another test, another conspiracy against him. In a way, perhaps it was. Marhala Wunn chuckled giddily at the thought all the way home.

A speedy runner relayed Marhala Wunn's decision to Banan's group late that afternoon. Vratu took the news joylessly. He had advocated loudest for leaving the Sleeping Grounds alone, amusing everyone and fooling no one with his reasoning. Only Voi was without opinion. Vratu became concerned at his unusual silence but left him alone in the hope that his morale would improve once they left the Winter Grounds.

Vratu stashed his cooking gear and heavy winter accoutrements inside his dwelling, stacked his traps by the river, rolled up his fish and bird nets and hid them below ground to prevent needless temptations of theft. His preparations never took long and he was ready well in advance of everyone else.

They were all, for the most, in high spirits. Rippling grasslands and meadows of fresh herbs with swarms of fat game awaited, streams would be churning with huchen on the move. Only one issue disheartened the People now, an issue that confronted them often when they moved from one place to the next.

The old woman was a late addition to the Clan of Banan, forced to join her one remaining son when there was no one left to look after her anywhere else. Vratu took pity on her as she sat on a mat in front of her dwelling. Nearby, her son and grandchildren checked over their travel packs.

Vratu walked over to her. 'Are you happy, Mother Inrik?'

Her eyes remained empty when she answered. 'It has been a long time since I have felt the happiness you do, Vratu. This is what happens when you lose your interest in things. But I have saved what is left in me for the last, and today I will be happy.'

'Will someone sit with you?'

121

'My son will stay for a while.'

'I am sad for you. Are your legs so heavy? Where we are headed is only three days away.'

'This is where my path ends,' she said with a smile, exposing all that remained of a set of crooked teeth. 'You are sad because it is all ahead of you, and you see someone for whom it is all behind. If your journey takes you as far as mine, when your time comes you can be happy too.'

Vratu put his hand affectionately on her shoulder. She put her own hand on top and gave it a squeeze. 'You are a good boy Vratu, a good boy. The memory of you will stay with me where I am going.'

He glanced around for Voi and saw him rolling up a blanket in front of his dwelling. So far his old friend was making every indication that he, at least, would be leaving with the group. Vratu released his hand from the old woman and let her be.

When the time came tomorrow they would bid her farewell with a few tears and embraces, and she would watch quietly as everyone walked away. Her son would remain with her a few days, perhaps less. It never took long.

Old man Voi sauntered about the camp quietly, stopping here and there to offer assistance to people as they arranged their loads into portable bundles. Feeling weaker than normal, he kept his exertions light and didn't have much to say.

That evening they feasted heartily as one unit. Their preparations were complete and everything was ready for the morrow's departure.

Voi climbed the hill for his evening ritual and was walking along the ridge overlooking the camp when he heard faint singing below. His people were blessing their Winter Grounds. Their singing followed him to his usual spot where he settled his old bones down and wondered where his thoughts would take him tonight.

The clouds were feathered streaks of pink and purple, the blood-red sun was soft on his eyes. The breeze came from the west, fat with the warmth of spring. He wondered what secrets it carried, what lands it had passed through, what it had left behind.

Mythical lands to the west, lands beyond his knowledge. The wind had been there, the same wind caressing his face now like his wife used to do, lifting his grey hair from his shrunken shoulders and parting it from his wrinkled forehead. He stood up and looked down, into a scene glowing in peace and happiness; a scene that might have been out of his past, when it was he who led them, when it was he who gave word as to when they left the Winter Grounds. Two boys wrestled in the dust laughing, a group of young girls finger-painted the side of a dwelling. And there were the men he had held in his arms as babies, babies he had watched grow into boys and fine men, men who had shouldered more and more of his burdens with each passing day, until there was nothing left for him to carry, and he could enjoy the peace of his final years effortlessly, like floating down a gentle river.

He turned to face the breeze. There seemed to be something riding with it, an invisible hand plucking away his weariness and throwing it to the wind. The years peeled away and he felt sensitivity return to his skin, tired muscle awake. Without knowing where he was going he made his way across the ridge and down the far side, into the gentle push of wind that sighed through the forest voids.

Where he was back in his hunting days. Every creature he had ever hunted fled before him, he quickened his pace. These paths he knew, they did not interest him now. He needed to get further away, to where the forest was less familiar.

He revelled in his march. Each step gave him new life; he had not walked with this energy in years. His night vision returned and his eyes flicked from side to side, guiding him through the growing dark and steering his legs faultlessly. The blood thrumming in his ears fine-tuned his hearing, enabling him to detect sounds he thought he could no longer hear, allowing him to differentiate between the scurry of paws in the undergrowth and the shuffle of his own feet. As if carried by a river in flood, with the dark forest rushing past either side, he went on and on until he came out onto a grassy plain glittering beneath a rising moon. At the far end a hill showed its jagged silhouette against the starlit sky. It looked familiar. He would climb to

123

the top and see what he could see.

The grasses were soft against his ankles, the spicy fragrance of flowering plants was rich in his nostrils. The ground tilted and he began his ascent, steeper and steeper through the whispering firs where the chill came back to him. His lungs heaved like a young man after a sprint, and as he climbed his legs grew so heavy that he had to stoop and reach out with his hands and claw the rest of the way, which he did without rest.

The ground levelled off and he was in the open again with the moon lighting his way. A large animal – a bear by the sound of it – crashed away through the undergrowth. The sound of its frightened retreat fell away and he filled the silence that followed with a burst of laughter. Possibly he knew this place, he could not be sure. His orientation had become confused. And now his mind was playing tricks on him. Flashes of silver, too bright for anything real, shot across his field of vision.

But Voi was not fooled. He was where he wanted to be, had invited the hand that led him here.

His age came back to him in weary waves. A rocky outcrop shone like broken teeth at the edge of the spur, he stumbled toward it. He sat down with his back against a large boulder and a clear view over the silver-lined canopy that shimmered into obscurity below, and wondered what lay hidden beneath, what rituals were being played out by the animals that hunted within.

His breathing returned to normal and he was overwhelmed by a dreamy light-headedness. He lay down on his back, tired beyond repair, and gazed at the starlit heavens that had always filled his mind with wonder and questions, and now he felt an incredible peace, for he knew the answers were coming.

On earth that might have held traces of his ancestors, the old man rested his bones. No animals feasted on his flesh, no birds picked at his face. Even in death his body endured. His people would cry and sing their mourning songs, but no one would look for him.

They knew he had given himself back.

Part 2

The People of the Longhomes

Thirteen

Haden Usonoli was dead.

Over a hundred mourners followed the funeral party carrying the bier up the hill. Beneath a cluster of sycamore trees at the top of the rise, a cairn sat in front of a rectangular pit. Down in the pit a small fire flickered, illuminating the flowers that carpeted the floor.

The funeral party reached the grave and the bier was gently lowered to the ground. Haden Usonoli lay on his back. An embroidered vest stitched with patterns of shell beads and quills was open on his chest, revealing a boar-tusk amulet, necklaces of shells and clay-fired beads. Ochre-painted tribal insignia covered his skin and spirally wound copper bracelets circled his wrists.

The dead man's son, Romoyr of Usonoli, was a bear of a man with a cold, predatory glare and neck as wide as his head. He jumped into the grave and three men carefully lifted the body off the bier and lowered it. As delicately as putting a child to bed, Romoyr lay his father down, angling the peaceful face toward the rising sun and tucking his legs into a flexed position.

The deceased's bow and quiver full of arrows were then passed down, followed by his hand-axe and favourite mug full of honey mead. A large vessel of the same drink, incised with stripes, meander and spiral motifs, came next. There would be drinking and feasting in his wake, and dead or no, Haden Usonoli would be offered the same while it remained in their power to do so.

Once each item was arranged within easy reach of the corpse, hands reached down and helped Romoyr out of the grave. Everyone waited quietly. The sun poked its face above the landline in the east and a shaman's voice broke the silence.

'I speak to the gods of the people of Usonoli. Enter the man-spirit that waits at your door, see to him in the afterlife as we have on

earth. There was good in this man. His spirit was your will, his blood the fish, the bird, the beast.' He upended a small pouch over the pit and shook out its contents; earth from the graves of the dead.

'Though you dance no more, we will dance for you. Though you sing no more, we will sing for you. In times of darkness we will pray to you, and you will see courage return to our eyes. Prepare our seats in the house of souls. We are all coming, good friend.'

Romoyr lifted his mug to his lips, drained it in a few swallows and tossed it into the grave. An assortment of wooden and ceramic cups rained in after.

They filled the hole with earth. One by one the mourners left until only the grieving son and an old man remained. Neither spoke as the sun rose behind and gave the grave their shadows.

Then Romoyr looked up. 'It begins,' he said, and walked away.

The old man stepped onto the freshly heaped soil, looked down at his feet. He thought the last of his tears had been squeezed from his eyes long ago. So what was this mist gathering in them now?

'We have done great things, my friend,' he said, 'but you leave us much too soon. Now your wolves of war are free. With you gone, how will I stop them?'

He kept his head bowed and stole a few moments more. Behind him in the house of Usonoli, where he had been made welcome since he was a boy, he knew they were waiting. Everyone except the man who mattered most. Romoyr of Usonoli would turn his back on them all, just as he had then, as if they meant no more to him than enemies he'd left hanging from trees.

But of all the old man had lost lately, he had not lost hope. Or his reputation, which he needed now more than ever. Wherever he went he became the centre of their known world. Beyond the furthest reaches of his people's influence, into lands his men rarely travelled, more people knew his name than any other.

That name was Unatks Vahichiwa.

* * *

It looked worthless there in the dirt, and until now ignored by all passersby.

Nurekt Gurajnik stooped and picked up the thumb-sized rock. He juggled it in his hand, then rubbed away some dirt to better expose the lustreless blue veins that told him it was no ordinary rock. He gave it to his son Ursil, who smiled and said, 'I like this.'

The lode had reached the surface where it had been stabilised by a surface coating of oxide. Pure and oxidised minerals just below the surface promised much more. Beneath the two men's feet lay weathered horizons formed by impurities leaching down over the millennia, successive zones of oxide and carbonate ores, and below this, a zone of enrichment where the impurities accumulated at the water table.

Ursil put the piece into his bag and scraped his shoe over the soil. 'We'll have to dig.'

'Let's keep going,' his father said.

The two men gathered their weapons and walked upstream. Fish shot through the pellucid waters, bordered on both sides by overhanging willows. As they headed west the forest opened into swaying grassland where they paused regularly to inspect and praise the fine-grained yellowish loam at their feet, soft and porous enough to be cultivated with the simplest digging stick.

Later that afternoon they entered a small valley. They turned a bend in the creek and Gurajnik saw a collapsed arrangement of stones and logs reaching into the water at right angles from the bank. As he slowed the shape of a dilapidated weir jumped into focus. His gaze darted up the bank and found a number of ovoid structures resembling large mounds of dirt.

'Wait,' he said, grabbing his son by the arm. 'See that?'

Ursil sighted down his father's extended arm. He opened his mouth to speak but Gurajnik quickly put a finger to his lips to hush him. But there was no sign of activity: no racks of drying meat, no smoking campfires.

'It's empty,' Ursil confirmed.

Gurajnik walked ahead, scanning the surrounding forest intently.

He stopped in the middle of the strange looking settlement and took note of the abundance of weeds, shrubs, seedlings and saplings that had grown unchecked for some time.

The twelve or so dwellings around them did not appear to be regularly maintained. The walls of several buckled and the daubing was so thin on others that the hazel framework showed through like ribs on a dried corpse. Leaves and twigs had collected on rooves. Grass sprouted between campfire scars and bleached animal bones.

'Where are they?' Ursil asked conversationally.

Gurajnik was too preoccupied to answer. He saw that each door was tied fast, presumably to stop snouts or claws prising them open. He went to the closest and untied the bindings, then stooped through and straightened to his full height at the centre. A leather flap drooped into his face from the smoke-hole of a flaking and punctured roof. Faded animal skulls, jawbones, horns and antlers hung from the walls. Ringing the floor were baskets and wooden pots, bowls, cups, a few mildewy furs and a rolled up reed mat. A cold hearth with a thick layer of congealed ash sat in the middle.

He picked up the odd utensil, gave it a quick inspection and carefully placed it back. Lastly he kneeled to examine the ash in the hearth. His guess at when it had last been fired matched the evidence outside. He ducked his head through the door and rejoined his son.

'What do you think?' Ursil asked.

'Two years have passed since people lived here,' Gurajnik answered. He spied something standing prominently at the edge of the camp. 'What is that?'

A pole, taller than a man by another half-length, was fixed into the earth. A large bison skull sat at the top. Frayed cords and plaited hair dangled from the horns, and a pair of dried eagle's talons hung from a cross-member tied beneath. Bird dung staining the skull completed an aura of barbarity. It must have been a tribal icon or totem, a silent sentinel presiding over the abandoned camp.

'So,' Gurajnik said, 'this is what a camp of the Wandering Tribes looks like.'

'This could be the place Nivik told us about.'

'No. Where he spoke of was much further west.'

'I wish we had found this sooner,' Ursil said, turning around in a circle to take everything in. 'What now?'

'Now?' Gurajnik shrugged. 'We go home.'

That night they camped by a bend in the creek where it was hard to be seen. They spoke softly, and went without a fire.

They returned to their tiny, two-longhouse settlement the following afternoon to find their extended family hard at work tilling the fields. The wife of Gurajnik, a pleasantly plump woman named Esrah, greeted them. 'How was your exploring this time?'

'Good, good,' Gurajnik replied, glancing around for his two younger sons. 'Where are Szlahov and Yukuv?'

'They went after some deer we saw.'

'They should be working.'

'They've been working all day,' his brother Djuri called as he shouldered his heavy hoe. 'I let them go. My boys went with them.'

'It's almost dark. If they're not back soon we'll eat without them.'

Gurajnik and Ursil walked into the larger of the longhouses. By typical standards theirs was relatively small, without the tripartite division into northwest, central and southeast parts, though planned extensions would lengthen them significantly. In a corner near the entrance Ursil unshouldered his pack and emptied the malachite onto a small pile of identical rock.

'We should show this to Nivik,' he suggested.

Gurajnik thought about this. Turning the ore into pure metal was not a simple task, and his contribution to the fledgling industry was restricted to finding the ore, crushing it up with heavy mauls, and bagging it. His other brother Nivik though, situated a little over a morning's walk south, was well equipped with the tools and moulds for casting, along with the ovens, blowpipes and billows to fire the necessary heat. Gurajnik held ambitions to start the trade himself.

They went back outside. Feeling the age of his legs, Gurajnik took a seat by the front of his house to watch everyone finish up.

Several rectangular plots stretched out in front of him. The largest

– an emmer crop planted the previous autumn – needed to be re-sown now it was evident winter had killed every shoot. All they could do for the time being was dig with their hoes, turn the residue and weeds over and disburse it all into the soil.

Gurajnik valued the opportunity to relax. The life of a farmer, combined with being the family head, was one of foresight and planning. Their first and foremost requirement was arable land. He could never get enough.

Each day he went over yield projections, estimating the needs of each household, the required surpluses to reseed the fields, the winter fodder needed for the animals, and the debt he owed to friends and relatives. From these he subtracted anticipated losses from storms, insects, wild animals, fungal spore infestations, and weeds, and came to the same conclusion every time. A hard year lay ahead. The priority now was to expand the clearing and have another field planted by the end of spring, but the extra tilling had thrown his schedule into confusion. Should he plant barley and einkorn, or could the soil here support the tastier spelt, club and bread wheats? Which strains would be tolerant of this cold and wet environment? Which had ears that would not shatter easily with harvesting? Should he plant flax and poppy, or legumes like peas, beans and lentils? Should he have rotated his crop or left the field to fallow?

This was only their second spring and already he had a failed crop. But like all farmers he had grown up with despair. Earth worked for generations near his former village had shown signs of impoverishment and an interlude of abandonment was unavoidable. Notwithstanding his lost winter crop though, the decision to relocate showed signs of being a good one. The yield from their first harvest had been extraordinary and were it not for his recent bad luck he would even have improved on that. A copper vein might make the difference. Labour could be bought with such commodities.

Yes, he reminded himself, there was much to look forward to by coming here. He had tired of his former life. Behind him were petty feuds, infuriating tribal politics and overworked earth. Here were wilderness and prosperity for the taking. Visions of being a major supplier of native copper to an eager market made him more optimistic still. And being the first to settle gave him entitlements. In time relatives could settle here without interference, perhaps along the terraces above the river or into the side-valleys. A new generation would take root here.

He looked at the sun, noting where it touched the tree line. In the same line of sight, just beyond his fields, a ring of poles stood in a brilliantly conceived geometric configuration. Properly aligned, the poles of the sun-calendar threw slim shadows with a precision that helped them decide when to plant and when to reap, or when the ripening of seed was overdue. Though still in its infancy, the tradition was already reaching beyond its practical applications. Perhaps, in time, people like him would trace the paths of celestial bodies, or join the brighter dots in the night sky, and see patterns of relevance they could extend to matters of everyday living. Perhaps they would teach their sons, and they would teach theirs, each generation building on the knowledge of the preceding. And perhaps one day they would worship the sun, and pay tribute through human sacrifices and other bizarre rituals played out beneath megalithic monuments dragged into position over ridiculous lengths of disobliging terrain.

Dusk was settling when his wife announced dinner. He noted the gold-lined clouds hiding the sun and decided tomorrow would be another fine day for work.

Only then did he spare a thought for the natives. True, there had been signs of their presence from the day he and his advance party of labourers first arrived. They had stared in bafflement at cave walls painted in what looked like blood. They had fingered foot-holes made in trees for climbing and scars in trees where bark had been cut away. They had picked at shell middens and campfires scattered over the countryside. And all had agreed that it was not possible to determine exactly how old the finds were, or if those responsible for them still lived there.

With only a few abandoned dwellings to consider, Gurajnik preferred to think that their owners had moved on. As far as he knew, natives did not prefer the type of country his people sought. They were not a numerous people.

The cool breeze made his skin feel clean. He rose from his chair and followed the last of his family inside.

That evening he was sitting alone at the main table sipping a mug of herb-tea when his son-in-law Guunt entered. The slim young man poured himself a mug from a bladder over the hearth, and sat down opposite him.

'It is getting warmer,' he said. 'We should sow soon.'

Gurajnik nodded and blew on his steamy drink.

'Perhaps we should just plant barley.'

'No,' Gurajnik disagreed. 'That last winter was one of a kind. We won't see another like it for a long time.'

They sat silently sipping their teas. 'I was led to believe we were alone here,' Guunt said after a time.

Gurajnik halted his mug below his lips. 'What do you mean?'

'Ursil told me you found a native camp.'

Gurajnik grimaced. On their way home, he had discussed the matter with his son and was under the impression they had agreed to keep it quiet for the time being. 'It was abandoned.'

'I've heard they do that sometimes,' Guunt said. 'Just like us. They usually come back.'

'Are you afraid?'

'No, but for the sake of our families perhaps we should be. You've heard the same stories as I.'

'From people whose motives I question.'

'What is there to question?'

'We know that in the east they come out of the hills to trade, to feast. Truces have been made – '

'And broken.'

Gurajnik shrugged. 'Where I come from, the only sign we ever saw of them was after they had gone. They passed through like soft breeze.'

'Then you were fortunate not to have suffered the fate of people I know.'

133

Gurajnik took another sip. 'What are you trying to say, Guunt?'

'The natives that lived in our parts were different to those here.'

'Oh? How so?'

'They knew of us.'

There was a long silence. 'Wars between them and us are a thing of the past,' Gurajnik reassured him.

'Do we risk our lives to believe this?'

'Risk our lives? We found an empty camp and you think our lives are at risk?'

'As do you. Why else would you not tell anyone what you found?'

Gurajnik felt his temper rise. 'You sweated here dawn to dusk in those early days sleeping under the stars swatting bugs and going hungry with the rest of us. What do you want to do now – leave when our reward is due? You saw last year's harvest, you have seen the rock we found today.'

'You won't be counting your grain and rock when you wake to find your house in flames.'

'This will not happen.'

'In other places it has, you know this. How can you dismiss this so easily?'

'Oh enough!' Gurajnik raised his voice. 'Wherever we go, someone has to settle first. You wanted to come here as much as the rest of us.'

Guunt bit down on his lips and took a calm breath. 'I came because your daughter came.' He stood and retired to his room, leaving his tea steaming at the table.

Fourteen

They made good use of fine weather in the following weeks. They gave the soil a quick tilling and went back to tree felling. The two heifers were hitched with a simple harness and used to drag trimmed logs over rollers all the way back to the village to be split and cut. When the danger of late frosts had passed and the soil felt warm and moist in their fingers they suspended all other forms of work and began sowing. A second shallower tilling to aerate the soil was quickly completed, after which lines of stooping men, women and children spent several days planting seeds in the shallow furrows. Gurajnik decided on a mixed planting strategy of emmer-spelt, with a few other plots dedicated to barley, peas and lentils.

After planting the spring crop Gurajnik and his team put in a day's effort pushing back the forest with heavy hoes and hard muscle, fighting stubborn blackthorn and hazel and bracken and birch stumps, piling it all up into mounds as high as their arms could throw. Late in the afternoon they put it all to the torch. They stepped back and leaned on their hoes with aching spines to watch the ash rise and merge into the smokescreen above. Birds hoping to snatch the odd insect fleeing the flames appeared from nowhere.

The flames were dying when they headed back. Beneath a gabled roof sat a large oak table and benches that served as their common area. The men sat down at the table and poured themselves mugs of barley water made cool in bladders of moist fur while the women prepared dinner and the children made up for lost playtime.

No one noticed Rukruk and Mulek run off to the fields, save a dog. Her ears shot up, she aimed her snout their way and decided whatever the two boys were doing was more interesting than sniffing for titbits at people's feet. She reached the boys in a few quick strides and nipped at their ankles as they ran happily ahead.

Rukruk slowed to a walk as he approached the closest of the smouldering piles, seeking a burning stick. Around him the ground lay black and smoking.

'Ouch!' Mulek cried as he trod on a hot patch. In his haste to follow his cousin he had neglected to put on footwear.

Rukruk taunted him with a laugh, then picked up a glowing branch and ran around drawing patterns in the fading light like a firefly. He found sport terrorising the poor dog with his fiery stick but she seemed in two minds; her tongue wagged playfully while her tail cowed between her legs. She retreated in full flight to the far end of the clearing with Rukruk in headlong pursuit.

Suddenly she froze in her tracks. Rukruk stopped a short distance behind. The dog lowered her head and pointed her nose forward, baring her fangs and growling, the fur on her spine as stiff as quills on a hedgehog.

Standing like stone only a few lengths away, with expressions set to match, were several strange looking men. One man was kneeling, scratching at the smoking earth. He saw the boy and stood quickly.

No one spoke. The strangers stood motionless in the dying light. Mulek ran up whimpering with exaggerated pain, but when he saw what the dog was growling at he stopped with a gasp. Rukruk grabbed him by the arm and they turned and ran.

'Did they say anything?' Gurajnik asked his grandson. All six men of this embryonic community had collected indoors, along with the boys' worried mothers.

'No,' Rukruk replied firmly.

'What did they look like?'

'They had things in their hair.'

'What were they wearing?'

Rukruk thought about this. 'Leggings and shirts with patterns.'

'Not all of them,' Mulek was eager to make his contribution. 'I saw two with loinskins on.'

'How many were there?'

'Four or five I think,' Rukruk answered.

136

'Five,' his cousin corrected quickly.

'Did they have weapons?'

Rukruk cut in quickly, 'Yes.'

'What sort?'

'Bows and spears.'

'All right.' Gurajnik waved them out. 'Go and help your mothers with dinner.'

After the women had taken their boys outside, Djuri said, 'That does not sound like any of ours.'

'No,' Gurajnik confirmed. 'It seems we are not alone, after all.'

They were quiet in their thoughts, then Ursil asked, 'What do we do now?'

'Nothing,' his father answered with a shrug.

Guunt had listened to everything quietly, and only now did he speak. 'We ought to keep someone on watch tonight.'

Gurajnik asked, 'What for?'

'They may come back.'

'They would have done so already,' Gurajnik pointed out, searching the faces of his men and seeing genuine worry for the first time in two years. 'They weren't here to cause trouble.'

Obuczni, a cousin of Gurajnik who had followed him west, scratched his nose thoughtfully. 'They may only have been passing through,' he proposed.

'True,' Gurajnik agreed. 'They could be headed anywhere, following their food.'

Guunt spoke again. 'And if they are not?'

'Then they are not,' Gurajnik answered indifferently.

Djuri's eldest son Nyaniv, the youngest amongst them, added his voice. 'Should we try to find them?'

'We would need an interpreter if we did,' his father said, 'and the closest Henghai is at least three days away. A six-day return trip, and we wouldn't even know if he spoke their tongue until we found them.'

'Here now,' Gurajnik offered cheerily. 'There is nothing to fear. We'll take a quick look where the boys saw them and then we'll eat.'

They went outside. Dusk had deepened and colour had been replaced by various shades of grey. Women and children stood around doing nothing, waiting for instructions.

'What is everyone doing?' Gurajnik asked. 'Do we eat tonight?'

'Where are you going?' his wife called after him.

'Start dinner. We won't be long.'

Using improvised torches from the smouldering piles they walked extensively over the area and found only a few faint footprints. They all peered long and hard out into the darkening forest, where night animals were already making their calls.

'Do you think they're watching us?' Ursil asked.

Gurajnik stood facing the forest, hands on his hips. 'I'm hungry,' he said, and turned to head back.

Later in the night he was jarred awake by horrendous squealing and yipping coming from outside. By the time he sat upright on his bed it was over. He grabbed an adze as he rushed through the house and found Obuczni and Nyaniv already outside, staring ahead. Both were armed with bows and arrows.

A waning moon cast silver light over the pigs, jittery in the pens. Djuri made a lonely figure way out in the dark, whistling and calling the dogs' names.

'What was it – wolves?' Gurajnik asked.

'We didn't see,' Obuczni replied.

The night was as empty of sound as it was of form. They stood quietly, overcome by a feeling of dread more sinister than any threat to their livestock. Djuri began walking back.

'Where are the dogs?' Gurajnik asked him as he got closer.

'Out there somewhere.'

Now Ursil and Guunt rushed out of the house, armed with adzes. 'What was it?' Ursil called as he came up.

'We don't know,' Gurajnik answered, listening hard. If it had been wolves or a bear the dogs would be taking up the fight. Out of the longhouses came the women now, some holding lamps that lit up the fear on their faces.

They did a count of the hogs and discovered that one was missing. The wattle fencing was intact. They held their lamps close to the ground but saw nothing to raise suspicions.

'Go back inside,' Gurajnik told the women. 'There is nothing to see.'

The women went inside to see to the children who kept calling out with excitement. Gurajnik followed his wife and daughter inside and went to his room. He was feeling about in the near dark when Ursil entered carrying a lamp.

'Are you staying up?' he asked.

Gurajnik found his bow and arrows and mumbled a confirmation on his way out. They found Guunt, Djuri, Obuczni, and Nyaniv still standing by the pens.

'I will sit up with Ursil,' Gurajnik told them. 'You should all go back to bed.'

'Ah,' Djuri replied, 'I will find it hard to sleep now.'

'As will I,' Obuczni agreed, rolling a stump forward to sit on.

Guunt and Nyaniv returned to their respective houses. The remaining men gathered a pile of wood and lit a large fire. Soon afterwards the dogs trotted out of the dark with frothy tongues and wheezing throats and went straight for the water troughs. Gurajnik and Djuri followed them over and gave each dog a cursory examination as they lowered the level of water. All were found without injury.

'What did you see out there?' Gurajnik asked affectionately as he checked the last dog over. 'What were you chasing?'

The four men sat close to each other during their vigil, weapons at the ready and a large fire blazing. Occasionally one of them stood and went for a stroll. There was nothing to report. After returning from one of his reconnoitres Ursil rolled up a fur to use as a pillow and stretched out on the ground. Soon he began to snore.

'Go on inside,' Gurajnik said to Djuri and Obuczni. 'My son and I will stay up.'

Djuri yawned and said, 'Maybe Guunt is right. Perhaps we've come too far. Nivik's village is a full morning's walk from here. Maybe we should consider leaving this place, for now at least. We can come back later.'

Gurajnik put another log on the fire. 'No,' he disagreed. 'If this was them – and we don't know that – what have they done? Taken meat to feed their families. They have no reason to do worse. It only bothers me that they haven't come to us yet. This is what they usually do. Once we start talking the situation will improve.'

'Should we go to their camp?' Obuczni asked.

'Not yet. Not until we have to.'

The next morning they did a thorough investigation and found several patches of blood inside the enclosure and a drop or two leading away. There was no other sign of a struggle and the human footprints leading to and from the pens were inconclusive. Someone made the suggestion that they dig a pit around the pen as added security, as if it might in fact have been a bear or wolves, and no one answered. The fencing itself was more than adequate for that type of thief.

It put them all on edge. Translocating livestock this far was an enormous undertaking and they valued every animal they possessed.

That day all hands were given to twisting and binding hazel, and by evening both houses had stables inside.

Fifteen

Over the following days Gurajnik noticed a change in the mood of his extended family. In small groups they focussed on land clearing and though the days passed without event, voices were quieter and humour was short-lived.

In the evenings the men gathered around the main table and went over what they knew about the habits of the Ancients, which served only to demonstrate the scale of their ignorance. If the men they had seen were not passing through they must have been part of a larger group, in which case Gurajnik preferred them to come to him, on their terms. He wasn't going anywhere and they knew where to find him.

He didn't have long to wait.

A few mornings after the incident with the pigs he was lying in bed savouring his last moments of sleep when a hand rocked him awake.

'Nurekt! Wake up! Wake up!' his wife cried urgently.

His mind cleared itself instantly. 'What is it?'

'Come and see. There is something outside.'

He dressed quickly and followed her outside. Everyone was assembled in the middle of one of their newly planted fields, staring motionless at some sort of fixture rising above their heads. Though at that distance he couldn't see it properly, a sense of foreboding turned his stomach into a knot as he set off toward it. He reached the group and not a single gaze diverted from the peculiar sight.

Stuck into the soil was a pole about two man-lengths high, with a bison skull headpiece identical to the one he observed in the native camp weeks before, save for one glaring difference. The face on this skull was freshly painted. An enigmatic frieze of red, black and brown dots, lines and crosses stood out boldly against the white of bone.

'What in the gods?' Gurajnik asked. No one spoke. All felt the same dread the object seemed to exude.

'Take it down,' he ordered.

It was fixed deep into the soil. Obuczni and Guunt gripped the pole and pulled it out. The weight of the headpiece toppled it backwards onto the earth with a thud. The hollow eye sockets stared at them accusingly.

The porridge simmered quietly, sending streams of vapour up to the ceiling. Gurajnik stood over the pot stirring the mix in large circles. He could hear the women and children outside carrying on as normal, which was more than could be said for his men.

'Who wants some of this?' he asked, holding up the ladle, and his companions each raised a hand. The porridge slopped loudly as he filled their bowls.

The bison-totem leaned against the wall. Djuri stood before it, scowling up at the bone-white skull. 'It's beyond me,' he admitted, scratching the stubble on his cheek. 'But they must be trying to tell us something. What,' he pointed a finger at the skull, 'do those lines mean? Has no one seen anything like this before?'

'My boy scribbles like that all the time,' Ursil answered.

The others chuckled in light relief. Gurajnik held out a bowl to his brother. 'Stop worrying about it. Come and eat.'

The six men ate quietly until Nyaniv said, 'It might be a greeting, or a tradition.'

'The tradition of giving their enemy fair warning,' Guunt commented dryly.

'Are we certain they put it there?' Nyaniv asked. 'Could it be Nivik's boys playing tricks?'

'No,' Djuri disagreed, then turned to his nephew. 'It's the same as the one you saw before, yes?'

'Oh yes,' Ursil replied.

'We should try to find them,' Nyaniv suggested.

Guunt asked, 'And then?'

'Talk to them.'

'In whose tongue?'

Gurajnik finished his bowl of porridge, placed the spoon inside and pushed it aside. He rested his elbows on the table, clasped his hands together and massaged his forehead with his thumbs.

'All right,' he said finally and stood, wiping his hands on his leggings. The confidence he added to his tone was not what he felt. 'I had hoped they would come to us like proper men but it seems this is not their wish. We could send a runner east in order to find an interpreter, but we'll be waiting at least five or six days before anyone came back, and that's if one can be found at all – the Henghai are elusive at the best of times. Or,' he raised his hands, 'we can go ourselves.'

There was silence for a while. 'We should discuss heading home,' Guunt suggested gravely.

'Home?' Gurajnik asked with a frown. 'What home? This is our home.'

'You know where I mean.'

'To an empty village and soil as dry as sand? Leaving everything we've worked for these last two years?'

'We can start again somewhere else.'

'Just because we found a stick in the dirt?'

Guunt gave his father-in-law a harsh look. 'Before this day we could argue reasons to be optimistic. Not so from this day on. You want to know what this message is; there can be only one. So let us talk plainly. We are not safe.'

'You are free to take my daughter and go whenever you like,' Gurajnik retorted. 'But think about this. Where would we be if we never went forward? Sitting in worthless dust, wondering what might have been. This is what we are. We would be nothing if we never took our opportunities.'

'This is different.'

'Is it? Let us talk fairly then, if we are to talk plain. The things you fear had their origins far from here. We don't know what really happened and the fighting ended there long ago. Men of the Wandering Tribes are not all cannibals and thieves. They are men, like

143

us. They laugh, they cry, they love their children and they want enemies no more than we do. What would they gain by causing trouble for us? What is a tiny patch of grassland to them? They have shown us they live here, but to do more than that? To come into our village and do . . . what?' he faltered, as if speaking the words might invoke the catastrophe lurking in everyone's minds.

'You speak as if you've forgotten what they are capable of,' Guunt said.

Gurajnik raised his hands as if there was nothing more to say, then turned and approached the totem. 'I am going to find these people. Today.' He glared long and hard at the skull, as if expecting dissent. 'It would be good to have company.'

'He is right,' Djuri said to the others. 'Sooner or later we have to go to them. Now is as good a time as any.'

Ursil said resolutely, 'I am keen.' He turned to Obuczni and looked at him questioningly.

Their good cousin answered, 'Of course.'

Guunt stirred his porridge slowly with his spoon. 'What will you do when you get there?'

'Of more interest,' Djuri remarked, 'is what they will do.'

'At least send for Nivik. Get some of his men to come with us.'

Gurajnik said, 'More men will look threatening.'

They sat quietly waiting for an answer. Guunt shrugged and said, 'If I am needed I will go. I think a few of us should stay here, though.'

Gurajnik eyed him distastefully, then returned to the pot of porridge. 'Who wants more?'

Djuri held up his bowl. 'Do we send a runner for the Henghai?'

'Perhaps when we come back.' Gurajnik leaned forward to take the bowl. 'Depending on what happens, we may not need one.' Too late he realised he could have put it a better way. He noticed Guunt scowling at him more ferociously than ever.

'The Henghai have spoken poorly of us in the past,' Ursil commented. 'They warned us not to come here. Why would they help us now?'

'It would be in their interest to,' Gurajnik answered.

They watched him with odd looks. No one appeared as confident as he.

At first glance, they looked peaceful. Women sat or stood around in small groups doing what appeared to be very little; here someone weaved fibres, there someone crushed seeds or daubed a wall. Children screeched and played while older boys and girls sat around flaking or carving things out of wood and bone.

A woman's shriek sounded from somewhere, then with alarming speed they dropped whatever they were doing and went for the children, shouting words in tones so guttural they barely sounded human. Gurajnik observed that the camp was made up almost entirely of women and children. And though they behaved like a frightened herd of deer there was an order to what they were doing, as if it had all been done before.

There were about twenty of them. Gurajnik stopped close enough to be heard without raising his voice. It took the women only a few moments to do what was needed, then the camp grew oddly quiet and he was challenged by a collective look of scorn.

They wore very little. Children went naked and young women wore only short loinskins. Older women wore long tunics. An adolescent girl with perfectly shaped breasts caused his attention to momentarily stray. The wolf-dogs, indistinguishable from their wild counterparts, watched the newcomers with restless inquisitiveness, reacting to the shift of mood with propped ears and hanging tongues.

The camp had been totally refurbished, its purpose restored. Overgrowth was gone and campfires were clean, bones and rubbish had been removed, spits and tripods and racks for clothing and cooking and drying meat were everywhere. Mattocks and various shaped digging sticks leaned against the huts, furs pegged and stretched out for tanning lay beside smoking fires.

In repose, the camp took on the aspect of a natural setting. Their dwellings might have risen up from the earth. A pack of wolves might have wandered into camp. Everything was dressed in shades of earthy brown.

The dust raised by the commotion floated about the camp in a lazy haze. An old man with a fierce look stepped into view. Two boys, short of a man's height and with shoulders yet to widen, flanked him. Their eyes darted about nervously.

The only sound came from water gushing over the weir, completely repaired now. Gurajnik took a deep breath. The air felt warm and sweat stuck his beaded shirt to his skin. Keen to impress, he also wore copper armlets and bracelets, and a necklace of polished mussel shells that sparkled in the sunlight.

'They carry weapons,' Guunt observed. Only then did Gurajnik notice hand-axes dangling inconspicuously in the hands of the old man and boys.

'So do you,' Gurajnik pointed out. He raised his hand in greeting and walked forward, his company following a pace or two behind.

'Greetings to you there! Do any of you understand me?' Not one of them moved. It was like walking into a camp of mutes.

'Their men must be out hunting,' Obuczni said.

The old man came forward and stopped in front of Gurajnik. Two men, descendants of common ancestors that had taken separate paths an aeon before, appraised each other wordlessly at arm's length.

'Hello there,' Gurajnik said. 'Do you know who we are?'

The man didn't utter a sound.

'This is hopeless,' Guunt grumbled.

Gurajnik's focus alternated between the man before him and the camp behind. A young boy tried to walk over and the old man barked loudly and stopped him.

'Give me the beer,' Gurajnik instructed.

Ursil stepped forward carrying a bladder and two mugs. Gurajnik took the mugs and his son poured them half full while the old man watched expressionlessly. Gurajnik took a small drink from one, then held the other out for the old man and motioned for him to do the same.

The drink was the best of their brews, sweetly fermented and easy to swallow. The old man took the mug and sniffed it, his brow angling quizzically. Gurajnik motioned again for him to try it. The old man took a reluctant sip and looked up aghast.

'That bad?' Gurajnik asked. He needed a response – a grunt or a laugh or a punch even – to help decide his next action. Nothing in the man's expression gave the slightest hint as to what he was thinking.

But as Gurajnik flicked his gaze from feature to feature, from eye to eye, he sensed more to their guarded demeanour than first appeared. Their eyes glinted with the light of enquiry and a perceptiveness as keen as any wild animal. These people were anything but mute.

The elder's attention diverted to Gurajnik's copper bracelet and stayed there.

'You want to look at this?' Gurajnik slid the bracelet off his wrist and offered it to him. For the first time the old man's face cracked in a positive way. He took the bracelet and balanced it in his hand with admiration in his eyes. Then, to Gurajnik's amusement and surprise, he put it to his tongue and tasted it.

Gurajnik shook his head when the old man offered it back. 'Keep it,' he said, using his hands for effect.

The old man looked at him blankly. A middle-aged woman with two bloated breasts sagging down almost to her navel walked up carrying a child. Gurajnik expected the old man to bark at her also, but she came alongside unchallenged.

'Ursil, show her your bracelet.'

Ursil clawed his bracelet protectively. 'Pigs to that idea.'

Gurajnik tried not to raise his voice. 'Give it to her.'

With a grimace Ursil offered his bracelet to the woman. Her face lit up as she took it from his hand. 'At least ask him if we can all sit down,' he suggested.

'No,' Gurajnik replied firmly. No invitation had been forthcoming, and something didn't feel right. His men had brought enough food for a meal, should the opportunity present itself, but the silence dragged on without the signs he was looking for.

'We should have brought gifts,' Obuczni reflected.

Gurajnik held his hands out and spoke clearly. 'You are welcome in my village, anytime,' he said, and pointed. 'All of you. My village – over there.'

'They know where it is,' Guunt reminded.

Gurajnik ignored him. 'We will eat.' He demonstrated with his hands. 'No need for skulls and sticks in the dirt.'

He let his attention wander one last time. He would have liked a closer look at their tools, their weapons, their dishes and their jewellery. Here was his first real opportunity to gain firsthand experience of a mythical people whose movements were as mysterious and unpredictable as the weather.

'We will go now. Thank you and goodbye. Goodbye.' He raised his hands in farewell. The old man stood rock-still.

'Shy man,' Ursil said.

A small boy raised his hand and imitated. The woman holding him smiled and waved as well, but her company didn't lift a finger.

'Let's go,' Guunt said.

As they put the camp behind them Ursil summed up his thoughts: 'They didn't like us.'

'What did you expect?' Gurajnik responded. 'A feast with dancing women? They didn't run away screaming or attack us with spears. That is good enough for me.'

'Men are men. We all know courtesy.'

'This was the first step,' Gurajnik said. 'That man was no leader and I don't think it was within his means to talk with us. When the men return, he will tell them we were there. Then we shall see.'

'Perhaps we should stay and wait then,' Ursil suggested.

'No, Gurajnik said. 'We did what we went there to do. Now it's their turn.'

Sixteen

Northwest of the village of Gurajnik, far beyond his regular patrols, was a native camp he was unaware of. Like the one he did know about, it too had only recently been occupied.

None of its thirty-three inhabitants, save one young man through extraordinary circumstances, had ever laid eyes on the People-of-the-Longhomes. His people knew who they were though, had even heard there were goings-on in the southeast that might be of concern. But for the time being none of this was their affair.

It was late at night and only this young man and a girl were awake. The fire in front of them crackled without pause, like the girl's voice, and tonight the People-of-the-Longhomes could not have been further from their thoughts. She had poured her heart out about a boy she was fond of, and the young man was doing his best to make her happy by telling her everything she wanted to hear. Doing his best because he was only half-listening.

Vratu was a troubled man.

Not because he had done anything wrong, this time. And not because of hard times; a thin layer of fat gave him a glow of health. And not because of rumours about trespassers. The source of his troubles was something far more serious: a girl.

More than two lunar phases had passed since he had last seen Nura, and by now it was causing him serious distraction. He forgot where he put things. He missed words sent his way. He missed signs of his quarry, missed their trails. Once or twice he had even missed what he aimed at. Missed! Fat, lazy boars close enough for him to hit with his eyes shut. What was happening to him?

The more the girl talked, the more he tried not to think about it. And the more he tried not to think about it, the more he did. The sound of a man laughing from somewhere conjured up an image of a woman, or perhaps two women, doing their thing with him. He should be that happy, he told himself.

'But he is always fighting,' she went on. 'Always. I have lost count how many times I have seen his face blue and red. I hate him fighting.'

'It is true,' Vratu agreed, making an effort to refocus. 'But he is a good fighter. I like him being my friend. With him beside me I never have to fight anyone; his fists always beat me to it.'

A smile shone on her face and she looked away. Sitting there quietly they were two of a kind, preoccupied with the same thing. The source of his preoccupations though was much further away than hers.

No runners had come from Iyanah's clan in all this time, no news from the small numbers of visitors that had stopped by. Time was dragging on. There had been no invitation from Iyanah's family for him to visit, and the cruel delay gave him dark thoughts. He even imagined Iswahl sneaking about her camp, spying on her like he used to do. Waiting for his moment of opportunity, like a coiled snake. Waiting for her moment of weakness, of indecision. Perhaps it was too late already. Right now they could be . . .

'Vratu!'

He forced the horrible image from his mind and saw the girl frowning at him.

'Did you hear what I said? People say you are a better talker than listener, but tonight I find you are neither,' she complained, though she was grinning forgivingly. 'I said – what about you? I have told you about my sad heart, tell me about yours.'

'There is no need,' he told her with conviction. 'I am decided. I will take care of my sad heart tomorrow.'

'Will you go to see Nura, then?' she asked shrewdly.

'I will.'

As pale light rimmed the east the next morning, Vratu left camp and headed toward it. Each step closer to his destination convinced him that he had made the right decision. A weight had been lifted; he glided through the forest without a ragged breath. Two nights he camped, lying awake for long periods rehearsing in his mind how to spend his precious time with Nura.

Evening was settling in on his third day out when he saw the faint light of a single campfire far ahead. Usually there were many; it was unusual to be homing in on one. The men must be away on a hunt, which was a good thing. It presented him with opportunities.

The final leg he completed in near dark. Carefree and full of spirit, he let leaves crackle beneath his feet and branches spring back noisily as he brushed past. Suddenly a twig snapped behind him and he swung around reflexively, raising a hand in defence and fumbling with the other for the hand-axe at his waist.

A voice sounded in the dark. 'Speak quickly if you are a friend.'

It sounded familiar. Clutching his hand-axe tightly Vratu walked closer until he could hazard a guess as to the man's identity. 'Turuk?' he greeted the elder and relaxed his grip. 'A fine welcome.'

'Vratu,' the old man gasped thankfully, lowering his bow. 'Go on to camp. You will find Nura and the women but the men are away hunting.'

'Why do you hide in the bushes?' Vratu asked. 'Is something wrong?'

'People-of-the-Longhomes came today.'

After seeing his sister-in-law and nieces to bed, his stomach satisfied but his reason for being there not, Vratu went outside to think. On arriving at camp he had found the mood jittery, hardly apt for a girl to fling herself into his arms and carry on as normal.

The only man left in camp, Turuk joined him by the fireside. Even the shaman was away in the forest doing a shaman's thing. Vratu was amused to find his presence welcomed; with his muscle now on offer their fighting force had virtually doubled. Far from amusing though was the broader issue.

People-of-the-Longhomes were here. Living in their land, their most sacred possession. The only thing that ever came under dispute or was fought over. Protracted negotiations, formal agreements and reciprocal arrangements entitled who could pass through, let alone enjoy an extended stay. And these people had come uninvited.

The old man told him that other than taking a pig and leaving a bison-head sentinel behind, they had left these people alone.

'Has anyone made words with them?' Vratu asked at a pause in the elder's dialogue.

'No,' Turuk said. 'After we found them we held council. It was decided that no one is to approach them.'

Deep in these thoughts he retired to his brother's dwelling to find his sister-in-law and two nieces sleeping soundlessly. He arranged his bedding on the opposite side of the hearth and stretched out on his back. Long after he normally would have fallen asleep, he was still thinking.

Anyaj, the wife of Ursil, checked that the dinner broth was bubbling nicely before taking her daughter and a young boy to check some fish traps.

The two children skipped merrily in all directions as they walked along the riverbank. She passed the first of the ropes dangling into the water and left them alone, intending to check the furthest traps first in anticipation of being loaded with fish on their return. After rounding a few bends she looked behind and noted unconcernedly that the village had fallen out of sight. Unlike the others she didn't believe natives constantly lurked about, even less that they posed a threat to a defenceless woman and two children.

The boy ran on ahead, skipping stones across the water at regular intervals. After Anyaj counted ten ropes she turned into another stretch of river and saw an empty trap sitting on the bank. Further up, the boy blissfully hopped along the track. She stopped by the trap and considered the rotted bait inside. The smell was ghastly. This was men's work.

'Kubul!' she called. 'Don't pull up any more traps. Wait for me.'

He mumbled something that sounded like a denial and disappeared around the next bend.

'Kubul!'

She rounded the bend and found him stooped over something on the bank. She came closer and saw scattered clumps of wickerwork at his feet, much of it still bound. A rope dangled limply from the bow of a willow leaning over the river. The lower end of the rope stopped short of the surface and the water beneath was murky with freshly stirred silt. Pieces of broken wickerwork floated downstream.

Someone had pulled the trap up, cut the rope and hacked it to pieces. Who would do such a thing? Now she saw Kubul bend down and pluck something off the ground. His staccato voice rang with joy as he made hacking motions in the air.

There was a sick little jolt in her stomach and she felt hair tingle at the nape of her neck. 'Kubul,' she said in an unsteady voice, 'bring it here.' The boy stopped gesticulating and came over.

It was a hand-axe. Unlike the elbow-hafted, polished-stone axes her people fashioned, this one was of the split-hafted type, its stone-head shaped by knapping and chipping. She took it from his hand and saw the figure of a boar crudely engraved into the haft.

'Give me your hand,' she said, unable to disguise the fear in her voice.

The boy held out a hand and she grabbed it quickly. She snatched the girl's tiny hand in the other, and with the axe poking out of the same grip she began walking briskly back the way she had come. At the first curve in the river she broke into a terrified run, dragging the children behind.

The little girl cried out and Anyaj released the boy's hand to pick her up. The burden tired her quickly and she started wheezing. Fear presented her mind with a series of violent images; rivers were notorious for carrying away all traces of murder.

They were almost back. Only one more bend separated them from the sight of her village when a man stepped out from behind a tree straight into her path. His appearance was so sudden that she stopped dumb, stuck to the ground with blood drumming in her ears and her lungs labouring for air.

In her fright her attention went first to the bow he gripped in one hand, then to a knife sheathed in a scabbard attached to his belt. But when she saw the inquisitive frown on his face, and noticed how his free hand dangled without purpose by his side, she knew his intentions were harmless. She relaxed a fraction and gave herself the opportunity to appraise him more objectively.

A lean frame and toned muscles portrayed a tireless stamina. The garments he wore, though not entirely drab, expressed practicality over finesse. A number of rudimentary repairs on the seams told her practised eye that they must have been made in the field. Leather armbands circled his biceps and a necklace of assorted teeth, claws and bones hung over his hairless chest. Painted ties hung from plaits in his fair hair, keeping the strands parted either side of wild, sky-blue eyes.

She put him at late adolescence. In spite of the circumstances she had to admit he was a striking individual, one to make any red-blooded woman look twice. A bit younger than her, nevertheless . . .

The silence dragged on. So much about him implied pride and confidence that her fear gave way to insecurity. She found herself wondering how she must have looked to him.

'Ba hupa.' His voice, slightly gruff, made her flinch.

She stayed quiet, hoping he had sense enough to appreciate the limitations of his tongue. He pointed to the boy and made hammering motions with his hand. Her heartbeat quickened again; she feared he was threatening to chop up the infant.

Kubul got there first. 'He wants his axe back,' he said smartly.

Anyaj had forgotten all about it. She held it out for the young hunter and he moved forward to take it. He slipped the haft through a ring on his belt, took a step closer to the children and crouched so their eyes were level. She felt they were safe but couldn't help tightening her grip on their hands and stepping backwards.

Then, as casually as he had appeared, Vratu of the Illawann straightened and departed, leaving a scent in his wake unlike anything that had found her nose before.

Taking his brother, son and nephew, Gurajnik headed upstream and found the demolished trap soon after. The stream eddied and flowed quietly alongside, a mild breeze tickled the willows lining the bank. He stooped and picked up a length of rope, noting the clean edge where it had been cut.

'This is getting worse,' Nyaniv said gloomily.

Djuri crouched down and picked at a few twigs. 'He was on his own,' he concluded.

They checked the fish traps further upriver and found two more pulled out and demolished. The rest were intact. Four traps had fat bream flapping inside. They said very little as they walked home. 'We were lucky my wife scared him,' Ursil broke the silence. 'Otherwise he would have ruined every trap we set.'

The men returned to their respective families. Gurajnik went inside and sat down at the main table. He propped Mulek on his lap and Anyaj set a pot of steaming gruel onto the table and ladled it into bowls. 'What do you think they will do next?' she asked in a voice lighter than normal.

There was an expectant silence. Gurajnik said, 'Pass the water.'

She passed him a flask of barley water. All eyes watched him. After he had filled his mug and taken a long swallow he said in a sober voice, 'If anyone goes into the forest, try not to go too far. If you want to check your traps, go in groups and don't stay away long.'

A short distance upstream of Gurajnik's village, Vratu had set up camp. A small fire flickered before him and for the second night in a row he was thinking deeply. It had not been his intention to delay returning to the camp of Iyanah. He should be back there already, spending time with Nura and her family.

The day had not gone according to plan, if in fact he had started out with one. The elder had warned him not to approach these people, and technically at least, he had not intended to. In his mind destroying a few fish traps was no different to leaving a bison-head sentinel behind. It was not in breach of these instructions.

But being caught in the act was.

His contact with the woman and children changed everything. And scaring them . . . he did not like the look of fear he had seen on their faces, making him feel like he was some kind of monster. To top it off he had retreated into the shadows like a frightened fox. It was not the impression he wanted to make. There were more honourable things to do over there than dismantle fish traps and scare children. After all he had been through on his Walk, had he not earned the right to do a little more? Who were they to tell him otherwise?

There were many reasons he came up with to justify what he intended to do. But if he thought about it, he would have realised they were all excuses. What really decided him was the same thing that had sent him over the Great River months before; a quality that defined higher intelligence and set a person on course for remarkable discovery.

He was curious.

Seventeen

Their first order of business the next morning was to send Nyaniv south to the village of Nivik where he would spread word that they were in dire need of an interpreter. After seeing his nephew off, Gurajnik decided to fell timber for extensions to the longhouses. The sowing of the legumes was complete and he thought he could use the diversion. Until recently he had been full of hope, but now it appeared his son-in-law's argument made sense. Knowing how massive a task it would be to start all over again made him miserable.

Axe in hand and his spirits at a low, he headed to the edge of the forest where the birch grew straight and narrow. He passed a series of mossy stumps and vented his mood on the next closest trunk. At the sound of the first crack he stepped back to let gravity finish his work. Beneath a shower of leaves and twigs he wiped sweat from his brow and saw that the early shadows were gaining an edge. He selected another tree and was about to hack into it when something caught the corner of his eye.

Standing so close to him that he almost tripped backwards with fright, a young man was watching him. The sun was directly behind him, making it hard to see his face. Something peculiar about his appearance, and his standing there like that, put Gurajnik instantly on guard. His clothing looked crude and his long hair was plaited in a manner more like a woman. Gurajnik squinted and shaded his eyes to better see. The face staring at him held all the traces of suspicion, or possibly apprehensiveness, and then Gurajnik felt his heartbeat quicken, because now he recognised the characteristic curvature of his face, the swollen lump of brow, and knew what he was looking at. He tightened his grip on the axe and lifted it a fraction.

The young man perceived the slight movement with steady eyes, yet remained as still as the trees. 'Oronuk?' he asked in a strange accent.

Gurajnik glanced around to confirm the native was alone. 'No, Serisi. Who are you?'

The native put a finger to his ear and shook his head.

'Ubren?' Gurajnik asked.

Again the native shook his head. It could have been a 'no' to the question or that he hadn't understood. But he knew something, and Gurajnik felt the tickle of hope.

'Can you understand my talk?'

The stranger looked beyond him toward the longhouses.

'No?' Gurajnik said. 'Here, over here,' he invited with his hands. 'Follow me.' The stranger regarded him with utmost concentration before dragging his feet forward.

Gurajnik guided him over to the longhouses. One by one the villagers saw them coming and a wary silence spread. Several women seated at the table in the common area dropped their sewing and leapt to their feet to join everyone else standing motionless. The stranger slowed his pace as he came closer.

'Here . . . here,' Gurajnik urged him toward the table. 'Eszrah, bring us some food.' He turned to his guest and made chewing motions with his mouth. 'Food, yes?'

Anyaj came forward, shaking her forefinger. 'That's him,' she said. 'The one I saw by the river.'

'Oh?' Gurajnik asked.

'The one who destroyed the traps.'

'Well, he seems to have had a change of heart. Where is that food, woman?' he asked his wife. She headed for the house obediently, neck twisted to look behind.

The initial shock subsiding, everyone shuffled closer now. The doors to each house opened almost simultaneously and more people came out. Gurajnik read signs on the stranger's face that his courage was fast abandoning him.

'Listen all of you,' he addressed the crowd, 'go back to what you are doing.'

'What does he want?' one of the children asked.

'Let me find out. Go away and I'll talk to him.'

'Why don't you bring him inside?' Eszrah called from the door.

'Good idea,' Gurajnik agreed. 'Follow me,' he invited the native, showing the way. Like livestock being led the stranger followed, step by hesitant step until they reached the door. Eszrah held it open and Gurajnik tried to usher him in. 'Come . . . come inside.'

The stranger peered suspiciously into the dark interior and didn't budge. Gurajnik turned to shoo the crowd away and had almost succeeded when a voice shouted from behind.

'Here!'

Gurajnik swung around and saw Guunt hurrying back from the field carrying an adze, followed by Djuri and Ursil.

'What happens here?' Guunt demanded as he came up.

'We have a visitor,' Gurajnik answered.

'This man is native.'

Anyaj cut in quickly, 'He is the one I saw down by the river.'

Guunt's frown intensified. 'So, now he shows.' He pointed to the pig stalls and addressed the native in a harsh voice. 'You steal our pig? Was that you?'

'Here, Guunt,' Ursil said calmly from behind. 'Don't talk so loud.'

Guunt said to Gurajnik, 'What are you doing?'

'Taking him inside.'

'Why?'

'I thought it might be a good place to start.'

'Wise thinking. Now he'll know what else he can steal.'

The villagers, dispersed only moments before, now crept forward again. Gurajnik was about to shoo them away a second time when he noticed the native's gaze had settled on Kubul.

'Kubul, is this the man you saw with Anyaj?' he asked, and the boy nodded shyly. 'Come here.'

Kubul moved forward as reluctantly as the native had.

'This little man of mischief,' Gurajnik said fondly, 'we call Kubul.' He touched the boy on the shoulder. 'Kubul.'

The stranger took a step closer, his forehead creased with concentration. '*Ku . . . bul . . .*'

159

Kubul's face broke into a huge grin. 'His tongue is twisted,' he said through shameless giggling. Then he began making stabbing motions in the air with his hand, crying, 'Ba hupa, ba hupa!'

Gurajnik was about to caution him when he noticed the stranger was amused by the mimicry. The young man pulled a hand-axe from a ring on his belt and offered it to the boy, handle first. Gurajnik saw it was decorated with an engraving of a boar. Kubul stepped forward and grabbed it with the innocent rudeness of youth, eliciting a thin smile from the native.

'Come in,' Gurajnik invited again, stepping inside and beckoning with his hand. The native put a foot through the doorway.

'Stop!' Guunt commanded, moving forward quickly. The native flinched and retreated. 'This home was made by my hands too,' he said to Gurajnik. 'It belongs to me as much as it belongs to you. This man is a thief. If you want to talk to him, do it outside.'

'What's the matter with you?' Gurajnik asked crossly. 'Does he look like he came here to cause trouble?'

'That's no reason to trust him. Where are his men, his leaders? Why is he here on his own?'

Gurajnik waved him away. 'Go then. We were making progress before you came.' He faced the stranger and held up his hands reassuringly. The stranger returned Guunt's insolent glare, then began walking away, brisk but composed back toward the forest.

'Oh no,' Gurajnik moaned. 'You see! He doesn't like you.'

'Good. It saves me the need to be pleasing.'

Gurajnik glowered briefly at his son-in-law before turning away and calling out to the native: 'Wait!'

'Let him go,' Djuri advised. 'If he means well he'll be back.'

'Not after this sort of welcome.'

'Those we want coming here don't include men who stalk our village looking for things to steal or break,' Guunt said, bending down to pick up his daughter. 'He got the message.'

Gurajnik cussed at him and hurried after their visitor. 'Wait!' he called as he caught up. The young man stopped. 'I'm sorry. Won't you stay?' He pointed at the village and noticed Ursil coming toward them. 'Stay?'

The native waved his hand dismissively.

'Tell us your name.' Gurajnik poked his chest with a thumb to demonstrate. 'Gurajnik.'

'Gur . . . uj . . . *nik*?'

'Yes.'

'Vratu.'

'*Vra*. . .*tu*?' Gurajnik asked, and received a nod. Ursil came alongside and stopped. 'Vratu, this is Ursil.' Gurajnik planted a hand on his son's shoulder. *'Ursil.'*

'Urs . . . ul,' Vratu said awkwardly, and then his attention strayed to something behind them.

Gurajnik turned around and saw Kubul running over, holding up the hand-axe. He reached the group and politely held it out to Vratu. The native smiled and made a hand signal for him to keep it.

'Uttnuh du arag, *Ku . . . bul*.'

Kubul's eyes widened thankfully as he clutched the souvenir to his chest.

'Guunt should see this,' Gurajnik remarked.

'Esnag vunus, echak.' Vratu pointed a finger up at the sky. 'Echak,' he repeated, making a shape with his hand like an inverted cup. Gurajnik paid careful attention but couldn't interpret the sign language. Vratu repeated the gestures and finger pointing several times, speaking gibberish.

'What is he saying?' Ursil asked.

From down below Kubul said, 'I think he wants to come back, just not today.'

'Yes,' Gurajnik agreed. 'I think he does.'

Vratu raised a hand in farewell and walked off, straight over the furrows of one of their carefully planted plots. Gurajnik draped an arm over Kubul and watched him depart with a feeling of regret. It had been so close. Right now they could be sitting inside, communicating, laying the foundation for the peaceful co-existence he desperately sought. Guunt's behaviour was unforgivable and he would have words with him when he returned.

Ursil asked, 'Do you think he'll be back?'

'Oh yes,' his father replied, and smiled contentedly. The visit could have gone better, but it was just what he'd been waiting for.

Days later Nivik and several of his men arrived. They were all overjoyed to see each other; spring was a busy time and visitations were rare. And yes, Nivik happily announced, they had found someone who might be able to help.

The man introduced himself as Bukkat, a trader who happened to stop by Nivik's village the day before. They all went indoors and food appeared in volume. Although quick to confess he was unversed in native dialects, the trader did claim to know something of their habits, but as they went deeper into the discussion Gurajnik suspected even this wasn't much. Crucial information like exactly who their neighbours were and how seriously they viewed encroachment into their land he could not give. When they showed him the bison-head sentinel he barely glanced at it.

'Territory markers,' he explained. 'Is this the only one you've seen?'

'Apart from the one in their camp,' Gurajnik answered.

'There will be more. They scatter them all over. The talons are a symbol of allegiance to other clans, the lines and dots below are their colours. If yours are there, you are welcome. If not . . .' He ripped another chunk of meat from the bone he chewed on and chuckled quietly.

'Who are they?'

Bukkat shrugged. 'This is hard to know. Bison skulls are used by the Ubren to symbolise their totem but this doesn't mean much. Lots of tribes choose this beast.'

'Can we get an interpreter?'

'The closest I know is away east and won't be back for days,' Bukkat mumbled through a mouth full of meat. 'How bad is he needed?'

'I would make it worth his while.'

'All I can do is pass word.'

Gurajnik felt disheartened; he had hoped for more. 'How many of these people are out there?'

'This is also hard to know.'

'We have lived here for almost two years and found one camp.'

'But you haven't been looking for them either, true?'

Ursil said, 'They would be easy to miss. We almost walked into the camp we found before we even knew it was there.'

'Of course,' Bukkat agreed as he chewed. 'Follow the creeks and rivers until you find a place you'd like to call home, and you're likely to find they got there first. There lies the problem with these people.'

'I don't want to push negotiations on my own,' Gurajnik went on. 'They weren't overjoyed to see us.'

'That stands to reason.' The childish grin reappeared on his face as he pointed to the totem. 'That was no invitation.'

Gurajnik became frustrated with the man's apathy. 'Are we on our own then?'

'Is this not what you wanted, Gurajnik? You made that clear by coming here.'

The trader tore another piece of meat with his teeth and kept smiling. Gurajnik had to check his frustration. Had this discussion taken place before the friendly visit from the native he would have felt less hopeful, but things were different now.

The conversation moved toward less serious matters and Gurajnik treated them with the custom reserved for guests. Nivik and Bukkat displayed considerable interest in the malachite. 'When can we see something made of that?' Gurajnik asked his brother.

'Soon,' Nivik answered. 'What do you want to do with it?'

'We need workers more than anything. And an interpreter. See if you can persuade them with that,' he said, gesturing to the copper-rich ore. When Nivik and Bukkat left the following morning, both men carried away generous chunks of the precious rock.

Life in Gurajnik's village continued its daily round. The crops were doing well and only a few more trees needed felling to begin extensions to his longhouse. In time they received word from Nivik that the Henghai of the east were having trouble with natives of their own and were not inclined at this stage to make contact with new ones. The good news was that his brother had cast several copper ingots from his malachite and there should be labourers to help Gurajnik with his autumn harvest.

The lands to the north were left alone, and when they hunted they steered clear of the native camp. There was little sign of their presence. One day the boys spotted thick smoke rising from the hills and they clambered frantically onto the roof for a better look. Gurajnik called from below that setting forest and grassland alight to facilitate hunting was common practice amongst natives, and in any case, it was too far away to be intentionally directed toward the village. Sure enough, it burned itself out long before getting anywhere near them.

Each evening he sat by his longhouse in anticipation of a visit, a mug of ale at his side. Once or twice on a clear night he saw the faint glow of a campfire deep in the darkness, and the following day he made sure he stayed close to the village. But no one ever came.

Discussions about natives fragmented into passing remarks. In time, even he stopped worrying about them. His neighbours had chosen to keep their distance and he would leave it that way.

Eighteen

A few weeks after his contact with the farmers, Vratu returned from a hunt to find a runner seated by the main fire. They exchanged greetings and the young boy announced the purpose of his visit. 'You are invited to the camp of Iyanah.'

The blood went warm in Vratu's veins. The belated invitation from Nura's family had come. 'How . . . is the Clan of Iyanah?' he stuttered.

'All is well. You will see.'

Throughout dinner he sat without appetite, eating only a small portion of berries and meat. Things could not be better for him of late. The hunting had been good and he and his mother had slept with full stomachs every night. They had repaired all that needed repairing, he was at the peak of health and no bugs made him itch. He was going to see his woman again, on invitation this time. And this visit would surely make up for the last.

After dinner, he sat exchanging news with their young guest. At one point Vratu asked, 'What news of the People-of-the-Longhomes?'

'Everything is quiet,' the young man replied. 'I think they want to speak to you about that.'

His jolly mood collapsed and his heart missed a beat or two. He had not told anyone about his contact with the People-of-the-Longhomes. Although he knew it was only a matter of time before someone initiated formalities, in which case his name would be amongst the first things mentioned, he hoped the leadership of the clans would not view it too harshly. But being asked to undertake a six to seven day round trip suggested they might. Headmen didn't take kindly to disobedience and Turuk's message had been clear. It was not unheard of to banish a member of a clan for serious disobedience. Perhaps this was why an invitation had been so long in

165

coming. Perhaps it wasn't an invitation to see his girl at all.

'Is something wrong?' Vratu asked shakily.

'It is not for me to know,' the runner replied. 'You know this. They give you a message and send you on your way.'

Lying in bed that night, his mind whirling with possibilities, Vratu appealed to Ilan. 'Come with me tomorrow.'

'Too far,' his friend replied through a yawn.

'I need the company.'

'Why?'

'I think I may be in trouble.'

Ilan turned on his side to face him. 'What have you done *now*?'

'When I was there last I talked to the People-of-the-Longhomes.'

It was a while before Ilan responded. 'I think there is something wrong with my ears. What did you say?'

'I talked to the People-of-the-Longhomes.'

Ilan raised himself up on his elbow. 'On your own, I am thinking.'

'Yes.'

'I am beginning to understand now. Why did you do that?'

'I needed something to do and Nura was poor company.'

'You never told me this.'

'No. Your mouth is not as reliable as the rest of you.' Then Vratu told him all about it, careful not to reveal anything about his experience with the Oronuk the winter past. Perhaps he would tell him about it one day, but not today.

'You have a talent for being a bug in people's noses, it is true,' Ilan said. 'Mine more than any. Perhaps I should go with you. Someone has to keep you out of trouble.'

They were preparing their travel packs the following morning when the runner came over. 'They only want you, Vratu,' he said.

Vratu stared at him. Ilan shrugged and said, 'You are on your own again, friend.'

As Vratu journeyed overland he did a lot of thinking. Several times he asked his companion a subtle question or two and the answers he received let him believe his contact with the People-of-the-Longhomes remained undiscovered. There had been no more stealing of pigs, no frightening with bison skulls, no contact of any kind. How then could they know? The purpose of the invitation must be a favourable one, and as they neared their destination he let himself get excited again.

Nevertheless, he prepared his defence for the grimmer alternative. He would explain that he had only acted in the tribe's interests. He would promise never to go back, if this is what they wanted. This he meant. His short role as emissary had scratched his itch of curiosity but left him with mixed feelings. These were not the same people who had swabbed his dehydrated body and nursed him back to life. His woman was his priority now and he wanted to do all he could to gain the trust and respect of her father and uncle.

They arrived at Iyanah's camp late in the afternoon. Immediately Vratu sensed something wrong. Task complete, his travelling companion wandered off without a word. While his nieces jumped up and down over him and several children pestered him for attention, those of older years only glanced at him briefly, nodding their greeting rather than saying it. Voices around him were like whispers. Fears he had laid to rest flooded back now, turning his stomach queasy.

Then he saw the weapons stacked neatly against the dwellings – spears with elongated leaf-shaped heads, bows and quivers stuffed with arrows, angry looking maces that had but one purpose. He reached his brother's dwelling and Nura skipped over, her manner at odds with the mood in the camp. She gave him a hug and she felt good in his arms.

'What is happening?' he asked in a shaky voice.

She smiled at him sweetly. 'Men's matters. They were waiting for you.'

'Vratu, is that you?' his brother called from inside his dwelling. A moment later the door-flap opened and he emerged. 'You came,' he said, the look on his face like one in mourning.

'What is happening?'

'Ukmaar and Krul are in Iyanah's dwelling. They will talk to you.'

Vratu felt the life go out of him. Krul. A name that made his thoughts darken, a man whose presence was like the prowl of wolves lurking in the shadows. Whenever his name was mentioned, Vratu despaired. And now they wanted to talk to him? His voice, when it sounded, was so faint he could hardly hear it. 'What do they want?'

'You wanted to know how they would come for you.'

The queasiness in his stomach gave way to excitement. He looked at Nura and saw her smiling, as if she knew something. Could this be what it is all about? The final test before they let him marry her?

'Yes,' he replied.

'Come, and you will see.'

Nineteen

The whimper almost went undetected.

Gurajnik's eyelids flickered open. It had been very faint, slipping into the underworld of his dreams. He lifted his head and waited for confirmation. Complete silence and feeble light told him it was that time of dawn when nothing was supposed to move.

Another whimper came to him and this time there was no mistaking it. It sounded like one of the dogs, probably bitten or clawed by any one of a horde of predators that prowled around their village nightly. He pulled on his leggings and tied the gathers on his way to the front door. In case a bear or wolf was nosing about he grabbed an adze leaning against a wall. He reached the front door, lifted the heavy plank off its bracket and swung the door open.

In the poor light he could barely make them out. A large group of men, too many to count, was creeping toward the longhouses. They saw him and stopped.

Gurajnik paused by the door, blinking uncomprehendingly. It made no sense having so many strangers in his village, as if they had come for a gathering or feast unannounced. They held their weapons in such an inoffensive and relaxed manner that he almost took a step forward to greet them.

As one they moved forward again. Most were bare to the waist. The paint on their faces and torsos showed no colour in the poor light, but the display in itself was enough to presage some boding evil.

The sight of the dogs lying dead on the ground, impaled by an assortment of spears and arrows, suddenly made it all clear. A pulse of giddiness throbbed in his temples, cold shock coursed through his veins and weakened his legs. In that horrible moment, Gurajnik knew his life was over. It would end here, violent and cruel in a lonely

169

wilderness where his bones would bleach in the sun.

The thought of thirteen people in his house, five of them children, called him to his senses. He swung around and reached for the door, and as he heaved it closed he saw a man raise his bow. The door slammed shut and he heard a light pop on the other side when the arrow hit. He dropped the adze, quickly slid the plank into place and ran a loop of lifting twine over its rest to lock it into position. Then he ran into the sleeping quarters, leaned over the closest bed and pounded the body concealed beneath the blankets with his fists.

'What are you doing?' Szlahov asked, frowning sleepily.

'*Get up!*' Gurajnik's voice vibrated with urgency. He moved from bed to bed, shaking awake sleeping bodies.

Szlahov sat up quickly. 'What's wrong?'

'We're in trouble.'

Eszrah appeared from her room. 'What is it?'

'Get up! Now! Everyone!' Gurajnik ran into Ursil's room. His eldest son raised himself upright, his sleepy face looking more irritated than confused. Anyaj lay fast asleep beside him.

'Ursil, quickly,' Gurajnik gasped. 'What weapons do you have?'

Ursil was instantly alert. 'What is happening?'

'They're here! Get up!' Gurajnik hastened to Guunt's room and found him already getting dressed.

'I heard you,' his son-in-law said, derision in his voice.

They all heard the faint tapping coming from the front door, like a courteous knocking, followed by a muffled voice that was punctuated by an explosion of laughter.

Gurajnik dashed over to a small rectangular window sealed by a removable wooden fitting. He removed the slat holding it into position, then pulled the fitting free by its two leather handles. Through the window he saw armed men running into his brother's house where they had managed to get the door open. A moment later he heard the first shout, followed by the heart-wrenching screams of men, women and children. And still more painted men rushed forward, queuing at the door to squeeze through. Close friends and relatives he had known all his life were being slaughtered a stone's throw away and he could do nothing. Shaking uncontrollably, his heart pounding hard against his ribcage, all he could do was moan his brother's name.

'*Djuri.*'

Everything was happening in slow motion. Panic threatened to unman him; he knew he had to keep focussed, keep moving. His hands were shaking so badly he barely managed to secure the fitting back into its frame.

'Nurekt, what's happening?' Eszrah asked, her voice quivering. A small girl started to cry. Eszrah pulled her close and covered her tiny ears with her own trembling hands.

Guunt walked in tying a knot in a legging-gather. His face bore a blend of resentment and fear. 'He didn't listen and now it's all over.'

'Who is it?' Eszrah asked.

'I don't know,' Gurajnik answered, unable to think properly. 'Them.'

Ursil emerged from his room with his wife and children. 'What's happening?' he asked. The look of terror contorting his father's face immediately erased the hangover of sleep. His body went rigid and he started for the door.

Gurajnik said quickly, 'Don't open the door.'

Ursil diverted to another window and removed the fitting. His jaw clenched tight and his eyes narrowed as he looked through the window, but his manner remained calm as ever. Carefully he reinserted the fitting.

Children began wailing and crying. The women bundled them up, trying to console them with unconvincing words of hope. The screaming from the other house died and an eerie silence descended, broken only by the muffled blurt of a pig.

Something banged heavily on the front door. Not a crack appeared in the solid oak, and after a few blows the thumping moved along the wall.

'We have to talk to them,' Guunt suggested weakly.

'No,' Ursil replied calmly. 'They did not come here to talk.' He went back to his room and returned promptly with his bow and

171

arrows. There was a thump on a window-fitting, the brackets holding it in position broke away and everything tumbled to the floor. A timber rod poked through the window and pale light streamed inside. Ursil quickly fit an arrow to the bowstring and aimed at the window as the rod withdrew. A painted face showed briefly and vanished. Ursil kept his arm at full draw and waited. The face never returned.

'What do you want?' Guunt shrieked.

Ursil lowered his bow. 'How do you want to do this?' he asked his father.

'You and I will have to go out first,' Gurajnik said. 'Let them come to us, draw them away from the others. Try to take out the closest. The women will take the children and run for the river or the forest. What have we got?'

Most of their work tools were in the shed outside. They gathered an adze, a hoe, three sets of bows and arrows and one spear. Guunt asked cynically, 'Are you going to fight them with that? We have more chance hiding in our beds.'

'Shh!' Gurajnik silenced everyone. 'Listen.'

A lone voice outside was shouting, answered by a chorus of shrills and a steady thumping that sent a pulse through the earth beneath their feet. Gurajnik glanced out the window and saw men with their weapons raised, stamping the ground with their feet. The war cry trailed off and they moved off to surround the house. A man holding a bow a short distance away saw him watching and smiled wickedly. He lifted his bow to take aim and Gurajnik quickly picked up the broken fitting and jammed it back into place.

'As soon as we're outside, don't help us,' he said to Szlahov and Yukuv. 'Stay with the children. Scatter in the forest, or go for the river. If you use the canoes be sure not to leave any on the bank for them to come after you.'

'Can't we wait here?' Anyaj asked. 'They can't get in.'

'They won't have to.'

'Where are they?'

'Everywhere we don't want them to be. We have to go out by the front door.'

Now they could all smell smoke. Every head tilted up. 'They've set the roof on fire,' Gurajnik said. 'We'll have to move while they're standing back. Eszrah . . .' His wife had grabbed a cask of water and looked ready to splash the roof. 'Leave that and bring the children here.'

Smoke leaked through the roof and the crackle of flames became louder. Gurajnik picked up the adze. 'Szlahov, Yukuv, take the bows.'

Ursil handed each of his brothers a bow and a supply of arrows.

Gurajnik turned to Guunt. 'Are you holding onto yours?'

Guunt nodded mechanically, his face ash-grey. Ursil acquired the hoe. That left the spear. Gurajnik picked it up and looked around for the most suitable person to give it to.

'Here,' Eszrah said, holding out her hand. 'Give it to me.'

'Eszrah . . .'

'I stay with you,' she said calmly. 'I'm too old for anything else.' Gurajnik handed it over. It hardly made a difference now.

Smoke poured through the thatching thick as water now, clouding the interior, stinging their eyes and making the children cough. In the stables the pigs scuffled and nipped at each other, fearing as much as the rest of them some imminent horror.

'Let the pigs out,' Ursil suggested. 'They might go for them.'

Eszrah helped him open the doors to the stables. The pigs rushed out and fought their way to the rear of the house, brushing past legs and groping hands. To a torrent of squeals the boys managed to catch about half the pigs and drag them forward.

'Is everyone ready?' Gurajnik asked, wiping tears from his stinging eyes.

Eszrah assembled the children and moved them to the front door. 'Stay close,' she told them.

Thick orange flames burst through the thatching. Eszrah crouched and hugged the children one by one, whispering words of encouragement. Gurajnik put his hands on the door-plank but now, knowing only death waited outside, he could not find the will to lift it. He bowed his head to avert the terrified faces around him, wanting it over, wanting an end to the pain and sorrow crippling him, and yet clutching at the last moments of life, as if some miracle might show itself and whisk them all to safety.

'What have I done?' He sank his head into his arm as tears of despair flooded his eyes.

Ursil disengaged from his crying wife and came over. 'Come,' he said, putting a gentle hand on his father's shoulder. 'We'll get this over with. You and me – we'll go and kill a few of these maggots.' He coughed a few times and turned to Guunt. 'Are you coming?'

His brother-in-law looked lost. 'I don't know,' he whimpered.

'You know there is only one way to do this. Be ready.'

The fire spread to the rafters and burning straw dripped from above, filling the place with sparks and making everyone cough and retch and swat at their shoulders and hair as if harangued by wasps. Gurajnik crouched and addressed the children.

'There are bad men outside. Bad men who want to hurt you. You all run hard now . . .' he coughed a few times '. . . as hard as your legs will take you. Hold onto someone's hand . . . don't let go . . . don't look back. Just run.' He lifted the door-plank from its bracket. 'Get those pigs up here.'

Ursil and Szlahov prodded the pigs towards the door.

'Now!' Gurajnik shouted, flinging the door open. He kicked the animals through and stepped into the haze of a smoke-ridden dawn.

The enemy stood back at a safe distance. They watched the pigs trot past without a shred of interest. 'Go!' yelled Gurajnik.

Ursil pushed passed him. Tall and proud he stopped in front of the enemy and raised his hoe. 'So here you are, brave men who come to slaughter helpless women and children,' he taunted, his jaw jutting forward and his eyes sparking like flints. 'Do you think you came with enough? Here is a man! Who will be so brave and strong?'

He feinted at the enemy with his hoe, daring them to break their line as they closed around him. A large, painted man stepped closer and Ursil spat at him in contempt. 'Look at you all painted up,' he snarled. 'What sort of fight did you expect?'

Gurajnik felt a surge of pride for his son; courage swelled inside and he had to fight the urge to join him in his lonely stand. An arrow buried into Ursil's rib cage and he didn't flinch.

Anyaj screamed. Gurajnik grabbed her arm and dragged her the other way. After only a few paces he felt the bite of an arrow deep in his back, but the adrenalin surging through his veins kept him running without a falter. Several men blocked his path and more closed in from behind, cutting him off from his group. The women and children panicked and broke up, running away from his protection. 'To the forest! To the forest!' he shouted, pointing frantically and willing them ahead, but they seemed lost, scattering in ones and twos.

To his left he saw Szlahov slow and take aim with his bow. An arrow hit him under the arm and another stuck into his neck. The bow fell out of his hands and he cried out weakly. Gurajnik turned to help, already too late. Men swarmed over the boy, overwhelming his feeble resistance with a hail of mace blows.

Yukuv yelled and rushed to help his brother, aiming his bow as he ran. The suddenness of his charge took his enemy by surprise and they scattered quickly. The arrow shot out and a man screeched as it stuck into his thigh. Yukuv stepped backwards to give himself time to fit a second arrow, for another man was racing toward him now, mace held high. The club began its murderous descent just as Yukuv let the arrow fly dead flush with the man's throat. The point of the arrow burst out the back of the man's neck the instant the heavy limestone head connected, breaking the boy's clavicle with a muffled crack.

Boy and man sank to their knees. The man shrieked in disbelief, making gargling noises as he dropped his mace and clutched his neck. Blood poured out of his mouth and painted his chin. The attackers turned on Yukuv with maces, competing with each other to get to this boy no older than twelve. The man with the arrow in his thigh limped over, eyes glowing with rage and mouth bubbling froth, pushing men aside so he could kick the boy with his good leg.

Two of Gurajnik's sons had been slaughtered before his eyes in the time it took to draw a few breaths. He was about to fly into the men attacking Yukuv when he heard Eszrah cry out his name.

Backed up against the flames, she stood clutching the hands of two terrified children while trying to keep within Ursil's protective stretch. Gurajnik cocked his adze behind his shoulder and rushed the man nearest to them. A spear thrown from behind grazed his side and skidded along the dirt in front of him. He stooped to pick it up, and then with a weapon pointed ahead in each hand walked backwards to flank the small group.

A man with an obscene spark in his eyes lifted his mace and came forward, ranting in a harsh tongue. A surge of madness took hold of Gurajnik's senses and he shouted with rage and rushed him. A body-length or two away he raised the spear and heaved, but his target sidestepped expertly. Gurajnik followed through, ducking under the wild sweep of the mace and swinging his adze with both hands at the man's waist. The man bellowed in pain and Gurajnik felt the rewarding give of flesh transferred up the stock of his weapon.

At once men were all over him, punishing him with a frenzy of mace blows that forced him to his knees. Dropping the adze to free his hands, he drove his shoulder into a man's waist and lifted him up off the ground. The man kicked the air madly as Gurajnik angled him sidewards and drove him down. They hit the earth and Gurajnik buried his shoulder into the man's stomach, there was a burst of expelled air and he took to the painted face with his hardened farmer's fists.

Angry hands grabbed at his hair, fingers clawed at his face and eyes. He was strong in his rage and somehow managed to avert serious injury by kicking and swinging like a madman, aiming his blows at the softer parts of those smothering him. Anytime a weapon landed ineffectively he clutched at it greedily, but they slipped through his fingers each time.

From the corner of his eye came the blur of a mace-head on course with his skull. All he could do to lessen the impact was turn his head at the last instant. His lower jaw took the hit with a bone-shattering crunch and his vision exploded in a blinding flash of red.

The ground thumped beneath him. Instinctively he rolled onto his back, tasting blood and spitting out fragments of teeth. Through the dimness he saw a man above with the adze raised. Gurajnik rolled as the stone-blade thudded into the earth beside his head. He grabbed the stock weakly and they both struggled for possession. Feeling the lesser hold, Gurajnik was about to let go when he heard a yell from the side.

The man turned in time to offer his face to Ursil's hoe. The stone head clipped the man's temple, his legs folded and he collapsed onto the ground. Ursil waved the hoe wildly, a space opened up and he stretched out an arm to help his father to his feet. Back to back the two crippled men retreated to Eszrah and the children, farm tools held before them in battle stance.

An archer drew his bow. Gurajnik watched helplessly as the arrow lined him up. 'Do it, you coward,' he muttered. The archer released and Gurajnik yelled in impotent fury. He was still yelling when the arrow sank half its length into his chest.

Fire flared deep inside him, blood welled in his throat and caught in his airway. He gritted his shattered teeth, gripped the fletching and snapped the shaft. He tossed it aside and braced himself for more, but it was clear his enemy wanted to prolong their sport now. At least some had done this before, of this he was sure – they were enjoying themselves too much for beginners.

A door banged open. Gurajnik turned and saw Guunt come out with the smoke, holding a bow and arrow. Gurajnik's daughter followed, coughing and sputtering, hugging her daughter to her chest with one arm and dragging her son with the other. Guunt pulled back on the bowstring and swept the enemy with a loaded weapon, catching them off guard. Those point blank to his aim quickly retreated.

'Yes, see what I have for you!' he shouted, edging ahead. Holding the bow at full draw he wiped his face awkwardly on his arm and glanced at Ursil and Gurajnik, imploring them to follow. For a short moment Gurajnik felt the sprinkling of hope. Men parted respectfully before his son-in-law as he headed for the river. But then, one after the other, arrows whistled through the air. One grazed his side, another took skin off his face, and yet he held his aim admirably. Gurajnik's daughter cried out in distress, forced to back away with her

177

children from their lethal trajectories.

Guunt's walk faltered with a direct hit in the chest. Now they could see his arm tremble as he fought to hold the bow taut. An arrow lodged into his back and the one he was holding in place shot out and disappeared harmlessly over the heads of those it was intended for. With a homicidal wail, they charged.

Guunt dropped his weapon and spread his arms out to meet them. Just before impact he doubled over and buried his shoulder into a man's waist and drove him backwards, but a disciplined barrage of maces and hand-axes from the swarm that quickly converged on him rendered his courage futile.

'*Chenka!*' Gurajnik called to his daughter, and she hauled her son toward him.

The furious heat from the burning houses drove them forward. Gurajnik could feel his punctured lung collapsing, his strength deserting him as rapidly as his blood. His head dizzied and the light was harsh on his eyes.

Ursil, unable to swing his arms freely for all the arrows stuck in his torso, took a few steps forward to shield his sister and niece and nephew. Three men turned on him, stepping into the diameter of his thrust to test his failing reflexes in hand-to-hand combat.

From behind Gurajnik came a scream and Eszrah ran past, aiming her spear at a man who watched her come with a look of amusement. He deflected her poor throw easily and with a deft lunge caught her hair in his fist and raised his mace above her head. Gurajnik yelled helplessly and stumbled forward, forced to watch the weapon come down. There was a sickening crack and his wife dropped like a stone. The club came down again, and again, and again.

Screaming with the last of his strength, the mortally wounded farmer raised his adze and charged one last time. The killer backed away from the limp body. Gurajnik reached his wife and let the adze fall from his hands.

'Eszrah,' he moaned, blood gargling from his misshapen mouth. To one side he saw his daughter being bludgeoned to death, a little further away a man hacked into Ursil's chest with a hand-axe. From all around came the sickening percussion of maces on bone.

Gurajnik sat down, hoisted his wife onto his lap and buried his face into her neck. Nothing else was worthy of his last memory.

A hand suddenly gripped his hair and jerked his head up. At once his eyes fixed on a man standing a short distance away. It was not just the peculiar contortion on the man's face that set him apart from the others. Despite a disguise of paint, the face staring back at him looked familiar. Using all that remained of his life's energy, Gurajnik fought his fading consciousness to search his memory.

With only a few weak heartbeats left in him, and perhaps one breath, he groaned the last word of his life the instant it came to him.

'*Vratu.*'

Standing above Gurajnik, his knife poised at the man's throat, Uru Ukmaar hesitated. His frown deepened as he followed the direction of the man's gaze, and then he saw Vratu.

For a long moment they stared at each other. Then, in a swift and effortless movement of hand, Ukmaar opened the man's neck. A stream of blood arced out and spattered the earth, raising dust and leaving the pattern of a snake. Ukmaar let the body flop to the ground. His gaze had not left Vratu once.

He wiped the knife on his legging and walked away.

Vratu had been under no illusions.

He knew there would be men and women and children and death. In his naivety he had, however, anticipated some sort of code, something akin to what lay at the heart of their hunting culture; the discipline to kill only what was needed, to leave what could be spared.

At first he'd been carried away. He'd felt the same stirring of blood as when he took on dangerous quarry, making every sense, every muscle, feel as if it owed its design to that sole purpose. It made the water he splashed on his face tingle like a shower of needles, tiny insects buzz loudly in his ears. It made it easy to bond with men he hardly knew, to forget those he tried to befriend. A morbid urge to be a part of it made him feel more alive, stronger. And with it came the pride of knowing that he alone had been chosen from his clan. The paint on his body made him feel special, one of them.

And so he had kept pace with the others marching forward, and when the longhouses appeared without edge in the dawn light there was no pause in his stride. But as he passed the whimpering dogs, the bow heavy in his hand, he was reminded of the last time he had crept toward longhouses, and wondered then if anyone had slept in their beds, or tasted their beverages, or been moved by the beauty of their women. Then he realised he was lagging behind, overtaken by men keener to lead, and so he slowed to let them pass. And now that it was over, he wondered what his purpose here was supposed to have been.

One of Krul's men was crouched by a dog, stroking its head. Another man knelt down by a mortally wounded boy and casually slit his throat. In the knee-high fields of wheat, men waded through with their heads down, brushing stalks aside with their spears.

He walked over to the man who had called his name and stood over him. He recalled a face kindly-lined and easy to read, not the punished mess it was now. And there not far away lay the other man – *Ursil* – his open chest like a bowl full of blood. It was a pity his courage had been to no avail. Courage like that should be kept in this world, emulated by others.

He heard a loud crash and turned to see a bloom of sparks from a collapsing frame rise into the thick pall of smoke blotting out the sky. Not far away a small group had gathered around the man with the arrow in his throat. Vratu walked over, stretching his memory to recall the man's name. Keorn. Not any more, he thought. Vratu watched him struggle with his last breaths, coughing blood over the feet of his friends, eyes darting everywhere.

What do you see, that none of us see? he wondered. *Was it worth it?*

He trudged over to the house that was still intact and pushed the door open. In the stables the pigs ran around in panic-stricken circles, squealing and crashing into the walls, while two young cows moaned uneasily in a stall opposite. He walked ahead and his nostrils flared at the sharp scent of blood. A man lay closeby with blood bubbling out of his mouth, clutching a gash as wide as a snake in his neck. Scattered over the floor in the sleeping section were the bloodied and spreadeagled corpses of men, women and children. A painted man lifted an adze and swung it into the first of several large ceramic pots lined up neatly against a wall. The fire-baked clay burst into shards and bounced over the floor. Along the row of pottery he went, smashing everything until he stood ankle deep in clay pieces and grain.

Nothing escaped their notice. Loving furnishings were flung about recklessly; chairs and stools kicked aside, tables overturned, shelves and wall-ornaments ripped down, clay pots emptied, straw bedding scattered. Items that drew interest were seized, those deemed useless were thrown to the floor.

He returned outside, not knowing what he should do. As he rounded the corner of the house he saw a young girl kneeling, trying to stifle her sobs with a trembling hand on her lips. A group of men stood around while Krul and another man argued.

'What happens here?' Vratu asked one of Krul's party.

'Idnuk wants the woman, Krul says no.'

Krul waved the man away, pulled a knife from the scabbard at his waist and went to stand over the girl. She moaned weakly and dropped her head. He grabbed a fistful of her hair and forced her head up, exposing her creamy-white throat. Her eyes stretched wide with terror and settled on Vratu.

Not again. Vratu turned away.

Kihad stood on his own, watching proceedings with a strange, far-away look on his face. Vratu glanced at his brother's hands and saw they were as clean as his.

'It is finished,' Vratu said as he came up. 'Let's go.'

'No. Wait for the others.'

A low, awful bellow turned their heads. A cow ran out of the

181

house with blood pulsing down its neck. Several men dropped their spoils and took up the chase, waving their weapons and shouting enthusiastically. Ukmaar called for them to stop but his voice failed to catch their attention.

'Vratu!' he called disappointedly. 'Tell the men with no heads it is easier to walk an animal than carry it.'

The Uru looked away but Vratu's gaze lingered on him a bit longer. He turned toward the men, intending to comply, but the words wouldn't come out.

At a command from Krul they collected the dead and dragged them into the undamaged house. Torches were thrown onto the roof and set against the walls. The barn was also set alight. Two canoes by the shore were flipped upside down into the rushes.

One by one they finished up and gathered in the centre of the village with bloodied feet and hands, weighed down by their spoils. Polished stones, shaft-hole axe-heads and trinkets of copper could always be put to use, or eagerly traded. Slaughtered swine hung over the backs of several men, while those that had escaped the knives for the time being were led away with ropes tied through their nose rings.

They left the village without as much as a parting glance behind. All but one. Vratu of the Clan of Banan, the youngest amongst them, looked over his shoulder and was left with an image of a blood-red sun, a smoke-screened sky and raging inferno beneath.

Twenty

Back in Iyanah's camp that evening they put the traumatised beasts out of their misery and cooked up a banquet. At first Vratu tried to participate in a fitting manner, nibbling on a few ribs and nodding absently to comments about how tasty the meat was, but his belly had turned into stone and the smell reminded him too much of burning flesh. After only a few mouthfuls, he put his plate down.

When he saw signs that the dancing was about to commence, he tactfully retreated to a darker portion of camp to sit it out. Between a blazing fire and drums the men turned their paint-smudged bodies into patinas of sweat, while women and children sat clapping and chanting with glee. When he had sat on his rock ledge in the Hills of Uryak, Vratu had felt closer to his people than he did now.

Long after he expected it he saw Nura's head twist this way and that amongst the crowd. Her roving gaze found him and she stood and came over.

'Your face looks like rotten fruit,' she said with a good-natured smile. Her own face was the colour of sunset. Vratu said nothing.

She reached for his hand. 'Come. I want to see you dance.'

'My feet are heavy.'

'Enough. Come.'

Vratu gave her his hand, but when they got to the rear of the group he stopped. The men's faces were clearer now, trance-like and sizzling with energy.

'Is something wrong?' Nura asked.

Vratu watched her closely. 'Where does this anger come from?' he muttered. She was intelligent enough to have thoughts on the matter, and he waited for words that might bind them together, or ruin any hope.

She regarded him with a puzzled look. In that moment, he felt

183

something fade between them. Her hand fell from his and she walked away mumbling.

Vratu found a seat away from the crowd to watch proceedings. A girl's fresh, happy face caught his attention. She laughed and threw her head back and he saw the flesh of her white neck part like a mouth and blood spurt into her face. Elegant limbs would crack and bend at impossible angles and bone would poke sharp-edged through torn flesh. And there, like a spectre in the dark between faces, was Gurajnik's . . .

'*Vratu.*'

He flinched and twisted his neck to see his brother holding out a plate of food. Vratu dismissed the offering with a shake of his head.

'You are being watched,' Kihad warned as he sat down.

Vratu involuntarily turned his head and saw Uru Ukmaar seated not far away, leaning on his elbows and aiming his dark scowl straight at him. Not once did it waver. Vratu looked away.

'All night you have behaved like one in mourning,' Kihad remarked.

Vratu flicked his wrist at the men dancing. 'I see their feet, stomping on the dead.'

'Does this make your heart heavy?'

Vratu looked him over, irritated at being so easily read. But his brother ripped into the meat as if it were his only concern. Vratu stood.

'Where are you going?' Kihad asked through a mouthful of meat.

'Somewhere I will not be watched.'

He walked down the riverbank. The river kept pace alongside, murmuring quietly. When all he could hear was the gentle breaking of water in the shallows downstream he sat down and closed his eyes.

'Yes,' he said. 'Clean my head.' But his head would not clean.

The possibility that he might be different from those dancing away the morning's carnage never entered his mind. It had to be something else, something to do with his stay amongst the Oronuk. For a long time he thought about the mark they had left on him.

How would they see me now? he wondered. *Would they have*

treated me so, had they known how soon I would be turning my weapons against their own kind?

And then it hit him.

Their medicine is inside me still.

Yes, he thought – this is what must be wrong with him. If what they had given him was powerful enough to keep his heart beating long after it should have stopped, it was powerful enough to be working still. Should it continue to give him grief, there was medicine for medicine. He would have to think about it.

He stood and returned to camp. As inconspicuously as possible he took a blanket from Nura's dwelling and returned to the same spot on the riverbank to sleep, beyond the outrageous pitch of hollering and cavorting.

That night he dreamed.

Keorn lay bleeding on the ground. Men stood around him, pointing at the arrow in his neck and mumbling. He kept trying to get up, repeating the same words: *'I'm all right, I'm all right,'* but fell down each time. He vomited copiously and Vratu saw that it was pure blood gushing from his mouth, splattering the legs of the men standing around.

Ukmaar came over. 'He is dying,' he said. 'Show him mercy.' Vratu knelt and held his knife-blade to the man's throat. Keorn croaked, *'Help me,'* and Vratu had to force himself to plunge the knife in, again and again. The arrow wobbled loosely in his neck, blood spurted with each stab and still Keorn fought in his grasp, spitting blood everywhere and pleading *'help me . . . help me . . .'* in a barely audible voice. Men were looking at them, whispering, talking about them.

Kihad came over, glancing nervously sideways. 'Hurry Vratu, we need to leave,' he warned. Something dreadful – Vratu didn't know what – was coming after them, something he could feel but not see. But despite his gruesome efforts he was powerless to kill the man at his feet. The flesh on Keorn's throat was a mess of dripping slashes and still his blood-soaked breathing kept its rhythm.

Everyone else left. It grew dark and cold and Vratu sat on with the man who wouldn't die. By then he had given up trying to kill him and was instead overwhelmed by remorse. He cradled the man in his arms, unable to drag his eyes from the horribly mutilated throat. Then the face shimmered and changed shape, and now he saw Gurajnik staring at him.

'*Vratu.*' His eyes rolled white in his head and his last breath choked Vratu with the stench of death.

It was a signal to the dead.

A sinister, all-consuming presence began to stir around him. Angry spirits were leaving their corpses, searching for him. In the world of the dead they might not see him, but they would feel him, just as he felt them. They came closer, their eerie incantations suffocating him with fear. His legs were too heavy when he tried to run. No matter how much he begged them to work they floundered hopelessly, as if he was running in thick mud.

The spirits were almost on him when he woke soaked in sweat. An airless chill raised goosebumps on his skin as he flicked his eyes about, half-expecting some horror to appear in the dark.

The worst the dead could do to the living was in their dreams, a saying went. It was supposed to lessen one's fear of evil spirits. But here, alone in the dark, it had the opposite effect.

He collected his gear and returned to camp.

The following morning Vratu woke earlier than usual and jogged off into the mist before anyone stirred. He was not worried that his absence would be noted; they would simply assume he had headed home early.

Retracing his steps, he arrived at the scorched village in the afternoon. Ash and dust swirled in the light breeze, thin feathers of smoke seeped out from the black ruins and ants scurried over dark patches of dried blood at his feet.

He had not the slightest notion as to what he was doing there. This was no place to return, let alone dally. Perhaps sane observations would exorcise the powerful images his dream had left him with.

The acrid smell of ash filled his nostrils as he shuffled through what had been an interment pyre. Barely recognisable amongst the blackened ruins were charred human remains, set upon by swarms of flies.

The squawk of a raven distracted him. He looked over the knee-high crop of wheat and spotted the flutter of black wings. Something was out there.

He waded through the field toward it. The birds raised their heads, aimed their red beaks at him and stretched their wings threateningly. They waited until he was only a step or two away before abandoning their feast with loud squawks.

Lying face up in the grass was a woman's corpse. Despite the mutilation of her face Vratu was able to recognise, barely, the woman he had seen down by the river with the two children. Mottled patches covered her bloated body and her eyes were plugged with clotted blood and flies.

As he turned away from the sickening sight his eyes made a random sweep over the ground around her. And then he saw them: ghosts of a sign where there should have been none. He squatted down for a closer look.

Beneath the trampled stalks were a faint series of child's footprints. In those footprints he could read what happened as if he had been there as witness. What he could not read were the ramifications to himself, his people, and his culture now that he had seen them at all.

The prints were close together and showed an orderly direction, not what one would expect from a person fleeing death. He stood up, perplexed. Whoever made them had wandered around the corpse at will, pushing stalks into the soft earth with each step before heading back to the village. Vratu followed.

The prints appeared here and there amongst the ruins, spreading grains of ash and crossing over other sets in places. Not once did he find any prints superimposed over those he followed. Whoever made them was alone. All things considered, the pattern was consistent with the behaviour of a boy.

187

'Where are you, brave boy?' Vratu asked aloud, turning his face skyward to examine the angle of the sun. There was time.

The trail headed away from the river, which he thought odd. The boy could have swum the short distance across; from there it was not much further to Heavy-Fish and beyond that, lands of the farmers.

Head down, he followed the tracks into the forest. It wasn't long before he realised that the set had doubled. He stopped and kneeled. The spacing between these smaller footprints was very close. Now he knew why the child, or children now, had stayed this side of the river. The foot that had pressed into the earth here belonged to an infant even smaller than the first.

Now he was certain a boy had made the original prints. Vratu felt a twinge of admiration and cast his mind back to when he was a youth, thinking how he would have reacted in a situation like this, and adjusted his tracking accordingly. Not that it mattered if he didn't find them, he thought. If he lost the trail he would let it be and head for home.

But Vratu rarely lost a trail.

In the end, their fire gave them away.

By then it had grown dark. Vratu recognised both faces in the firelight – the children of the woman he had seen by the river. They had backed themselves against the toe of a rocky outcrop, easy enough to ascend should a hungry beast show its teeth. The girl tossed and turned while the boy sat close by with eyes that kept flicking in every direction.

Vratu was appalled at their lack of resources. It appeared all they had salvaged from the ruins were a few embers, furs and clothing. For some time he squatted in the dark, wondering how to declare his presence without sending either child fleeing into the darkness.

There was only one way to do this. Making no attempt to soften his footfall he began walking straight towards them. The night was deathly silent and his footsteps crackled loudly. The boy stood quickly, lips quivering and eyes bulging wide as an owl. The girl raised herself off the ground and almost tripped over her tunic in fright.

Vratu walked into the light and stopped. The fire crackled softly.

No one moved. The girl sucked on her fingers and the boy stared at him terrified.

Vratu crouched down to the boy's height. '*Kub . . . ul.* Yes?'

The boy's breathing slowed and he blinked a few times.

'That was a good idea, to lie down in the grass where no one could see you,' Vratu said conversationally. 'But you go the wrong way.' He lifted his arm and pointed east. 'You need to cross the river.'

The girl opened her mouth, and from there came a murmur as soft as would have been the beat of her tiny heart, and an image of his niece sprinting up to him, hands outstretched, flashed in his mind. He opened his arms and the little girl took a half step forward, then another, and he motioned gently with his hands until she came within reach, crying now. He picked her up and was surprised at how light her little body was.

The boy held onto his courage as long as he could, until the futility of it all broke him, and then he let the pain flow out of his eyes as well.

For the second morning in a row, Vratu woke far from refreshed. He had hoped a new day might shed light on a decision. It hadn't.

There were three options, as he saw it. The first was to return to the ruins and leave the children there with food. The second was to swim them to the far side of the river, point them east and leave them to their fate. The third was to retrieve one of the canoes from the shallows and send them downriver. Eventually they would reach the Great River and, after a few days of drifting perhaps, come alongside a village of their own kind. In each case, he first had to return to their village and see what they could find. By then he would also be in a better position to assess the boy's capabilities.

But as soon as they arrived there Vratu knew he had to rule out his first option. The stench of death was strong in the air now. It was a disturbing place, not one for frightened children. Best send them off in a canoe.

After a short search in the rushes, Vratu found one of the sunken dugouts and hauled it ashore. Satisfied it was still intact, he flipped it upside down and let the water gush out.

'You see there?' he explained, pointing east. 'You can use this to get to the other side, or you can head downriver. You can decide what is better. But you will need a paddle.'

The two children stared at him dolefully. Vratu felt his anger rise. This was not his doing, not his problem. It belonged to someone else; to Ukmaar and Krul, to the People-of-the-Longhomes for coming here in the first place.

He turned the dugout the right way over and let go. It fell to earth with a thump and rocked a little with water sloshing around inside. He contemplated the far side of the river, and then the children, rubbing his hand over his forehead and grumbling.

After a while of this he cussed and reached into his backpack. He took out several items of dried food and tossed them at the children's feet. The boy looked at him with an empty face and didn't move. Vratu turned his back and walked off, slowly though, as if dragging a weight behind him.

As he passed the first of the trees he heard the patter of feet behind him. He kept going without looking back. The deciduous canopy closed overhead, the air cooled and he kept his pace slow and his hearing fine-tuned. The sound of their tiny feet followed at a discreet distance.

When it sounded like they were almost at his heels, he turned around. The children stopped a stone's throw away. As if embarrassed, the boy shuffled into the ferns. The little girl stayed where she was, watching Vratu with a guilty face.

Vratu resumed walking. After a few steps he looked behind and saw no one. Moving slowly and keeping his hearing sharp, he soon heard the crackle of leaf litter behind.

It made him smile.

They walked for three days, stopping only to feed or sleep or gather a few berries and mushrooms. At night the children fell asleep as soon as their heads touched the ground but Vratu sat on deep in thought, moved by the look of peace on their faces.

In a sombre mood he returned to his people late in the afternoon. His arms ached from carrying the girl for most of the day and all he wanted to do now was rest. It seemed the entire clan was present for this momentous occasion. People sat about enjoying the last of the sun, boys and girls swam in the glistening stream.

The air stilled as he walked into camp and he felt the eyes on him as the children did: the small hands tightened around his neck and the boy bumped into his knees repeatedly as he tried to keep up. He reached his dwelling and found Ilan to one side extracting pitch from birch bark by heating it over hot coals. Ignoring his friend's stone-faced look of astonishment, Vratu set the small girl down and unhooked a bladder from a tripod.

'What food do we have?' he asked as he tilted the bladder to his lips. The sweet taste of rosehips smoothed his parched throat. He lowered the bladder. 'Ilan, are you there?'

Ilan shrugged stupidly without taking his eyes off the children. Behind him, Banan marched ahead of a group of men and women. The Uru reached him and stopped.

'*Buno*, Vratu,' he said coolly, as if this were some sort of prank. 'We have been waiting for you. Runners came and told us what happened. The clans are heading west. We need to leave.'

'What did you hear?'

Banan ignored the question and pointed to the children. 'What is the meaning of this?'

Vratu took another long swig from the bladder before he answered. 'The children are hungry.'

'Who are they?'

'They were in the forest,' Vratu said brusquely. Today he was in no mood for reprimands, advice, or instructions. As he looked around he realised that yes, once again he was the centre of attention.

There was a lengthy pause as Banan pieced it together. His face contorted, as if in pain. He looked as if he had been presented with a dish of poison and told to eat it.

'These are Children-of-the-Longhomes, yes?'

Vratu said nothing.

191

Banan rubbed his forehead and lowered his voice. 'They have no place amongst the Illawann, Vratu.'

Some older women crouched down beside the children and Vratu heard a few whispers. The little girl smiled. More people, mainly girls, came forward and poked the children playfully.

Vratu placed the bladder back onto the tripod. 'They will be food for wolves and ants, back in the forest.' He put his hands on his hips. 'They eat no more than two of our pups.'

'These are not pups, Vratu. It is not their appetite that worries me.'

'What then?' Ulke cackled as she squatted in front of the children. 'Their teeth? Their temper?'

Banan dragged Vratu away from the ears keenly listening. 'This is foolish. Who will take care of them? No one here has understanding of their tongue. They will be more lost here than in the forest. Have you thought these things through?'

'I have walked for three days and I am tired,' Vratu said, and walked off.

'We will talk more about this,' Banan called after him.

Vratu nodded dismissively and found a log to sit on. One by one the men left and women pushed forward to inspect the new additions to the clan. A few children followed, but they quickly lost interest and were the first to return to what they had been doing.

Ulke took the boy by the hand; he didn't let go. She led him to her dwelling and sat him down by the front. More women joined them. A young woman took the hand of the little girl and led her away. They returned a short time later with the girl in better fitting clothes and joined the group gathered around Ulke's dwelling. An older woman offered the children some food on a plate, and when neither child took anything she placed it down beside her.

All afternoon Vratu kept them in sight. The children sat quietly and barely moved while everything went on as normal around them. Many heads turned toward the children, and then to Vratu. He held their eyes and they looked away.

That evening he helped his mother feed the children and prepare new beds in her dwelling. Afterwards he went outside to take in the evening air. He passed Banan's dwelling and saw wisps of smoke rising from the glowing smoke-hole.

They are talking still, he thought uncomfortably. Earlier on he had thought it best to let them talk freely; now he decided it was his turn. He walked over and opened the door-flap. All the clan's men were seated inside.

Banan motioned him in. 'Here, Vratu.' They made a tight space and Vratu sat down. 'We have been talking.'

Vratu stared deeply into the fire. He was worn out before he joined them, now he felt worse.

Banan asked, 'Are they settled?'

Vratu nodded and drew a heavy breath. 'I thought of taking them east, back over Heavy-Fish.'

'We talked about that,' Banan said. 'It is not wise. Everything they have seen will go back with them.'

Vratu leaned forward and flicked a stick into the fire. He'd come to the same conclusion.

'The clan will leave tomorrow,' Banan advised. 'Do you plan to take them with you?' The hearth crackled loudly as they waited for him to answer.

'They shake in their sleep,' Vratu said softly, feeling his eyeballs water from the heat. 'The girl cries, the boy moans like the wind.' No one answered. He looked up and saw them all staring into the hearth as deeply as he had been.

Banan leaned back. 'We are clan, Vratu,' he said. 'If it is your wish to take these children into your dwelling we will respect your decision. But there will be others less loyal to you who may not. We cannot speak for them.'

'Everything they were is no more,' Vratu said. 'Here they can be what we make of them, just like any other orphan we have fed and kept warm.'

'You saw the men of Krul and Ukmaar,' Banan reminded him. 'Their way with these people is to turn them into ashes, and you

193

bringing back two children who escaped their weapons is not part of that way.'

'They did what they went there to do. It is finished.'

Banan shrugged. 'It seems not.'

Vratu stood feeling displeased. They had given their support, but without heart, which made it feel like no support at all. On his way out he stopped. 'Am I to feel I have done wrong?'

'If you have Vratu,' Banan answered gravely, 'we won't know until it's too late.'

The children were sleeping soundly when he returned to his mother's dwelling. Ilan was waiting for him. Vratu knelt down beside the girl and brushed away a strand of hair that was tickling her nose.

'Have they talked?' he asked his mother, sitting on her bed. A seam had parted on the boy's shirt and she was mending it with a bone needle.

'No.'

It didn't surprise him. The girl had spoken two or three words in as many days, the boy hadn't uttered a sound. 'Does this agree with you?' he asked.

She only smiled in reply. He knew that smile. The readiness with which she and other women helped raise orphans was second nature. All that made these two different was their inability to communicate verbally; their behaviour, withdrawn and quiescent, was otherwise the same.

'Is this the cause of all our fears?' Ilan observed from above. 'Are these children stronger than ours?'

'Banan is right,' Vratu murmured. 'What am I to do with them?'

'Did you see his mark?' Ulke asked, without looking up from her sewing.

'What mark?'

She put the shirt down and picked up a lamp. 'Here,' she said, shuffling forward on her knees. She pulled the blanket off the boy and his eyes opened in fright. She calmed him with a soft hush and a gentle hand on his forehead, then moved the lamp closer and turned his head to one side to expose a faint line running down the rear of his neck.

Vratu hadn't noticed it before; the boy's shoulder-length hair hid it well. Each end of the tattoo curled into a spiral like the frond of a fern, the top starting below his ear and the bottom stopping short of the collarbone.

'That is strange,' Ilan remarked.

Vratu was mystified. Boys were never painted, at least not amongst their own. It was the last thing he wanted to think about. 'It has been a long day,' he said.

As he lay in bed he found his thoughts returning to Voi. He missed his old friend. The old man had always known what to do. A shaman once told him the spirit of a close friend might visit a man in his dreams in times of need, and guide him through his difficulties.

But it never happened to Vratu.

The following morning the boy was gone.

Vratu stood above the boy's bed. He had taken his belongings, nothing else. Vratu looked at his mother, tempted to rebuke her, but the worried look she gave was enough to pacify him. This was his fault anyway. He should have predicted this, should have known better. He stood and went outside.

Ilan was still there, waiting for him. 'Perhaps it is for the best,' he suggested.

Vratu looked him over. Ilan was right – here was the opportunity to let it be. For a while Vratu stood there, thinking about it. Then, with a huff, he strode over to his dwelling and put a hand on the door-flap. After a short hesitation, he pulled it open and went inside. Almost immediately he re-emerged with his bow and a quiver full of arrows.

'We won't wait for you,' Ilan told him.

'I will catch up,' Vratu answered as he walked off.

Nearby, Banan was fitting a bundle onto a boy's back. 'We leave soon, Vratu,' he advised unhappily.

Vratu adjusted the quiver strap over his shoulder and ignored him. Ilan made one last appeal. 'The boy will find his way home.'

'No,' Vratu replied over his shoulder. 'He is lost out there.'

'Do you want me to come?'

Vratu glanced back with a smile. 'You slow me down.'

Following the trail they had come in on the day before, Vratu surprised himself by finding the boy easily. The child made a forlorn sight beneath the giant beech, so fixed on the trail ahead he seemed oblivious to someone approaching from behind. Vratu made a quick scan of the murky woods either side of the trail, wondering if he wasn't the only one following him.

'Here, boy!' Vratu called. Kubul kept walking. He didn't even turn around. 'Boy!' Vratu called again, louder.

Still Kubul kept walking. Vratu ran to catch up. He came abreast and slowed to the boy's pace.

'*Buno*, my friend. Where are you going?' He put a hand on his shoulder. Kubul stopped and looked up, tears dribbling down his grubby face.

Vratu felt a stab of pity. 'We are going to Walk-on-Clouds, two days west of here. It is a good place. There is a big lake. The birds are so many they fly into you, the fish are so thick in the water you tread on them. You will see.'

The boy stood quietly, his face as lifeless as one in a trance.

'You have to come with us.' Vratu shook his shoulder gently. 'The forest is not kind to a boy who walks alone.'

Kubul broke from under his hand and sprinted away. The reaction was so sudden and unexpected that Vratu didn't move.

'Where do you go?' he called after him. 'Shall I leave you here? Is that what you want?' He watched Kubul disappear ahead. 'Boy!'

The rustle of Kubul's feet receded into silence. Vratu took off at a jog and caught up to him in a few easy breaths. He grabbed Kubul's arm roughly. 'Enough of this!'

Kubul wrenched his arm away and dropped to the ground. He wailed and kicked and thrashed his arms around in a frantic fit. Vratu took a step back, feeling half-pity, half-annoyed, and waited for him to tire. Finally Kubul stopped and lay whimpering on the ground like a wounded cub.

Vratu squatted down beside him. 'What do you want?' he asked softly. 'Your friends and family are with the spirit world. You have us now, there is no one else. Be brave.'

Kubul rolled over and faced the other way. Occasionally a strange groan punctuated his crying, more like a death-wail. It was an eerie sound for a small boy to make, and made Vratu nervous. The same sort of sound had come after him in his dream a few nights before.

He held out his hand, feeling a sudden urge to touch the boy's head, then pulled it back. 'When you are finished,' he said as he stood up, 'we will go.'

And with that he chose a log to sit on, and waited.

Twenty-one

Crystal clear streams fed Walk-on-Clouds, which was surrounded by dark woodland and several strategically positioned bison-head sentinels painted with the mark of Banan's clan. The lake had swollen considerably since they had last occupied its shores, and the aqua-blue waters now lapped at the doors of the lowest dwellings.

They fattened themselves over the first few weeks on waterfowl dropped by arrows fired into the startled swarms, or by hurling bolas, or by casting nets with loom weights attached. When their quarry showed signs of spooking the hunters resorted to craftier techniques, like stalking their floating targets from behind a screen of floating reeds and closing the final distance underwater to grab their webbed feet from below.

To Vratu's dismay, Kubul showed not the slightest interest in hunting or trapping. Tasks given to him were carried out with a dull face. Pups tickling his toes with their needle-like teeth failed to stir his spirits, the sweetest foods on his plate went uneaten. The girl, who squeaked the name of Ly with the same ease she offered a smile, took to her new friends naturally, but the boy's dark mood was impenetrable.

The sentiment of the women was no passing whim and Vratu felt comfortable leaving the children in their care whenever the need arose. The mild interest his people showed in the children soon grew into genuine concern for their welfare. Several members made a habit of volunteering food and mothers encouraged their children to play with them daily. The boys of Kubul's age group however were quick to sense the darkness in his soul, and their behaviour alternated between harmless indifference and a level of bullying that required their mothers' intervention.

The lake had a tradition as a meeting place for native clans needing overnight shelter, and visitors were common. They stopped by to trade, to exchange information, to investigate potential mates. Children of farmers meant little to these men. They looked them over with passing interest, a question or two might be asked and they enquired no more.

On one occasion Vratu returned from a hunt to find Iyanah and about half his group present. Several men were gathered around Vratu's dwelling. A man named Gru was hunched down in front of the boy, and Vratu's mind flashed with the image of his face painted a hideous red and a bloodied mace in his hand. To his alarm he observed their examination directed at the tattoo on Kubul's neck. He did a quick scan for Ly and saw his mother showing her to a group of women. As he hurried over to his dwelling Kihad intercepted him.

'Why are you here?' Vratu asked, peering around his brother to keep Kubul in sight.

'We are headed for Smooth-Waters,' Kihad answered. 'Nura is here.'

Vratu hardly heard him as he kept walking, eyes ahead. The men parted as he nodded his way through. Kubul saw him and lifted his head, his shoulders relaxed and his eyes softened like a boy on seeing his father return from a long hunt.

Iyanah gave Vratu a serious look. 'We had not heard about your boy,' he said flatly.

Vratu went into his dwelling and shed his hunting attire. By the time he returned outside only Gru and Kihad remained. 'He finds it hard to talk, yes?' Gru said, and gave Vratu's shoulder a gentle pat. Then he walked away, oblivious to how much that simple gesture meant to the young man.

'How did you find them?' Kihad asked.

'It was easy,' Vratu said. 'Easier than knowing what to – '

A finger stabbed him from behind. He swung around and saw Nura's ivory-white teeth flash in a wide smile.

'Buno!' she cried, looking brilliant as ever. She flung her arms around him. 'You left last time without me knowing.'

Kihad started off. 'We can talk later,' he said with a grin. 'After you feed us, you squirrel.'

Vratu kept his eyes on Nura. She looked the boy over and a flicker of amusement showed on her face.

'What will you do with him?' she asked.

Something in her prolonged smiling annoyed him. 'You find this funny, yes?'

'You are funny,' she answered, pursing her lips. 'You always find a way to make things difficult.'

'I am not laughing.'

'That is because you are not a happy man, no?'

Vratu scoffed.

By the day's end the children had been examined thoroughly by almost every guest. Nura was the rare exception, Vratu noticed. She flittered around camp like a butterfly; giggling, swapping secrets, comparing jewellery and doing everything except showing the slightest interest in something of great importance to him. Should he bludgeon the children to death in front of her he doubted she would protest, to his growing disquiet.

They ate dinner in small groups and made no mention of the children. Nura's brother, a likeable brute named Ubutt, bedded down in Vratu's dwelling. They argued cheerfully over the merits of two hunting strategies planned for the next day and resolved the issue with a bet on which would be more successful.

The morning dawned clear and promising as they divided themselves into two teams. Vratu felt excited, too excited to fret needlessly over children. Months had passed since he'd included himself in a hunt of this scale. His group voted to head for some marshes where aurochs loved to wallow when the day turned hot, and in his mind the bet was as good as won. Perhaps, if they were back that night, he might even partake in a little dancing.

Nura skipped over and gave him a hug before they left. 'Be careful,' she said. An aurochs had recently impaled a cousin of hers to death.

'My mother cannot look after the children all day,' he replied, looking her in the eye to show he meant it. 'It would be good for you to help her while I'm gone.'

'I can do that. Will you be back tonight?'

He smiled arrogantly. 'Our group will.'

The hunting parties departed, each bound for destinations more or less equidistant from camp. As Vratu turned to wave farewell he saw the boy standing in front of the line of well-wishers, watching with a sad face. Vratu turned around one last time as they entered the forest and saw him still standing there after everyone else had left. It was an image he would never forget.

A voice called him.

Kubul turned around and saw Mother Ulke – one of the women he truly liked. Her smile was as friendly as her touch and there was none of the strain to her goodwill he correctly assessed in others. She gave him a pile of clothes and mimed unnecessarily the act of cleaning. He looked around for Ly and saw her playing with some children.

Despite appearances he didn't mind the tasks given him. They gave him a sense of purpose and kept his mind occupied. When he was alone and bored, the images returned. Images a grown man would find hard to reconcile, let alone a small boy.

He walked down to the shore. A group of boys played in the water, flinging sand and gravel at each other. As he knelt by the water scrubbing the clothes he felt a stone hit his back. Preferring to think it wasn't directed at him, he paid it no mind.

When more muck hit him, he looked up. An older boy stood smiling a short distance away, the shapely tone of his pubescent chest looming above water. Kubul didn't know him. He must be one of the visitors.

The boy said something that made everyone stop playing and gawk Kubul's way. He quickly gathered the clothes into a bundle and started walking up the bank. A stone stung his shoulder and a burst of laughter followed. Forcing composure into his walk, he made it to the safety of the women without looking back.

Ulke sat by the front of their dwelling bending hazel rods into a wicker basket. She saw Kubul and pointed to a rack for him to hang the clothes on. When he finished this she pointed to the children playing in the river but he returned an empty look. Ulke sighed and pointed to her work. The craft of wickerwork was a familiar one and he sat down happily enough. Now and then she showed him the correct length to trim or cut, but for the most he proved proficient. It wasn't long before an impressive basket was complete.

Ulke clucked approvingly at their combined effort and left to put it to use. It appeared he was dismissed. He had a lot of spare time at his disposal, which he might normally spend with Ly, but she looked happy playing with her new friends.

Kubul was familiar by now with the homely routines of these people. Men who went hunting or fishing left early in the morning and groups of women and children normally headed off into the forest soon after. Toddlers remained in camp with grandparents. The visitors had altered this routine. Groups of boys took the opportunity to play amongst themselves and more women than usual remained in camp, talking, always talking. Water was permanently on the boil and fires constantly nourished. Perhaps they were preparing special dishes for later on.

Lately he'd been accompanying Ulke when she went digging for edible roots and grubs, but today the girl of Vratu called him away. They went into the forest and found a group of boys engaged in collecting honey. One of them, clad head to foot in furs and partially obscured behind clouds of smoke, pulled wads of dripping honeycomb from a beehive. Boys standing safely back made a game of swatting at bees with bundles of leaves and Kubul teetered on the brink of laughter at their profanity every time a lone bee managed to dodge the flurry and deliver its sting. They returned to camp laden with nature's prize sweetener and he helped the women drain the free-flowing honey and pack away the honeycomb, licking his fingers at every opportunity.

It was midafternoon. He looked around for something to take an interest in. A circle of boys stood down by the lake, some he knew were fairly friendly. He walked closer and saw the boy at the centre of their attention showing off a necklace. Its dominant feature was an impressive set of talons, evidently valued by his peers.

Sometimes his emotions wavered. So many things were new to his experience that natural curiosity threatened to break him out of his shell of gloom. The bee-swatting experience had put him in good cheer and rekindled a long-lost urge to participate. He noted the looks of the boys standing around, saw in their eyes how impressed they were, and hurried back to Ulke's dwelling in order to find something he thought might impress them. They had given him a whole new set of attire, as if to make it easier for everyone, including him, to forget who he was. His original clothing sat neatly folded in one corner and his belt pouch protruded from the bottom of the pile. He opened it up, pulled out a small leather pouch and went outside.

The boys were still there. Kubul approached slowly, looking down every few steps at the pouch. Inside was the only personal item of jewellery he retained; something his father had always warned him not to lose. He wouldn't wear it in front of strangers, for he knew that would draw attention, and the less attention he drew to himself, the better.

A few steps away he halted. Some vague instinct warned him now that this might not be a good idea. But the boys noticed him and stopped talking. One of them, a newcomer, came forward. His sharp eyes went straight to the pouch and Kubul balled his hand into a fist to hide it; a reaction that put a frown on the boy's face. He stopped an arm's length away and waved a finger at it.

Obediently Kubul opened up his hand. The boy made an impatient gesture and Kubul's fingers trembled as he untied the string and pulled out a necklace.

The boy froze and stared at it, as if in shock. Several moments had passed before he roused himself and held out his hand.

Kubul took a step backwards. The boy gestured for him to hand the piece over but Kubul clasped it tightly and hurried away.

He walked along the shore far enough not to be bothered and found a large log that made a comfortable seat. Recently he had developed a habit of rocking when he sat. It was a comforting motion, placid and steady.

An inverted sky was reflected on the surface of the lake. Close to shore mayflies amused him with their ritualistic dance, fluttering swiftly upwards before falling death-like in a spiral down to the water. Swallows swerved and banked as they caught insects on the wing, a flock of geese skidded to a stop far out on the lake.

Kubul looked down at his jewellery. Fond memories were coming back.

Something cracked behind him. He swung around and saw the older boy who had thrown muck at him earlier and the boy who had taken an interest in his necklace. Kubul stood quickly and tightened his grip on it as they looked him over smiling, but neither smile he cared to trust. The older boy moved closer and grunted something unintelligible. Kubul began to back away.

Without warning the older boy's fist came up and hit him in the face, hard. The skin beneath his eye socket split and he sank groggily to his knees. The other boy swung a foot into his chest, knocking the wind out of his lungs. The older boy crouched down beside him, clutched a handful of his hair and pulled his bleeding face closer, shouting into his face and groping for what he held. Kubul fought him off and stood back, wheezing with a sore chest as blood trickled down his cheek.

The older boy lunged forward and his fist shot out in a blur. This time Kubul caught its full weight on his jaw. He hit the earth with a thump and the necklace fell out of his hand. He scrambled to his feet and launched himself at his assailant, encircling both knees with his arms and hanging on with all his strength.

The older boy lost balance and toppled over. Abetted formidably by his accomplice, he tried to kick himself free while punching Kubul's head and pulling his hair. Kubul managed to grab a stray finger and force it into his mouth. He bit down hard and heard a bellow, the hand twisted away and he tasted skin on his teeth. As he crawled away his hands closed over a thick branch. He picked it up and held it before him threateningly. What he did was a bluff, but only he knew this.

The older boy paused. A puzzled look showed on his face, then it flushed red and his eyes glowed bright as a wolf. The muscles in his arms snapped tight as he balled his hands into fists and advanced on his prey with a low growl.

Kubul swung ineffectively once or twice, mainly to keep him at bay, until the older boy's size and strength prevailed. He relieved Kubul of his weapon and began using it himself.

Kubul curled into a ball to protect his face and undersides as the blows came down, painful but not crippling. Not happy with this, the bully lifted the branch high above his head and took deliberate aim.

The rock-hard ash landed squarely on Kubul's kneecap, there was a muffled crack like a stick breaking and he screamed in agony, eyes pinched shut against the pain. The hands protecting his face went to his knee and he reopened his eyes to the flash of the club on its way down again. His nasal bone splintered with a horrific crunch and shards of pain bit into his eyes like needles. His hands dropped limply and he lay on the ground choking on the blood flowing down his windpipe, barely clinging onto consciousness.

The boy lifted the weapon high as his friend watched dumbstruck. The club came down and deflected off Kubul's skull, peeling his scalp open and sending his mind into complete blankness. The happy thug beat the motionless body a few more times and then, panting, he raised the club high above head, contemplating a more lethal blow.

The sight of helplessness below him mercifully killed the urge. He let out a high-pitched yell instead, the same as he had seen many a hunter do, their kill twitching at their feet.

Twenty-two

As soon as Vratu sighted camp he knew something was wrong. Gloom had descended on the tiny settlement with the surety of a fallen cloud. Fresh meat was being worked in a barren silence. No children rushed forward, grave faces glanced at him briefly and turned away. At once he knew it was the children. He quickened his pace, striding well clear of his party.

Ilan met him with a sombre face. 'There has been trouble.'

Vratu let the leg of meat he was carrying fall from his shoulder. 'Where are the children?'

'The girl is with Mother Yuruk, she is well.' Ilan pointed feebly at Ulke's dwelling. 'The boy is in there.'

'What happened?'

'Come and see.'

Each frantic step Vratu took toward his mother's dwelling was quicker than the last. He reached the door-flap and flung it open.

The sight of a battered and unconscious child lying still as death on blood-soaked furs did not, in those first few moments, shock him. Pragmatic as always, he glanced over the injuries and quickly ruled out a wild animal or accident as the cause.

Only then did he begin to shake with a violent, mounting rage. It was as if a sleeping monster inside him had been poked awake with a burning stick. His jaw clamped shut and his breathing deepened, blood throbbed in his temples and his eyelids twitched. He forced himself to look for something positive and saw the boy's chest rise and fall, fighting on.

Kneeling next to Ulke were Ilan's parents. Vratu felt his rage checked by their presence. They had always been close to him, were always quick to defend him. Lavaar, Ilan's father, adjusted a poultice of comfrey leaves over the head wounds while his mother mashed fine strips of willow bark. A bowl of steaming liquid sat on the floor amongst several soaks of sphagnum moss, red with blood.

'What happened?' Vratu asked in a tight voice, stepping closer.

'It was over when they found him,' Ilan said behind him. 'Something happened down by the shore.'

Ulke arranged a set of splints beside the boy's leg as Lavaar felt around the boy's swollen knee carefully. The look on their faces was enough to confirm his fear that the damage was serious. 'Where is Nura?'

No one answered. Lavaar carried on with his examination. 'Tie it here,' he said to Ulke, pointing.

'Who did this?'

'Gru's boy,' Lavaar answered without looking up. 'Uaan.'

Vratu lips lifted in a snarl. The boy had a nasty reputation and he had never liked him. Now he liked him even less. 'What has he done?'

'His knee is broken here.' Lavaar touched the massive swelling. 'You can see what he did to his face.'

At that moment Nura stepped in. She glanced fleetingly at the boy before turning to face Vratu. Despite his blinding rage, he thought he saw something false in the look of sympathy that appeared on her face.

'Where were you?' he demanded.

The defiant look she gave him matched the tone of her reply. 'Working.'

'See what they have done? I asked you to watch over him.'

Again she glanced at Kubul as if he wasn't there. 'This is not my doing. I cannot look after him all day.'

'Did you look after him at all?'

'Am I to feel responsible for this?'

'If you took it upon yourself to start, it might never have happened.'

She glared at him without blinking. Quickly she turned, smacked the door-flap open and was gone. It bounced back into position on its leather hinges and all went quiet. Water from a squeezed rag trickled into a bowl.

Vratu was barely able to suppress the urge to drag her back by the hair. He forced his attention back onto the boy and watched Ilan's mother gently wipe a patch of dried blood off the swollen face. 'Tell me what happened.'

Ilan answered slowly. 'Uaan and Bruk said the boy attacked them with a branch.'

'Then he would have had good reason.' Vratu lunged at the door-flap and punched it open.

'Vratu!' Ilan called. Vratu ignored him and marched ahead. Ilan followed him outside quickly. 'Vratu!'

Only out of respect for his friend did Vratu stop. Ilan overtook him and blocked his path. 'Come inside.'

'Do you think this was nothing more than a fight between two boys?' Vratu asked angrily, and saw that Ilan was lost for words. 'No? Then leave me alone.'

'Listen to yourself!' Ilan retorted in a low, harsh voice. 'You divide your own people! What will you do – punish Uaan in the same manner? While they watch?'

Vratu relented a little and looked around. Every face had turned their way. Children stood still, men sat around fires with dour faces and a group of women that had been scraping flesh from a bison hide were upright on their knees, gazing at him like startled hares.

Vratu raised his voice loud enough for all to hear. 'Why not? What do they care if a boy is beaten into darkness?'

Ilan put a hand on Vratu's chest. 'Stop.'

Vratu flicked the hand away and lowered his voice. 'Do we allow for this?' he hissed. 'Is this where you stand with me?'

A look of hurt showed on Ilan's face. Without another thought, Vratu brushed past him and stormed toward Iyanah's men, sitting in a conspicuous circle of their own. They watched him come and raised their heads. Vratu stopped in front of them and addressed the boy's father. 'Where is your boy, Gru?'

'I put him in Nonah's dwelling,' Gru answered in an apologetic tone. 'He is in shame.'

Nura was seated with some girls not far away. She should have made herself scarce, retreated somewhere in shame as well. She had her back conveniently toward him.

'Nura,' he called matter-of-factly. 'There is work for you in my mother's dwelling.' She half-turned her head in his direction, then turned it back.

Tradition required that guests in camp behave with respect. They were not supposed to shout or curse or do anything to offend their hosts. Uaan's violation had brought every visitor into disrepute. The men knew this; they sat around in an embarrassed silence. Nura was pushing his limits. Still he waited patiently, showing no outward sign of the fury threatening to break him.

'Nura,' he repeated, sternly this time.

'The work is yours,' she replied, 'since it is your doing.' She leaned forward to adjust a bladder that hung over the coals, more interested in how warm she could make their tea. She mumbled something and one or two girls sitting opposite giggled.

A spark went off inside him, all sense fled. He felt his legs pumping; he could not have stopped them even if he wanted to. He reached her in a few strides and his hand shot out and enclosed her arm so tightly he felt nothing but bone beneath his fingers.

She felt unusually light as he jerked her up and dragged her away. 'You will go back in there and wash his wounds,' he snarled through gritted teeth. 'You will help my mother and you will stay until I say you can leave.'

Everyone watched dumbstruck. Men and women had their altercations, so be it. It was no one's business to intervene. But Nura did not officially *belong* to Vratu. Not yet, at least. True, her behaviour was disgraceful and some form of punishment was warranted. But was Vratu the one to give it? The dilemma showed on their faces.

Ubutt had taken a few steps after his sister and hesitated, jittery and tight-muscled in his restraint. Nura stiffened her legs and fought Vratu's pull, twisting her torso and trying to wrench her arm away. Vratu shoved her so hard in the direction of his mother's dwelling she tripped and fell flat on her back.

She opened her mouth to protest and he was down on her in a flash. He grabbed a fistful of her hair and pulled her face so close to his that it blurred before his eyes. 'Do you want to say something?' The fire in her eyes died as swiftly as a pinched wick.

An arm as solid as a bough circled his throat from behind and lifted him up with a violent jerk. His legs left the ground and he kicked the air, his fingernails clawing at the arm choking his windpipe.

'*Enough!*' the voice behind him growled.

The arm slackened and let go. Vratu swung around off-balance, fists cocked. Ubutt stood there breathing deeply, arms stiff on each side, hands open. He took a step further back, signalling clearly that he did not wish to fight. Though primed to lash out regardless, Vratu reminded himself that they had always been good friends. He looked around and saw everyone watching him, this time though with a greater display of confusion.

For the first time in his life he felt like a complete stranger amongst his people. It was enough to take the fight out of him. He forced himself to turn away.

He reached his mother's dwelling and swung the door-flap open. Ulke and Ilan's parents looked up from their work with doleful expressions.

It almost ended there. He had settled enough to focus on the more important task of doing what he could for Kubul. But as he put a foot inside he couldn't help turning around and shaming the men of Iyanah with one last look of disgust. It was then he saw that Uaan had emerged from Nonah's dwelling.

The son of Gru stood by the door, smug as ever. Vratu felt every hair on his body bristle with contempt. There was unfinished business over there. His outburst had achieved nothing and Kubul still lay broken and bleeding. Yet despite the overwhelming urge to punish, to storm over and thrash the boy red and blue, Vratu found the strength to restrain himself. He knew the issue would be dealt with accordingly – by the elders, the headmen, the boy's father. Maybe all of them. He could let it go for now.

The stiffness left his muscles and his breathing steadied. He was about to turn away when he saw the boy's eyes glint triumphantly and a wicked smile form on his lips.

The rage kicked deep in Vratu's core again, fighting to break free. He glared at Uaan long and hard. 'See how temper makes fools of us?'

Uaan replied, 'The only fool I can see is you.'

Vratu moved on reflex. In the same instant, the look on Uaan's face went from bold to timid. As Vratu closed the distance between them he saw the boy's body turn rigid and his hands ball into fists.

'Vratu!' Banan shouted.

It felt like a long walk with everyone's eyes on him. At the edge of his vision he could see one or two of Iyanah's more able men take to their feet and come after him fast. Ahead of him Uaan bravely stood his ground.

A muscular hothead named Enol got to Vratu first and tried to block his path. Vratu transferred his weight onto one leg and violently shouldered him out of the way.

Uaan's fists came up in fighting mode when Vratu was all but one or two steps away. The boy might have been in trouble had Vratu not hesitated at the last instant, checked by the very quality Uaan lacked.

A body slammed into Vratu's back and again he felt an arm encircle his neck. He swung his arms as one berserk, thrashing his limbs in all directions, trying to position his legs for a throw. A thick growl sounded from his throat, his sight whirled turbid and grey, and the faces of friends, rushing forward to assist, became strangers. Voices around him made no sense at all.

More of Iyanah's men rushed into the fray. Choked from behind, he lashed out at them indiscriminately, but his co-ordination was poor and the flurry of his fists was as aimless as bees buzzing around a hive. Deep down he knew he did not wish to fight anyone; if any remnant of sense remained it told him he was feeding his own rage. Nevertheless if a face presented itself he went for it, and with so many to choose from he soon connected. This only raised the intensity within the tight huddle of rage, and now his face bore the brunt of one or two solid blows. A heavy, overhand punch caught him squarely on the temple, dazing him enough to stall his fight.

In the thick of it all was Kihad, but Vratu, blind to all reason, did not recognise his own brother. 'Enough!' Kihad shouted, failing to hold him. 'Vratu! Stop fighting!'

It took three men to hold Vratu and they made a poor job of it. Enol took advantage of Vratu's pinned arms and drew back his fist, lining up Vratu's face. Banan pushed through and stepped in the way.

'Leave him!' he ordered. 'We have him.' He planted both hands firmly on Vratu's shoulder. 'Listen Vratu! Be still!'

At last Vratu regained his senses. 'Be still!' Banan repeated sternly, then used the same tone on Iyanah's men. 'Let him go!'

Vratu felt the grip on him loosen. His body jerked free and he stood panting, mouth flecked with spittle and eyes glowing like embers from his deep-red face. Iyanah paced the ground like a surly old bull, shaking his head. 'You have a curse,' he said to Banan. 'He needs to go.'

At first Vratu thought he meant him. Then he saw the headman flick his hand in the direction of Ulke's dwelling, and realised who he really meant.

Vratu walked over to his mother's dwelling. Aside of some jittery nerves he was relatively composed when he picked up a spear leaning against the wall. But the feel of a weapon re-ignited his rage and his knuckles tightened so hard on the shaft it felt like they had sunk into the wood.

'Take him then,' he sneered.

'Vratu!' Banan yelled. 'Put it down!'

Turning wildly, Vratu saw the confused looks of people witnessing the transformation of a human being. Had he the ability to see what they saw, he too would have beheld a stranger. People he lived with day to day, people who knew him intimately, had seen his good and bad and all in between – save this – now saw a savage ready to inflict harm on his own people.

His voice, when he found it, was a low-pitched snarl. 'Is it not enough what we have done to him already?'

Iyanah scowled at him without answering. In the drawn out

212

interlude, Nura began to cry. Vratu felt his anger ebb. His hands shook as he lowered the spear and let it fall from his hands.

As he turned away he saw Uaan standing by the dwelling watching him, wiser though that it was best not to smile. Gru stood protectively beside him. Vratu glowered at the boy, daring a reaction.

Uaan muttered something to his father. At this, Gru grabbed his arm and shook him roughly.

'Do not say that of Vratu,' he said.

'Why not?' Uaan answered, this time loud enough for everyone to hear. 'Everyone else does.'

Gru backhanded him across the face. Uaan stayed firm and the look of defiance never left his eyes. The sound of the slap hung in the air a long time. Gru turned to Vratu. 'My son has no respect,' he said, and gave the boy a shove. 'Go inside.'

Uaan staggered a step or two and stopped at the door. There he glared at Vratu, his face flushing red where it received his father's hand.

Vratu cursed himself. He had been warned by Ilan and yet had to have his say, the final word. It was his fault Kubul was possibly crippled, he had roughed up Nura, offended her brother and father and clan, insulted his best friend, and turned a father onto his son.

Everything was deathly quiet. He retreated into his mother's dwelling before he could do more damage.

There was no happy feasting that night, no bragging over either kill. The meat was divided and everyone retired in groups to eat in an uncomfortable silence.

Early on in the night Kubul regained consciousness. The pain was unbearable. His knee was swollen and stretched as tight as the belly of a pregnant woman and no amount of boiled willow bark could lessen the magnitude of his suffering. The head wounds, though ghastly, weren't the problem. His nose and face were puffed tight and his eye sockets so sunk into the swelling that he could barely see, but superficially at least the skull seemed intact and his returning consciousness was a good sign. The knee was the problem. The

213

swelling was too tight and the boy's pain too intense for further examination, but it was likely that something was broken or chipped, and this had serious implications. The ability to walk and run, in their world, was imperative.

No one joined them. It was as if a contagious fever and not an injured boy occupied his mother's dwelling. Ulke whispered to the boy and swabbed his forehead repeatedly with a warm rag as he tossed and moaned deliriously, and Vratu took wicked satisfaction in knowing it kept people awake.

It was late when Ilan poked his head inside. '*Buno,* Vratu.'

Vratu knew there had been a discussion going on in Banan's dwelling for some time. 'Do they talk still?' he asked glumly.

'More than a Women's Sit. I started to yawn.' Ilan ducked his head and came inside. 'They wanted to know if I'd seen you knock your head lately, or if you'd been eating medicine mushrooms.'

'Not funny.' Vratu slid his fingers through his hair, parting the sweaty strands that kept falling into his eyes. 'Look at him.'

Kubul whimpered and his hands went again to the splint on his leg. Ulke leaned forward to stop him from pulling at the bindings. Ilan watched Vratu closely. 'How is it with you?'

Vratu took a deep breath. 'My mind feels empty.'

'Ah!' Ilan replied consolingly. 'You held it in for too long. It needed to be let out.' He gave Vratu a smile, and then he left.

Vratu felt his spirits lift a little. He stood up and took stock of himself. It was time to do what he knew had to be done.

The clan had retired for the night and the campgrounds were bare. The only other dwelling to show the leak of light was the one he headed for. He walked over and stopped at the door to collect his thoughts. He needed to choose his words carefully now. What had happened that afternoon was only half the affair, what happened now would be judged equally. They would be particularly interested in his follow-up behaviour. What he was prepared to do to remedy the situation.

So he would express contrition for his part, as best he could, but stop short of accepting full responsibility. It was as close to the

214

concept of an apology as he was capable of giving. They had no word for *sorry*.

He lifted his chin, squared his shoulders and pulled back the door-flap. Inside sat Iyanah, Kihad and Banan. Their faces lifted but not their eyebrows, as if his appearance was no surprise. At the rear Banan's family of six seemed to be asleep.

'Vratu, come in,' Banan invited. Vratu dipped his head through the door and entered. They waited for him to speak. He looked down at his feet and struggled to make his voice sound masculine.

'I have come to say I did not wish to behave as I did,' he garbled, waving his hands awkwardly. 'I respect the Clan of Iyanah and did not mean to . . . anger my friends.'

Iyanah's eyes looked hot when he spoke. 'Would you always treat my daughter like that?'

'I have no wish to treat anyone like that,' Vratu said sincerely. 'That is all I wanted to say.'

A satisfied look appeared on their faces. By the quietness that followed, and a barely perceptible nod from his brother, he sensed general approval. Nothing more needed to be said.

'I will go now,' he finished up. 'The boy is in pain.'

'It will pass, Vratu,' Banan assured him.

Vratu made eye contact with Banan long enough to read genuine concern. But when he tried to do the same with Iyanah, the headman looked away.

The following morning after breakfast, Vratu approached Nura and suggested they take a walk. Most of her people stood around in small groups, ready for departure. Iyanah chatted to Banan and Ubutt was nowhere to be seen. No one had acknowledged him all morning. If it was a simple matter – a misplaced word, a breach of trust – they might have settled their differences with a parley and round of jokes over shared food and vows of friendship, bleeding gums and all. This was not one of those matters.

They walked along the shore of the lake, Nura with her head down. All morning Vratu had rehearsed this meeting in his mind. He wanted to be humble yet firm; a fitting response for a man displeased with what his woman had done, yet ready to bear some responsibility. No different to what he had chosen to do the night before in front of his leaders, and no less important.

'We should not part like this,' he said, 'so let us be fair to each other.'

She gave no reaction. She walked slower than normal and he had to consciously check his pace. He took her hand and she held it loosely.

'What is this all about?' she asked. 'What is happening?'

'They started it.'

'What do you mean?'

Vratu shrugged. 'They came to me, I never went to them.'

'I don't understand.'

'I went because of you.' He watched her closely, to see if she understood.

'Vratu . . .' she said irritably. She stopped and dropped her hand. 'You make no sense. Do you know what you are doing?'

For a long moment he just stood there, saddened it was all lost on her. She bowed her head and he bent forward to hug her, but the tautness in her body told him she was not as forgiving. Looking past her shoulder, he saw Iyanah watching and was grateful her father was witness to his act of contrition.

'Go now,' he said, letting her go. 'We will talk again when both of us are happier.'

As Vratu watched her go, longing for a conciliatory gesture that never came, Gru appeared between them.

'Vratu,' he greeted him, and they both watched Nura settle in amongst friends. 'She will be smiling the next time you see her.'

Vratu nodded absently.

'I found something on Uaan last night.' Gru held his hand out. 'He said he took it from your boy.'

Gru dropped a small necklace into Vratu's palm and walked away. A few painted clay-beads, pretty as they were, he hardly noticed. It was the glittering spiral pendant identical to the shape of the tattoo

216

on the boy's neck that piqued his interest now.

Unaccustomed to any workmanship like it, Vratu fingered it delicately. It took only an instant for its value to sink in. At once he knew why two boys had almost beaten Kubul to death.

No jewellery he had ever laid eyes on could compete with this. He gazed at it a long time, feeling an almost religious awe grow inside him. He was about to show it to someone else for a second opinion when he was halted by an irrational greed to keep it entirely to himself.

Such was the power of gold.

Twenty-three

After the attack on the village, Marhala Wunn took to the forests regularly. There was a lot he had to think about now. Their return to Oyub-ka had been a mistake, he feared; misery and death had indeed followed. And if a reckoning was imminent, from mortal source or otherwise, prudence demanded he look for signs.

But for weeks he saw nothing. Everything in the forest appeared as normal. After each walk he returned to find his camp in order. Women returned from foraging with full baskets, hunters returned laden with meat, and never was a smile far away.

Then came a day when he did witness something unusual.

A golden eagle stood in an opening in the forest. A lone wolf circled it, eyes flashing excitedly, tongue lolling. The eagle made no move to fly away, suggesting it was either injured or very sick.

The wolf appeared to have made a game of it, scampering sidewards and back with eyes as playful as a puppy. The raptor stood its ground, hopping around on its talons while keeping beak and angry eyes pointed at the aggressor. Occasionally it unfurled its wings to create an impression of size and bulk, then the beak would part and a high-pitched squawk pierced the silence.

The wolf kept trying to get in behind the eagle, lunging every so often and nipping a feather or two, backing off when the eagle retaliated with a sharp peck. The bird looked hardly concerned. Its defensive reactions were weary and without urgency, despite the danger it was in.

With a quick lunge, the wolf managed to get in behind. Too late the bird turned, and the wolf caught an extended wing in its jaw. The wolf did not mangle its prey as it normally did; instead, with head lifted proudly, it tried to drag the eagle away.

The eagle hopped along awkwardly, soundless mouth parted in a frozen yawn. After being dragged for a few steps it squawked loudly. The wolf let the wing drop and they both stood where they were; the eagle preening its wing, the wolf with its tail erect and tongue wagging.

The eagle took a few steps and gathered speed. It flapped its wings, lifted gracefully off the ground and flew away.

Flew away?

The wolf sat on its haunches, licking its paws. It glanced at the shaman as if noticing him for the first time, then trotted away without a backward glance. High above, the eagle slanted a wing and altered course. Soon it disappeared from sight.

Marhala Wunn was confused. If the bird could fly all along, why subject itself to this? Why risk being torn apart by a wolf? Had it enough of life?

Or could this be the sign he had been looking for?

The eagle, far ranging and all seeing, was a powerful totem. The wolf was its matching counterpart. Both were kings of their domain. To see either in action was cause enough to consider a sign, and here both had been engaged. Had they been playing, or fighting? Never before had he seen them behave like this. The only sense it made was if they had tried to tell him something. Perhaps they had colluded to warn him of some imminent peril. For this could only be a warning. Whatever was coming warranted a display profound enough to impress on an observer the clear sign of danger.

A worried shaman returned to his people that day. Each time he passed someone he eyed them closely, searching for symptoms of evil spirits or hostility. But his people were faring as well as ever.

For many days afterwards he stayed alert. Hunters returned safely, there was no deluge from the heavens, no bouts of sickness, and no children went missing. A niece went into labour and he went to lengths mollifying the gods with an assortment of invocations, half-expecting both mother and child to perish. Not only did she live, she gave birth to healthy twins.

Perhaps something more ominous was in the making. Were men of the east looking for them, armed and angry and hunting for those responsible for slaughtering their people? But no word came to him to substantiate his fears. Even when he took his psychoactive toadstools nothing presented itself.

As time passed he thought that the wolf and the eagle might have had an agenda of their own. Or perhaps the altercation had no meaning at all.

Then Iyanah returned from his journey to Smooth-Waters. He immediately took Marhala Wunn to the side and told him the news.

Vratu had brought back two Children-of-the-Longhomes.

To a howling protest the boy's knee was regularly poked and prodded, and with youth in his favour it healed quickly. During this time Vratu stayed close to camp. Hunting parties left without him and he wandered the shores of Walk-On-Clouds to hunt and fish on his own. Traps and fine-meshed nets yielded fish and tasty freshwater crayfish, and slow-moving tortoises provided good exercise for a boy with one leg in a splint. They always came home with something and a simple trade added red meat to their diet of waterfowl, crustaceans, molluscs and fish.

Iyanah's group had not visited on their return east. In a roundabout way Vratu heard that after leaving Smooth-Waters, they had arced south of Walk-On-Clouds. It might have been a matter of convenience, but he suspected otherwise.

The days passed pleasantly. There were no more visitors and their wandering kinsmen had vanished into the vastness surrounding the lakes. But Vratu knew his days of peace were coming to an end.

A runner came bearing the message he'd been expecting. Developments in the east had called for a tribal council and included in the message was a request, if one could interpret it so, for Vratu to attend. Ukmaar, the great Uru himself, wished to speak with him.

'This time I trust the boy to you,' Vratu said to Ilan morosely on the morning of their departure. 'Do I need to say more?'

The look Ilan gave him suggested he had taken offence.

It was a two-day walk to Ukmaar's camp. As the distance to his destination shrank so too did Vratu's spirits. The uncle of the woman he hoped to marry had sent for him for reasons that could not be mistaken, and he knew his defence had nothing to do with the interests of his people. Those who accompanied him were not there to back him up, nor did he expect them to. He was on his own, again.

The Clan of Uru Ukmaar was, until his experience with the Oronuk, the most densely populated group of people Vratu knew of. In his days as a runner he was always well received and over the years had grown strong in friends amongst them.

On entering their camp he found himself not so much a subject of intense scrutiny as just another visitor. There were the same smiling faces, the same unassuming goodwill and genuine concern for his welfare. Even Iyanah greeted him with a gruff smile.

'Vratu,' he said. 'Nura came with us. She is out with the women and should be back soon. She is eager to see you.' Others were equally accepting. Kihad gave him a customary thump between the shoulder blades, Enol growled at him jokingly and Ubutt grinned at him slyly. Vratu was left dumbfounded by their clemency.

They had been waiting for Banan's group. After a muffled discussion, the clans' leaders retired into Ukmaar's dwelling for council and Vratu was told to wait. He found a place to sit and several friends joined him. There were the standard updates before talk turned towards likely movements in the immediate future.

At least two families were contemplating permanent trips north and were requesting access to the hunting grounds of Banan's group. Every year now more families were heading west, and Vratu sensed in his friends the same darkness of spirit as the men of Uryak he had spoken to at the Winter Grounds in the autumn past. When he found himself questioned on the specifics of the attack in Oyub-ka he tried to skirt the subject, but his listeners, clearly disappointed at having been excluded, kept at him. From what he heard the attack had successfully renewed bonds between Ukmaar and Krul, making him wonder if this had been their main incentive all along.

The women returned around sunset and his friends left to see how well they would eat. Vratu was about to go and greet Nura when

221

he saw the door-flap to Ukmaar's dwelling open and the men spill out. They stretched and breathed in the evening air.

Kihad came over and sat down. 'They are having a dance tonight,' he said.

'A dance?' Vratu asked eagerly. It had been a while.

'We've been invited to eat with the brother of Gru.'

Vratu felt his muscles tighten when he saw Ukmaar emerge from the dwelling. The Uru saw him and came straight over. His feet sank into the earth and nothing above his waist moved. It was like watching a walking tree. He stopped at the edge of the fire, his muscular frame cast in a livid glow.

'And now we come to Vratu of the Clan of Banan,' he said in a deep voice.

Kihad stood to leave. 'No,' Ukmaar stopped him. 'He and I will walk for a while.'

Vratu felt his confidence weaken. The Uru's deep, sparkling eyes were uncomfortably penetrating. Few men had the ability to unnerve him, none more so than this one. Ukmaar started walking and Vratu followed obediently.

'I knew your father,' the Uru said. 'He was a good man. Do you remember him?'

'No.'

'I see his likeness in you.'

Vratu ignored the flattery. He took a deep breath, clearing his head.

'My father was a half-breed, Ubren madman,' Ukmaar told him. 'When he wasn't making enemies, he was beating his own sons. You have that over me, my friend. Is Mother Ulke well?'

'Yes.'

They passed a dwelling with a middle-aged woman out front. 'Mother Kuna-ku,' he said out of earshot. 'A few days ago she buried her fourth son. He joins his two sisters. She thinks she is cursed. Perhaps she is.'

They walked past families eating and talking. 'Brunug there,' Ukmaar pointed, 'buried his brother last winter. He has taken his wife and family into his home, and now he has three wives, seven daughters and four sons to feed. But others will help him, and perhaps they will all see the winter through.'

A small boy crossed their path. 'Avul!' Ukmaar cried, and the boy stopped. The Uru growled playfully and the boy ran away giggling. Ukmaar needed only a few paces to catch him. Taking care not to be rough, he up-ended the infant and gave him a light shake.

'Here is a boy who lost his mother soon after he was born,' he said.

It was curious to watch the man, freakishly muscled and hard as oak, express the affection one might expect from a softer aspect. 'But he has a fine father,' Ukmaar put the boy down, 'and there are many people who will deny their own to give to him.'

Every family had a story of woe; these were no exception. 'Why do you tell me this?' Vratu asked.

'Barely a winter passes that our children do not go hungry,' the Uru replied, nudging the boy away. 'Yet you put food in the mouths of our enemies.'

'Are even children our enemies now?'

'Ask them.'

They came to the lip of the riverbank and stopped. The Uru pointed to the far side, barely visible in the dark. 'They are out there,' he said in a voice that was cold and rational. 'The Oronuk. The Serisi. Other Ubren and more. All manner of men who look this way, and they are like a river that has burst its banks. How would *you* stop them, Vratu?'

Vratu weighed the benefit of responding in the way he itched to give. Debating tribal politics had never been a skill of his, let alone under these circumstances. 'Are weapons all we have?' he asked sullenly. 'Have we tried to talk to them?'

'Oh, there has been a lot of talk over the years, too much talk,' Ukmaar responded. 'Most of it comes from men who would rue their own decisions if they had their way. They keep their hearts at peace by letting others do what they cannot. Truth is something to face when it suits them. They speak as if they have all the answers, yet the

223

more they learn, the less they want to know.'

There was no drama in his voice, more a timeworn weariness at odds with the energy of his presence. 'The gods,' he gestured flippantly toward the sky, 'care little for talk. They put strength into the arms of those who see it their way. You will know them better when you see what we have seen.'

'It was only one village.'

'One village today, one village tomorrow . . . no matter,' Ukmaar agreed. 'But it never is one village today, one village tomorrow. They will keep coming and they will not stop. Would you prefer to fight them in the years ahead, when they are much stronger? Or perhaps let our sons fight them instead?'

'Would this be true? We never see these people.'

The Uru chuckled, and the tone in his voice when he answered was clearly condescending. 'Have you never wondered why?'

'I hear talk of treaties.'

'The People-of-the-Longhomes like treaties. It gives them the opportunity to stretch their borders.' Ukmaar sighed and shook his head. 'No. There is no easy way to do this, and it is up to us to defend our land with greater force than those who want to claim it. Nothing less than fear keeps these people away. By fear we have kept them from our lands this long. With the passing of the years they forget, and so it must be done again.'

There was a long pause, after which his voice took on a lighter tone. 'It is not my way to explain this to you, Vratu. I do so only because you are almost of age and we must all do our part to get you there. I know you find this difficult. That day in the village . . . when I looked at you I saw someone lost. You were not really there with us at all, no?'

'You did not need me there.'

'Ah, but we did,' Ukmaar disagreed, waving a finger. 'We need to know what sort of man *you* are. We still do not know. You did nothing then and you have made matters worse since.'

'Am I seen as a coward?' Vratu raised his voice a fraction. 'Is that what this is about?'

'Oh, we know you are no coward,' Ukmaar responded tiredly. 'If men came at us waving spears and maces you would be amongst the first to bleed for our people. This alone does not make us men.'

'Am I here for you to tell me this?'

'It is time to finish it,' the Uru's voice was firm again. 'What are you ready to do? Are you the man I spoke of before? A man who lets others bear the weight he has no strength for? Even this man knows deep in his heart what must be done. Only by living up to hard truths is he made worthy of his place. Worthy of a girl like the one you seek.'

Vratu saw Nura sitting amongst a group of women and children preparing food. Wolf-dogs hunched around them, drooling heavily. The whole group burst into laughter and he envied their ignorance.

Ukmaar followed his gaze. 'They know no more than they need to,' he said. 'It is worth the look in their eyes to keep it that way.'

'They have new enemies now,' Vratu said glumly. 'One day they will come for us, and that look in their eyes will be gone.'

'It is possible.'

Vratu stared at him in confusion. 'I do not understand,' he said. 'Why do this then? Why give men reason to fight us?'

'If we let fear stop us we have lost already. Let them think like that. We control the fear.'

Vratu began to tire of the advice. 'You said it was time to finish it.'

The Uru rubbed his chin. 'Let me tell you about our shaman,' he said patiently. 'He speaks now of his dreams, which he has never done before. He fears these children come with a curse, that they are a peril to our people and should be gone. But I am willing to trade with you. The girl is too young to be of concern, too young to have the memory. She can be yours. The boy,' he shrugged, 'will always have anger in his heart. There is no hope for him.'

'I brought him back,' Vratu pointed out. 'I have fed him, bound his wounds. I cannot do what I think you are telling me to do.'

'True,' Ukmaar agreed. 'It is the *choice* that must come from you. All you have to do is give word, then we will take him and everyone can go back to the way it was.'

'How could we go – '

'When it is done,' Ukmaar cut him off, 'you will be ready for Nura.'

It should have left him floating. The words he had waited so long to hear had just been uttered. 'Why not just do it?' Vratu asked lamely. 'Why come to me?'

'Have you not heard anything I said?'

Vratu said nothing, grateful the dark concealed the loathing in his eyes.

'I keep hearing your name, Vratu,' Ukmaar went on, 'but I never expected to hear it from one of *them*.'

Vratu recalled Gurajnik's last word and shut his eyes, as if to block the image that always came with it.

'Stay away from these people,' the Uru warned. 'As you were told.' And with those words, he left.

She saw him standing there alone and put down her work. Vratu watched her come, her figure worthy of worship, resplendent in loinskin and tightly laced vest. She gathered him in her arms as if nothing bad had ever happened between them, and when his gaze diverted to her cleavage she saw where he looked and tilted her head backwards, laughing. Then she dipped it down again and saw lines of worry appear on his face. She grasped his hands and stepped back.

'What's wrong?' she asked.

'Your uncle has asked something of me.'

'What has he asked?'

The emotion in her voice had sounded genuine, but he knew she was a good actress. He looked deep into her eyes and saw nothing but orange rings flickering in her pupils. 'Has anyone said anything to you?'

'No,' she answered, frowning deeper.

He pulled her close again. 'We have decisions to make.'

'I do not understand.'

'You will.'

After a generous meal the dancing began. Mugs of honey mead were handed out amongst the men and they sat down to watch the girls' performance. With each sip of his drink, Vratu's mood improved. Not a girl he saw was prettier or more womanly than his.

When he noticed his shaman alone for a rare moment, he went over and sat down beside him. 'Uru Ukmaar talked to me,' he said.

The one man he hoped might offer a rational perspective said nothing. Vratu opened his mouth to speak and was cut off.

'You will have your share of other people's pain in life, Vratu,' Marhala Wunn said. 'Why take on more than you need to? It will destroy you.'

'As will what is asked of me.'

'There is no gain in seeking my counsel if it is only to hear what you wish to hear,' Marhala Wunn said frankly. 'We have discussed this before.'

It took a sprinkle of rain to end the dancing. A few men, feeling the mild effects of the mead, tried to keep the proceedings going. 'Do you run from a little rain?' they cried, and were overwhelmed by a chorus of disapproval.

They were still loitering around in small groups, arguing over weather forecasts, when the skies opened up in earnest. Rain pelted down in drenching sheets, sending everyone bolting for cover, all but the men sitting around a hissing bonfire and complaining loudly.

Vratu had made a dash for a friend's dwelling when he noticed Nura standing alone under the dome of a large oak. He veered off course and joined her. Golden beads dotted her forehead, her vest clung to her skin and silvery veins of water trickled between the cleft of her breasts. Wet hair hung down in strings of disarray to give her an untamed, feisty appearance.

He checked that her father and uncle were looking elsewhere before grabbing her hand and tugging her out of sight.

'Vratu, what are you doing?' she asked with a giggle. He hauled her away into the dark as heavy droplets landed around them like clammy footsteps. 'Vratu, I'm cold and wet,' she complained, dragging her feet.

He stopped and pulled her wet, slippery body into his arms, and for a heartbeat or two she obliged him.

227

'You have the claws of a bear,' she said cheerfully, pushing him away.

He grunted and tried again, but she resisted his efforts more determinedly this time. He dropped his hands sulkily. With water streaming into his eyes he watched her skip back to camp where the fireglow gave her a graceful silhouette.

She ducked inside a dwelling and was gone.

They picked up the spoor of some aurochs on their way home.

For some time they stood around the tracks, sharp-edged and fresh, debating the merits of a hunt. Every so often someone kneeled and fingered the impressions gently, treating them like something precious, followed by someone else doing the same, and they delighted in it. They examined every hoofprint and discussed every option, including taking no action, for with their suicidal bravery and spear-like horns, aurochs were a particularly dangerous quarry for even a large team of hunters, and the tracks indicated at least seven beasts, three of which were full grown adults.

The hunt required a detour of possibly a day or more, and though Vratu knew the boy would be anxiously awaiting their return, his allegiance to the hunt went without question. Five men were barely sufficient, four men hardly, and one less porter meant more meat wasted on ravens and wolves. As he listened to his peers he could feel the excitement prickle up his arms, the stirring of idle senses. Thoughts of Nura, the boy, his talk with Ukmaar, flew away like an arrow from his bow. For him the hunt had already begun.

It did not go entirely to plan. They managed to separate and surround a brave old bull, a spear found its mark and Vratu found himself charged at by something out of a nightmare. Despite the inconvenience of a mortal wound the blood-snorting bovine closed the distance that separated them with horrifying speed.

In that moment of sheer terror, with the bull the size of a mountain and the massive forehead with its elegant curls of fur and deadly horns aimed straight at him, Vratu knew he had to take the hit. He threw his useless spear aside, bent his knees slightly and danced on his toes into position, bracing himself for impact. In that last instant the bull snorted, sending warm, stinking breath and a fine mist of blood into Vratu's face, and he thought he saw his reflection flash in the dark eyes as the beast dropped his head for the hit.

The air exploded from his lungs, his ribs flexed inwards and his stomach heaved in agony. The bull flicked his head and Vratu's feet left the earth. Vaguely he saw the world turn upside down, trees and sky and friends flashed together, then his face smacked onto hard spine and he somersaulted gracelessly down to earth, barely avoiding the stomping hooves.

Had his chest caught a massive boulder he'd have felt better. He lay on his back hopelessly winded, trying to suck air into his lungs. Instinct commanded him to move, for he knew the bull's entire purpose in life now was to trample and gore him to death, but his legs would not respond. Now his companions leapt forward waving and shouting, confusing the bull enough for Banan to step in behind with his hand-axe and slice an ankle tendon. The crippled animal bellowed again, his hindquarters collapsed and three spears angled into his heart and lungs from close range left him harmless.

They quickly returned to Vratu lying helpless and wheezing on the ground, but once it was established that no serious damage had been done they let loose with the sort of jests reserved for sufferers of indignity. It took a while for him to indulge their humour.

But he was walking again, sympathetically burdened with a lighter load than the others, and even with his ribs bursting with pain he rejoiced in their camaraderie. They went over it repeatedly, humouring his poor evasive technique and trivialising the severity of his bruising, but underlying their jest was genuine flattery for his courage in standing ground. Nothing was like the feeling of a successful hunt, knowing that his part had earned him respect from his peers, and he would wear the marks of his injuries like proud emblems in the days ahead. For too long he had not enjoyed anything like it.

Back home it started all over again, with enthusiastic accounts of the pitch of his terror, the speed at which he had tried to evade the beast frothing at his heels, how high it had sent him skyward. When he tried to correct their embellishments it only made them laugh louder. Not one enquiry was made about his talk with Uru Ukmaar.

They decided to make the most of fresh meat. Ulke prepared a sunken oven-pit, surrounding the parcel of meat with hot coals to bake it in its own juices the way he liked. When he went to check on the boy resting in his mother's dwelling he found the odour of sickness and decay inside offensive. Kubul sat upright on soiled furs with his extended leg wrapped in a splint. The swelling had gone down enough to see lumps of bone beneath the mottled bruising, while all that remained of his facial injuries was a slightly misshaped nose and the faintest edge of purple skin beneath his eyes.

'Are you better?' he asked, but Kubul just watched him with empty eyes. 'Why are you always silent with me? Am I not your friend? Are you blind to what I have done for you? When your tongue stays still I think you are not my friend.'

He went outside and accosted his mother. 'Have you been cleaning his furs?'

'Yes.'

'It's a pig swamp in there.'

He saw Ly sitting in the dust with a woman, playing with a string of nettle fibres. Her face lit up and she squealed in delight at a knot trick the woman performed. Vratu looked at his mother's dwelling. It had an air about it as gloomy as within.

It tempted him greatly to send word to Ukmaar. Everything would be in order and he could commend himself on having preserved the life of an infant girl. What was one crippled child to his people? Ukmaar's parting words echoed in his mind, followed by the enslaving image of Nura and the feel of her in his arms . . .

He cast his eyes to the ground and rubbed his forehead as a series of conflicting emotions battled within. The laugh of Ly lifted his head. He stood there motionless, his mind blank. She giggled again and he walked over, curious to see what the child found amusing.

Twenty-four

The sun crouched low over the hills. The sky was painted pink and a soft breeze creased the lake. In the shallows waterbirds felt for titbits; spoonbills swung their heads side to side, ibises trawled with open bills, herons stalked, egrets jabbed, cranes frisked, and shorter billed swans, ducks, mallards and teals dabbled and chattered as they paddled peacefully amongst their company of stiff, long-legged waders.

The coracle drifted to the whim of the breeze. Kubul leaned over the side with a fishing line between his fingertips, staring into the grey fathoms. Vratu could see activity in camp; people preparing dinners and sorting through fishing nets. Several fires dotted the bank.

'Are we finished?' he asked.

Kubul looked up. *There it was again*, Vratu thought – that look in his eyes. As if in confirmation the boy pulled in his line. Somehow he'd understood. Either he had a gift for picking up foreign languages or an intuition far beyond what Vratu felt comfortable with. Or both.

They were in the middle of the lake. Kubul's stroke was unco-ordinated and lacked muscle, barely nudging them into the breeze, and the vessel aimed itself in all directions as they headed back. Tempting as it was to take over, Vratu decided against it. Exercise was good for the boy.

They reached shallow water and Vratu hopped into the sludge to pull the coracle through. Clouds of insects scribbled aimless patterns in front of him, tickling his ears and face. Birds close to shore parted respectfully and a flurry of tiny skaters shot away from his shins.

Up on the shore Kihad walked into view and waved. Gru followed behind, a hand also raised in greeting. Vratu returned their salutations happily; he hadn't seen either of them since his visit to

Ukmaar more than a month ago. He hauled the coracle up the bank.

'Where are your fish?' Kihad asked, peering into the watercraft.

Vratu spotted their bows and quivers leaning against his dwelling. A glance around camp confirmed no carcasses on display. 'Our friends of the lakes outsmart you again, yes?'

'We were not hunting.'

'As we were not fishing.'

Kihad laughed. Vratu lifted the boy out of the coracle and placed him gently on the ground. Gru asked, 'How is his knee?'

'His walk is still weak.'

Kihad asked, 'The others left this morning?'

'Yes,' Vratu confirmed. The men were off hunting and would be absent overnight.

They sat in front of Vratu's dwelling in pleasant discussion. Ilan was away with the party and he had it to himself. A chill hung in the air and now and then someone leaned forward to stoke up the fire. The perfunctory manner in which Kihad and Gru conversed suggested they had something on their minds they wanted to discuss, but there was no hurry to bring it out. Time did not need shrinking here at Walk-On-Clouds.

They waited until after dinner. Ulke took Kubul away and Gru wandered off, leaving the two brothers alone.

'Listen to me brother . . .' Kihad wavered before going on. 'There are things that must be talked about, things that will cause you pain, and I am here to bring them to you. I will begin with Nura. It has been decided. Wipe her from your memory.'

There was a lengthy silence as his words sank in. Had Vratu been told this more than a month ago he would have been devastated. He might have cursed and raved, kicked at anything in his way and bellowed for justice. Now he simply took a long, defeated breath and stared into the fire. He felt no shock. The news his brother bore was like an end to his anxieties and for this he found solace. Unless of course . . .

'Iswahl?' he asked, and Kihad nodded.

This hurt more. Images of her tight little body in the arms of his

232

nemesis sent sparks of jealousy through his blood. 'Was this her choice, or one she has been made to take?' he asked, revulsion in his tone.

'What would you prefer?'

Vratu realised then he didn't know which answer he wanted to hear. He stood and kicked the dirt, every muscle screaming to inflict damage.

'What grief have you caused?' Kihad went on. 'I had words with Iyanah and he spoke poorly of you.'

'And his brother had words with me. About him.' Vratu pointed to where Kubul sat with Ulke. 'Do you know what they wanted me to do?'

'No.'

Vratu sat down and went into detail about his conversation with Uru Ukmaar. Throughout, Kihad listened thoughtfully. At the end he remarked, 'You make it as hard for them as they do for you. No one wants to see more of what happened the last time we came here.'

'I would do it all again if they tried the same.'

Kihad nodded respectfully, surprised at his brother's grit. 'All will be well, you will see,' he said. 'There are many girls waiting for you, they just don't know it yet.' He added a hearty laugh.

Vratu wasn't moved. 'Is she with him already?'

'No. There is talk they will be married once we are settled at the Winter Grounds. When I learned of this I asked her if it was what she wanted. She shook her head and I saw tears in her eyes, but no words came from her mouth.' Kihad tapped his head. 'She has the mind of a squirrel.'

Vratu rubbed his forehead roughly, anger bubbling inside. 'I will go and think about this.' He stood to leave.

'Wait,' Kihad stopped him. 'Trouble shadows you of late. There is more.'

The look on his face made Vratu forget Nura for the time being. He sat down and remained taut, as if braced for something physical.

Ulke and Kubul had moved within earshot. Kihad indicated the boy with a slight dip of his head and spoke softly. 'Can he understand our talk?'

'It is hard to say.' Vratu thought again about this. 'There have been times I think he must. Either that or he is very clever.'

'Has he spoken yet?'

'No.'

Kihad watched Kubul as he spoke. 'Have you thought about taking him away from here? Our friends in the west would take him.'

'This is my doing,' Vratu said firmly, 'and I will not burden someone else with it.'

'Hear what I say and you may think again,' Kihad said gravely. 'A few days ago some of Krul's men brought word of happenings in lands south and east of Heavy-Fish. Men never seen before are making contact with the People, asking questions. They heard about the raid in Oyub-ka, but this does not trouble us, and these men were wise enough not to ask about it. It is something else they want to know, something they seek that makes us uneasy.'

He leaned forward and lowered his voice. 'These men of the east mention names that have no meaning to us, but they mention a boy. They want to know more about him. They describe a boy as one would describe him.' He pointed to Kubul. 'It might have ended there had they not said something else.'

Kihad made the familiar spiral pattern in the dirt with his finger. 'The boy they are looking for has a mark on his neck like this.'

Later that night, leaving Kihad and Gru snoring softly in his dwelling, Vratu took the boy's necklace and went outside. He felt tired, but not from lack of sleep. The talk with his brother had put heaviness in his heart and head, and he hoped the cool evening air would clear both.

The grounds were deserted. He rebuilt a smoking fire, sat on a log and tightened his hand over the emblem.

Every step he had taken since beginning his Walk had aged him that little bit more. He wondered if others could see the wrinkles he felt growing on his face. His spirit was abandoning him, which was not a good way to be. It left him susceptible to all manner of afflictions and curses.

You have a curse, the father of Nura had said. He had not said it out of spite. Or anger. He had said it as a leader concerned for the welfare of his people. Curses were like diseases. They were real. A person cursed was an extremely serious matter. It put others at risk. A curse could spread through an entire clan, an entire tribe, heaping mishap and sorrow on anyone in contact.

Nothing good had come from bringing the children back with him; indeed all it had brought was conflict. He had been selfish, had conferred with no one and upset the harmony of the clans. Trouble had followed and now it appeared more was on its way. Iyanah was right; the boy had to go.

But first Vratu wanted answers. He held up his fist and uncurled his fingers, as if they lay inside.

What was he looking at? he wondered. What miracle created this mystery? As he turned it over in his hands the firelight breathed life into it, made it dance with shimmering reflections. More striking in contrast to everyday curios, here, captured in his palm, was the essence of sun, a tongue of fire made cold and hard by some inconceivable craft of men. Its weight, out of proportion to its size, seemed to have the effect of empowering one with the same.

Instinct had warned him not to show it to anyone. As far as he knew only Gru and two boys had seen it. There were men he knew who would kill for something like this. Jewellery like this commanded influence. Its rareness and beauty had to attach significance to whoever possessed it. But what was a boy in a small, isolated village doing with it? Or could it be that he simply thought it worth retrieving from the ruins?

But the cord fit neatly over a child's head. Vratu was convinced it belonged to Kubul. The necklace must have been a thing of importance, to be worn by someone of importance. That men were looking for him supported his theory. A pack of wolves will not chase after a rabbit.

Never before had he needed to think this deeply. It felt like only yesterday that the biggest decision in his life was whether to be so bold as to arrive unannounced at the camp of Iyanah in order to see

Nura. All his life he'd been taught to focus on survival imperatives –
to heed the seasons and climate, to follow their food, to explore new
places, to be wary of enemies. But most importantly, to be sure
everything he did was for the good of his people. The dubious plan
taking shape in his head was not. He lacked the experience, the self-
confidence to be convinced it was the right option. He also knew a
decision like this was not the call of a man as young as him. It should
be referred to council, but he knew what their answer would be.

In the end, preferring the call of his heart to the sense in his head,
he decided his course of action. More tired than ever he returned to
his dwelling and undressed. Down on the floor Kihad groaned. 'Are
you still awake?'

Vratu put the necklace back into its pouch. 'Tomorrow I will go
back with you,' he said. 'I want to see Nura.'

Iyanah was away hunting when they arrived, which Vratu found
convenient. In no mood for pleasantries he found Nura without
wasting time.

Her family greeted him affably and she obliged his request that
they take a walk. Without speaking they followed a stream and
reached a familiar glade where the air was cool and crisp and the
earth smelled fresh. As children they had thrown stones at
caterpillars ascending the trunks of the sycamores around them, they
had run amok with other children through the twisting lantanas,
throwing berries, wrestling each other over the soft carpets of grass
and returning to camp with their clothes stained with forest-squash.

They sat down on a large boulder and he made the comment,
'We sat here in happier times.'

At once Nura began to cry. Vratu watched without feeling the
need to console her, waiting patiently until her little outpouring of
emotion had spent its force. Then she looked up, though not at him,
tear-puffed and sniffing.

'Iswahl,' Vratu sneered, still unable to believe it. 'Is this what you
want?'

'I don't know.'

'He never even completed his Walk.'

She began sobbing again. 'Why did you come?' she muttered through her tears.

Even in weeping she looked so pretty he felt his longing return. 'I call on you to make a choice,' he said, almost putting a hand on her. 'You are Ubren, of Uru blood. They cannot make you do what your heart tells you not to. I ask for you to wait. By the time we next meet at the Winter Grounds everything will be better.'

She blinked a few times and there was an easy pause in her crying. 'What do you mean?'

'It would be wrong to tell you. But I know how to put an end to this. All I ask of you is to wait.'

She looked at him puzzled. 'What are you going to do?'

'It is not your concern.' Vratu waited for her to speak. She wiped tears from her cheeks and said nothing.

'You choose to say little, but I hear much,' he went on. 'I think you are already decided. I think you have struck me from your heart already.'

The tears came back and she rose her voice. 'You have always done what you want!' she moaned. 'See what it has brought on us! What you ask of me is too much!'

'Do women teach nothing of the value of honour?' he retorted. She stood up and started walking away, and he stood up after her. 'It is not important that you understand what I have done, or what I choose to do. I only ask that you be there for me, as a woman should.'

'Stop it!' she cried. 'I *was* here, waiting for you! And *you* ruined it! I did nothing wrong!' She quickened her pace.

'What have you to lose? What do you risk? Anything more than what I do?' Vratu shouted after her. 'Where is your courage?'

She covered her ears with her hands as she put the forest between them. The ferns swayed back into position behind her, everything went silent.

'Where is your faith?'

He returned to camp and joined his brother by a fire. Nura was nowhere to be seen. Eyes veered away from his and the lines people walked kept well clear of him. Vratu was not offended. Soon they would forget that he and Nura had ever been a point of discussion, until then he carried the curse of rejection.

'What did she say?' Kihad asked.

Vratu poked at the embers with a stick and didn't reply. Kihad broke the long moment of silence. 'You take on too much.'

Vratu lifted the stick and held the fiery end before his eyes. 'Have I done wrong?'

'We only want to see you smile again, Vratu. It pains us to see you like this.'

Vratu blew on the tip and watched it flare. 'You think I would smile again if I did what they wanted?'

Kihad shrugged. 'The wise thing to do is not always what your heart tells you to do.'

'Why do you waste your words on me?'

Kihad drew back and frowned. 'What do you mean?'

'That day in the village . . . I watched you brother. I saw your eyes, I saw your hands. You feel as I do.'

Kihad made a face and looked away. He stood and flicked his cup of herb-tea empty. 'Come,' he said brusquely, 'I need to check some traps.' He turned aside and stretched.

Vratu stayed sitting, looking his brother over. They were only half-brothers, really. Their personalities were different, their views rarely compatible, and people told them they bore no resemblance to each other. Yet this was his blood equal, the all-powerful leveller of differences in times of most need. It was as if an old, friendly voice was whispering in his thoughts, a ray of wisdom shining on his heart.

Kihad turned around and a puzzled look formed on his face. Vratu straightened out of his slouch. 'What?' he asked.

'You are smiling.'

Vratu shook his head lightly, his smile broadening. 'All those stories you told me about our father . . . it was hard for me to know him.' He stood up. 'I think I know him better now.'

As he stepped away from the fire his brother put a hand on his shoulder. It felt good. He had never done that to him before.

At the first tender hues of dawn next morning, Vratu headed home alone. The forest embraced him like an old friend. Birds sung, breeze tickled the leaves, lattices of light blinked on and off through the foliage and boughs creaked in drowsy tunes. This was what he needed. It allowed him to think clearly.

He took consolation knowing that when his time came there would be more than enough women to choose from. The ratio of men to women seldom rose to equal – the legacy of a hunter's more perilous lifestyle. Add to this his fresh bloodline and looks women apparently found pleasing, and he knew he would have his pick, probably more than once. So he need never dwell on one woman. If he could fight off wild animals, survive blizzards and cheat death, a bit of heartache should hardly compare.

But it did. It would be some time before he could *wipe her from his memory*.

When he returned to Walk-On-Clouds that afternoon he found his people preparing to leave. The doors to several dwellings were tied, indicating that some families had already left for satellite camps in order to meet up with friends or relatives before rendezvousing at the Winter Grounds.

After helping his mother pack he spent the rest of the afternoon springing snares and pulling up traps. Back at camp he examined Kubul's leg. The knee felt bumpy beneath the skin, like a pouch of stones, but when pressure was applied now the boy could bear the pain.

'Lavaar!' Vratu called. 'What of Kubul's leg?'

'The bone has mended,' Ilan's father said. 'He will have his running legs again.'

'Where is Ilan?'

'Over by the shore.'

Vratu found his friend in waist-deep water retrieving a net from the shallows. Content to watch, he waited on the bank.

239

Ilan shot him a sour look. 'Careful,' he jeered. 'You might get your toes wet.'

'Anything?'

'No. And I can feel a big hole this end. You can fix that.'

Ilan waded ashore and Vratu joined him at the water's edge. Hand over hand they hauled in the net and spread it out over the bank. Nothing flapped between the meshing; all it caught was lake-litter and unidentifiable muck. They squatted to untangle the mess.

Ilan asked, 'How was she?'

'Nura?'

'Your mother told me you went to see her.'

Vratu grimaced. 'As I thought she would be.'

'She will grow up lazy and fat and turn into a nag,' Ilan predicted faithfully. 'You will see. Iswahl will come to you one day and beg you to take her back.'

Vratu's face cracked into a grin. Piece by piece they untangled dripping muck and tossed it aside. 'Men are looking for the boy,' he announced.

Ilan looked up. 'Who?'

'People-of-the-Longhomes . . . Ubren of the east. They have been to the camps of Krul and his cousins.'

Ilan stopped working. 'Why are they looking for him?' he asked, and received no answer. 'Will they be looking for you?'

'Why would they not be?'

A worried look spread over Ilan's face. 'What does it all mean?'

'I don't know,' Vratu said. 'But he is hunted. And if men of the east are hunting him, they bring nothing but trouble. I have seen what their hands can do.'

'Why not give him to them?' When Vratu stayed quiet, Ilan said regretfully, 'I see. Why am I still your friend?'

Vratu smiled. They worked on in silence, both in deep thought. At length Ilan asked, 'Who told you about this?'

'Kihad.'

'Who else knows?'

'Not anyone here,' Vratu said thoughtfully. 'Much here goes

240

unsaid.'

'Does Banan know this?'

'No. I will tell him tomorrow, when I tell him something else.'

'Oh?'

Vratu kept his head down and his hands working as he spoke. 'When they leave here tomorrow, I am not going with them. Nor is Kubul. The boy comes with bad medicine and I fear a curse if he stays.' He wiped his hands on his leggings and picked up a stick to draw on the ground. 'Tomorrow we go on a Walk of our own. Wide of the plains here, following trails east over Oyub-ka to the village where there are canoes we sank in the shallows. I will take one and ride with the current onto Heavy-Fish, then south to the Great River and downstream to a place where the hands of men are gentler.'

Ilan gaped at him. 'What place?'

'A village of the People-of-the-Longhomes.'

Ilan sighed and spoke in a subdued voice. 'I think it is time you spoke to me like a proper friend.'

Vratu brushed his hands and shifted into a comfortable sitting position. The cleaning could wait.

For the second time only he spoke about his stay with the Oronuk, but this time he included a few details about Abinyor. And like Voi, Ilan sat quietly throughout, although with a slightly more bewildered expression.

'Is that what this is about?' he asked when Vratu finished. 'You think you owe them something?'

'I keep hearing them,' Vratu murmured. 'Those we took our maces to. I hear their voices when the wind moans, when the wolves howl. Sometimes when I wake I see their faces in the dark.'

'Ah! I see. You go to kill a demon.'

Vratu shrugged. 'I go to finish what I started.'

'What about Ly?'

'The curse comes with the boy, not her. She will stay. She is well liked here anyway.'

'Your mother?'

'I will ask your father to see to her while I am gone.'

241

'What of these Oronuk friends or yours? Why would they help? You take him there, they throw him into the river and you will be angry because you walked so far for nothing.'

'It is not their way,' Vratu said. 'I am still here, am I not?'

Ilan narrowed his eyes. 'What is the real reason you wish to return?' he asked, but Vratu said nothing. 'This woman must be the work of gods, yes?' Ilan then suggested with a grin.

'Abinyor?'

Ilan stayed grinning as he waited for a reply. Vratu moved onto his knees and began sorting through the net again. 'You make me sad,' he rejected the suggestion with indignation.

Ilan laughed. 'What will you do? Walk into their village uninvited, introduce him and be on your way?'

'Perhaps I will do just that.'

Ilan's face sobered when he saw Vratu meant it. 'This needs to be put to council. They will forbid it. Banan, Iyanah, Ukmaar . . . they will have words. As for Krul . . .'

'That is why I will not put it to council,' Vratu replied, tossing another twig aside. 'I alone will decide how this will end. I am weary of being sent for, being called for, being told. Tomorrow I will tell Banan I am going on another Walk. Then I will be gone and who learns after that matters not.'

'If you take him back, he will tell his story. His people will sharpen their weapons and come looking for us.'

'The forest between us is big and will lose them.'

'But if men are already looking – '

'Oh, enough with your questions!' Vratu cut him off. 'I have asked them all already! Every day – in my head! And we are still going. Are you?'

The life went out of Ilan's face, and there was a delay before he could speak. 'Where you speak of is a long way from here. Six, seven days each way, moving fast. The boy will slow you down.'

Vratu watched him quietly, waiting to see if the real meaning of what he asked would sink into his friend's head. Waiting for words that would mean far more to him than having an extra set of eyes and hands to help him hunt and stand guard.

But Ilan only stared back, stunned. 'Why do you bring this on all of us?' he asked. 'No good has come of it.'

Vratu thrust his handful of net aside. For a long moment he held his friend's eyes, letting his hurt show. Then he marched off back to camp.

It was late in the night and Ilan still hadn't shown.

Vratu sat in his dwelling, staring into the hearth. After leaving the lake he had stopped by his mother's dwelling and told her of his plan, along with his misgivings, and she had smiled and told him that all her life she had watched men struggle with decisions. When their intentions were noble, she had said, the rest always seemed to take care of itself. Of this he had to keep reminding himself whenever doubts pricked his mind.

At last he heard the shuffle of feet outside and the door-flap opened. Ilan stepped inside, rubbing his hands. 'It is getting cold,' he said, contemplating the hearth from above. He sat down opposite and rearranged a few sticks in the fire. Then he bowed his head, took a deep breath, and spoke in a monotone.

'I am not like you. I could never do what you have done. All I want is what I have always wanted – to hunt and laugh with my friends, to wake up next to my own woman, soon I hope. I want to be at peace, I want to be in awe of all things beautiful. I want to be free of the worries that make the mind heavy and the face grow old. These are things for headmen and medicine men.'

'Then go to sleep,' Vratu said disappointedly.

Ilan looked up with a sad face. 'You think you have brought a curse upon us. I believe you. See the trouble it has made between you and your woman, you and your people, you and me. I have been sitting in the dark thinking of ways to stop it. I even thought to take this boy myself; take him to those looking for him, save you the pain.'

He inhaled deeply and let out a sigh. 'Now you ask me to do something we could both be banished for. You want me to go with you and seek people our headmen warned us to stay away from.

243

Even more, you want to take this boy with us. You think it will end there, but I fear more will come of it. And I never even sought to be part of this.'

Vratu opened his mouth to protest but Ilan held up a hand to cut him off. 'Only then the answer came to me. Listen to me now. I have never thought much of shaman talk but what I say now comes from knowing you since we first crawled over the earth together.'

His tone dropped a notch. 'As soon as you found these children you were sworn to protect them. You did not know it at the time, but you had no choice but one. There was only one path you were ever going to take. If this were to happen again you would do the same.' He let out a deep breath. 'This is how I see things. You are what you are, and I am what I am – as bound to you as you are to him. And so, I must follow you.'

With those last few words, Vratu felt his heart glow. The warmth pulsed through his veins all the way to his fingertips. When he felt water rim his eyes he cast his head down, embarrassed it might show.

There was a long silence. Vratu offered consolingly, 'You will learn much from what you see of these people.'

'Learning I can live without. Just bring me back without arrowheads stuck inside me.'

A smile broke out on Vratu's face, but it was nothing compared to the smile within. He lifted his head and saw how tired his friend looked; his shoulders sagged and his face hung low and brooding.

'We will meet up with everyone at the Winter Grounds when it is finished,' Vratu promised.

'There is one thing I ask of you.' Ilan stood and took off his shirt. 'When we get to this village, we do not stay. We leave the boy and go home at once, yes?'

Vratu was far too grateful to consider any alternative. 'Yes.'

Ilan yawned. 'Then it is settled.' He finished undressing, eased into bed and pulled the blanket over himself. 'Now go to sleep,' he chuckled lightly. 'Even a shaman sleeps.'

Vratu smiled on, staring into the fire, content through to the core of his soul. Long after his friend started snoring the same smile was still on his face. In the space of two days he'd tested the loyalty of those most dear to him, and had his judgment confirmed. His faith in those who had given it had been as strong as his doubt in those who hadn't.

In the dead of night Vratu was wakened by howling wolves. After a long period of tossing and turning he gave up on sleep and went outside.

The air was fresh and moist, cleaning his lungs as he drew it in deeply. The howling of wolves trailed off and the silence was filled with croaking frogs and chirping crickets. He sat down on the bank.

As soon as you found these children you were sworn to protect them. Ilan was right. The need to be true to his nature was far stronger than the urge to adjust it.

Perhaps life was like this. Be it man or beast, tree or rock, wind or rain – all obeyed their own rules and instructions, like a watercourse flowing toward some greater confluence. Perhaps finding two children in the forest was no accident at all, but pertinent to the execution of some higher plan. So regardless of whether or not his proposal met with disaster, it was still the right thing to do. Everything was now set for the final phase of the Walk he'd begun. Thinking this – *believing* this – made it so much easier to bear, and he smiled in the dark; the smile of a person coming to terms with what he was, and what he *wasn't*, and not at all disappointed with what he found.

A splash sounded out in the lake, above it a sprinkle of stars appeared in a break of cloud. He looked closer and saw the brighter ones beating like tiny hearts, and his smile lifted higher.

'Will you walk with me too, old man?'

The wolves sounded again, the vast melancholy of the wilderness toying with his mood. He sat there until soft waves of sleep washed his mind of thought. His legs felt heavy as he trudged back to his dwelling. As soon as he lay down he fell into a dreamless sleep, serenaded by the whisper of the wind and the howling of wolves.

Ric Szabo

Part 3

The Darkening

Twenty-five

Romoyr of Usonoli was a man true to his word. A few days after the death of his father, it began. Or so went popular opinion. Those with longer memories argued it had never really ended.

The boy had been leading his cattle home after a day's grazing, swishing a leafy branch against their backsides, when eight men stepped from the woods into his path. Questioned later he would say that though their faces were not familiar, their tribal scarification and markings could not be mistaken.

The Clan of Usonoli.

A man with a flat nose and a scar that ran down the side of his face like a worm stepped forward. 'Go now.'

The boy wavered, torn between duty and fear. The man drew his bow and pointed an arrow at the boy's face. 'Go fast.'

By the time an armed party returned they found five beasts dead and another two bawling on the ground, mortally wounded. All were found whole. The perpetrators were not after meat.

Opinion remained divided. A foolish act carried out by a few troublemakers did not necessarily represent the broader sentiment of their people. The incident, it was agreed, could be dismissed as isolated. They decided to err on the side of caution. Cattle could be replaced.

But it did not remain an isolated incident for long.

Herd boys rounding up their cattle at the day's end began to find the count short. When armed escorts put a stop to this, their nemesis took to stalking the herds like wolves, waiting for the right moment to fling their spears from the edge of the forest before slinking back into the shadows. They even stole into villages at night. Cattle with spears poking out of their bloated chests became a frequent sight in the morning.

Paths that led to Ubren villages were no longer walked. Pastures were abandoned, relations between the two tribes ceased. Resources had to be directed toward security. People in isolated areas began encircling their villages with palisades. For the first time in many years, sentries walked the village grounds at night, keeping watch-fires burning through to dawn.

Across the land men crowded around tables, put family differences and petty squabbling aside, and channelled their energy toward a common threat. Views once concealed were openly expressed, plots and schemes once thought extreme were given serious consideration.

The sun blazed, the sky glowed, but a shadow had descended now – a shadow that darkened the spirit and seemed to quieten their beasts. A reckless cry or shout, the sudden bellow of cattle or squeal of pig had everyone's neck twisted, their voices cut short and hands on tools tightened. They kept their weapons close and turned their eyes repeatedly toward the forests beyond their fields, where the trails stayed empty and the dark hills loomed.

* * *

They came in long dugouts, at least five people in each, paddling close to shore where the current was at it weakest. In the bow of the leading canoe, Kulej looked over his shoulder. The men in the canoes behind kept speed, stroke for stroke. Born and bred on the banks of the waterways they were as much at ease on water as on firm ground, as skilled with a paddle as with an adze.

His gaze shifted to Abinyor seated between her brothers in a canoe a length or two behind. The lines of anxiety on her face had deepened. The Henghai turned around and resumed paddling, unconcerned. In his line of work the sight of unhappy faces was as common as happy ones.

The village came into sight and they ran their canoes aground. By the time they splashed ashore a large crowd had lined the bank. Hrad-Uik clambered shakily out of his canoe and joined his men clustered on the bank, waiting for the invitation to proceed.

The crowd parted and several men approached, an old man leading. The girth of his torso and the thickness of his limbs were like that of a bear. Spirally wound copper armlets and bracelets shone on his fair skin, necklaces of teeth and bone hung over an embroidered vest stitched with beads, feathers, painted shell and bones. To his side stood a younger, lankier man sporting a matching vest and armlets, a necklace of disc-shaped limestone beads and bracelets of vertebrae.

Kulej slapped a hand on the old man's chunky shoulder. '*Buno,* friend Attuaal.'

Attuaal's mouth parted in a wide smile, his teeth shone white. '*Buno!*'

Kulej turned to the old man's son. '*Buno,* friend Segros.'

Segros mumbled, '*Buno.*'

'Welcome to my village,' Attuaal greeted Hrad-Uik civilly.

'Thank you,' Hrad-Uik replied. In a brisk manoeuvre, a tight group of women surrounded Abinyor and ushered her away.

Kulej said to Attuaal, 'Shall we talk?'

'If it pleases you.'

The convoy shuffled quietly up the bank. At the door of Attuaal's longhouse Kulej turned and saw layers of men keen to participate. 'Let us have privacy,' he appealed to their headman.

Attuaal waved a hand and his men dispersed. He held the door open and Hrad-Uik and Borchek entered, followed by Segros and two stern-faced Ubren clansmen. Kulej followed them in with his long-time friend Varsi. Attuaal entered last and closed the door behind him.

They were shown into the main room where a girl was placing mugs around the table. A large vessel of beer stood at its middle. Attuaal's men sat down on one side, giving Kulej the unfortunate impression of opposition. When all were seated the girl filled their mugs, guests first.

'So!' Attuaal began. 'It comes to this. How is the family of Hrad-Uik? All must be well, yes?'

'Yes,' Hrad-Uik responded. 'And yours?'

'Good! Is your health improving?'

'Yes,' Hrad-Uik lied.

'Is the beer to your liking?'

Hrad-Uik picked up his mug and took a long swallow. 'Yes.'

The girl left the vessel on the table and closed the door on her way out. The conversation flowed as freely as the drink, and Kulej winced when Attuaal and Segros filled their mugs a third time. The brew was strong and at their present rate of consumption the opportunity for rational dialogue was dwindling fast.

Kulej timed himself expertly. 'Attuaal old friend, let us get unfortunate matters out of the way.' He had set the mood with his tone. The men settled back and he went on. 'You have heard we are having problems in the east?'

'I have heard.'

'We fear it is spreading like disease. Has it caught us here?'

'See how many people have come here today,' Attuaal pointed out. 'It seems not.'

'We have had representations from several of your neighbours. They claim your brother and his men are causing difficulties, again.'

At this, Attuaal folded his arms and said nothing.

Kulej spoke in a tired voice. 'For years there has been progress between our people and yours. We share what we have and talk when there is disagreement, yes?'

'Some people are never happy,' Attuaal answered suavely. 'They should not take their whining to you.'

'There are issues of trespass – '

'The issue is who owns the land, not trespass.'

'They claim they have lost livestock at night. This sounds like the old days, does it not?'

'I am shocked.'

'Do you look into the cause of these troubles?'

Stiff-necked but polite, Attuaal answered, 'No.'

'Does it concern you that your brother and nephew are accused of these things?'

251

'Is that the talk?'

Kulej raised his hands limply. 'That is the talk.'

'Have they been caught? Have they been seen?'

'These things happen under the cover of darkness. But there – '

'Ah, I understand now.'

'Attuaal,' Kulej said patiently. 'When I put the same questions to the men who made these claims, they showed me – '

'It made me sad to hear of your daughter's passing last summer,' Attuaal cut him off. 'I hear she was long in the earth by the time you came home, is this true?'

Kulej frowned and leaned back.

'How many children have you now?' Attuaal waved his hand airily. 'Eight? Seven?'

Still Kulej did not answer. He clasped his hands together and looked at him hard.

'Why do you take these matters on, my friend?' Attuaal asked in a commiserating tone. 'A family man is a happy man.'

'Am I wasting my time?' Kulej asked.

Attuaal grunted. Varsi said, 'Amongst our people, a leader does not remove himself from the actions of those he claims to represent.'

Attuaal glared at him. 'Are you here to give me lessons, *friend?*'

'Varsi is saying there is need for cooperation here,' Kulej interceded smoothly.

'And when the need arises, we give it,' Attuaal answered, the insolence in his tone deliberate. 'But it is not my way to force others to give theirs. Nor do I take it upon myself to speak for everyone, as is your way, friend Varsi.'

'I have authority to speak for all the Oronuk of this district.'

Segros cut in quickly, 'Are they too frightened to speak for themselves?'

'Friends,' Kulej interrupted with a raised hand, 'that's enough.'

Segros snorted softly. His father put a hand on his arm and said to Kulej, 'For you old friend, I will look into it.' He drained his mug, looked inside it and frowned sceptically. 'This is good beer. It cannot be one of ours.'

'Recently I have met with our neighbours of the east,' Kulej continued determinedly. 'Unless we learn from their mistakes, I fear their problems will become ours.'

'What can I say?' Attuaal responded. 'You know I am in a difficult position here.'

'I understand,' Kulej said. 'You have done much in keeping the peace. But it seems you have kinsmen equally committed to break it.'

'I have heard what our neighbours say about us,' Segros said. 'Moaning men, all of them. So now you can hear me.' He leaned forward menacingly. 'We have been to enough of your councils to see how you work. Rarely are we invited, and even when we are it is for us to hear your words, not for you to hear ours. They are numbered against us and our voices are always silenced. You speak of fairness and cooperation,' he waved his finger and his tone turned sarcastic, 'it is all too much for me. I have darker suspicions. Our harvests were poor and a bad year approaches. A year bad enough to see where *your* loyalties lie.'

'Our councils need not always require your presence,' Varsi said. 'This you should understand.'

'Yes, my friend. When we go behind closed doors, we too will scheme. And when we do, we too will put our people first. What you have taken in the past by force you take now with treaties and promises. You try to appease us with gifts and the offering of wives. Yours is always the best land, your people the best fed. If you are in league with your Vahichiwa, so be it. We will stay in league with our own.' He leaned back. 'The *Unatks* Vahichiwa,' he added a trace of scorn. 'What is "Unatks?" It has the sound of a stag bellowing in the rut.'

The two men seated beside him chuckled. Kulej used the break to explain. 'It is not a title the man gave himself.'

'Yes, how fitting,' Segros said. 'But I know what he is doing. It would be easy to voice my own accusations, but with respect to our guests and my new father-in-law, I will not do it here.' He picked up his mug and smirked. 'On this day I am to be married, so I will drink.'

He took a long swallow and appraised the contents of his mug.

253

'My father is right – this *is* good beer.' A tight smile appeared on his face. 'Too good for us, on any other occasion.'

'I have always been curious,' Varsi said to Segros. 'You work soils we set aside for you, live under rooves made by the hands of our people. Your blood is mixed with ours, yet you call yourselves Ubren and side with them in all matters.'

Segros' eyes shone bright and bold. 'Ubren blood is stronger than yours,' he hissed. 'It sings in our veins. This *you* should understand.'

Attuaal sighed. 'My son's words are strong but he says what many of us think. Your Unatks Vahichiwa . . . without ever meeting him I feel he is a good man.'

'He dreams with the birds,' Segros interjected.

His father held up a hand to quieten him. 'But I question how practical he is. Look at the lands that separate us. There are matters here that cannot be addressed, let alone understood from where he is. If what he wants is treaties between people whose paths never cross – people as strange to each other as the moon is to the sun – then what he wants is fantasy.'

'It is what we make of it,' Kulej said.

Attuaal nodded his head appreciably. 'That is true. But his hands cannot stretch this far. We will never know the truth of how these troubles started again. When we hear our people in the east are being wronged, we become angry. So let us talk openly, like honest men. I too want to keep the peace. Many of our daughters are now amongst you, and many of your daughters are here amongst us. It is good we now have one more. But my people will always come first, as yours will for you.'

Attuaal lifted the mug to his lips. To his side Segros and his men sat like stones. Hopeless, Kulej thought. Their blood was still too thick.

Varsi offered, 'We are always ready to be of service. You convey this to your kinfolk, I trust.'

When Attuaal looked up and saw them all staring at him, his face cracked with a broad smile. 'What is this talk?' he boomed. 'We are all friends here! Let us go outside and we will match each other drink for drink. I am thirsty!'

Noticing that Kulej's eyes hadn't wavered, he added in a conciliatory tone, 'With respect to all of you, I will do what I can. If you want me to talk to my brother and his men, then talk I shall.' He clapped his hands together. 'Now! Shall we go outside and make ourselves sick?'

They stepped outside and were greeted by a procession of friends and acquaintances with sincerity in their greetings, and Kulej's mood softened. Over two hundred people were there to enjoy themselves, he reminded himself. As should he.

Petals coated the tables and benchtops – white violets, wood sorrels and snowdrops, purple violets and hepaticas, yellow primulas, primroses and buttercups, blue gentians and bluebells, red anemones and pink geraniums. At the Banquet-shed sheaths of the same flowers hung down from overhead beams and filled the air with the fragrance of spring, bowls of fruit and berries and flower-filled vases covered the tables. Several more benches and tables, hewn just for the occasion, sat in neat arrangements ready for their attendants. Women busied themselves with final preparations, carrying baskets and bowls, fussing over the bouquets. Children ran amok and small groups were engaged in lively discussions.

The atmosphere did not extend to Kulej, Varsi, and Hrad-Uik when they regrouped after their exhausting round of welcomes.

'What are your thoughts?' Varsi asked Kulej.

The Henghai waved at a guest and smiled. 'He means well, but his message is clear – he has his loyalties. Hopefully now he will see he has more.' He saw Hrad-Uik's eyes flare briefly and immediately regretted the comment.

Then he spotted Borchek. Though he stood amongst company one look at him was enough to see why everyone gave him space. The colour was deep in his face, his lips were drawn into thin lines and his glare was like that of a marauding hawk. Kulej followed it and saw his prey. Segros had an arm draped over one of his men, the mug in his hand at a tilt.

Kulej reached Borchek before he could swoop. 'Your ears are steaming,' he said good-naturedly.

Borchek's eyes didn't waver. 'The impudence of the man,' he said through clenched teeth. Only the mug in his hand stopped it balling into a fist. 'To speak with such contempt on his wedding day. Their harvest fails again and he uses this against us. In his own village he mocks us. Never would he dare speak like this in ours. Is this a man worthy of my sister?'

The meeting had raised dark clouds, but of one thing Kulej found promising. More than once he had expected the son of Hrad-Uik to leap the table and break his new brother-in-law's nose. That he had sat quietly throughout was major progress.

The Henghai put a hand on his shoulder, wondering how long it would be before he did.

In what would be her room from that day forth, Abinyor was, in appearances at least, almost ready.

She stood still as her sisters brushed the last specs off her brilliantly decorated, light doeskin tunic. Flowers sprang from her braided hair, woven feather-tassels hung from the shoulders of her tunic. A band of shell-beads circled her forehead, a necklace of jet and amber stones with spacer-plates of clay beads hung around her neck, and schist bracelets adorned her wrists – all pre-nuptial gifts from the groom's family. Yet despite her magnificent appearance there was something in her expression the ochre-based rouge and malachite paste failed to mask: uncertainty.

The politics behind the marriage were irrelevant to Abinyor, not that they had been properly explained. If anything had played to her desire it was the prospect of change. She had always feared the trap of the mundane. There was different blood and different people here, nuances of manner and custom outside her limited experience, all of which appealed to her restless and enquiring mind. And so she had nodded her reluctant consent, after which things had moved with an urgency that prevailed up to the last stroke of the oar that brought her here. And though only now did she feel the weight of what she had ceded to, she refused to sour the occasion. As they were preparing her, she was preparing herself.

When all was ready Borchek came to collect her. The young bride and her eldest brother led the entourage through the house to the front door where she stopped to take a deep breath and summon her courage.

The path to the Banquet-shed was strewn with petals. On both sides, the three-deep layer of guests fell into silence. She forced a smile and walked ahead, trying to ignore the whispers around her.

Surrounded by a row of spears stabbed into the earth, Segros stood waiting. A man she had met enough times for her instincts to sound warning.

A shaman raised his hands. She glanced over the family of Attuaal standing to one side and settled her attention on the man she was about to marry. He looked at least ten years older than her; old enough hopefully to match her intellect, yet young enough to retain his boyish charms. There were words being spoken.

'. . . that no evil conspires to spoil their happiness; that suffering comes swiftly to those who seek to destroy the good that their union shall bring forth . . .'

She had found it difficult to warm to him on appearances alone. The bulge of his brows cast his eyes in permanent shadow, his nose was squat and the chin beneath his thin-lipped mouth seemed to point like an accusing finger wherever he looked. Dark hair fell about his shoulders in a mass of unkempt swirls.

'. . . that he receives as she receives, that he will give as she will give, that they serve rightly the laws of their people, that there be children to inspire them to great joy and bear testimony to the goodness of their families and the efforts of their forebears . . .'

The shaman finished talking and she was jolted from her thoughts by a deafening trill that marked an end to the official ceremony. Her family and close friends came forward to stand around her, protectively she sensed, while Segros stood quietly beside her, acknowledging people's congratulations with an occasional bow of his head and polite smile.

257

Moments before she had been the daughter of a well-loved man of Oronuk blood. Now she was the wife of Segros, son of a powerful headman of Ubren blood, a man she hardly knew amongst people she knew less.

Everything was different now. There was a long trail ahead.

Feasting and drinking followed, and a pleasant ambience settled in. People from different tribes mingled freely, some with a history of disputes that on this day at least were put to rest, or at worst reduced to a harmless pretence of sociability.

All day men came over to Kulej and whispered to him out of earshot, voicing the same grievances and misgivings about Attuaal and his clan. Kulej listened to them all with the diplomacy he was renowned for. Duty bound to both guests and hosts, he still managed to keep watch over Abinyor for most of the day. Though she behaved with exemplary maturity, only through his experienced eyes was he able to appreciate the effort she made. She ate little and drank not at all, asked few questions and spoke in short sentences. Her new husband, mug in hand for most of the day, seemed oblivious.

Long rows of lamp-tipped poles were put to the flame as evening settled, and everyone gathered in a large circle to watch the dancing. The girls of Hrad-Uik's clan were entertaining the crowd with an amorous dance when one of Attuaal's more burly men, reeling from drink, staggered into the arena. At first the dancers played along, limbering up to him with extended arms and enticing him with innocent gestures of encouragement, but then he suddenly lunged forward, grabbed one of the girls by the arm, hefted her over his shoulder and began hopping about in a poor imitation of dance. Her face crumpled with pain and a groan escaped through her clenched teeth each time her stomach bounced on his shoulder. The fool was beside himself in his fun, adding a series of ribald shouts to his roughness.

At once the drummers, all clansmen of Hrad-Uik, stopped. Even Kulej felt a deep sense of protection for the girl. He knew her father well, had watched her shape into a woman, and all he could do now was sit there as stunned as everyone else.

The girl's father pushed aside his drum and stood with an angry face. The girl cried out in pain and the man finally noticed. He stopped jumping about and swayed like a tree in the wind.

'Hutt, da nuag ku adna,' Attuaal's voice cut the silence. 'You dance like a bull on broken legs.'

The man put the girl down. She clutched her stomach and walked meekly over to her father.

For what felt like an eternity, silence reigned supreme. Then a solo drumbeat recommenced its rhythm. One of Attuaal's men tilted his head back, whooped loudly and danced wildly into the arena waving his arms. It was like a knife slicing through the thick atmosphere. People laughed and Hrad-Uik's men saw fit to beat the tension away with their drums.

'Mother of all gods,' Varsi muttered to Kulej beside. 'What are we trying to do?

Late in the night, with the wedding coming to an end, guests who lived close by took the night-walk back to their villages while others headed for beds in longhouses or settled for wherever they collapsed. Beds in Attuaal's house had been prepared for several important guests, none of whom would enter before the married couple had settled in first.

A woman approached Abinyor and motioned for her to follow. With the day almost over and the most dreaded part about to be faced, Abinyor let the cheer fall from her face as she was led into the house and over the fur-lined floors to her room.

The woman sat Abinyor down on the bed and began combing her hair. Though her face was not one Abinyor would call beautiful, the smoothness to its edges and soft radiance in her eyes had a calming effect.

Abinyor had met her only once before. Her name was Szanaj-kik, she was the widow of Segros' brother and that was almost all Abinyor knew. They had said little to each other all day but now they were alone there was something the young bride wanted to discuss.

In the leadup to the wedding she had been briefed on many of these people's customs, had even witnessed a few. Yet the one she wanted to know about most, the one that made her girlfriends giggle whenever it was discussed, remained a guarded secret. If the rumours were true the woman combing her hair was an active participant. Not only active, but active with the man Abinyor had just married.

For all the traditions these people were said to have abandoned, forgotten, or lost, the hold of one seemed too hard to shake. Married or not, their men did not restrict themselves to one woman.

But if it did go on she had seen no clear evidence. Ubren men didn't attend a ceremony or feast parading an assortment of wives or bed-mates any more than they discussed extramarital behaviour endemic in their culture. When she had tried to raise the issue with Kulej he had been quick to catch on to what she was really asking. 'An Ubren man is pledged to his wife,' was his cautious reply, 'and must respect her traditions no less than his own.' It was a thin reassurance, yet enough. Jealousy had not been an emotion she had juggled with these past months.

She sat quietly, wondering how to broach the subject. Hairs of smoke curled from several pedestal burners on the floor, giving the room a familiar scent. Shadows danced in the flickering light and not a sound drifted in from outside. The comb slid through her hair expertly, and with each stroke she felt her eyelids grow heavier. All thought slipped from her mind and she swayed drowsily.

A sharp tug on her hair brought her back. 'The night is not over yet,' Szanaj-kik reminded her as she worked a knot out.

Abinyor yawned and shook the heaviness from her head. She opened her mouth to ask a question, then closed it again.

'Ask,' Szanaj-kik urged. 'You will eventually. Now is as good a time as later.'

'Where is . . . your bed?' Abinyor asked, which was followed by another tug on her hair. 'Ow!'

'Your hair is stubborn,' the older woman observed. 'Like the rest of you, I am told.'

'I am here, am I not?'

Szanaj-kik absorbed it quietly, as if deriving something important from the comment. 'Do you think he will not make you happy?'

'Does he make you happy?'

The comb slowed and stopped, and a long moment of silence passed. There was pride in the woman's voice when she answered. 'I call myself lucky that he makes me so.'

'How did it happen?'

'It matters not.'

'Tell me,' Abinyor said, watching her with interest.

'Later. Now is not the time for sad stories.'

Abinyor had to force the vital question out. 'Are you . . . still with him?'

'That is for you to decide.'

'I don't understand.'

Szanaj-kik didn't reply as she resumed her combing. Soon they heard the sound of heavy footsteps. Szanaj-kik stood and exited the small room. There were a few womanly murmurs on the far side and then a man's deep voice: 'As much as I have to.'

Segros appeared at the door. Light from behind backlit his large frame and made his eye sockets dark and soulless. Abinyor sat still on the bed as she had been instructed, but couldn't help shrinking backwards when he lurched forward. At the foot of the bed he stopped, vapours of stale beer following his draft. For fear of him interpreting any look as inviting she cast her head down.

He angled his head, trying to peer into her down-turned face. 'It is easier to talk to me if you see who I am,' he suggested.

Abinyor lifted her chin.

'You have spoken to Szanaj-kik, yes?' he asked. 'She is a good woman. You will get to know her well.' He lifted the necklace from his head. 'Take heart that she speaks highly of you. Many men want her as a wife. Headmen, shamans, Henghai – they all listen to her. As for me . . .' He shrugged and hung his necklace on a hook. 'It falls on me to see to her and her daughter now, even though we are forbidden to marry. Yet she stays in my home, even when she knows she can do better.'

Was this a hint? Abinyor wondered. Had she just been given the answer to what she had asked Szanaj-kik earlier?

'My people are happy you are here,' he said. 'I am happy you are here.' After waiting a while in silence he asked, 'Are you happy you are here?'

She didn't answer. His shirt looked stained in patches; beer spill she suspected.

'I think you will be happy here,' he decided. One by one he blew out the lamps and the room sank into darkness. 'Did they tell you not to talk to me on your own wedding night?' He glanced over his shoulder as he leaned forward to blow out another flame.

There was pride in the calm lift of her head, a bold glint in her eyes. His quizzical expression gave way to a frown that seemed a more natural configuration of his face.

His eyes never left her as he took off his shirt and dropped it onto the floor. She stood from the bed and slowly removed her jewellery, piece by piece, carefully placing each item on a shelf. Lastly, she lifted her tunic over her head and let it drop at her feet.

Segros finished undressing and lay down on the bed. After a short hesitation, she lay down beside him. Flat on her back, her breathing short and forced, it was impossible to relax. The air reeked of stale beer. She knew what it was like to feel sexual passion, knew what it took to ignite it, and every instinct cried that this was neither the man nor the occasion to bring it out.

She closed her eyes and waited . . .

Time passed . . . neither moved.

At the sound of snoring she chanced a roll of her head and saw Segros lying on his back with his eyes closed and mouth open, oblivious to how hard he fought for each breath of air that jammed down his throat.

She left the last lamp burning, worried that her slightest movement would wake him.

Twenty-six

She opened her eyes to a roof that little bit lower, to walls that little bit shorter. The air was a stale mix of body odour and decay. In better light now she could see that the hunting trophies on the walls were mildewed and spider-webbed. The place had a dankness about it that made it feel colder than normal.

Beside her on the bed, Segros snored. For the first time in her life she had spent an entire night with a man and had found the experience grotesque. She dressed quickly and exited the room.

Her body felt heavy as she yawned her way through the sleeping quarters, past spreadeagled bodies lying naked and exposed on the beds and floor. Outside, she surveyed the mess of the previous night's festivities and despaired at the scale of work that lay ahead. At once she longed for her former start to the day; being the first to wake, brushing past the pigs that surrounded her when she stepped outside, breathing in the cool mist as she headed for the stalls and feeling the nudge of calves' noses as she prepared their feed.

She entered the longhouse where her family had slept. Upon locating her brothers sprawled unevenly over their beds she picked one at random. 'Yanukz! Up!'

As esteemed siblings of the bride her brothers had complied with tradition admirably, drinking themselves to oblivion the night past. Yanukz's eyelids squinted open to reveal two bloodshot eyeballs.

'Why do you do this to me?' he groaned, rolling away.

There were moans and grumbles around them, eyes blinking open. In a room hidden by the classical partitioning of the longhouse came Nankyi's voice. 'Abinyor, is that you?'

'Yes mama.' She had always felt close enough to her stepmother to call her that. A moment later Hrad-Uik appeared, his sleepy eyes brightening when he saw her.

'Abinyor!' he cried, and they embraced tightly.

During breakfast Segros, Attuaal and Kulej joined them. They joked about one or two events that had happened the night before and even Hrad-Uik let loose with a guffaw or two. Attuaal was a man quick to laugh and his mood was contagious. Abinyor found herself enjoying the company immensely. Only Borchek remained circumspect. Once or twice he included himself in the conversation with a few brusque comments but contributed little else. Not that this was unusual to those who knew him; his gift for small talk was as impaired as the rest of his social skills.

'So,' Attuaal's voice boomed, 'did you all sleep well?'

They all answered *yes*.

'And you all had a good night, yes?'

They heartily agreed. Nuridj let everyone know that Yanukz had emptied his stomach over himself during the night, and they laughed. At a lull in their humour Segros asked out loud, 'But did Abinyor enjoy the night?'

The room went quiet. Something in his tone suggested that her behaviour, either publicly or privately, had not met his expectations. Abinyor glanced at her father and saw him watching her closely. She quickly turned her head away and was struck by the murderous glare Borchek had levelled at her new husband.

'Yes, thank you,' she replied.

'That is good,' Segros said, a faint note of impudence in his voice.

Kulej stood from his seat and placed a hand on Hrad-Uik's shoulder. 'When do you want to leave?' he asked him.

'After we've eaten and said our farewells.'

'Excuse us for now,' Kulej said, 'there are people we need to see,' and then he left with Segros and Attuaal.

After breakfast Abinyor went outside with her father. He asked to see inside the house she was to live and she showed him through. The sheaths of flowers and guest bedding had been removed, decorations taken down. They walked into her new room and Hrad-Uik took it all in with a sad look.

Too soon the time came for everyone to depart. Abinyor walked arm in arm with her father down to the shore where the rest of her family waited by the canoes. Nankyi walked alongside while Segros and a host of his clan marched behind.

'We shall see you soon,' her father reassured her. 'Your brothers will come in a few days to see how you are.'

'Will you come too?'

'Ah, we shall see, we shall see.'

She knew her father would never let on that the shortest of journeys made him suffer. The tears in her eyes grew heavy, her throat seized up and she knew she couldn't talk without blubbering. Her sisters embraced her with free-flowing tears rolling down their cheeks and after a short, ceremonious farewell, she waved them away in their canoes.

The last to leave, her father and brothers stood on the bank prolonging the moment with idle chatter. Hrad-Uik gave his daughter a farewell hug and climbed into his canoe. Kulej assisted him while Borchek held the canoe steady.

'Goodbye old friend,' Kulej said. 'I will stop by soon.'

'We will hold you to it,' Hrad-Uik replied, sitting down in the front. Nankyi took a seat in the middle, some cousins sat fore and aft.

Segros came forward and draped an arm over Abinyor's shoulder. The young girl didn't move, didn't seem to feel it.

'Take care of my daughter,' Hrad-Uik said as he picked up a paddle. It had almost sounded like a plea.

Borchek pushed the canoe from the bank and straightened to his full height. 'Yes Segros,' he said, his dark eyes full of warning. 'It would do you well to listen to my father.'

Segros responded with a mirthless smile.

When Borchek spoke next his face had changed dramatically. His lips curled into a treacherous smile, his jaw came up and there was a savage glint in his eyes. Those who had caused him grief in the past knew that face well.

'Hurt her, and I am already coming for you.'

Kulej sprang toward him. 'Borchek!'

'Forget your cousins, your proud uncles . . .'

Kulej pushed him toward the canoe where Yanukz and Nuridj were already seated and waiting. 'Enough!' he cried. 'Go!'

In no hurry, Borchek walked over to the canoe and stepped inside. There he stood, a shameless smile plastered across his face.

'Treat her well, or by the blood of the gods I swear you will see how the Oronuk win their fights.'

'Enough!' Kulej strode forward and gave the canoe a hard shove with his foot. Borchek lost balance and dropped into a sitting position. The canoe drifted away.

Slightly embarrassed, Kulej turned around and was surprised to find the exchange given scant attention. People walked up the bank without looking back. Only Segros remained, facing the river and smiling menacingly.

Abinyor walked away alone. She glanced longingly over her shoulder at the canoes disappearing downriver with tears streaming down her face.

They gave her space as she made her way indoors, and no one followed. The reality of her situation was slowly sinking in. Never had she felt so utterly alone. Walls seemed to press inwards and her breathing sounded too loud in the stillness. She imagined her family paddling away and had to restrain a silly urge to run after them.

After a while Szanaj-kik came in. '*Yehu!*' she said cheerfully. 'Has anyone given you anything to do?'

Abinyor shook her head mildly for a no.

'You're not going to sit here and sulk all day, are you?'

Abinyor sniffed and gathered her dignity. 'No.'

'Everything will be well, you will see. How was last night?'

'Good.'

'Oh?' Szanaj-kik invited happily.

'He left me alone.'

A look of astonishment clouded Szanaj-kik's face. 'He left you alone?'

The reaction threw Abinyor a little, and she stopped feeling sorry for herself. 'Yes,' she answered warily.

266

There was a pause while Szanaj-kik considered this. 'Did you make him angry?'

'I don't think so.'

'Did he say anything to you?'

'No. He fell asleep.'

'Do you not want him?'

Realising a 'no' might sound offensive, Abinyor checked herself. 'I don't know,' she said. 'Something doesn't feel right. Perhaps . . . with time .'

'Abinyor – be careful with him. Don't make him angry, don't test him. He can be cruel in ways you cannot imagine.'

'I did nothing of that. I lay down and waited, like you said. He just went to sleep.'

'All right.' Szanaj-kik nodded slowly. 'Perhaps his mind was too wet with drink. It wouldn't be the first time, and it won't be the last. Now, is there anything you feel you need to do today?'

'No.'

Szanaj-kik sat down beside her. 'If you give me your – ' she broke off and screwed her face. 'Eek! Woman, you smell! No wonder he left you alone! When was the last time you washed?'

Abinyor would have felt embarrassed if not for the good-natured smile on the woman's face. 'Oh, I don't know.' She heard a giggle coming from the entrance and turned her head to see a small boy duck out of sight.

Szanaj-kik stood and motioned with her hand. 'Come with me.' She had a compelling look of sincerity, an expression that invited trust.

They gathered clothes and a blanket and went outside. Szanaj-kik led the way briskly past staring eyes and turning heads, and when a few children tried to follow she bellowed at them so fiercely they stopped in their tracks. They left the village and followed a trail that led to a bend in the river where a pocket of water offered privacy beneath a guard of willows that draped their sinewy branches into the crystal-clear water.

'The water is calm here,' Szanaj-kik said. 'Take off your tunic and I

267

will wash it for you. You can put this on after.' She held up a spare one. Abinyor glanced around and Szanaj-kik added, 'There is no one here but us.'

Abinyor shed her clammy tunic and stood naked by the water's edge, contemplating what appeared to be waist-deep water. She held her breath and stepped boldly into the river, which swallowed her up to her neck.

The water was still thick with the winter chill and it bit into her mercilessly. She squealed loudly and gasped in rhythm to her pounding heart. Once her body temperature had adjusted a little she took a deep breath and ducked under the water. She resurfaced shaking her head and shrieking in delight, then lay back and let the water float her under the willows.

Szanaj-kik kneeled by the water's edge, grabbed a handful of river-sand and began scrubbing the tunic. 'Cold?' she asked.

'As snow.'

Abinyor flopped about lazily, enjoying the freedom and forgetting about everything. When the cold became unbearable she emerged shivering on the bank. The swim had shed the gloom from her face and a belated smile now beamed in its place.

Szanaj-kik wrapped the blanket around her and patted her down. 'Tell me your story, Abinyor of the Clan of Hrad-Uik, and I will tell you mine.'

'Shouldn't . . . we . . . get back?' Abinyor stammered through chattering teeth.

'When we are ready.'

'All . . . right, but you first. I can't . . . talk properly anyway.'

'My story? That's not fair. I asked you first.'

'No . . . you didn't . . . I asked you last night.'

'Uh, so you did. Here, sit down.'

Szanaj-kik cleared a few branches from the ground and they sat down. She kept massaging the young girl as she told her story.

She was a full-blooded native and the last of her clan. She could still recall stories her great grandmother told her about the new people who came into their land. Traders and prospectors had led the way, following established routes or led by native guides. Then came the farmers, manoeuvring themselves into areas wherever native people were most pliant.

On so small a scale her people eagerly embraced the trade and technology these newcomers brought with them, and this early period proved beneficial to both cultures. Whether contrived or a matter of course, as the years rolled by her tribe found itself relying less on shifting subsistence patterns for their survival. Satellite camps fell into ruin and patches of territory infrequently roamed were either surrendered or shared with an expanding populace of agriculturists.

But they kept on coming.

The fighting was well advanced when Szanaj-kik was orphaned. No one ever explained to her why her family group had been slaughtered; those accountable would have said it was the way things were, had always been, and would go on being.

She was adopted by the same farmers who massacred her family group and raised by a woman who had lost a young daughter to natural causes only days before. Given the surrogate her maternal instincts cried for, she bestowed upon the infant girl all the passion and love her true mother would have given her. The child had foster parents to bond with, playmates in her new siblings, was given everything she needed and spared any deprivation or mistreatment for her lingering grief to feed on. Her transition was complete and her past forgotten – even her name. She would only ever know herself as Szanaj-kik, one of many reborn.

Then one evening when she was about eight years old a runner came and demanded she accompany him back to his village. As soon as they arrived she was led into a room where a man lay bleeding on a bed. Several serious looking men stood around. The man was doubled up in foetal position, his mouth was flecked with blood and he drew his breath in loud wheezes. The broken shaft of an arrow protruded from the base of his neck and the furs beneath him were soaked red. The sight made her tremble.

'Szanaj-kik,' someone said, 'we need you to remember the talk

269

before you came to live with us. The talk you knew when you were little.'

She moved closer to the wounded man and he rolled his head to face her. Sweat ran down his forehead and his eyes were fired by pain, but when he saw Szanaj-kik a tortured smile creased his lips.

'I see a little girl,' he gasped. 'Why have they brought you here?'

It came as a shock to hear her native tongue spoken so fluently. Light had been shed on a dark, closed off section of her mind, stirring memories long forgotten.

'What – ?' She caught herself replying in the wrong tongue.

'Do you speak my words?'

She nodded.

'What is your name, little one?'

Perhaps it was the connection that made her feel pity; perhaps it was his kind, fatherly face. 'Szanaj-kik.'

'Szanaj-kik. I can see you are of the People.' He closed his eyes and grimaced, the effort too much.

She waited until he opened his eyes again, then pointed to his wound.

'Yes,' he said. 'See how well they aim.'

A man standing beside her said, 'What is he saying?'

'He says you shot him.'

'We need to know who he is,' the man went on unperturbed, 'and who were those with him. We will help him if he tells us. Ask him.'

She thought hard while the men around her waited patiently. Lost words scratched at her memory, reaching up from the dim of her early years. 'Who – ?'

The man broke into a chuckle, then the pain hit him and he spoke with difficulty. 'They want to know who I am, yes? I will meet with my gods soon, Szanaj-kik. What good would it do to tell them?'

Words came back to her now. 'They . . . help.'

'Do you think I should tell them?'

She nodded weakly.

The man wheezed a few more times. 'I am just one more of our kind who will die like this, and I have no more regret for the things I have done over the years than they would. But on this day I am without hatred toward these men, Szanaj-kik. It is important you tell them this. They shoot arrows into me because they must. All I ask is that they return me to my people. I want my spirit to wander the lands where my forefathers lie, here it will be lost. If they are proper men, this is all they need know. Tell them that for me.'

She translated dutifully. Despite the insistence of the men standing around nothing more could be learned from him. A woman took her away and fed her and put her to bed. In the morning she was told the man had died in the night. They had taken his body into the forest and buried him in a lonely grave. They took her back to her village and nothing more was mentioned about it.

But the incident served its purpose. She had been tested under challenging conditions and proven herself admirably, and after that was encouraged to revive her dormant tongue. Although not, in those early days at least, the preferred interpreter asked for, she was used when no one else was available, which turned out to be quite often. As she got older she sat in on some serious discussions and became more learned in regional politics than most men. A trusted interpreter, she soon drew the attention of the Clan of Attuaal.

Attuaal was a half-breed. Typically his native blood came from his mother, whose band had been one of the more friendly that had crossed paths with the settlers. If things were going well the band would be invited to special occasions. Rumour had it that on one of these occasions his mother was seeded by the son of an Oronuk headman, and when the wrong coloured eyes flashed open in Attuaal nine months later her husband wanted nothing to do with mother or child. This was her milder form of punishment. Banished by tribal council, she had her only other child Utt-vunn ripped from her hands and his impure brother thrust into them. With nowhere else to go she took Attuaal to the Oronuk village and threw herself at the feet of the boy's bewildered father.

She had found a new home, but she was a ghost amongst the living. She tried to return to her own tribe and they turned her away. She tried again and they chased her away. The next time she returned she begged only to see Utt-vunn, and they beat her away. She tried one last time accompanied by a party of armed men. Approaching the Ubren camp, they were met by an equivalent force.

Then her ex-husband stepped forward. 'Why do you keep coming here, stinking of them?' he asked, gesturing to her company. She replied calmly that she wasn't leaving until she had seen their son. He grunted and walked off. A short time later he reappeared towing a boy.

She almost fainted with joy at the sight of her first-born. He had grown in the year she had last seen him, and now stood half the height of his father.

'This woman keeps coming here,' her ex-husband said to the boy. 'She lived amongst us once, then brought shame upon our people. She can be punished, but she cannot be taught humility. She says she is your mother. Do you know this woman?'

And the son she loved as only a mother can love had said: 'I have no mother.'

At that moment, it was said, clouds shut out the sun. It was winter then and the first snows fell heavily on their way home. They didn't hear her speak again until later that evening when, sitting at the table staring down at her untouched meal, she mumbled something about how beautiful her boy looked. During the night she walked off into the forest, lay down in the snow and let her broken heart stop beating.

Despite these early disadvantages, the infant Attuaal, raised by a devoted father, grew into a strong and healthy boy. Then without warning around his twelfth year the half-brother he hadn't seen since birth appeared from nowhere. They were both overjoyed. In the years that followed they did their best to make up for lost time.

Though Attuaal was raised in an agrarian culture his loyalty remained with the indigenes, and with his links to his brother's people he became a prominent figure amongst a growing hybrid subculture of farmers descended from native stock. As an ethnic minority though they found themselves increasingly marginalised, pushed into empty villages on the borders of settled lands after their former occupants had squeezed the soils dry. With Attuaal at its heart, the northern precinct became the refuge of several clans with Ubren origins, and by virtue of her heritage Szanaj-kik became a trusted friend of Attuaal. Marriage to the eldest of his two sons followed, and they were rewarded with a wonderful daughter.

Against a background of cultural disparities and factional fighting there was always, as Szanaj-kik explained optimistically, those at work equally inspired to preserve the peace. Men like Kulej, hand-picked from an early age for his exemplary mediation skills and wisdom well in advance of his age, with the stamina to endure long treks, often at speed, to the furthest villages to attend councils, mediate, negotiate, organise trade, and to oversee the movements or repair the consequences of what was generally an unco-ordinated sprawl of pioneers incapable of considerations beyond their own interests.

Like it or not, Szanaj-kik went on proudly, the Oronuk needed clans like those of Attuaal. His was an important link with the Wandering Tribes – the term given to elusive bands of hunter-gatherers roaming the countryside – who in turn provided access to lands beyond established villages and trade routes to the north and west. Natives made invaluable guides, exceptional hunters, and with their local knowledge were more proficient at supplying natural resources and providing information about where they could be found. They could also provide valued labour, if they could be coerced. Men like Attuaal were their best and often only means of introduction.

Two major events took place that led to Abinyor marrying the son of an Ubren headman. The first was when disease ravaged their people; a disease that turned the air so thick with the stink of fever and rotting flesh that entire villages had to be abandoned. Nothing could be done. They tried their medicine, their medicine failed; they called for their shamans, their shamans fell ill. Then as quickly as it came it was gone, leaving the soil rich with the dead and a walk through the forest without straying onto a burial ground a challenge for the most diligent passerby. Amongst those returned to the earth were Segros' son, wife, and older brother.

Szanaj-kik had heard only fragments about the other event. It had to do with the resurgence of an old grievance between two clans – one Ubren, the other Oronuk – both of which had at their centre a powerful headman and thousands of men loyal to their respective causes. Although it was predominantly an issue of the east local Oronuk clansmen were getting nervous; a groundswell of Ubren ill-will seemed to be heading their way.

For the good of both causes it was decided that Attuaal's surviving son should marry an Oronuk woman. Only Segros couldn't be persuaded. No Oronuk women took his fancy but one. 'Bring me the daughter of Hrad-Uik,' he had responded arrogantly, 'and I will think about it.'

When Szanaj-kik finished her story Abinyor sat thinking quietly. No one had ever explained to her the politics of her people in this detail, and her mind reeled with this new information. 'When will I meet the brother of Attuaal?' she asked.

'In two days. They are eager to meet you.'

'Why were they not at the wedding?'

'Because men were there who would have taken a mace to their heads,' Szanaj-kik responded frankly.

'What are they like?'

Abinyor listened fascinated to Szanaj-kik's descriptions. There was an air of mystery about the Wandering Tribes and their world, and she felt drawn to them in a way that went beyond curiosity. Indeed if she felt anything resembling an attraction for her husband it was that primal, unspoilt element consistent with her preconceptions of the wild and carefree race he shared blood with.

But there had to be more to it than that, she knew. Perhaps it had something to do with the native she had met last winter. A man she often thought about, probably more than was good for her. For she knew they were unlikely to ever meet again.

Twenty-seven

Abinyor and Szanaj-kik returned to the village in midafternoon and prepared dinner, which consisted mainly of banquet leftovers. After dinner the men left to drink ale elsewhere, the children were put to bed and the women were given their first real opportunity to speak to the new wife of Segros. She had intended to go to bed early herself and be either asleep or feigning it by the time he returned, but when they started firing question after question about her brothers she stopped glancing at the door and lost track of time praising their better qualities.

So it was when Segros and Attuaal returned. The gathering fell quiet and she used the interruption to politely excuse herself. A wall-lamp guided her to her room where Szanaj-kik's three-year-old daughter was curled in a corner under a blanket. Abinyor undressed and draped her clothes neatly over a railing.

She was about to blow out the lamp when she heard the sound of heavy feet. Segros appeared at the door and she felt his eyes crawl over her nakedness. Her hand reached out reflexively and she pinched the flame. Under the cover of darkness she quickly slipped beneath the covers and rolled away.

'Abinyor.'

She turned her head obediently. In the dim light she saw him kneel down and reach out a hand to touch her face in what seemed to be a genuinely affectionate manner, but she couldn't help recoiling from it.

'Not the way you want it, no?' He sighed loudly and stood up. She waited until he left the room before breathing again. All she could do now was pretend an unlikely sleep.

He was back before she might have been convincing. Keeping a cold eye on her, he set his lamp down and began stripping off his clothes. She turned her face away and heard them drop onto the

275

floor piece by piece.

'Look at me,' he said.

Abinyor forced herself to comply. Fully naked now he sat cross-legged on the bed, watching her impassively. Blood pounded in her temples and sweat chilled her forehead.

Footsteps approached and Szanaj-kik appeared at the entrance. Comprehension showed on her face in a blink. She brushed a strand of hair behind her ear, leaned down to check on her daughter, then lifted the tunic over her shoulders in one fluid movement. Her legs were straight and narrow, the dome of her belly was smooth and firm. She knelt behind Segros and dragged herself forward on her knees until she was up against his back. She wrapped her arms around his neck and nuzzled her nose against his cheeks.

Segros' eyes mellowed as he reclined into her breasts. 'She is not happy here,' he said, a thin smile wrinkling his lips. 'But she does not wish to talk about it.'

Abinyor looked deep into Szanaj-kik's eyes. It might have been jealousy, it might have been empathy, but something lurked beneath them that Abinyor found unsettling. It made her feel like an intruder in her own room.

'What can we do for you?' Segros asked with a chuckle. 'Tukgla num ekech?'

Szanaj-kik answered in kind and a short conversation in their native tongue followed. Segros shrugged dismissively and turned his attention to Szanaj-kik. Their hands moved over each other and Abinyor rolled over and faced away.

Listening to their passionate lovemaking not an arm's length away, Abinyor was surprised to feel nothing. She wasn't the slightest bit interested in what they were doing. If she felt anything at all, it was a sensation resembling loneliness.

Beside her the groans subsided and a grateful panting ensued. The air in the room restored its order.

'Abinyor,' Segros said in his gruff voice.

She didn't move.

'Abinyor!'

She turned her head and saw their naked bodies entwined like the courtship of snakes. Segros lay on his back underneath Szanaj-kik, smiling contentedly. Sweat glistened on their skin and dripped onto the furs.

'Blow out the lamp.'

The next day they prepared for the arrival of Attuaal's brother and cousins. Abinyor took to her tasks with rare purpose; reassembling sheaths and decorations, mixing honey and maple syrup into elegant bread cakes, and pouring a fresh supply of beer through sieves to clean out the mucky residue left by fermentation. Her thoughts kept returning to the night before, and her family, father and future, and the more she thought about them all, the lonelier she became. Szanaj-kik noticed yet said nothing to her, merely delegated to her the easier chores and monitored how she went about them discreetly.

The girls ate outdoors around midday, seated around the table in the common area. Abinyor picked at a few pieces of fruit and lifted her head politely to acknowledge a well-intended remark but remained as voiceless as she had been all morning. When everyone finished eating Szanaj-kik called her to one side.

'You can stop working for a while,' she told her. 'You need to learn some dancing.'

'I know how to dance,' Abinyor replied in a dull voice.

'Of course. But you might want to make a few adjustments.'

The girls assembled into a group and followed Szanaj-kik and an enthusiastic young drummer into the forest until they reached a clearing where the earth had been churned bare by countless feet.

The drummer pulled up a stump and they began. With a girl either side Abinyor was shown step by step when to pause, when to kick and when to swirl, and after some initial reluctance she even managed to contribute to the occasion. Szanaj-kik stood to one side with a critical eye, correcting errors and making suggestions. Their style of dancing was familiar, allowing Abinyor to adjust to the variations easily.

At first it was a playful occasion. They fooled around and blamed the drummer unanimously when something went wrong, and to get his own back he would thump out of rhythm and break into fits of laughter at the sight of them trying to keep up. A chorus of good-natured rebuke would follow, then they would try again, and in the spirit of the occasion Abinyor played along until at last a smile broke from her lips, and not long afterwards a giggle or two, and as if awaiting that very signal, Szanaj-kik clapped and barked at the group. The drummer stiffened, the banter died and the session became serious. They started over, making fewer errors this time, gathering momentum until their timing became flawless, and the dancing took on a life of its own, like a single being. The emotion that begged release surged through Abinyor's arms and legs to merge with those lost in the ecstasy of dance around her.

She felt like a woman again. Her new friends felt the transformation, and they kept going long after she had learned what was needed. When they could barely lift their legs Szanaj-kik brought it to an end with a few loud claps and a flow of compliments, and they made their way gasping and laughing to a stream. As the boy knelt by the edge to drink one of the girls ran up from behind and pushed him in. For his poor drumming, she cried. He leapt out of the water and caught the girl and threw her in as well. Within moments the whole group was laughing and splashing, turning the stream into whitewash.

Wet and cheerful they headed back. Abinyor was sad they were leaving. It had been the best of days and the afternoon's fun reminded her of similar times back home. Judging from the way the girls treated her, she was confident they liked her already. At one stage she noticed Szanaj-kik trailing the group with a knowing smile on her face, and Abinyor returned the smile, for she knew what the woman would have been thinking. She would have been thinking how good it was that the quiet plan she had formed in her head that morning had worked. She was telling Abinyor things were not as bad as they seemed. She was letting her know that everything would get better and she was there to see it so.

They returned late in the afternoon but there was no reprimand for their extended absence. As they cleaned up after dinner Abinyor asked Szanaj-kik, 'What do we need to do tomorrow?'

'Not much,' Szanaj-kik answered. 'We won't dress you up much; the effort is wasted on the men of Utt-vunn anyway.'

'How do we know they will be here tomorrow?'

'A runner came today when we were dancing.'

She excused herself early and went to bed. Segros climbed in a bit later and politely rolled away from her. Soon he was breathing deeply, sparing her the need to consider evasive tactics. The day had left her so jovial she even gave thought to how she might have reacted if he'd tried anything. She was being conditioned, she knew now, and if nothing else they were being very clever about it. Even Segros had to be commended; his patience and restraint were working. Tonight she would sleep well, tomorrow she would feel that little bit better about the whole situation. And him.

She looked at the dark figure in her bed and wondered if her conduct had been unreasonable. Whichever way she looked at it, she had agreed to be here. This was her doing. She hadn't warmed to him, hadn't given him anything owed to a husband, yet assumed all the entitlements and respect that came with being his wife. Szanaj-kik was a good woman and adored the man, and Abinyor felt she could trust her implicitly. Surely there had to be some good to him.

What did she expect? That the whole village would break from tradition and fall over itself attending to hers? Indeed, as Szanaj-kik had implied, they were willing to try. Despite their different traditions, they were prepared to honour hers. Even if there had been, or still was, an arrangement with a third party, who better than Szanaj-kik to share it with?

For some time she watched Segros in near darkness. His face had taken on a look of innocence, calm and peaceful and not altogether unattractive. She lifted her hand and held it above his chest, daring herself, and gently let it fall. She felt the hardness of man and the power behind his rising chest, and was surprised at how pleasing it felt. His breathing stayed slow, his body lay still and harmless.

She heard someone enter the room and jerked her hand away. Szanaj-kik walked quietly over to the corner of the room to check on her sleeping daughter, then undressed and placed her clothing to one side. Softly now she stepped over the bedding and lay down beside Abinyor. It was a deliberate choice, putting herself on the far side of Segros, and Abinyor guessed correctly that this was customary. Szanaj-kik covered herself with the blanket, then reached out and gently touched Abinyor's forehead. The young girl flinched and Szanaj-kik murmured, 'Shhh.' She stroked Abinyor's forehead a few times, her fingers went slack and she turned onto her stomach and flopped an arm over Abinyor's chest. A short time later her breathing deepened with sleep.

With Szanaj-kik on one side, Segros on the other, and a child in one corner, Abinyor felt a curious sense of family. It made her smile. She had come a long way in a single day. Hope was not lost yet.

They came after midday, stepping out of the forest and walking single file along a path between the fields. There were at least twenty of them. Tall and proud, they embodied the leanness of life in the forest. The briskness in their walk was effortless and their eyes shone with the ever-present watchfulness of those whose survival depended on it. Vests flapped loosely over rippling stomachs, necklaces of teeth and bone bounced on their gleaming chests, and long, braided hair flowed behind every man.

A number of wolf-dogs trotted alongside, tongues flapping and eyes as sharp as their masters'. A large boar dripping blood from its nostrils dangled beneath a pole carried by the two men leading and three smaller pigs bounced against the backs of those behind. They arrived at the Banquet-shed and dumped their loads.

The entry of this wild-looking party silenced everyone at first, then there followed a frenzy of greetings and backslapping. Attuaal pointed a finger Abinyor's way and they all came forward.

She saw that their jewellery and garb was similar to those who worked the soils. Their uniqueness showed in their physique. They were taller on average than her kind, their body tone more economical. Their faces were characteristically broad and chiselled. The leading man looked matured rather than old, with limbs like an ancient oak.

Attuaal introduced him. 'Abinyor, here is my brother Utt-vunn.'

She dipped her head politely. Although she knew Attuaal's brother was older by several years, he looked healthier and younger. There were fewer folds in his skin, his waist was narrower, and the whites of his eyes were without the slightest blemish. He gave the impression of a man ready to break into a sprint or climb a tree at an instant's notice.

'My brother speak truth,' Utt-vunn used the common tongue. His voice was thickly accented and his forehead was bonier than anyone she had met, but the eyes beneath were bright and friendly. 'You pretty face.' He clicked his fingers and a man stepped forward carrying a neatly folded bison robe. 'This my son, Agrud.'

Agrud's eyes sparkled. 'For you, pretty face,' he said, offering the robe.

'Thank you.' Abinyor smiled shyly as she took the gift; this was one handsome man.

'Szanaj-kik!' Utt-vunn cried, and extended a greeting in his own tongue. Szanaj-kik responded in kind and there were smiles and laughter all around. A growl diverted their attention to the dogs flashing their teeth and bottom-sniffing from one to the next as they carried out their own introductions. Several boys assigned themselves the task of peacemakers.

After the initial co-mingling, Attuaal and Segros led Utt-Vunn and some important looking men indoors. Abinyor helped with the preparations, finding time here and there to sit down with her new friends. All were keen to talk to this new addition to the Clan of Attuaal.

A universal ritual, men and women divided early in the night to talk their separate interests. It wasn't long before Abinyor's restless gaze settled on another curious distinction. Despite the ample bench space Utt-Vunn's men chose to sit on the ground in neat circles with their legs crossed. Their chatter was short and fast, yet more calmly pitched than that of Attuaal's men. They were less inclined than their hosts to have their mugs refilled. By their quick smiles and laughter they gave the impression of men easily pleased, content in a more traditional way. For all their common roots, traditions and tongue, the two bands remained worlds apart.

Feeling like a break from the women, Abinyor took a jug of beer from a table and went inside. She found her husband and his company seated at the main table and poured mugs for those requiring a refill. In no hurry to leave she lingered by the group, going so far as to ask Utt-Vunn's men a question or two relating to their wives and whereabouts, and received a frosty silence. She waited awkwardly, hoping the conversation would pick up, and when it didn't she knew she had somehow broken with etiquette.

'There are thirsty men outside,' Segros confirmed.

Her head steamed as she left. Things had changed significantly since becoming his wife. Prior to the wedding, Segros and his kinsmen had shown her nothing but respect.

Food was placed on tables for the diners to help themselves. The natives returned to their places and feasted heartily, ripping meat off bones like hungry dogs. No one else approached them or said anything to them. Abinyor watched it all with a wry smile. When the sound of crunching bones jarred the air she had to stifle a laugh when she observed it was not the dogs making it.

After dinner the dancing commenced. At first Abinyor was nervous, but with hearty encouragement from the audience she quickly lost her shyness. The musicians made it easier for her, picking dances she could easily apply herself to, and any error she made was lost to the greater spectacle of her competence.

By the first break in the dancing Segros was well into their heady brew. It was then she noticed another side to him. Not once did he acknowledge her, or talk to her. While dancing she had seen many eyes directed toward her and her alone, none of which were his.

Agrud caught her attention with a shout. 'Pretty face! Come and sit!' Beside him sat Segros.

Abinyor went over and sat down between them, trying not to

grimace as beer-breath flowed over her from both sides.

'You dance well,' Agrud praised her.

'Thank you.'

'Cousin! She dance well, yes?'

Segros mumbled something incoherent.

'Where is her drink?' Agrud asked impatiently.

'Woman,' Segros said, 'take a mug.'

Agrud shook his head disappointedly. He filled an empty mug from a jug and offered it to her. She took it from his hand and raised it to her lips.

'Now you are complete,' Segros mused.

The dancing continued without her. By her third refill she was mildly intoxicated.

Agrud's grasp of the common tongue was passable enough to allow for a simple conversation. They talked about her village, her family, of people they knew, and his intelligence and sincerity worked like a charm. Here was a man who showed far greater interest in her than Segros ever did, and she found herself liking him immensely.

A while later, having hardly participated in the conversation, Segros stood abruptly and walked away. Abinyor watched him leave, her face betraying her thoughts.

'Hard shell outside, soft inside,' Agrud remarked. 'You will see.'

'Oh?' She took a long swallow of beer. 'When?'

'When you do what he want.'

She felt her temper flare. 'He wanted me here; I am here.'

'Perhaps try harder.'

'I see.' She stood up unsteadily, aimed herself at a group of friends and dropped down amongst them. A girl thrust another full mug into her hand. As she sat brooding she hardly heard the conversation going on around her. Her attention kept straying to Agrud.

The natives retired first. Abinyor watched them choose bedding here and there beneath the trees until only a group of hardy men remained talking and drinking. The girls in her group broke up and she decided to go to bed herself.

283

Her head spun more now. A lamp or two showed her through to the sleeping sections where she observed most of Attuaal's family asleep. She found the entrance to her room and stumbled inside. Quietly now, she groped forward in the dark on her hands and knees until stiff animal fibres met her outstretched fingers. She slipped under the covers, happy to have the bed to herself.

She had almost drifted off when she felt her arm trodden on. She opened her eyes and saw Segros stumble briefly and reposition his feet. Melted fat from a lamp he held dripped onto the floor. With difficulty he placed it onto a shelf and squatted down beside her. She rolled away.

'You there,' he said.

She didn't move. The blankets flew away and Segros gripped her wrist and jerked her into a sitting position. 'My bed is not to your liking, no?'

'I am *trying,*' she retorted, yanking her wrist away.

'Would you try harder with someone else?'

'What if I did?'

They held each other's eyes for a tense moment and she saw the humour on his face replaced by the snake-like appraisal she was learning to loathe.

'You like my cousin better than me, yes?'

'Please,' she said wearily. 'I have worked hard all day and I am tired.'

He heaved a sigh and stood. She lay down and pulled the blanket over her as he departed. Her pulse returned to normal and she closed her eyes, hoping against hope that Segros would find Szanaj-kik – or anyone for that matter – to oblige him.

Before long she heard footsteps approaching. Segros and Agrud walked into the room. 'Get up,' Segros ordered.

Her stomach contracted and she tightened her grip on the blanket. Like lightning he pitched forward, grabbed a fistful of her hair and violently hauled her to her feet. Strands of hair popped out at the roots and she cried out in pain.

'I told you to get up.' He showed no sign of having trouble with his balance now. 'And stop your pig-snivelling or I will get angry.'

She covered her breasts with her hands. 'Please . . . no.' She felt her legs shaking.

Agrud moved forward and ran a rough-skinned hand over her shoulder. His touch, felt through her drink-distorted haze, was not as unwelcome as unsettling. For a moment she even tried to calm herself by closing her eyes and letting his fingers play over her skin.

But something didn't feel right. Standing there like this made her feel like some obedient pet. Worse, it felt perverse. At once her mind sobered and his fingers felt like a spider crawling over her skin. She opened her eyes and stepped back.

'No,' she said staunchly.

'Ha!' Segros cackled. 'And I thought it was just me.'

'Leave me alone.'

'Get it over with,' Segros said wearily, a sadistic smile slashed across his face. 'We all saw the way you looked at this man.'

'No.'

'Lie down,' he said, enjoying himself.

'I don't want to.'

Agrud was already taking off his clothes. If she screamed, would people come running? This was the house and family of Segros. What was normal here, what was custom? Who would *their* sympathies lie with?

This was going to happen sooner or later, she knew. Anaesthetised by drink and spiteful enough to do it with anyone but *him*, she felt the pull of resignation.

'Lie down,' Segros said, sternly this time. 'I will not say it again.'

She felt herself submit. Immediately Agrud was over her, pressing his prickly face into hers. She rolled her head to one side, clamped her eyes closed and concentrated on separating mind from body. She felt her insides rip but didn't utter a sound. Intent on reflecting this feeling of degradation back onto him, she offered as much life as a corpse stiff with rigor mortis.

So detached was she that she didn't notice him spend himself. He crawled off her and stood, bearing a look that blended satisfaction with pity. Segros watched from one side with a lewd smile. She closed her eyes and lay perfectly still.

When all was quiet she opened her eyes. The room was empty, a single lamp burned. Over in the corner Szanaj-kik's daughter was sitting upright, watching soundlessly.

Abinyor's head felt dizzy as she stood and dressed. She tucked the infant back into bed and went outside. Segros and Agrud had joined Attuaal and a group of men drinking. No one paid her any mind. Her legs felt heavy as she walked down to the riverbank.

A good distance downstream she dropped to her knees and was physically sick. She emptied her stomach, stuck her fingers down her throat for good measure and dry-retched a few times. She stripped out of her tunic and waded into the water.

The bitterly cold water felt purifying. She washed herself thoroughly, waded out and sat down on the bank. She drew her legs up to her chest and rested her chin on her knees.

The night was clear and the river glowed beneath the three-quarter moon. When she began to shiver she dressed and made her way back to the village. A few men were still up but Segros and Agrud were nowhere to be seen. She went to her room and found Segros pounding his hips into Szanaj-kik. Both were on their knees facing the entrance; Segros leered at her and Szanaj-kik looked up with a face contorted by either pain or ecstasy. Abinyor grabbed a blanket from the floor and a leather pouch from a shelf, and then left quickly.

'Wait!' Segros cried after her, laughing. 'I am almost finished!'

Back outside she wrapped the blanket around her shoulders and walked along the riverbank to a smooth spot beneath a willow. She sat down, opened the leather pouch and took out a small figurine. Clutching it tightly in her hand, she lay down and tried to will herself to sleep.

Much later in the night her mind and body relaxed. Her hand opened and the aurochs figurine Vratu had given her rolled out and rested beside her.

Twenty-eight

More than one respected elder had told Szanaj-kik that had she been born a man, she would have made a remarkable shaman. She would dip her head, show due respect, and inwardly cringe. Only men spoke that arrogantly.

Though Szanaj-kik had been completely honest with Abinyor by the stream days before, anyone who knew her well would have complained of a glaring omission. Szanaj-kik had given herself a woefully inadequate review. She was far more than just an interpreter. She was a healer, nurse and counsellor, always keeping her judgment silent, sparing the gifts vested in her for those who needed them most.

She had an acute antenna. In the blink of an eye she, better than any, could see the spirit fading in someone's body, the soul crying for solace. And she had seen these things in Abinyor. Her different blood made it stand out even stronger.

Though pretending not to, she had noticed Abinyor's gesture of affection toward Segros two nights before and approved. The girl was making progress. It seemed to prevail into the After-Wedding and so Szanaj-kik had discreetly kept away from them both all night. Even later, obliging Segros with bed-duty, she had not suspected anything wrong. Only when she had woken during the night to find the family bed short one person did she begin to worry. She would have confronted Segros right then had she not known that the state he was in precluded him from waking to anything save beating with a stick.

When Abinyor emerged in the morning she kept a wary eye on her. She watched the young girl keep her head down and avoid eye contact with everyone, saw when Utt-vunn walked over to bid her farewell that she barely acknowledged him. Utt-Vunn looked enquiringly over to his brother standing nearby; Attuaal arched his eyebrows and transferred the enquiry to Segros, who shrugged innocently. Szanaj-kik knew a good act when she saw one.

They went in for breakfast. The crooked smiles Abinyor gave in response to the friendly humour on offer seemed forced. After breakfast Szanaj-kik followed her into a barn.

'Are you well?' she asked.

Abinyor's face hung in a shadow of gloom.

Szanaj-kik steered herself delicately. 'Did he go to you last night?'

Abinyor tipped some grain from a pot into a small basket. 'No.'

'Did he do anything?'

Abinyor said nothing as she tilted the pot up.

'I see,' Szanaj-kik sighed. 'Keep it a secret.'

Later that afternoon Szanaj-kik realised the girl was gone. She made enquiries as to her whereabouts and discovered no one else knew where she was either. She found Segros in a shed rummaging around the bench with his hands.

'What did you do to Abinyor last night?' she demanded.

The movement of his hands slowed. 'Have you seen a maul in here?' he asked, and she waited patiently. When he looked up he pretended surprise at her still being there. 'What?'

'Where is she?'

'Am I to keep watch over a woman?' he asked irritably, making to get past.

She blocked him. 'Talk to me. The girl's upset. What did – '

'Oh, enough! Your voice pains my head!'

'No! Not enough! What did you do?'

He might, on occasion, thrust her aside, break things and shout, but he needed drink to be physically violent, and even then she never feared him. The paradox to his nature was that he would never hurt *her*. She, however, could pack a fairly solid punch with impunity.

Not long into the shouting match they resorted to the native idiom, a more explicit way of hurling insults. No one paid them much mind. It was no one else's business.

Segros flung the door open and strode away, leaving Szanaj-kik seething in his wake. She marched off into the forest, as good a place to start looking as any.

She found the young girl sitting beneath the willows by the stream they had been to days before. She sat down and put a hand on her knee. 'Shall we talk about it?'

Abinyor sniffed and her red, wet eyes dripped another tear. 'I want to be alone.'

'Here, here!' Szanaj-kik responded harshly, withdrawing her hand. 'Why the tears? You knew what was coming. Be strong girl, you live a woman's life.'

'A woman's life?' Abinyor replied obstinately. 'Where I come from, this is not a woman's life.'

'Oh? Why is it different where you come from?'

Abinyor wiped her eyes. 'Segros is a pig.'

'He is your husband.'

'You can have him.'

'Abinyor,' Szanaj-kik lamented. 'What do you want?'

'I want to go home. I cannot do this.'

'Have you tried? Tell me what you want us to do – what you want him to do. There is so much good in him, you just haven't seen it yet.'

'I'll try to remind myself of that the next time he gives me to someone.'

Szanaj-kik frowned. 'I don't understand.'

Abinyor turned to face her. 'Does he do that to you too?'

Szanaj-kik took a deep breath and narrowed her eyes. 'Tell me,' she asked firmly, 'what happened last night.'

'He gave me to his cousin – Agrud.'

'Oh no,' Szanaj-kik groaned, absorbing it slowly. 'Was that your first time?'

'Yes.'

Szanaj-kik shook her head in disbelief and cussed away in her native tongue. Anger replaced the shock on her face now. 'Tell me how it happened.'

Abinyor opened up candidly and Szanaj-kik listened with a distant look in her eyes, as if it sounded all too familiar. 'You poor girl,' she said when Abinyor had finished, and then put an arm around her shoulders.

'I'm not having a child like that,' Abinyor vowed. 'I'd kill it first.'

'It won't happen again.'

The support made Abinyor teary-eyed again. 'No it won't,' she said with grit in her voice. 'Not ever.'

'Shhh.' Szanaj-kik held her close. 'I will talk to him. What he did was wrong. I see I have work to do, as does he.'

Abinyor wiped her nose. 'I miss my family.'

'It will pass.'

They sat in silence. A faint wind blew ripples over the stream and shook the willows around them. Szanaj-kik asked, 'Did you leave a boy behind?'

Abinyor hesitated slightly before answering. 'No.'

Szanaj-kik kept her eyes on her. 'No?'

Abinyor opened her mouth to speak, then closed it again. 'No.'

'No one you were fond of?'

'No one real.'

'Do you want to talk about it?'

'No,' Abinyor said, smiling sadly. 'I want to keep it in my dreams.'

'Would you rather not work on someone real?'

A far-away look appeared on Abinyor's face. 'I would like you to teach me the language of your people,' she said in a wistful voice.

'My people?' Szanaj-kik was taken by surprise. No one had ever asked her to do this before. Translate – not a problem. But teach?

'Yes.'

'You speak to them every day.'

'You know who I mean.'

'But you have no need to learn the other way.'

Abinyor gave her a look of sheer determination. *'Please.'*

Szanaj-kik could only guess she had something to prove. Interpreters were highly regarded and their respect in the community must have made quite an impression on her. It was also patently clear that the girl possessed the sort of intelligence that required frequent mental stimulation. 'This is not easy,' she warned.

The expression on Abinyor's face showed that she wasn't about to be dissuaded.

'All right,' Szanaj-kik consented, confident that the young girl would tire of the pursuit after a few lessons. 'If it means that much to you.'

'It does. Thank you.'

Yes, Szanaj-kik thought. A few basic words, two or three lessons maybe, and Abinyor would let it drop.

She had no idea how wrong she would be.

The village allowed few secrets. Abinyor knew the tension between her and Segros was common knowledge, however something must have been decided. Attuaal showed her excessive charm and went to great lengths to see that his family treated her well.

Segros showed neither contrition nor unkindness in the days that followed. The division of male and female labour kept them conveniently apart and he conversed with her for practical reasons only. She took any opportunity to avoid him, trying not to make it more obvious than necessary. Employing an uncanny insight on the timing of his libido, Szanaj-kik won Abinyor's undying respect, and gratitude, by satisfying his need when it arose and even sleeping between the two of them once it was met.

A morning came when Segros and several men donned hunting attire and left the village. The following afternoon Abinyor was mixing temper into clay at the centre table when she heard a familiar voice.

'Abinyor!'

She turned her head and saw Borchek and her brothers walking up the riverbank. She dropped her work and ran towards them, clay-stained hands outstretched. The force with which she collided into her eldest brother sent him staggering backwards, her arms went around his thick neck and she jumped up to let him take her weight. He set her back down and untangled her arms.

'Yes, it is good to see you too,' he said sheepishly.

She embraced Nuridj and Yanukz, then noticed their empty canoe on the bank. 'Where is Papa?' she asked worriedly.

'At home,' Nuridj answered. 'He is tired.'

People converged on the small group. Attuaal was as jolly as ever and several girls crowded around her brothers and didn't move. Soon they were inside sitting around the main table and the mugs were out and the mead was flowing. They talked about simple, insignificant things happening back home, and she loved every word of it. How her favourite calf was doing, who was sleeping in her bed, whether her friends were still moaning about this and that. They touched briefly on their crop expectations, recent visitors and what news they had brought. Her sisters were all well and weddings were coming up that they might be attending. She was updated on Borchek's courting of a woman from a neighbouring village; a subject he tried unsuccessfully to silence. Abinyor surmised that things weren't going well for her brother in this regard and took the news with silent rejoicing. The woman her brother took a fancy to was a hag.

They talked about the visit of Utt-vunn and his men. At this Abinyor let Attuaal do the talking. Not a lot was said about the night. Borchek and his brothers knew the sensitive position her father-in-law was in and kept their questions discreet. Well into the discussion, Segros and his hunting party returned with a large deer. Segros and Borchek traded civil nods and left it at that.

They cooked the venison and laid it on the table beneath the Banquet-shed in smorgasbord fashion. The siblings found themselves dining alone and Borchek asked his sister what he couldn't before.

'Are you happy?'

Abinyor didn't answer until she'd finished chewing. 'Yes.'

'You lie, little sister. You tell me if he's bothering you, hear?'

'Everything is all right. I have things on my mind,' she said more truthfully.

'As you would. What were Utt-vunn and his men like?'

'I didn't talk to them much.'

'Were they friendly?'

'Yes.'

'Hmmf,' he scoffed. 'They better be careful. You will see visitors

292

coming here in the months ahead who care little for the cousins of Attuaal.'

They poured a few more mugs. Abinyor remained until the last of her brothers went to bed before taking the dreaded walk to her own. Segros entered alone shortly after. Two or three mugs, she knew, was all he had drunk. His breath was acceptable and his manner surprisingly affable. He undressed and climbed into bed.

'You had a good day, yes?' he asked pleasantly.

'Yes.'

'I like your brothers. I like Borchek. There is fire in him.'

She accepted this gratefully, even if her brother didn't share the sentiment.

'You are close to him, yes?'

'All my family are close to me.'

'Tivikeh has eyes for him.' By now the daughter of Avnatt was a good friend of Abinyor. 'But I was told he has an interest in another woman. Is this true?'

'Not while I draw breath.'

'Oh, why is that?'

'The woman is as ugly as a fish.'

Segros propped himself up on his elbow to see her better. 'Have you a reason to feel ill of fish?'

Abinyor smirked. 'Only when a brother of mine fancies one for a wife.'

'A wife now? That is not good. Tivikeh has little hope.'

'Yes she does. She has more to offer than that pig-scrap.'

'Oh? She's a pig-scrap too?'

'And worse.'

'So, does she like you as much?'

'It is the last thing on my mind.'

'I think you are being unfair. Some fish are very pretty.'

Abinyor smiled. 'Well, the thing my brother's taken a liking to is not one of them.'

'Tivikeh is not good for him, then.'

'Why?'

293

'She does not look like a fish.'

So he could make her giggle. It was risky, she knew, with Szanaj-kik conspicuously absent, but it had been too good a day and the mead singing in her head left her warm and complacent. He hadn't moved, just watched her quietly, respectfully she thought, as if awaiting permission. It made her feel the return of her old self.

She knew she could go on sulking and feeling sorry for herself. She could keep resisting. Or she could try, at least, to improve the situation. And there was one thing yet to try.

She could offer her consent.

He must have sensed it. Before she knew what was happening she felt his weight on top of her, and though she neither resisted nor engaged, by the tautness in her body and her absence of any sound, she let him know he was the one enjoying it, which was easy to do, and it was over with very quickly.

They said nothing to each other afterwards. She rolled to one side and fell asleep.

Twenty-nine

The village comprised six longhouses, all empty. A light breeze swirled the dust and lifted loose stalks from the roof thatching, seedlings and weeds swayed in the abandoned fields.

It was late afternoon, and the five young men cast long shadows over the sun-baked earth as they entered. They assembled some kindling and lit a fire. Each man then took a torch and set to work. Dried by a long, hot summer, the rooves caught quickly. Smoke streamed from the thatching and gathered in the heights above, blotting out the light.

By the time the first men arrived the arsonists were long gone. All that remained of the longhouses were a few burning columns, collapsing one after the other in a swarm of sparks.

It angered both sides. Recent strategies devised to put an end to the tit-for-tat hostilities Romoyr had initiated appeared to be working. This ruined a lot of effort.

Then another village was hit. This time though, it was not unoccupied.

There had been two sentries. One was an unreliable, dozing man who had lived up to his reputation; the other would take a full day to recover consciousness. By the time the alarm was raised the barns were infernos and two longhouses were well on the way. They left the barns to their cindery fate and pooled their efforts on the longhouses. Throwing water, beating with wet furs, clambering over thatching and hacking away sections of burning roof, they barely managed to save their homes and half their grain supplies.

They'd had enough. This time people could have been killed.

As dawn broke and fifty armed men gathered in the village, a representative of Vahichiwa, urgently summonsed by a network of hastily dispatched runners, arrived. Only the imperious command of the Unatks, conveyed with appropriate guile by his representative, stayed their anger and averted what had the makings of a bloodbath.

'If you cannot stop these Ubren savages,' someone shouted, pointing at the charred remains, 'we will!'

A hastily convened council followed. Representatives from the opposing parties put their grievances forward. There were all the standard accusations and every time it looked like they were on the brink of settlement a new demand was made and another argument followed. How many beasts were worth the loss of houses? What about all the other incidents? Who had lost more? Who should be made to pay?

An Oronuk elder stood up and brought his fist down hard on the table. 'See how we fight each other!' he shouted. 'Do we let Romoyr ruin us all? What must we do to end this? How do we make peace?'

An Ubren prefect, a bull-like man with a face made to snarl, spoke up. 'Then return the boy you have taken from him.'

And they were back to where they started.

* * *

The rest of Attuaal's clan grew on her.

She found a kindred spirit in Szanaj-kik. They never got on each other's nerves and always found time during the day for Abinyor's language lessons. When the young girl expressed concern that her lessons might be taking up too much time, her tutor had replied that she derived more satisfaction watching her rapid progress than anything else that went on in the village, and if there remained any reservation in their friendship it shrivelled into nothing right then.

There was her next closest friend Tivikeh, in whom she confided as much as Szanaj-kik. The rest of the girls placed her in high regard and the boys were always at her with a prank and a laugh. The only faults she could find in Segros' parents were his mother for carrying him to term, and his father for failing to pass on the virtues a son's birthright assumed.

She fell into a routine that differed little to her previous one.

After the animals were turned out in the morning she might check on the granary or clean around the kitchen area, doing an inventory of dried meats and other preserved foods while inspecting them for spoilage. She would milk the cows that nursed calves, store the milk in stomach-gourds to curdle and sour, and help Szanaj-kik wash and feed the children and animals. When this was done she might clean clothes down by the river.

Much of her day was taken up with the mundane. She hastened the ruin of her back grinding grain; kneeling with her arms outstretched, pushing the pestle back and forth over the quern until her strong young spine seized up with pain and the task was passed onto some other unfortunate girl. There was always barley grain to be steeped, dried, roasted and crushed for ale; there was always hair or plant fibres to be twisted and woven into cord and rope. She might find herself patrolling the crops with one or two others, scaring away beasts or flocks of birds, or keeping the smattering of crop-weeds in check. She dried flowers, roots and leaves, and immersed them into melted fat or beeswax to create fragrant ointments she would rub into her skin to make her feel womanly. Earthenware impressed with her unique brand of free-flowing motifs reached as far as a trader's legs could take him.

Any time left over might be hers. Her first priority was her language lessons with Szanaj-kik, her next most favourable pastime was to accompany the boys when they drove the cattle out into the grasslands to graze, or when they took the pigs into the forest to grub for beechmast and acorns. There she collected all manner of vegetable matter from the sylvan larder; virtually every plant had a use. If the day turned hot she joined her friends swimming in their favourite waterholes.

She visited neighbouring villages to help transfer livestock, to inspect newborn babies, to pay her respects to the sick or dying or dead. Her stock of friends grew. There were rituals and ceremonies and the Clan of Attuaal needed little persuasion for eating and drinking and dancing. They were her welcome break in an otherwise ordinary life.

Garlanded in flowers she would dance in front of headmen and shamans and traders and other far-travelled men rich in stories. People normally indisposed to speak to Attuaal's extended family opened up to her as if she was a dear friend. As a special favour Segros let her return to her former village to celebrate the summer solstice. Better still, he did not accompany her. She spent three days there and had to force herself to leave. Her father's health was getting worse and being with her family and friends left her yearning for her former life.

Rarely did Segros' cousins stop by. Whenever they did Abinyor made herself scarce. They never stayed long and were gone by dusk.

Men of bordering villages had eyes for several nubile women and came bearing gifts and enticements. As predicted by Borchek, emissaries of distant tribes came and went, along with a mysterious collection of far-ranging traders making their annual run up the Great River. On arrival they promptly disappeared behind closed doors. No women attended these meetings — not even Szanaj-kik — and yet the issues raised still found their way into women's discussions.

The unrest in the east drew most attention. Territories were in dispute, men were keen to poke west and not for the first time Attuaal was asked what he knew of the Wandering Tribes west of Heavy-Fish. Most importantly, if he could provide guides. This led to her learning of a family of colonists who had been massacred over that way. Confusion persisted as to who was responsible or why it happened.

Abinyor listened to these matters with mild interest. She had her own worries. The hope she once held that she could adjust to her new life was long gone. She could play the part of a wife, play her part in the politics, but despite her best efforts she could not play the part of herself. Having given her all she bore the posture that showed the limit of her endurance. At the end of a long day, when she knew she should have a warm bed and man to make her happy, she instead was given a reason to despair. She could not always avoid him at night. To reject him was to invite force, if his mind was set, and her only means to discourage him was to try and make each occasion duller for him than the last. This lack of interest, along with the charity of Szanaj-kik, kept the frequency of his demands to a minimum, and even those threatened to break her spirit.

The days blurred into the next. The shadows thrown by their primitive calendars crept closer to their special marks, the air tingled and everything grew full and fat. Each morning men gathered in the fields to pick at husks and hold short conferences about when they should begin their most important phase of the year: the harvest.

On a cold autumn morning a week or so before reaping was due to commence Abinyor woke up nauseous. She went outside and quickly rounded the corner of the house. Making sure no one watched, she dropped to her knees and vomited into a ditch.

She wiped her mouth, steadied herself and went back inside to help with breakfast. After this she slipped away and headed for a sunny embankment in the woods where tansy grew in quantity.

The handsome perennial herbs with their loose, umbel-like clusters of yellow flat-topped flower heads looked innocuous beckoning to bees. She plucked a number of flowers and put them into a bag.

Back in the village she bound the stalks and hung them alongside other bunches of drying herbs. Once they had dried she would grind up the flowers and store them. The flower had a strong smell and was often used as an insect and vermin repellent. Medicinally it could be used to expel intestinal worms, it had value in treating gout, mild fevers, hysteria, muscle spasms and nervous affections, and there was nothing unusual about it being included in their stores. In moderate doses it promoted appetite, assisted digestion and acted as a mild stimulant; in larger doses it became a violent irritant and induced venous congestion of the stomach organs.

But it also had a more diabolical application for those prepared to take the risk. It was also used as an abortifacient.

Nature had been overgenerous this autumn, and Abinyor was late.

Like all girls she had been taught what plants to avoid eating

299

when pregnant. She had no idea what sort of dosage she should take, or how often, and she couldn't ask anyone for help. She hadn't told anyone; not Szanaj-kik, not Tivikeh, and especially – the thought made her sicker still – not Segros.

Abinyor loved children. All her young life she had dreamt of being a mother, dreamt of having a family. But not once did she give what she was doing a second thought.

Thirty

'Mother earth.'

The shaman stood with his arms outstretched, facing the sinking sun. Behind him stood a silent crowd of over a hundred men, women and children, mixed blood and full native.

'Who carries the mountains and forests on her back?

Who lifts the sky and holds it there?

Who raises the mighty beech from dust?

The seasons pay you tribute, the sun pays you homage,

You are the deliverer of all that grows, the nurse of all living things,

Keep us close, hold our feet firm,

Take our seed and bear the fruit,

We are your children,

All that is yours shall be returned to you.'

Standing at the rear, Segros shuffled impatiently. This had been going on for long enough. Every year, on this tribute to the harvest, they went through this ritual. Some years were good, some poor. The only thing that remained the same was the ritual. In the village the girls were storing away the day's harvest in underground pits. Soon they would be finished and then he could begin the only ritual he was really interested in.

Days before, in accordance with tradition, they had taken a supply of barley from the very first bushels and added the honey the natives had brought to make the first brew of the season. Ever since then the vapour from the fermenting malt in the sheds had interfered with his thoughts. It clawed at him. Earlier that afternoon, as the women refined the final brew by sieving, he had teased himself with a taste and been thoroughly impressed.

He looked around the village. As with every harvest, natives had bolstered their labour force. This year though a greater number had stepped out of the forest keen to earn some winter sustenance; the horrors of starvation the winter past had evidently left their mark. He wondered what *they* thought of the shaman's words. Theirs were different gods, he knew. Their deities were of land and animal, not celestial influences on a crop of wheat. Theirs were different needs, different pleas, different offerings. That they chose to be here at all always confused and unsettled him. Only their women took to the harvest with any semblance of enthusiasm; most natives persuaded into the fields reacted lethargically to manual labour and distracted easily when lessoned on crop rotation, the math of yield or fungus infections. Their young hunters hardly ever participated. They may be here on this night of ceremony, replete in traditional attire, but would be gone again at first light to do their thing in the forest, leaving only old men, women and children to bend their backs to the soil.

He glanced at Szanaj-kik, a rarity amongst any people. She caught his look and smiled knowingly. *Be patient* the smile told him, and he felt his heart swell. How a woman could have as much power over him always left him mystified.

And as he waited for this one-sided discourse to end, another troublesome feeling returned. It would be there when the hunters left in the morning, and again when their families left at the end of the harvest. Despite its risks, the forest always pulled them back. He shifted on his feet and his mood darkened.

He *envied* them.

The beer beckoned stronger now. Not much longer. A few more invocations, a chant from the gathering, and then he could lose himself in a manner that would warm his mind and make such thoughts meaningless.

No sooner had their shaman finished and the crowd returned to the village the mugs were out, the beer tasted and unanimously approved. Food was brought outside and the drinking continued as a salute to prosperity.

Abinyor kept to herself. That afternoon she had taken another dose of the abortifacient and now felt ill. Despite taking several infusions over the last few days there was no sign that any had worked, and this time she had taken a fairly strong dose. Perhaps too strong, she worried now.

Amongst those present was Agrud. After dinner he went over to Abinyor as she cleared the tables. She had her back to him and didn't see him coming.

'*Buno,*' he said.

When she turned around and saw who it was her face tightened like a fist. 'What do you want?'

'You not talk much.'

'Have you lost your memory?'

He returned an oblivious look. 'But I am friend, yes?'

'No.' She picked up some plates and made to leave. His hand caught her arm and she whirled on him, eyes flashing. '*Don't touch me!*'

He let go and she walked away, shaking with anger. Inside the longhouse she found Szanaj-kik pushing a large ceramic baking pot into the oven. Abinyor sat down at the table and crossed her arms. 'I think I will go to bed,' she announced.

Szanaj-kik raised an eyebrow. 'So soon?'

'I don't feel well.'

'I see. Can you take this outside first?' Szanaj-kik held up a flask of tea she had made out of dogrose-hips. 'Try to get them to start on this, before they lose their heads.'

'It might be too late already.'

Szanaj-kik laughed. 'We will try anyway. Go.'

'Can you come too?'

The two women carried out a flask each. Abinyor offered hers to a group of native women and they smiled warmly as they held out their mugs. In the group were several women Abinyor had been quick to befriend. It never ceased to impress her how readily they maintained their cheer while going about the drudgery of the harvest. They had encouraged her to test her grasp of the native tongue, and though they occasionally greeted her efforts with a laugh, she correctly interpreted their humour as a sign of goodwill.

'The baby-carrier is good. Yegda is very happy,' Abinyor said to a woman who had traded her carrier for a spondylus shell bracelet.

'I am glad it is gone,' the woman replied. 'It has carried my lazy boy for too long. Now he can walk like everyone else!'

The company perked her up. She sat down and poured herself a mug of tea, her stomach settled and she found her second wind. The attention she received was so full and warm she hardly noticed the gathering thin out and people waving goodnight.

'Abinyor!' A loud voice interrupted the conversation she was enjoying. She saw Agrud holding up a mug. 'This waits for you.'

She raised her own. 'I have one.'

'Abinyor!' Segros' unpleasant voice called from nearby. 'Share a mug with the man.'

'Just a mug this time?' she mumbled, looking away to avoid his reaction. She stood and said goodnight to the group. As she walked past Szanaj-kik she placed her half-empty mug on the table.

'I'm going to bed.'

Szanaj-kik noted the flush on her cheeks. 'Is something wrong?'

Abinyor kept walking and gave her stomach a rub. While talking to the women she had forgotten she was feeling ill.

She made it to her room and was about to undress when she heard heavy footsteps and saw a light approaching. Segros stumbled in and she swore to herself, possibly a little too loudly. He set his lamp on the shelf.

'You have a sour tongue tonight, woman.'

'You'll wake the child,' Abinyor cautioned, pointing at Szanaj-kik's daughter.

'You are too good for my friends, yes? Come outside and we will talk about it.'

'Stop it.'

'Are you going to lie down and sleep?'

'Yes.'

There was a wicked shine in his eyes. 'Do it then.'

'No – I think I will wait until you leave.'

'You know, if you were a real woman you would have done it properly by now,' he said, untying his vest. 'That you show no interest bothers me not; I have no interest anymore either. What I do now I do for you, to make you a better woman.' He took off his vest and dropped it on the floor. 'And do not speak to me like you did outside.'

'Leave me alone or I will scream.'

'No. This would trouble our guests, and I would have to make you quiet.'

She tried to leave but he caught her with a strong arm. 'Get away from me!' she shouted, pushing him back.

One of his hands shot out and smothered her mouth, the other went to the back of her head and she felt her hair pulled tight in his fingers. She opened her mouth and bit down hard on the soft flesh of his palm. He tried to wrench his hand away but she clamped her jaws, wanting to feel his pain, taste his blood. A groan escaped his lips. Failing to free his hand from her jaws, he balled his other hand into a fist, took a step back and swung a hard uppercut into her belly.

She doubled over, gasping for breath. With a deft flick he threw her onto the bed. He fidgeted with his belt and moved forward with an evil gleam in his eyes. Clutching her stomach, she forced herself to her feet and tried to get past but he reached out and grabbed her by the hair. She rolled a wild swing that landed on his cheekbone but before she could take satisfaction a heavy fist slammed into her jaw.

Something rattled in her head and the next thing she knew she was lying on the floor. Her jaw was numb, and when she tried to sit up her arms and legs wouldn't obey. She flopped on the ground like a fish out of water.

She managed to struggle into a kneeling position. Her head was giddy and she tasted blood in her mouth. Vaguely she became aware of shouting, her vision cleared and she recognised Szanaj-kik kneeling beside her, screaming at the man so loudly the effect was like a splash of water on her senses.

Every so often a word registered: 'selfish. . . heartless. . . cruel. . .' Slowly, they fused together. '. . . nothing wrong! She has a will of her own!' She placed Abinyor's arm over her shoulder and guided the girl to her feet.

Abinyor's legs found strength as she hobbled off, dragging one foot in front of the other with Szanaj-kik taking most of her weight. Szanaj-kik's child stared after them, a scared look in her tiny eyes.

'And don't expect either of us to come back tonight!' the fiery woman added.

'Yes, put her in a stable,' Segros answered, 'where she belongs.'

'Slowly now,' Szanaj-kik said gently. 'Watch the chair.'

By the time they reached the door Abinyor was able to stand on her own. 'I can walk.'

'Where did he get you?'

Abinyor massaged her lower jaw. 'Ow.'

'Open your mouth.' Szanaj-kik examined it thoroughly. 'Your cheek is open. Can you move your jaw?'

Abinyor tested it. 'Yes.'

'Szanaj!' Segros shouted.

They ignored him. 'I can walk,' Abinyor repeated. 'I'm all right.'

Szanaj-kik let her stand on her own. 'Are you certain?'

'Yes.'

'You can sleep in Avnatt's house tonight.'

'We can't go there.'

'Yes we can. He knows what Segros is like. Many times I have slept there.'

'Szanaj!' Segros hooted with laughter. 'Can you bring me my mug?'

They went outside. Abinyor concentrated hard on trying to walk normally past everyone, but as she passed the group of remaining men Attuaal saw her and his voice stopped mid-sentence. Confusion appeared on his face, followed quickly by an intense glare.

Abinyor turned her face away. From the corner of her eye she saw her father-in-law striding after them. He caught up quickly and stopped her with a hand on her shoulder.

'Did he hit you?' His voice was laced with anger.

'I'm all right,' Abinyor answered, unconsciously licking blood from her lips.

Szanaj-kik's answer in the native tongue wasn't lost on Abinyor. '*She is all right. It was my fault.*'

Attuaal's face became ugly and Abinyor saw the same look she feared in his son. He hurled his mug to the ground and stormed off toward the house. She fought against the drag of Szanaj-kik and tried to call after him, but her voice was no louder than a croak.

'No . . . please.'

Something was still wrong with her head. Her thought process was dream-like and vague, and now she became aware of a visceral cramp much more severe than the bellyache she'd felt all afternoon. By the time they entered the sleeping quarters in Avnatt's house her insides felt like they were being cut open.

Tivikeh woke up immediately. 'What's wrong?' she asked, her face creased with worry.

'Help me get her into bed,' Szanaj-kik responded.

Avnatt appeared briefly. One sleepy glance was enough. Without a word he turned and went back to bed.

'Szanaj,' Abinyor said in a raspy voice. 'I feel sick.'

'Do you want to be sick?'

'Yes.'

As Tivikeh searched for a toilet-pot, Abinyor fell to her knees and vomited over the floor. Their feet scattered and Tivikeh cried, 'Careful!' Abinyor pitched forward, breaking her fall with hands that slithered in her own vomit.

Szanaj-kik kneeled and lifted the girl's chin. 'Abinyor?'

Abinyor's eyes glazed over and her head flopped loosely. The last of her strength left her and she slumped to the ground making gagging noises and breathing in convulsions.

'Abinyor, open your eyes,' Szanaj-kik said calmly. There was no reply. The convulsions continued. 'Abinyor, can you hear me?'

'What's happening to her?' Tivikeh asked, panic creeping into her voice.

'Get her into the bed.'

They laid Abinyor down and Tivekeh rushed off to wake her mother.

The following morning she was too weak to do much more than lie in bed. She reassured everyone she was well and they let her be.

Around midday Szanaj-kik entered balancing a bowl of steaming liquid. 'How is your sickness?'

'Better.' Abinyor sat up on the bed. 'What is that?'

'Motherwort. To flush out your stomach.' Szanaj-kik sat down beside her and gave her the bowl. 'Are you still bleeding?'

Abinyor nodded feebly and took a sip. She saw the blend of compassion and worry on the woman's face, and the words came out of their own accord. 'I was carrying.'

'Yes,' Szanaj-kik agreed. 'We thought so. But not any more. You never told anyone.'

'No. I wanted it dead. Perhaps I wished too hard.'

'Oh, Abinyor,' Szanaj-kik winced. 'Why do you say that?'

'Because I mean it.'

A long silence followed. Szanaj-kik's eyes, so soft and deep, served to both calm and intimidate. 'Did you take something?'

'Tansy.'

'That can kill you.'

'Not if I do it right. You might want to show me for next time.'

'Oh girl,' Szanaj-kik sighed deeply. 'What are we to do with you?'

Abinyor finished the drink and put the bowl down. 'Please don't tell anyone.'

Szanaj-kik gave her a harsh look. 'All right,' she said. 'And you won't take that poison again, agreed?'

She didn't leave until Abinyor nodded yes.

Thirty-one

The old man's voice was like the drone of bees. He stood at the front of the main room, folds of yellow skin swaying beneath his arms with each wild gesture.

Kulej sat with his elbows on the table, face down, massaging his temples. Despite the old man's distortions, the message was clear. The unrest in the east was not only getting worse, it was creeping closer. And there was nothing anyone could do about it. Kulej saw his purpose there reduced to offering his ears to the wronged, just as he might offer his shoulder to the bereaved. Leadership came not without feigning interest in a lost cause.

'And he gives me an empty cask and says, "when you have filled twenty casks like this, you can bring them to me." And so I filled it with dung and sent it back to him.'

Kulej lifted his head. Hands dropped away from chins and sleepy eyes refocused.

Unatks Vahichiwa spoke for them all. 'You filled it with dung?'

'I filled it with dung,' the old man replied proudly. 'If he wants nineteen more,' he shrugged, 'this can be arranged.'

Vahichiwa drew a heavy breath. 'The man you speak of has killed men for lesser insult than that, particularly old men like you Struputz.'

'This is not our doing. We never agreed to any of this, yet we are forced to give them grain we do not owe. We play no part in what they accuse us of, yet we must walk our villages at night just to stop them being torched. We cannot graze our cattle where they have always grazed, we cannot walk paths we have always walked. How long must this go on? And you tell us to take no action? To suffer our losses in silence?'

'Yes, we know what is happening,' Vahichiwa reminded him wearily.

'How can we live like this? If this boy is still alive, why have you not found him? What has become of your search?'

'As has recently been shown, the natives of the west do not take kindly to strangers,' Vahichiwa explained. 'Is this not so, Henghai Kulej?'

Every face turned toward Kulej. He straightened out of his slouch, wishing he hadn't been drawn into the discussion. 'This is true,' he said. 'Though we have persuaded some of our Ubren friends to make enquiries west of Heavy-Fish, all they return with are rumours.'

'What I am hearing then is nothing,' Struputz said.

Kulej stared into his half-empty mug. Vahichiwa answered for him. 'We live in hope, Struputz. We thought we had a truce with Romoyr that involved compensation, but he is stretching the agreement far beyond what we negotiated.'

'You live in hope?' Struputz groaned. 'We live in the shadow of terror! It is we who are feeling their wrath! If you do nothing we will be forced to take action ourselves, and what my men are threatening is not in your interest.'

Vahichiwa glared at him with eyes as unblinking as a snake. 'We have as much reason as any of you to be angry. If we can wait, my good friend, so can you.' The Unatks never threatened outright, but he knew how to make it sound so. 'Many clans are caught up in this. You would not only spoil the hope for yourselves, but for everyone.'

'Why do you hesitate?' Struputz asked, calmer now. 'You can gather as many men as a swarm of locusts and cross Heavy-Fish with impunity. Who would raise their hands against such numbers?'

'The natives there would scatter like seeds in the wind, and we have not enough men to follow every trail.'

'I have said all I can,' Struputz said, raising his hands defeatedly. 'You tell us to come to you in times of need, and we have come. You promise you can keep the peace, but I think these are only words. Perhaps you think of me as no more than an old fool, so be it. But even an old fool can pass on a message.'

He leaned forward. 'We are tired. We have negotiated, we have given, and we see now we have been too soft. There are limits to our *patience. If we suffer just one more wrong, just one more spear or arrow where it has no place, then it will be back to the way it was, with the stench of rotting corpses thick in the air and heads on spikes for all to see. Let the strongest be left standing. And this time we will leave no one, for we know now what happens when we do. We will rid our lands of this bad blood once and for all and you will not be able to stop it. There are too many of us, and your hands cannot stretch as far as they would need to.'*

Men shifted nervously in their seats. Kulej took a long swallow from his mug and looked in despair at the faces around the table. A veteran of the early wars, he knew the signs. All he could do now was go home and plan with his own men how to steer clear of the carnage that was coming.

* * *

Her face was smooth, her body calm. Floating waterfowl bunched in the shallows copied her mood.

Vratu stood on her bank, gazing at the far side. All he needed to do now was cross over, land a short distance downstream of the village, point the boy there and be off. Go home with Ilan and think no more about it.

'They will see you,' his friend warned.

Vratu turned around. Ilan squatted behind him, staring at the village. Awe was not visible on his friend's face, nor any appreciation of the significance of what lay over there, merely a crinkle on his forehead that barely passed as curiosity.

'It is a too big a place to live in,' Ilan commented at length.

The mighty river awaited their crossing. Vratu's mind flashed with the image of a much smaller river, blackened ruins, a boy trembling in fear and a little girl crying.

'See his face,' he said, pointing to where Kubul stood further up the bank. 'He fears what lies over there.'

'His face is always that way.'

Vratu's eyes flicked between the two. They watched him

311

suspiciously, albeit for entirely different reasons, he thought.

Ilan asked softly, 'Why not . . . just *do* it?'

Vratu stared at him without answering. At once, Ilan understood. He stood up and walked over to the boy. 'Come,' he said, putting a hand on his shoulder.

Kubul followed reluctantly. Ilan led him down the bank to the canoe grounded in the shallows. He reached inside and heaved several items of gear onto the shore while Vratu watched quietly.

'In, little man.' Ilan took hold of Kubul by the arm. The boy stiffened and tried to pull away. 'Come!' Ilan raised his voice. 'There is the village, there are your friends.'

The boy broke away and retreated hastily up the bank. Ilan waited undecidedly until the youngster sat down, then he stomped after him. He grabbed Kubul by the arm and hoisted him to his feet.

'Come!'

Down the bank they struggled, the boy driving his feet into the soft earth, Ilan tugging him forward in stops and starts. They reached the water's edge and Ilan had to let the boy go to handle the canoe. Free again, Kubul tried to march off but Ilan lunged forward and grabbed him by the vest. Kubul fought back in earnest now, wailing loudly and thrashing his arms.

'Stop it!' Ilan said assertively. He manhandled him back to the canoe, lifted him bodily and dumped him inside. 'Sit there and be still!' He planted a hand firmly on Kubul's shoulder to keep him there. 'And stop blubbering or we will leave you here.'

'Ilan,' Vratu said. 'Let him be.'

Ilan swung around to face him. 'Why are we not finished with this?' he demanded, waving his arms. 'Leave him here! Let him find his own way across!'

Taking advantage of the distraction, Kubul quickly stepped out of the canoe and returned to his seat up on the bank, sniffling and wiping sand from his eyes.

Vratu watched him with a pang of sorrow. He walked up to him and kneeled.

'Did you hear that?' he whispered. 'It is pain in my ears, but at

312

least he talks to me. See how far we have brought you? It ends over there,' he pointed to the village, 'one way or another. And still your tongue stays silent.'

Kubul sniffed weakly, a haunted look in his eyes.

'Who are you?' Vratu asked softly.

Not a sound came from the boy's mouth now. Vratu sighed and walked down to the river's edge. He picked up a paddle and swung the nose of the canoe toward the far side.

'Take him into the forest and wait where I can find you.' He pushed the canoe out to knee depth. He knew what his friend was thinking, could feel his disappointment.

'I recall a promise,' Ilan reminded him.

So did Vratu. He wasn't game to turn around and look him in the eye. He hopped into the canoe and headed for the southern shore for the second time in his life.

In the middle of the river he was able to think clearly. Considering everything, he should have known he could never abandon the boy in the manner he had originally promised. So too should have Ilan. But the closer he got to the village, try as he did to deny it, he knew there was something just as powerful at work here, if not more so. Without meaning to he was already imagining their reunion.

In the village was Abinyor.

Strange that now, embarking on the final leg of a mission with such dire consequences should he get it wrong, what he thought about most was a woman. How she would greet him, what she might look like. The detail of her face was only a blur, but the queasy sensation that stirred his stomach was more than enough to remind him of the power she once had, and still held, over him.

A vacant village loomed ahead. No one was in sight except a small boy gawking at him from the riverbank. Vratu held his paddle out of the water and let the canoe drift until it nudged bottom.

'*Buno*, little boy,' he said as he splashed ashore. 'Where is everyone?'

The boy turned and sprinted up the bank. Vratu followed at a leisurely pace. Everything was quiet. Apart from cattle in the enclosures and a few pigs nosing about, the grounds were bare.

Memories came back to him and he was surprised at the nostalgic pang that followed. Here was the path that led to Hrad-Uik's house, there was the barn he had broken into that bitter winter night. In the shade of a tree in the middle of the village several dogs stretched out lazily. Could that be . . ?

'Vek?'

The dog sat up, pricked up her ears and rotated her head. She took to her feet and lifted her nose in enquiry.

'*Come to me.*'

Something must have registered in her primitive memory. Her jaws parted and her tongue lolled as she strolled closer. She reached him and he kneeled and grabbed her muzzle in his usual way, giving it a friendly shake.

'Attacked any thieves lately, you brute?' By the time he stood again she was pawing at his legs, tongue dribbling.

No one was in sight. A door opened and an old woman with a vaguely familiar face came out. 'Da vindlik?' she asked suspiciously.

'Hrad-Uik?' he answered. 'You must bring Hrad-Uik.'

'Hrad-Uik?'

'Yes.'

Slowly, like clouds parting, the confusion scattered in her eyes. 'Salu kujno!' she cried, clicking her fingers. 'Ah, se vindikos!' She looked down at her feet, smacking her forehead repeatedly with an open palm. Vratu waited patiently. Suddenly her head shot up and her jaw dropped, revealing a mouth missing most of its teeth.

'Vratu! Vratu! Hesi . . . hesi!' she cried, beckoning excitedly for him to follow.

They walked past the longhouses, the fields came into view and Vratu had his question to the boy answered.

The fields were alive with activity. The height of the crop amazed him. Where bare fields had stretched last winter, a mass of golden stalks now stood. Arched backs bobbed up and down, flint-bladed sickles lifted and fell to the rhythm of steady swishing. Boys carried sheaves over to the barns where girls stood beating the stalks.

People began to notice him, lifting their heads one after another like a herd of deer catching his scent. The old woman shambled over to a man hacking into the crop with a long sickle and said something that included mention of Vratu's name. The man straightened and turned around.

'Vratu!' he shouted.

Everyone stopped working. Faces dripping with sweat turned his way and a few people actually smiled at him. He scanned the fields looking for Abinyor but saw instead Nankyi hurrying toward him, babbling happily. Before he knew it several familiar faces were following her. Hrad-Uik's kinfolk he assumed, keen to berate him for leaving so disrespectfully last time.

The small group stopped a pace or two away and Nuridj came forward with a huge smile and gave Vratu a friendly slap on the shoulder. One by one the reapers in the fields bowed their backs and went back to work.

'Hrad-Uik?' Vratu asked.

'Ah!' Nankyi replied, and handed her sickle to a boy beside.

Vratu followed Nankyi and Hrad-Uik's three sons into their house and found the headman asleep in his room. In less than a year he had aged fast. The sockets of his eyes were sunken and baggy folds showed beneath, his skin had a deathly hue and his temples looked like a mace had caved them in.

Nankyi bent over her husband and whispered into his ear. He opened his eyes and a smile spread his lips, colour returned to his cheeks and he struggled to sit up. Borchek laid a hand on his shoulder and had it brushed away.

'Vratu!' the old man cried.

Vratu couldn't understand it. If anyone had taken offence over his quiet departure the last time he was here, no one showed it.

After a short spurt of gibberish Hrad-Uik raised himself with difficulty from the bed, ignoring the protests of Borchek and Nankyi, and ordered Vratu in no uncertain terms to follow him into the main room where they sat down at the long, friendly table. A mug of ale was thrust under his nose and food appeared in volume. The family of

315

Hrad-Uik were keen to attend to any direction he gave, suggesting his burst of vigour would not last long.

But Vratu, conscious that Ilan and Kubul were waiting, would have preferred none of it. At a pause in their foreign babble he held up his hand to draw their attention.

'I have seen a mark,' he said, dipping a forefinger into his drink. He traced a wet spiral pattern on the table and looked up to read their expressions. Their faces went blank. He tapped the mark on the table with his finger, then traced the same outline on his neck. 'Here.'

The sickness on Hrad-Uik's face reared away and a sobering frown shadowed his eyes. 'Usonoli peik, vi hok?' he asked eagerly, drawing a confused look from the native. 'Uputt na?' Hrad-Uik pointed to his neck. 'Where you see?'

This was as much as Vratu wanted to reveal at this point. They knew the mark. Now he needed to know what it meant.

'Where you see?' Hrad-Uik repeated, raising his voice excitedly. 'On boy?'

'Where is Kulej?'

'Kulej?'

'Yes.'

Borchek said something, his father answered sharply and they all started arguing. Hrad-Uik and his sons waved their arms and pointed fingers, voices rose and everyone tried to talk over each other. When Nankyi joined in, Vratu stood. With nothing else to go on he resorted to intuition, which told him to leave.

This silenced them all. Hrad-Uik put a hand on Vratu's shoulder. 'Stay,' he said, rocking slightly. He put a hand on the table for support and Borchek and Nankyi pushed him down onto the seat. The talk was quieter now. Nankyi kept her hand firmly pressed on her husband's shoulder, forbidding him to move or get excited.

'Kulej come,' Hrad-Uik gasped. 'You stay.'

Vratu shook his head in the negative. Through sign language he learned that Kulej could be there in two days, and a compromise was reached that they all meet again then, in the afternoon.

Further attempts by Hrad-Uik to get Vratu to stay were thwarted

316

by Nankyi, eager to get her sick husband back to bed. With a show of reluctance the old man gave up. Assisted by Borchek on one side and Nankyi on the other, he stood heavily and laid a hand on Vratu's shoulder.

'Vratu . . . Vratu,' he crooned. There was grip in the tired man's fingers and the eyes that met his were soft and affectionate. 'Is good, you here.' He patted him on the shoulder and turned to go.

'Abinyor,' Vratu said. 'Where is Abinyor?'

Hrad-Uik froze. The air became charged with static and Vratu felt another presence there now, something forbidden and unspoken. Without waiting for an answer, he turned and departed.

Vek followed him down to the river. He reached his canoe and kneeled to stroke the dog's head. 'What is happening here, you dumb brute?'

'Vratu!'

Turning quickly, he saw Borchek striding down the bank and tensed a little, still undecided as to whether the brother of Abinyor was friend or foe. Borchek came up and looked over Vratu's humble canoe. His mouth broke into a grin, then he shook it away and his face restored its proper seriousness.

'Abinyor,' he said, pointing northeast.

'Abinyor?' Vratu pointed in the same direction. 'Over there?'

Borchek nodded, then pointed more easterly. 'Kulej.'

Vratu watched him go, perplexed at his motive. Was it to let him know that Abinyor was out of his reach? Or was her brother just being courteous?

He thought the former more likely.

'Has he gone?' Hrad-Uik asked Borchek when he returned.

'Yes,' Borchek replied. 'Where do you think he saw that mark?'

'We shall know soon enough.' Hrad-Uik raised himself up on his bed. 'Listen to me. Send Yanukz to Kulej. Now. Today.'

'I can go.'

'No, I want you to head in another direction. It is time we saw Abinyor again.'

317

'You're too ill to travel.'

'Nor do I intend to. Go to the village of Attuaal and tell him I want to see my daughter.'

'The harvest is on. She will be needed there.'

'Tell Attuaal I am very sick.'

'You're not dying just yet,' Borchek reminded him sternly.

'No?' Hrad-Uik feigned surprise. 'That might not be a good idea anyway. They would all want to come back with you, just to make sure.' He grinned at the thought. 'Tell him the truth then, but do not tell him everything. A friend of the family has come to see us and won't be here long. I would be in his debt.'

'You want Abinyor to come all the way here for that?'

'I want to see my daughter whenever I can. Now I have another excuse.'

'Segros will ask questions.'

'Tell him nothing.'

'He may want to come too.'

'Not if I send you,' Hrad-Uik said with a wink. 'Anyway it is the harvest and he has his cousins to play host to.'

Borchek's face deepened a shade as he understood. For a moment he looked ready to speak, then thought better. As he left he said over his shoulder, 'This might not be a good idea.'

Hrad-Uik settled back into his bed, comfortable with his decision. It was pointless trying to explain certain things to young people, he thought. Well did he recognise the justness of his son's warning. But when a man had spent his entire life planning, his entire life worrying about the consequences of his decisions, he had earned the right to throw caution to the wind once in a while.

Vratu had asked for her. And so she would come.

Thirty-two

With no hope of reaching Kulej before nightfall, Yanukz diverted to a friendly village for the night.

In accordance with custom, the son of Hrad-Uik was treated as a guest. They gave him a splendid dinner, and for his part, also in accordance with custom, he did his best to be polite and truthful when answering their questions. Because he was amongst friends he had no reason to doubt their motive. Thus he let it pass that a native they had cared for the previous winter had returned with some extraordinary news. He had seen the mark of Usonoli. More interestingly, he might have seen it on a boy's neck. That was as far as he had ventured.

His hosts took immediate interest. Who was this native, where had he come from? But their guest, in all honesty, had little more to tell. With utmost respect, they suggested he was tired. Perhaps it would be more practical, and expedient, to send a fresh runner to Kulej. Though young and inexperienced, the son of Hrad-Uik had his father's skill of diplomacy. They would understand that the message had been entrusted to him.

By then it was going on dark. The men returned to their homes and relayed, as a matter of interest, the news to their families. Before long it was the talk of the whole village.

Another guest was present in the village that evening. On overhearing the news, he quickly lost interest in the woman he was courting, bade his hosts a speedy farewell, and set off on the hazardous night trail back to his village.

There was a lot of arguing in his father's longhouse after he returned, most of it over where their loyalties lay. The lamps had almost burned dry when it was decided they lay in a different direction to where the son of Hrad-Uik was headed.

By the time Yanukz set off the following morning another runner

319

was well on his way. His body was sleek, built for endurance, and he was the best long-distance runner in his village. He would bypass all villages along his route, and if he stopped it would be only to drink and eat and lay down to sleep. By dawn he would be on his way again. He would reach his destination the following morning and a fresh runner would continue in his stead.

The runner knew he had to make the most of his head start. Even now, as attested by his own haste, word was spreading like ripples from a stone cast into a pond. And as he ran he wondered what to make of the name that had raised so many questions the night before. No one could offer insight as to who he was, who his people were, and what his interest may have been. All they had was a single name.

Vratu.

* * *

For three days she stayed in Avnatt's house, barely leaving her bed. Spirited voices drifting in from outside reminded her of a life she used to live, a happiness that was hers not a year before.

It was not something physical that kept her there. What she had done, or at least willed to success, festered in her mind like a raw wound, and she had spiralled into the dark world of depression.

As she lay curled in bed she did a lot of thinking. Despite all that had happened to her, she no longer feared her husband. Something had broken inside her, leaving her with a whole new perspective. A man could not be both a monster and an adored clansman. They had turned each other into something neither wished to be.

But this newfound way of thinking did little to solve her problems. Her marriage was far too important to terminate, should she pursue the option, and the counselling against it would be insufferable. Nor did she put much faith in a resolution coming from her adopted family. Segros was, after all, one of them.

A bowl of untouched medicine sat next to her bed. The only thing she thought might help her now was distraction. She was playing with the idea of getting up to test her resolve on the threshing floors when

Segros walked in. It was his first appearance in three days. As if on cue the cramps returned to her stomach.

'How is your sickness?' he enquired.

'My stomach feels awful.'

'Shall I let you rest?'

'Yes.'

'You brother Borchek is here. He calls for you.'

'Here?' A burst of strength lifted her into a sitting position. 'Let me see him.'

'So you don't want to rest?'

This, she thought, was so childish. 'Please . . .'

'Later.' He dragged a stool forward and sat down. 'I want to talk with you.'

Three days ago such behaviour would have caused her alarm. But sitting there now, he looked like a beaten man. No, she thought with satisfaction, a turning point had been reached.

'What makes you angry, Oronuk girl?'

'I am not angry.'

'Do you hate me?'

'Those are ugly words.'

'I spoke to Szanaj last night. She is a good woman, yes?'

'Yes,' Abinyor agreed, wondering where he was leading. His manner was very strange.

'I knew this native girl, many years ago,' he said. 'There was fighting somewhere . . . her family perished. They brought her here to live with us, as they did with Szanaj when she was a child. A few days after this girl came here she ran away, but she returned soon after with many dark bruises on her. Szanaj tried to talk to her and learned only that she had gone back to her tribe, but the women there turned on her with fists and sticks. After she came back she never spoke to anyone. She had no friends. She was angry, too angry for a girl not yet a woman. One day this girl lay down on her bed and refused to get up. She took no food, spoke no words. Her eyes closed and within days she left the world of the living. This girl, so young.'

Fearing a show of interest might prolong the conversation,

Abinyor said nothing.

'I will always remember the look in the girl's eyes,' he said. 'It is the same I see in you.'

Abinyor watched him quietly, curious at this unexpected hint of a soul.

'Szanaj tells me you were carrying,' he murmured.

She felt her stomach tighten. 'Yes.' For a fraction of a moment she saw his eyes soften. Then his shoulders sagged and he lowered his head.

'I cannot remember what my son looked like. What my wife looked like.'

Abinyor felt a softening of her contempt. He had never spoken of his dead wife and son before.

'I remember other things,' he said, balling his hand into a fist. 'The way my son used to grip my finger in his tiny hand . . . I think he would have been very strong.'

A smile fluttered on his face and vanished, and he spoke with a dreamy quality to his voice. 'When the curse came he was the first to die. We buried him and my wife cried for days. The first child a mother loses is always the worst. She could still smell him in our bed, even after I took the furs away and burned them. Then she got sick. When she found her peace I picked her up and took her into the forest. She was light as a child and her arms swayed when the wind blew. She lies next to her son; a patch of primrose grows there now. One day I will show you where it is. This is where I want to lie when my time comes.'

He looked up and spoke in a voice surprisingly free of malice. 'Do you know why *I* am angry, Oronuk girl?'

Abinyor gestured in the negative with a cautious shake of her head.

'I am angry because a curse fell upon my people, yet passed over yours. I am angry that there is medicine amongst your people that is not shared with us. I am angry because the gods chose to take the two things dearest to me and left me behind. But most of all I am angry because I am weak. I am weak because I cannot let the memory

322

of them die as easily as they did.'

His voice weakened then, and a watery veneer shone in his eyes. 'I look for someone to blame, and I see your people. This is how it is with me.'

'Why did you choose me for a wife?' she asked. 'Why not Szanaj-kik? It is clear to everyone that the two of you are suited for each other.'

'So I thought,' he replied. 'But they said it was not proper, that it would be disrespectful to my brother. They also warned me it is hard for her to bear children. I know better now.' He sighed heavily. 'Had we married you would not be here. You see Abinyor, we both have a purpose to serve. But neither of us can give what the other wants – what was taken from us. In this, we are the same. We were happy with our past.'

Abinyor was moved enough to talk further on the matter, and she might have done so if she had been less eager to see her brother.

'You said Borchek is here.'

For a few moments he stared at her, as if offended at her failing to appreciate the effort he had made. 'A friend of your family has stopped by your village,' he answered, dropping his chin back to his chest. 'Your father calls for you.'

It struck her then that this effusion of sentiment might not be as much a sign of contrition as something else. Did he fear the wrath of her family, or was she starting to reach his softer side?

'Who?'

'Someone not from these parts, your brother tells me,' he said. 'A man named Vratu.'

Her breath caught in her throat and she could feel each heartbeat thumping on her ribcage, gaining intensity. Segros withdrew from his thoughts and looked up, and she quickly dropped a mask of composure over her face. Only by the flush left on her cheeks and the glistening of her pupils might he have detected the emotion charging through her veins.

'I would like to go,' she said, trying to keep her voice from shaking. 'He is a good friend.'

'Who is he?'

She shrugged and looked away. Sheer instinct told her something highly irregular was happening in her father's village and her mind raced with possibilities. But Segros had picked up on something; he watched her like a viper and she didn't trust her voice.

'He is a friend of the family,' she said innocently. 'I could be there and back in three or four days.'

He stood from the stool and shook his head, as if to clear away the weakness that had overcome him. 'It is the harvest and we need you here.'

'My father is ill,' she appealed in a voice that needed no acting. 'The days I have left with him are precious to me. Every time I see him I fear it will be the last.'

A hint of sadness showed on his face. 'Yes,' he said, turning his back. 'Go to your father then. Go and learn what those words really mean.'

As soon as he left she flung the covers back and dressed. The cramps in her stomach were gone.

Thirty-three

Tired after their long journey, they stopped outside the village.

The shorter of the two men, painted with insignia on his arms and chest, took a deep breath. Men with better intentions than his chose to avoid this place. The quiet, homely appearance of the village was deceptive. It was hard to believe that behind these unspectacular walls the ruin of entire villages had been planned, the lives of so many people ended long before they knew it.

'Remember what I told you,' he warned his silent companion. 'Talk only when spoken to.'

They walked ahead. A crumpled village dog sniffed alongside. After a few obligatory greetings they were pointed toward a shed. Through the open door they could see the unmistakable frame of the man they sought, digging hoe in one hand and rummaging around on the workbench with the other. Beside him was a boy.

The boy saw them and tapped the man on the shoulder. The man looked up and his sharp eyes glinted briefly, then he turned his attention back to the workbench.

The visitors approached the doorway and stopped. The painted man said feebly, 'Romoyr, we need to talk.'

Romoyr picked up a small wooden wedge and examined it. He inserted it between the head of the hoe and the stock, picked up a stone hammer and pounded the wedge into the gap. 'What is there to talk about?'

The painted man stepped inside and moved past the boy. 'Friend, listen to me,' he said, placing a hand on each of Romoyr's shoulders. The headman stopped hammering and glanced at him irritably.

The painted man gave him a gentle shake. 'Your boy lives.'

For a fleeting moment the stiffness left Romoyr's shoulders, but he recovered quickly. 'I have heard this before,' he answered flatly, sourness reappearing on his face. 'Alive . . . hiding . . . dead. All words and nothing else. Why do you come to me with this?'

'Is there harm in such a message?'

'When hope has died in me enough times already, I'd be a fool to suffer it again.' He looked beyond the door. *'Who is that man with you?'*

'He is of the Brothers.'

Romoyr gave the hoe to the boy. *'This will stop it from wobbling,'* he told him. *'Take some bindings and strap the head tight. Go.'*

They waited until the boy left. Romoyr said, *'I am listening.'*

'You heard that your boy was in hiding to the west,' the painted man said.

'I heard. There is nothing there any more, I saw what remained.'

'This man knows more. Most of his words are like ours, he will tell you himself.'

'Why bring him to me when you could have brought the news yourself?' Romoyr asked suspiciously. *'I know who you are; your words are amongst the few I trust.'*

Now came the part the painted man dreaded. His pitch was slightly nervous as he spoke. *'You are known in many places, even to this man. He has sacrificed much to be here so quickly, and humbly requests you reward the information he can give you with the grace for which you are renowned. He comes to you knowing there are others who would reward him well for the same.'*

The sides of Romoyr's mouth tightened in disdain. *'He said this to you?'*

'Yes.'

'What does he want?'

'Perhaps some ingots . . . and a few gourds of brew.'

The headman stepped out of the shed and stood before the native. *'What is your name?'*

He stood tall and proud, spear in hand, face like stone. *'Udnu.'*

'Tell me what you know.'

'With your favour, friend.'

'I see,' Romoyr said, eyeing him with distaste. *'If what you say proves true, you will have what you ask. If it does not, you will feel how sharp I make my spearheads.'*

The native's face went pale and the mask disintegrated, his chest expanded as he sucked air deep into his lungs. 'I have heard your name many times headman,' he said. 'I see I have incurred your anger. The news I bring was entrusted to me by our Brothers, and I come on their behalf. I ask nothing more. If my service causes you disrespect I ask that you seek them instead.'

Romoyr bowed his head and spoke in a low voice. 'Some time ago I heard my boy was alive. I went west with my men and found nothing but ashes and bones. I came home and let it be. Now you bring me word that my boy lives. I will do what any father must do. I will go and fetch my weapons. I will tell the boy's mother and fill her heart with the same miserable hope I am given. I will take some men and go where you tell me, not knowing if every step I take is in vain.'

He lifted his head and returned Udnu's stony stare. 'It is too late, my friend. My interest is now your interest. Your offer stands, as does mine.'

Udnu's fingers tightened on his spear. Romoyr's glare never wavered and his voice relayed all the anger he had endured for months.

'Now tell me what you have heard.'

* * *

A light drizzle made the far side appear murky. Halfway across the river he could see many men hurrying down the bank. He stopped paddling and the canoe swung its nose downstream.

A man waved and shouted, 'Vratu, Vratu!' It looked like Kulej. They stopped at the water's edge and Vratu recognised Varsi and Ivnisi. He resumed paddling.

No one spoke as the canoe bottomed out and he stepped onto the bank. Kulej came forward with a reassuring grin.

'Vratu!' he said, putting a friendly hand on his shoulder. 'It is good you are here. You recover good, yes?'

No sooner was the question asked than Vratu was surrounded. His lungs tightened in the heavy air as Kulej prodded his elbow.

'Come, we talk.'

'Where is Hrad-Uik?'

Kulej's face became solemn. 'I take you, but he is not good. Come.' His friendly insistence made Vratu feel he had no alternative.

At the entrance to Hrad-Uik's house Vratu stopped to look behind. Men closed in around him and he sensed that if he tried to take a step backward they would block him. About ten of them followed him inside. As they took their places around the main table he walked on by to look through the walkway into the sleeping section.

'You see Hrad-Uik later,' Kulej promised. 'Now he rests.'

Vratu sat down. Filled with grim-faced men, the room felt different to the one he had supped in so quietly and uneventfully the winter past. There were no mugs or bowls of food. It was hard to hide his jitters.

'You ask for me?' Kulej asked.

'Who are all these men?'

'Friends.'

It all came back to him – the day he had sat at this same table and been questioned. What he had felt then was nothing compared to now. 'Why are they here?'

'To hear you speak.'

'Their faces are not known to me.'

'Faces here you do know – Ivnisi, Szujkuk, Yanhos.' Kulej pointed them out. 'You trust them, you trust other men.'

But Vratu didn't trust them. Nor had he asked for them. He trusted Hrad-Uik and his family, none of whom were present. 'How many will hear my words?'

'I have brought Nruvag.' Kulej pointed to a man seated at the front of the table. Vratu recognised a native element, and felt at once a sense of trust. 'And there is Horgeszba.' Kulej pointed to another man seated beside whose face bore a look that suggested life was a daily grind of unpleasantness.

The silence dragged on. Vratu had to remind himself there was no going back. He leaned forward, put a finger on the table and traced the spiral outline. 'I have seen this mark.'

'Where?' Kulej asked.

'This you must know.'

'*Yuh*, mark of boy.' Horgeszba cut in abruptly. 'You tell where he is.'

Vratu turned to Kulej. 'Why does this man speak?'

Kulej switched languages and spoke to the man in an admonishing tone. Horgeszba raised his hands. 'Why trust him?' he asked. 'Why?'

It was all too much. Vratu stood to leave. Several men around the table rose to their feet immediately and he tightened his posture, prepared to fight his way out if necessary.

A calm voice interceded: 'Vratu, look at me.'

Vratu turned his head. Nruvag watched him with a relaxed look, arms folded across his chest.

'Speak to me Vratu, just you and me,' he said. 'Hear me first, and if you wish to leave when I am finished you can do so and no one will stop you. Sit down for now and we will talk. Do not look at these men.'

Vratu looked them over anyway. They reminded him of the wolves he had fought at Crumbling Rock.

'You have seen this mark on the neck of a boy, yes?' Nruvag asked. 'This is what you seek, yes? The truth? You will not find it by walking away.'

Vratu glowered shakily at the silent faces around the table, then sat down. After pausing briefly to remind him who was in charge, the men that were standing resumed their seats.

'Now we talk properly,' Nruvag continued. 'This is what I am here to do. What do you know about this mark and the boy who bears it?' He spoke with very little accent and his dialogue was clear.

'Nothing.'

'Do you know of the Clan of Usonoli?'

'No.'

'Then I will tell you what I can. I am Ubren, and I am amongst all that remains of those who lived here from the beginning. We hunted side by side with men like you long before these people came; now we are scattered. My people live in two worlds – the one we knew, and the one that has been made for us. In my father's time I would not be sitting here. I might be hiding in the forest, I might be sitting with my ancestors already. But I am here today and the Oronuk are my friends. I will tell you how this came to be.

'But first I must talk of a darkness that quietens men's voices and is not polite to talk of. I will talk of it now only briefly and then I will talk of it no more. What needs to be said concerns some men that lived here long ago, men whose names are lost. We do not know the entire truth of what happened back then, only what has grown from it. It is said these men became tired of the blood and tears. They found men amongst their enemies who shared the heaviness in their hearts, and though they came from different worlds they found ways to listen to each other. In time they invited each other to feasts and dancing. They became friends. As the years passed they sent their sons to live with each other for a time, to learn their ways and tongue when their minds were fresh and not yet poisoned by the talk of evil men.'

He leaned forward and clasped his hands together. 'This is the Tradition. It started long ago and keeps the peace, makes men brothers. Two tribes send their sons to live with each other. Many of us have kept the Tradition alive – me, Kulej, Horgeszba and others. This is how we speak each other's words.'

Vratu looked at Kulej. The Henghai sat in a relaxed manner, arms clasped behind his head.

Nruvag rubbed his temple. 'A man passed recently; a man of my people. His name was Haden Usonoli and each harvest he sent his favourite grandson to live with friends of an Oronuk headman named Vahichiwa. About a year ago there was a quarrel between the two tribes. Usonoli sent the boy's father Romoyr to make peace, but something went wrong. Only those men who were there know the truth, and no two men tell the same story. There was a fight and some Oronuk perished. The brothers of those slain have wounds that open too easily, and they are friend to no one but clan. They knew

330

Romoyr would never come within reach of their weapons, so they went instead to take revenge on his son and destroy the peace they never wanted. We sent a man to keep him from their knives but he took to his task too well. They vanished like two leaves blowing in the forest.

'Romoyr fears his boy is dead. Alas, that men sitting here are responsible. Now that Haden Usonoli is gone there is no one to keep the peace. Romoyr has turned his anger into dead cattle, burned villages . . . fear. Then word came that his boy may have been in hiding in a village far to the west, but this hope was crushed when we found it burned to the ground. The darkness of old is the flight of an arrow away. The only thing that has stopped the bloodshed is a small rumour so many of us have dared to hope is true. And so Vratu, if you have listened well, you will know why all these men have come.'

Vratu had listened in deep thought. He felt as if he stood at the edge of some dark and unfamiliar territory. Warring factions and the taking of hostages were nothing new to him, and this sounded comparable. But something in their story had set off an alertness in him as strong as if he'd heard a bear growl in the dark, something his ancient instincts warned him was a camouflage of false affability and friendliness.

'What has this to do with the mark I have seen?' he asked.

'The Clan of Usonoli mark their sons as you have drawn,' Nruvag said, touching his neck. 'Here.'

'What is the boy's name?'

'Konli of Usonoli.'

'The boy I know does not bear that name.'

Nruvag's shoulders came forward and his voice was charged. 'You have seen him?'

'I have seen a boy.'

'Where?'

'The name you spoke is not known to me.'

Kulej and Horgeszba leaned forward as well, and a deathly silence hung over the table.

'Vratu, listen to me,' Nruvag said earnestly. 'His name would have

331

been hidden along with him. The man he fled with would have given him another and told him not to speak in his own tongue. This boy would be very scared, very quiet.'

Something is missing Vratu thought. He rubbed his forehead, trying to see through the shadows of their story.

'I will make this easier for you,' Nruvag interrupted his thoughts. 'A boy bearing this mark was seen northwest of Heavy-Fish, in the lands of your people.'

Vratu thought quickly. 'You spoke of a village where this boy was in hiding,' he said. 'Who were they?'

Kulej answered, 'The family of Nurekt Gurajnik.'

The name refreshed Vratu's memory as if spoken by the dead man himself. He lowered his head guiltily, unable to meet anyone's eyes.

Kulej reared back and spoke in awe. 'This man you knew.'

When Vratu looked up he no longer saw a friendly face. It had turned as suspicious as everyone else's.

'He knows more,' Horgeszba muttered. 'See how he hides it in silence.'

Someone asked a question, Nruvag answered and everyone started talking at once. They pointed fingers and lifted their backsides off the chairs, arguing loudly.

Vratu looked for a way out. The door was closed. He looked through the walkway into the sleeping quarters, wishing the old man, or any of his family for that matter, were present. He could feel a dangerous presence in the room now, and it was growing stronger. He bowed his head and spoke barely above a murmur.

'The boy is alive.'

The arguing continued unabated. He looked up and saw no one paying him any attention. No one but Kulej. The Henghai alone had caught something and was watching him with fierce interest.

'Aye, bistuk, bistuk!' he shouted, waving his arms in a frantic bid for attention. 'Bistuk!' One by one the men's voices broke off and they settled down. 'Speak Vratu.'

Every set of eyes in the room was aimed at Vratu like the tips of

332

arrows. He held onto those of Kulej and repeated himself. 'The boy is alive.'

Kulej expelled his breath loudly. 'Se vu nuen!'

'Se Konli vistu buchos?' someone asked.

'Eyg, Konli buchos,' Kulej answered.

There was an ominous quiet. Men leaned back with calculating looks. One of them tried to speak: 'Estyan su –'

'Where is he, Vratu?' Kulej cut him off.

Vratu glanced at the door. All that stopped him from walking through it was the certainty that they would stop him if he tried. 'I fear for his life should I tell you.'

'Why do you fear?'

'He is hunted.'

'True, he is hunted. We will protect him.'

'It seems not.'

Nruvag raised himself in his seat. 'The life of one of my men speaks otherwise,' he protested sharply.

Vratu swept his eyes over each of them. 'I have heard your words,' he said, 'but I see many strangers here, and I know nothing of what his enemies look like.'

'True,' Kulej agreed. 'Many men look, friend and foe, as we speak. Some will come and speak lies. Spill my blood if they sit here.'

'Why is the boy's father not here?'

Kulej looked away in an evasive manner. 'He comes already, we think,' he said darkly. 'What do you fear Vratu? Not trust us?'

'The trust is not mine to give. It must come from the boy, and be more than what he has given me.'

'Ah! So,' Horgeszba cut in quickly. '*You* have him.'

Vratu realised his slip. So be it.

'Vratu, Vratu,' Horgeszba's voice was deceptively soft. 'We praise you. You have our respect. Your part over, now we do ours. You tell where he is.'

No, Vratu thought. *This man I do not trust*. 'I know what must be done now,' he announced. 'We will wait. I will return the boy to his father, when he comes. When he stands before me, when I can see him for what he is.'

Nruvag and Horgeszba glared at him. Vratu chose to look Horgeszba in the eye; the man he trusted least. 'As you should have done from the beginning,' he added. Nruvag grunted and sat back shaking his head.

Horgeszba said, 'How we know you have him? Is boy Konli of Usonoli? Boy someone else, Romoyr break your head. Break all our heads.'

Vratu pulled the necklace from his belt pouch and tossed it to him. Horgeszba snatched it out of the air and examined it closely. Everyone leaned forward and not a single face showed surprise.

'Vratu, listen well,' Nruvag said diplomatically. 'Spare the suffering. Every day that passes bears agony to everyone. Others will be here soon, men we do not trust. They will hunt you down and you do not want to cross their path. You have never met such men.'

'I know such men.'

Nruvag translated for the others, but his words weren't well received. Any remnant of diplomacy poised on the brink of disintegration. As one their faces went cold and sceptical, opinions were expressed and then the meeting turned volatile.

Voices rose as each man tried to get his words in. They lost their temper when they weren't listened to and slapped their hands on the table, trying to speak over each other. Kulej did most of the talking and Vratu suspected a lot of it was in his defence.

At a lull in their heated discussion Horgeszba turned to Vratu. 'Some of us are not in agreement with you,' he said coldly.

All at once, Vratu was tired of it. For too long he had behaved like a squirrel, ready to sprint up a tree. He was tired of playing the meek, tired of others taking advantage of his youth and inexperience. Was he not a hunter? Was he not a man? Did a man cower when words turned strong against him? He had emerged from situations far more dangerous than this. And with these thoughts came the same surge of courage that had inspired him to stand his ground when a bull aurochs had charged.

Abruptly he stood. 'Speak clearly so there is no

misunderstanding,' he said, groping for the knife in his scabbard.

'No Vratu,' Kulej cut in, holding up his palms to ease the tension. 'We trust you. Yes Horgeszba?'

Horgeszba eyed Vratu and said nothing.

'I have nothing more to say,' Vratu said, turning to leave. Then he remembered the necklace and made the appropriate gesture to Horgeszba.

'You talk about trust, my friend,' Horgeszba said, tossing the necklace back. Vratu caught it without taking his eyes off him. 'How we trust you?'

'You are all clever men,' Vratu answered as he tucked the necklace into his belt pouch. 'You will see the truth.'

'But I am not clever. How he come to be with you?'

Hoping for some sort of intervention Vratu looked to Kulej, but the Henghai regarded him with the same keen interest. 'I found him in the forest,' Vratu answered curtly.

'More.'

Vratu did not answer.

'And you not know who he is?' Horgeszba asked sceptically.

There was another empty silence, then Horgeszba went on. 'This man Gurajnik . . . harmless man. Now he and his family join with the dead. Your kind thieves, killers – '

Kulej interrupted, 'No. This man – '

'Wait.' Horgeszba waved his hand dismissively. 'I want to believe he speaks truth, but he knows more. See it with eyes like this,' he said to Vratu, tapping an eyebrow. 'You come from people who make much blood, break hearts of our women and children. You say you find boy in forest. Not know who, but keep safe anyway. Now you bring him here. Why?'

Vratu lowered his gaze. 'We have nowhere else to go.'

In the hush that followed he turned and headed out, holding his breath and braced for an attack from behind. He would have liked to see Hrad-Uik but didn't want to push his luck.

He had almost reached the riverbank when he heard his name called, and knew it was Kulej without looking. More than ever now he looked forward to the quiet of the far side. There was his plain dugout sitting on shore, an anomaly beside the finely shaped and ornamented watercraft lined up neatly beside. He looked down the river a way and saw a canoe with three people heading toward them.

The Henghai approached bearing a look of pain. 'Here, Vratu,' he said in a strained voice. 'That was close. No matter now. Come and talk, just you and me.'

'I saw wolves in there.'

'Do you see a wolf now?'

Vratu turned on his heel and spoke with his back to him. 'Why do they not like my plan?' No answer came. He turned around and saw Kulej staring at him, a look of blatant disappointment, if not hurt, on his face.

'Boy's father Romoyr,' Kulej said in a beaten voice. 'Not a friendly man.' For a moment he seemed on the verge of saying something, but let it go.

'How many days?'

Kulej shrugged. 'Two, three days if they run fast.' Then his voice turned serious. 'Understand Vratu, bad men come too. Word fly like birds. I gather good men and we take him from you.'

Vratu waved his hand airily, taking in the village. 'You are here.' Then he pointed to the hills on the other side of the river. 'And I am there. Where is someone more a ghost?'

'You found him.'

Vratu's answer was solemn. 'I was meant to find him.'

Kulej rubbed his chin and regarded him thoughtfully. 'How will you know when they get here?'

'I will know.'

'Ye Vratu, you a mystery,' Kulej said with a weighty sigh. 'You need food?'

'No.' Vratu looked down the river. The canoe was getting closer.

'Boy is in good hands, yes?'

'Yes.'

'You stay then,' Kulej invited, but Vratu was only half-listening. His eyes flicked between Kulej and the canoe. It looked like Hrad-Uik's son Nuridj sitting in the front, and yes, that had to be Borchek in the rear. The occupant in the middle wore a hood to keep the drizzle off his or her head.

'I am not welcome in there,' Vratu said.

'Ach, they leave soon. You want to see Hrad-Uik, yes?'

'Yes.'

'Good! Come.'

Vratu gestured toward Hrad-Uik's house. 'What are they doing back there?'

'Argue, talk loud I think.'

'I want no more words with them.'

'That is wise.'

The canoe was close now. Vratu felt his heart flutter when he realised who was probably sitting in the middle. Without seeing her face he knew it had to be her, if for no other reason than the eels slithering around in his belly making the connection.

'Borchek comes,' he said.

Kulej turned and faced the river. 'Ah!' He walked down the bank waving his arms. '*Yehu!*' he cried, and the occupants in the canoe waved back.

Now that Kulej looked the other way Vratu felt safe to study her freely. She watched him with equal interest. As she came closer he thought he saw her lips part and mouth a silent word: '*Vratu.*'

The canoe bumped ashore and the boys got out. Nuridj smiled at him. '*Yehu*, Vratu,' he said, slapping his shoulder as he walked past to grab the prow of the canoe. Borchek mumbled a greeting and Abinyor smiled and said nothing. All at once Vratu felt indescribably more at ease now they were here.

Abinyor flicked the hood off her head and shook her tangle of hair free. Vratu watched as one under a spell. Almost a year on and her features had ripened to improve upon what needed no improving. They were all talking but he heard nothing until his name sounded above the nonsense.

'Uh?' he flinched.

'What do you do Vratu?' Kulej asked. 'Stay or go?'

Thirty-four

By the time they returned to the house Nankyi had shooed the newcomers away. They went straight to Hrad-Uik's room and found him awake. His arms opened wide when he saw his daughter. Tears of happiness flooded his eyes and he struggled to get up while everyone struggled to keep him down. Abinyor fell into his arms and the room filled with excited talk.

The switch from a heavy interrogation into this warm and friendly atmosphere left Vratu slightly dazed. The old man saw him standing at the back and stretched a wobbly arm out toward him.

'Vratu . . . Vratu,' he croaked.

The fuss died, leaving Vratu feeling awkward. Nevertheless he moved forward and took the outstretched hand, and was surprised by the strength in its squeeze. Hrad-Uik mumbled something and Kulej translated for him. 'Stay and eat.' Then Hrad-Uik dropped his hand and said something else. Kulej said, 'Now he asks about you.'

Vratu said, 'It is good to be here.'

'Shouting wake him before, he want to come out but Nankyi stop him. No matter now – you stay. You want to offend, say no.'

Vratu felt a sudden, overwhelming guilt. In his usual narrow-minded way he had forgotten what this family had done for him. These were not suspicious strangers making demands or prying into his past. These people had washed him, forced food down his throat in order to keep him alive, nursed him back to health and accepted his ungracious departure without a word, asking nothing in return save to join them in a meal.

He bowed his head shamefacedly. 'I will stay.'

The bull-calf looked no more than a year and a half old, with two stubby growths rising from the hump of his brows. The muscle tone in itself separated him from domesticated stock. His shoulders hunched forward, every muscle bunched and restrained, immured like the spirit within. His forelegs scuffed and stomped beneath proud bulk, while eyeballs as shiny and black as his hide blazed behind strings of overgrown hair. Vratu could feel the rage behind those eyes; rage vented through nostrils that pumped like a beating heart.

He waited for the beast to relax before taking a handful of feed from a trough in the adjacent pen and throwing his leg over the fence.

'Uh, Vratu! Not feed him.'

Vratu turned to see Kulej walking over with a grin. 'Why do they take the forest from our friend?' he asked.

'Sharp eyes you have,' Kulej said as he came alongside. 'Caught in pitfall not long ago.'

'He is not happy.'

'No,' Kulej agreed as he leaned on the fence. 'Bad temper. Some people like him. Not good for breeding though, spirit too strong. But good for a feast, when someone brave enough to try.'

The bull-calf kept pawing the ground, bobbing his head up and down and snorting.

'Who caught him?' Vratu asked.

'Boys of Hrad-Uik. Pen belongs to them,' Kulej explained. 'Each family has their own cattle, pigs, grain. I will show you.'

As much as he was beginning to like the man, Vratu cared for his company as much as the lesson on village dynamics that followed. What he truly wanted was to spend time with Abinyor, preferably alone, and by loitering around outside he had hoped she might notice.

A light drizzle floated down. Pigs snuffled about, the last of the workers returned from the fields carrying baskets and tools, girls bundled up the sheaves and older women tidied up around the threshing floors. By the time they completed a circuit of the village dusk had settled. Vratu caught sight of Abinyor by one of the sheds talking to some girls. As Kulej started back for Hrad-Uik's longhouse Vratu said, 'You go. I will come inside later.'

He returned to the pen of the immature bull and leaned on the fence. *Yes!* Out of the corner of his eye he saw her break from her group and head over. She stopped beside him and rested her elbows on the fence.

'Pretty yes?' she said, raising her chin at the bull-calf. 'Like you.'

Vratu straightened and let the surprise show on his face. 'What did you say?'

'This is Mo-ah.' A perfect smile lifted her lips.

So startled was he that it took a moment to sink in. 'You speak my words.'

'I learn, but only little.' Her voice was pleasantly accented.

'How?'

'In village I live now.'

'That is good.' He nodded his satisfaction, then managed to utter one of the greatest understatements of his life in a normal voice. 'This pleases me.'

They were quiet for a while. Mo-ah flicked his tail and licked his nose. 'Where do you live now?' Vratu asked.

'Not here.'

'Why?'

Her smile flattened out. 'They marry me.'

Once the shock of hearing those words had passed, he realised how foolish he had been. What did he expect? That she'd run into his arms and continue from where they had left? Still, his manly pride forbade a show of disappointment.

'How long you stay?' she asked. 'You stay night?'

'Where?'

'With us, in house.'

'Do you know why I am here?'

'A boy, yes?'

'Yes.'

'I hear.'

'I am not liked by the men here.'

'Ach!' she exclaimed. 'They no matter.'

'How did you learn to speak my words?'

'Abinyor!' a woman shouted.

They both turned. Nankyi stood at the door waving.

'I go now,' Abinyor said. 'More work for a woman.'

He watched her leave with mixed feelings. She had cheered him with the same intensity as she had grieved him. The bull-calf paced the enclosure unhappily. There were those with worse problems, he thought.

Rain started coming down heavily. People hastened inside, it was getting dark now anyway. Kulej called from the doorway of the house.

'Vratu! Come inside, eat.'

Vratu walked over. 'Where are the men that were here earlier?'

'Go home, those who live close,' Kulej said. 'Some come from far away and wait for Clan of Usonoli. Not for you to worry. I speak to them, they leave you alone.'

Dinner consisted of sloppy gruel and vegetables, unleavened bread, tea, and a dripping dessert of berries preserved in honey.

The prattle bored him. Every so often Kulej translated. No mention was made of the boy or the issues at hand, or Abinyor's matrimony, which made him wonder where her new husband was and why she was here on her own. There were many questions he needed answered and he knew he couldn't ask any without raising eyebrows. Nor did he converse with her directly. They traded subliminal glances, she smiled at him discreetly, and he wondered who else was wise to what was going on between them.

The rain fell solidly as they ate. Vratu glanced up at the roof, expecting it to leak. Not a drop fell into the room.

'You stay here tonight,' Kulej told him.

'Where?'

'Spare bed in house of Ivnisi.'

Vratu looked down to hide his disappointment. He had expected the offer of a bed in this house, preferably the same one as before, one with walls and privacy in case Abinyor decided to . . .

With their bellies swollen to capacity Kulej and Vratu bade their hosts goodnight and made a dash through the rain for Ivnisi's house. Vratu was shown a bed opposite Kulej. This is not what he wanted. The house was wrong, his bed was wrong. Nothing here felt right. It occurred to him then that they were intentionally keeping Abinyor and him apart. An irritable mood, aggravated by earth-shaking snoring, made it impossible to sleep, and he grew crankier and crankier as he tossed beneath his blankets. Sleep might have been easier had she not kept looking at him the way she did.

Thunder struck, and he smiled in the dark. The heavens sympathised, speaking his mind for all to hear.

The wind picked up and whistled through a gap in a window-fitting. Wearing only his loincloth he rose from bed and removed the offending fitting. Through the window came the fresh scent of rain and solid splatter.

Lightning flashed and the village pulsed briefly. Raindrop tracks formed long slivers of shining silver, through which he could see Hrad-Uik's house enclosed in a wraithlike, misty spray.

The sky rumbled as he crept through the house now, past jittery pigs in the stables and into the downpour outside. His skin shrivelled from the cold, but it was the sort of cold that made him feel more alive. Splinters of rain bit into his shoulders and his hair hung heavy on his head from an instant soaking.

A wall of water surrounded him. Another lightning flashed. Thunder boomed, vibrating the air and jarring the earth beneath his feet as they squelched in the cool mud toward Hrad-Uik's house. He hopped over the dark narrow pit running parallel to the wall and slipped slightly when he landed on the inner strip. He skimmed his fingers along the wall until he reached a point where he thought Abinyor's bed might be on the other side.

There, not more than a body length away, she must be sleeping. He pushed against the wall and slapped it a few times. All that stood between them was a wall of twisted hazel and clay.

He grunted dejectedly and hopped back over the pit. But as he headed back a sudden volition made him pivot on the balls of his feet, and he found himself facing the house again.

342

'Come out Oronuk girl, and we will dance in the rain,' he whispered.

In the heart of the tempest he paced back and forth like a caged beast, scowling at the house as the rain sluiced down his shoulders. Surely, by willpower alone, his thoughts would reach through the wall and draw her outside.

Another lightning bolt crackled around him. The sky grumbled, softer this time, and he stopped and laughed loudly. This needed better thought. The wall between them was the least of his obstacles.

Raising both fists he began dancing around in circles, head thrown back and eyes closed, mouth catching the pouring rain. Lightning flashed and he hooted with laughter when he saw the cattle in the pens watching him.

Having exorcised his demons, he returned to his bed dripping wet and fell asleep with a ridiculous grin perched on his lips.

In the morning he woke early, dressed quickly and went outside. The village grounds were empty. Grey clouds hung low and fat, promising more rain. He went inside a barn where he'd seen fishing gear previously and found a small basket containing a stack of bone fishhooks. He picked several to his liking and tested the fishing line with a sample of his strength. Then he went back outside and sat down beneath the roof of the Banquet-shed to wait.

Children emerged to snatch a bit of play. Older girls and boys followed soon after, leading livestock, heading for barns and sheds and swinging doors open. Slowly the village came to life. Abinyor emerged from the house and joined him.

'*Yehu*,' she greeted him with a comely smile.

'*Buno*,' Vratu replied. 'Do you work in the fields today?'

'Yes.'

'I am going to fish by the pond where you and I sat once,' he said. 'Do you know where I mean?' This was most important.

'Yes.'

'Perhaps I will be there all morning.'

He walked away. From what he knew they always took a work

break at some point in the morning. The rapids where he had sat with Abinyor were close. Now it was up to her. By the end of the day he would have it sorted, one way or another.

The floor of the stream rose to beds of gravel, smooth as eggs. Fishing line in one hand and bow in the other, Vratu hopped nimbly from boulder to boulder and reached the quiet pool without a drop of water on his shoes. There he peered fondly into the mysterious depths, likening its translucent pull to the eyes of the woman he waited on.

The fishing line was made up of sections of twisted vegetable fibres wound over a short wooden stock. He attached a bone hook and turned over a few rocks. Satisfied with unearthing a fat worm, he skewered it with the hook and flung it into the middle of the pool.

'Now, we shall see.'

Fishing like this never appealed to him. He preferred the power given to him by the use of a weapon, to select his prey rather than the other way around. That way they had no choice. He tugged on the fishing line and looked around. *Fishing for a woman,* he mused.

The woods accepted him. Small wrens fluttered close by, a hedgehog sniffed at the rocks he had overturned and a fox stole down to the water's edge. Periodically he checked his limp bait and cast it back into the waterhole. He had hoped she might get away after breakfast before going to work in the fields, but the time for that possibility came and went. As the morning wore on he considered jogging back to the village, but he knew she would be working and there was nothing he could do about that.

By midday he felt petulant. Perhaps things would never change for him, he thought. Men ridiculed him, women didn't want him, fish ignored him. To keep his mind from such thoughts he collected more worms, changed the bait, tried a few different fishing spots and threw rocks at bugs crawling on trees.

The newcomers sitting around the main table showed no interest in the food and ale on offer. The largest of them, red-haired and heavy-shouldered, twirled his beard in his fingertips as he aimed his speckled eyes at Kulej.

'You had him in your hands,' he said disbelievingly, 'and you let him go.'

Kulej lifted his mug to his lips and said nothing.

'There is more than one boy with his neck in the jaws of savages, you know that,' the red-haired man reminded him gravely.

'I know that.'

'And you sit here while this man is . . . where?'

'What would you have us do?'

'You should have men out there now, with dogs sniffing at every drop of sweat.'

Another man said in a more conciliatory tone, 'You should have followed him, at least.'

'You think you know these people?' Kulej scoffed. 'Nothing follows them but their shadows.'

The red-haired man asked, 'Where is Romoyr?'

'He would have word by now,' Kulej answered indifferently. 'Which means he is two or three days away, at most. There is no stopping him.'

'This native . . .' the red-haired man said. 'He waits for Romoyr, yes?' He leaned forward and poked his breast with his thumb. '*I* am Romoyr.' Then he pointed to a companion. '*He* is Romoyr. Any one of us could be Romoyr. When your friend comes next, you tell him the boy's father is here.'

Kulej barked a short laugh. 'I was right. You *don't* know these people.'

'We *need* to try something else,' the red-haired man grumbled.

'Yes,' Kulej agreed. 'Trust perhaps. Trust in this native, trust in the gods. Trust in Romoyr. It is out of our hands now anyway.'

'The corpses in our graves speak for those who have trusted Romoyr before,' another man said ruefully. 'And the native – what makes you believe he is different to any other Ubren savage?'

'Vratu is no more savage than he is Ubren.'

'People are moving everywhere,' the red-haired man resumed.

'Men are coming who none of us know, let alone trust. I say we look for him.'

Kulej looked him in the eye. 'And I say again, we will wait.'

'Our greatest losses have come about from waiting.'

'Then go home,' Kulej answered bluntly. 'There is nothing for you here. There is nothing for anyone here. It will all be resolved without the need for anyone else to come.'

'Oh, you will find it is too late for that,' the red-haired man assured him.

They went back to their canoes, crossed the river and set up camp in an elevated position that gave them a good view of the surrounding country, and waited.

The red-haired man was right.

They were the first of many that would come.

The forest announced her presence. Birds cried, twigs cracked and bushes rustled at her passing. The unmistakeable approach of a woman, Vratu thought wryly. He left his fishing line where it was and hid behind a tree. It might be anyone coming and he didn't want people to know he was there.

She came into sight wearing a short, practical tunic for fieldwork. As he approached her from behind she swung around and jumped backwards in fright.

'*Yuh!*' she gasped. 'You scare me!'

They stood face to face. 'I am happy you came,' he said. 'I have been sitting here waiting for you, waiting with the fish.'

'Heavy storm bad. Not good for. . .' Failing to find the right words, she tried to mime them instead.

'Never mind.' He laid a gentle hand on her shoulder.

Her face coloured, she dipped her head and brushed away a few bits of chaff that clung to her tunic. Vratu watched with amusement, then turned to face the waterhole.

'Do I listen to the words of men, or to what speaks so strong inside me? To what speaks to all of this.' He lifted his arms to take everything in, then turned around. 'What talk do you listen to?'

She looked him over with a quizzical frown. 'I not understand,' she said in her curiously attractive accent.

'It is the same for me.'

She reached out and touched his face. Her fingers felt like feathers and he wanted her to keep them there. 'I not understand your talk.' She withdrew her hand and looked up at the treetops. 'This is a beautiful place,' she said perfectly.

He touched her chin and steered her face back to his. She looked at him shyly and tried to speak but the words came out so stuttered and meaningless he had no idea if she was using his language or hers. He brushed a strand of hair from her cheeks and she closed her eyes and inclined her velvety face onto his palm. Her body urged closer, her lips parted and her breathing became slow and laboured.

Surrounded by the verdure of ancient forest, with only a few inquisitive squirrels watching, Vratu surrendered to fate and did what nature insisted, heedless of the consequences and fed up with caring. Below him Abinyor writhed and thrust, while elsewhere furry ears twitched and slanted to cries of liberation she seemed to want the world to hear.

They lay for a long time after. She felt warm and soft beneath him. No sound found his ears except the whispered approval of trees and the gush of running water. The sun broke through a break in the clouds to tickle his naked back, and he decided that nothing was better than this, and he would stay like that forever.

The sound of light tapping brought him back. He turned his head lazily and saw the wooden stock of his neglected fishing line dancing over the rocks, the line unravelling at an astonishing rate. Groaning loudly, he untangled himself from Abinyor to tend to the inconvenience.

They stopped outside the village and he let the catfish drop to the ground. 'What am I to do with you?' he asked, more to himself.

Abinyor embraced him tightly. 'You come back tonight?' she invited, smiling promiscuously.

'I have to go back to my friend.'

Her face went glum. 'Tomorrow then, yes?'

He looked into her eyes and felt an impossible weakness. 'What will you tell your people?'

'Not for you to worry.'

Vratu thought about this. Now his craving had been satisfied he expected his senses to recompose and leave him feeling guilty or worried. Nothing came close. On the contrary, he had never felt this fulfilled.

'Tomorrow,' he said. 'I will come again, to the pool. At midday, the same as now. Will you be there?'

'I try.'

'No, no try. You have my word; I need yours.'

She thought for a moment. 'I see you, yes.'

Vratu picked up the string tied through the fish's gills; it was heavy and bit into his fingers. Abinyor watched him with the same half-smile on her face and hypnotic pull of her eyes. Vratu left quickly.

Only after he had crossed back over the river and hidden the canoe in the rushes did the gravity of what he was doing occur to him.

The last two days had thrown his mind into turmoil. There was much to the People-of-the-Longhomes that was disconcerting. Their politics were too sinister, too driven by ulterior motives for his liking. It was hard to know whom to trust. To be part of it required skills he did not have, did not care to have. He would happily keep his distance. Abinyor though was another matter.

This he had not allowed for. Soon he would return to his people and sadness would fill in his heart, but something more sinister crouched in this vision of certainty, like a phantom cackling in the background. Having lost one woman and finding something better in another, he feared being worse off than before.

And what punishment would they give her if they found out? Or him? She could be excused as acting on impulse, he should have known better. Sneaking about like was also disrespectful, to her people and family. Yet nothing could dissuade him now. It simply felt right, felt good, and the forces at work here were without his scruples.

So deep was he in these thoughts that he walked straight into their camp.

At least seven men sat around a fire at the far end of a clearing. He tightened his grip on his bow and stopped. Camp gear and bivouacs were set up around. By their dress and dogs – at least five of them sniffing about – he knew they were not of his kind.

A man saw him and drew the attention of his companions with a foreign grunt and a hand signal thrown in Vratu's direction. Silence fell and the dogs hunched a little, as if awaiting a command.

A red-haired man stood up and wiped his hands on his leggings. He walked forward holding his hands out palm first in a universal gesture of friendliness.

'Kos ni yastyun, neh?' He stopped after a few steps, the need for a reply plain on his face.

Vratu was not inclined to give it. He retreated the way he had come, briskly yet calmly, sighting behind him every other step to keep as many trees as possible between him and those watching.

As soon as they were out of sight he broke into a run.

They had set up temporary camp not far from the river in a rocky cleft concealed by overhanging trees, picking the place on this merit alone, but the smoke that helped guide Vratu there now defeated that purpose. Annoyed with this wanton breach of common sense, he strode into camp scowling. Ilan was sitting on a log looking bored and Kubul was fiddling with arrowheads nearby.

'I told you to keep the fire from smoking,' Vratu growled. He flung the catfish to one side, took a bladder hanging from a small sapling and emptied it over the fire, which exploded in a cloud of hissing ash and smoke.

'Ah! Vratu returns!' Ilan retorted. 'Shall we cook for you before you leave us again?'

Vratu saw the look on his friend's face and decided to let it rest. He tied the bladder closed and hung it back in place.

'I waited for you yesterday,' Ilan said. 'What was I to think? What was I to do – look for you? Do I go to the village and say, "Have you seen my friend?" Dragging this boy with me? Where did you leave your mind?'

Vratu ignored him and headed over to Kubul, who watched him come with his typically glum face.

'Why did you not come back last night?' Ilan continued angrily behind him.

'The storm, remember?' Vratu answered airily.

'When have a few raindrops stopped you doing anything?'

Vratu stopped in front of the boy and looked down. 'I think I know who you might be now, Ubren boy,' he said. 'Do you hear me, *Konli of Usonoli?*'

Something flickered deep in the child's eyes. The small lips moved weakly and words seemed only a small effort away.

Ilan approached from behind. 'What did you say?'

'His name, if it is what it is. One of many things he needs returned.'

If Kubul had been about to say something, the moment was lost. Vratu took the necklace out of his belt pouch and kneeled.

'What is that?' Ilan moved closer, eyes wide with awe. Vratu slipped the necklace over the boy's head. Kubul gave not the slightest reaction, didn't as much as glance at what was put around his neck.

'Where did that come from?' Ilan persisted.

Vratu checked around them. Nothing came to his eyes or ears to suggest men were out there, at least for the time being. 'Are you finished? Shall I tell you about it?'

'Have I better things to do?'

'Come over here then,' Vratu said. 'If I am wrong about this, I would rather not raise his hopes.'

Vratu took Ilan to a spot out of earshot of the youngster and gave him a condensed version of what he had learned and what had been arranged. Ilan waited until he had finished before asking the vital question.

'How long must we wait?'

'Two, three days,' Vratu said. 'If they move like fat cows – more.'

They returned to the fire and Vratu gave the boy's head an affectionate rub. He stooped and checked the contents of his backpack, watching Ilan from the corner of his eye.

'I will go back tomorrow, to see if I can learn more,' Vratu said. 'Do not whine like a child again if I am gone overnight.' Ilan said nothing and Vratu seized the opportunity to distract him from protest. 'We need to leave. Gather everything and I will take you to the cavern where I stayed last winter. We need to be there before nightfall.'

'I like it here,' Ilan replied like a stubborn child.

'There are men this side of the river.'

Ilan scoffed. 'Do you never have anything good to tell me?'

Vratu didn't answer as he tied his blanket tight.

'Listen to me,' Ilan appealed in a subdued voice. 'This is not good for us. Why must we wait here, jumping like startled rabbits every time we hear noise? Your boy does not like me. He wanders away and I am weary of following him. His tongue may be quiet but he knows how to throw a tantrum. We should take him over the river and leave him.'

'I would but for something that troubles me.' Vratu stopped what he was doing and took Ilan to the side again. 'These men I spoke to,' he said, barely above a whisper. 'They claim to have the boy's interests at heart. Why then was he not taken back to his father when the trouble began? Why was he taken far from home and left with strangers? Why is it left for me to do what should have been done from the beginning?'

'You have two ears, and neither is listening,' Ilan replied with a grin. '*Two tribes send their sons to live with each other . . .* you said. Do you not see? There must be another boy like him somewhere,' he pointed to Kubul, 'one of their own, in hiding, waiting to go home. They need your boy for the trade. It is all they have to stop the spears.'

It took a while to sink in, and when it did all Vratu could do was stand there blinking stupidly. He felt like a fool. The interest of the men waiting back at Hrad-Uik's village, he knew now, was more a bargaining one than the boy's welfare. If things didn't go their way, what would they do to him? He trusted them all a little less now, even Kulej. He sighed and rubbed his forehead, disappointed as much by this new development as something he had long suspected: his best friend was a nudge sharper than he.

'But see how strong is the curse he carries,' Ilan continued gravely. 'See how it destroys everyone who tries to protect him. Let them have it. Give him to them and you and I will go home and prepare for winter. If we hurry we might be back in time for the Arrival Feasts.'

Vratu could barely make out a coil of the Great River through the trees. He faced it and put his hands on his hips. Without meaning to, Ilan had convinced him even more of the need to wait. Everyone had a motive behind their reasoning, including his best friend. Only one man would have told him, would have *begged* him, not to listen. And that was the man they all waited for.

'I am sworn to protect him, as you said,' Vratu agreed, 'and we have been through too much to throw it away by giving him to the wrong men just because they speak clever words and we want to be home for Arrival Feasts.'

Ilan frowned at him. 'I think you don't know what to do.'

Vratu looked him in the eye. 'I know the need of a boy for his father,' he said. 'We will wait.'

Thirty-five

The next day they met as arranged. But as soon as she came into his arms the grin he greeted her with fell from his face. Something was happening to him, something wild and untested, and though it felt warm and good, it left him with a dangerous disregard for the men stampeding through the forests of the east toward them.

At Abinyor's suggestion they left the pools and went to a part of the forest completely spared from human hands. Blocking out the light with their golden crowns were gigantic oaks and lime and ash, with ivies and lianas bulging from their limbs and trunks like varicose veins. The forest-mulch smelled fresh and clean, and there was music in the rustle of the breeze.

The sun punctured the formless spread of cloud and fell through the canopy in welcome beams. They swam naked in a stream, splashing about like children, and whenever they embraced Vratu held onto her as long as he could, helpless in her body heat. Afterwards they lay like lizards on the sun-warmed rocks, soaking up the heat and talking. One of his first questions was if she was happy.

'No,' she answered bluntly, and went on to tell him everything. Vratu couldn't understand it. In his world beauty came with privilege; she should have been married to a man of her choosing, not sent to some distant place to face an unwanted future.

There was much to her story. Common tragedy had ensured most of her siblings were returned to earth, others had been waved goodbye and never seen again. Only when she spoke of her real mother was her straightforward recital of facts tinged with pride. She brightened immediately when she moved onto Szanaj-kik and Tivikeh and the friends she had made, and when her father became the subject he detected the strong bond between the two.

'He likes you,' she said.

Vratu felt flattered. 'I like him too. But I don't think your brother likes me much.'

'Which?'

'Borchek.'

'Ach! You see.'

She asked him about his people, and he told her where they roamed and how they lived and all about the tradition of the Walk that brought them together almost a year before. At this she smiled and stood. Vratu watched her walk over to her shoulder-bag and reach inside. She pulled out a small object and concealed it in her hand as she returned.

She sat down and opened her palm. Vratu saw the aurochs figurine he had made for her.

'Thank you,' she said, her eyes shining with affection. But then she saw the puzzled look he always gave when her words made no sense. 'Thank . . . *you*?' she repeated.

Vratu stared at her, confused. As with apologies, sentiments like gratitude were never expressed in words. In his culture it was just as rewarding to give as to receive. Why was an exchange of words necessary?

'Why do you look at me so?' she asked.

As best as he could, he tried to articulate his perspective but saw on her face the same scolding look a mother might have given an unruly child. She followed this with a laborious lesson on how it was proper to thank people, in words, for good deeds. That it cost nothing, that it was expected and that it defined goodwill. Even the Ubren she lived with, far from being the most culturally advanced of folk, had adopted this common courtesy.

For the first time Vratu grew bored with her voice. To him it was all women's words. Nevertheless, he was wise enough to sit through her explanation patiently. When she realised her words were completely lost on him she stood abruptly. They stared at each other long and hard, and he read in her face the same gloomy signs that had dashed his hopes with Nura.

She must have seen something also. A spark lit her eyes but it was too weak to have flared from anything but a sad heart. She shook her head dejectedly and turned away.

Two things reminded Vratu of his foolishness. One was that Abinyor and he were from opposite ends of the earth. The other was what Nura had already shown him. Clearly he lacked something women wanted. He wasn't ready, after all.

'Tell me of the boy,' Abinyor suggested, still facing the other way. When Vratu didn't answer she turned around and he saw the return of genuine interest in her eyes.

And so he opened up to her, and she earned his deeper respect by having the sense not to prise into issues that, by the scant attention he gave them, he felt uncomfortable with. Like how the boy came to be alone in the forest in the first place. What had motivated Vratu to bring him here at all.

She let him know that the boy's father was probably well on his way, but the subject was a damp one, bringing the present back to mind.

'When do you have to go back?' He had consciously avoided asking the question but had his own return to the Hills of Uryak to consider, and he needed to leave soon if he wanted to be back by dark. If she were to spend the afternoon with him though, he would sleep cold under the stars and consider it fair trade.

'When I want,' she replied firmly.

'What did you tell them?'

'I did not. I just leave.' She stood to gather her clothes and Vratu watched with an infatuation bordering on obsession. She saw him watching and her cheeks dimpled with a smile. She lifted the tunic up over her head and let it drop. 'Can you help me with nut and berry?' she asked as her head popped out the top.

'They will want to know why you were gone so long, gathering your nuts and berries.'

'Ach, I tell them I get lost,' she answered with a giggle. 'Not first time.'

Vratu laughed. Now that autumn was here an abundance of trees sagged with hazelnuts, rowanberries, haws and rosehips, and they filled her bag quickly. Their walk back was delayed by her continually pulling him back and clutching him all over, and in stops and starts they arrived at the outskirts of the village much later than intended.

By the time they disentangled from their farewell embrace they had agreed to meet up that night.

And so, long after everyone had fallen asleep, Abinyor crept from the house and met up with Vratu in the dark. They lit a fire beneath an overhang and lay down on a bearskin she had brought. When their exertions were complete they curled into each other and fell asleep as content as babies in their mother's arms.

They woke at the first shade of light and Vratu saw her back to the village. They made arrangements to meet the following day and he waved her goodbye from the trees.

Abinyor crept through the house, entered the sleeping quarters and froze. Nuridj was sitting upright on his bed with his back against the wall. His eyes were watery and puffed. The beds around him were empty.

'Where have you been?' he asked.

By then she had invented enough excuses for her furtive coming and goings, should she be questioned, but the shock of being discovered, along with the look on her brother's face, prevented the best of them coming to mind.

'I couldn't sleep.'

A trace of scepticism flickered on her brother's face, but faded quickly. Abinyor heard Nankyi sobbing softly from her father's room and felt an icy claw grip the back of her neck.

'What's wrong?' she asked anxiously.

'It's Papa,' he croaked, and his eyes welled over.

She strode quickly into her father's room. Hrad-Uik lay motionless on his bed, staring lifelessly at the ceiling. Borchek and Yanukz stood over him while Nankyi knelt holding a rag against his forehead. Their faces were riven with grief.

Abinyor's legs went weak and she dropped down by his bed. Tears blurred her eyes as she took his hand and saw with relief that he still breathed, if only feebly. His eyes turned her way, wide and scared.

'Oh no,' she choked. '*Papa . . .*'

While she had lain in Vratu's arms earlier that night, something had happened to her father. Nankyi had woken to find him crippled, barely able to move or speak. There was none of the burning heat one associated with fever, no head wound and no clues as to what was wrong with him. Outwardly there was only a slight change in the rhythm of his breathing. Everything else looked the same.

Their shaman Variknud arrived around midday. Borchek showed their only hope to Hrad-Uik's bed where his immediate family stood around in a collective daze, including those of his daughters who had made the urgent dash from their own villages.

Variknud unslung his backpack, took out a leather fold and spread it out on the ground. Onto this he placed the paraphernalia of his trade – a bone tube stoppered at each end, a small hair paintbrush, dried fungi and powdered horn.

'Can he talk?' he asked. He unplugged the bone tube and inserted a thin wooden plunge. Orangey-red paste oozed out.

'He has trouble,' Nankyi answered.

Abinyor leaned forward and put a hand on her father's forehead. His eyes opened and one side of his mouth lifted in a smile, the other stayed flat. He mumbled words she barely understood, and she turned away to hide her tears.

Variknud picked up Hrad-Uik's left arm and let it go. It dropped onto the bed with a soft thump. Nankyi motioned for them to leave. They went into the main room and she walked over to a large pot suspended above the hearth.

'Would anyone like soup?' she asked torpidly. Abinyor didn't answer on her way out.

Work continued in the fields; emmer and spelt did not hold back their seed in a climate of gloom. Even Borchek and Yanukz, seeking distraction, chose to work the harvest. Abinyor lingered close to the longhouse with her sisters, who could no more abandon their hope of a miracle cure than understand the pathology of his condition.

When Variknud came out later with Nuridj, Abinyor asked if her father was in pain.

'He only feels one side. The other is dead,' Variknud answered matter-of-factly. 'He asks for *Huvsoi*.'

A concoction with deadly nightshade as its major ingredient. Taken in carefully measured doses the plant could be a strong sedative, mixed too strongly and it was fatal. Abinyor shuddered, wondering which dose her father preferred.

His work done, Variknud left them. It was out of his hands now. The decision lay with Hrad-Uik's family, everything else with the gods.

The two siblings watched him walk away. Nuridj said, 'We looked for you early this morning.'

Abinyor looked away. She had neither the energy nor the heart to deny anything now, much less for a fight.

'Where were you?' Nuridj pressed.

'Does it matter?'

'If you were where I think, ' Nuridj shrugged, 'to me – no. Nor to father, the state he is in. But I think Borchek suspects something and he would have good reason to be angry. This will fall on his shoulders.'

Tears stung her swollen eyes, yet again. For now all she craved was solitude. She strode away quickly.

'Abinyor!' her brother called.

She didn't stop until she arrived at the pond where she had met Vratu for two days now. She sat on the same log where she had first embraced him, feeling more miserable now than then, needing him more than ever.

The year was turning into the worst of her life. Her pillar of support was on his death bed, the young man who had granted her a taste of what it felt like to be a woman would soon return to his happy world, she would return to her miserable one, and that would be the end of it. The utter despair of it all kept her weeping by the pool all morning.

If the day had been going badly it was only to set the tone for when she returned. As she walked through the house intending to check on her father, she saw seated at the main table as if he were part of the household the only man on earth she despised. Seated next to him, solemn-faced and tired, were her brothers and Kulej.

Nankyi put aside the plate she was cleaning. 'Abinyor,' she said. 'Where have you been? Your man has come. We were worried about you.'

'Yes,' Segros answered in a low voice. 'I have been worried.'

She looked at him coldly. She knew why he was here. Despite giving his permission, and despite her father's condition, in his mind she had probably spent too much time here already. She wanted him to bring it up, to show her family his true nature, but to her added contempt he hid it now, and the look on his face was a wonderful mask of sympathy.

She didn't say a word as she walked on past.

The runner arrived soon after. Thin and sleek he had come from the east, exceptionally fast by the sound of it. A reliable boy, he sank their spirits with his report. Men were converging on them from everywhere, he said, the movement of the hordes capturing more in its wake. Vahichiwa's men would arrive soon, followed closely by the Ubren. At their heels, Romoyr and the Clan of Usonoli.

The hastily convened meeting took the news grimly. It sounded like an unstable mix bearing down on them and many who were coming would meet face-to-face with men they were predisposed to avoid. Thrown into the morass were more than enough trouble-makers to start a battle.

The runner thought that the boy was already with them. This worried them greatly. If this was the understanding relayed throughout the land, what would the Clan of Usonoli's reaction be upon discovering that he wasn't?

By midafternoon an advance party of Vahichiwa's men arrived. They went inside and demanded the Ubren boy be handed over before anything else was negotiated. Kulej had to draw on all his skills to convince them this was not possible. Men slammed fists on tables accusing Hrad-Uik's people of hiding him, shouting veiled threats and warnings.

The meeting broke up. There were rumblings of discontent as they filed out. A cranky looking individual stopped at the doorway.

'There are others on their way, Henghai Kulej, who will be less patient than us,' he said. 'But we will wait and see if your word is good.'

An ominous presence settled over the village like a dark cloud, and the air turned heavy with the discharge of human fear. Workers in the fields stopped early and retired to their houses, and most of the women and every child hurried off to the closest village to sit out the whole affair. Kulej sent runners to neighbouring villages to collect as many trusted men as would come, on the presumption that the safest way to avert hostile inclinations was by a show of superior force.

Then, right on dusk, the first of Usonoli's clan arrived.

Earlier that morning when Vratu returned to camp, Ilan had grumbled the need for some time alone and wandered off. The evening was settling in and he should be back soon.

The humble shelter had grown considerably on Vratu. To be perched like an eagle on the same rocky ridge instilled in him the same sense of peace he'd felt the winter before. Nothing could hurt him here. Everything was as he had left it. It had been waiting for him, he fancied. Twice now the Hills of Uryak had not let him down. By now he felt an almost telepathic communion with the creatures that called it home. They would warn him of danger.

Occasionally the silence was punctuated by the clash of horn and antler, the bellow of stags, the squeal of the hapless. A chill breeze made him turn his eyes longingly northwest toward the Winter Grounds, as if he could feel the same impulse that sent birds overhead toward their distant callings. The coming of winter was in the whisper of the trees, the rustle of the leaves, the gurgle of the streams and the cry of every lung. It took his mind back to the last time he sat here. Not a year had passed and yet it felt much longer.

Behind him, the boy was practicing the art of straightening arrows by pushing a shaft through a bored quartzite pebble. He looked happy enough. The soot on the cavern walls, slightly faded since last winter, had been painted over with his abstract scribbles.

Vratu faced below and caught a glimpse of Ilan through a break in the trees. His relief at his friend's return was short-lived when he observed him moving at a steady pace. Vratu stood quickly and picked up his bow.

'Kubul, come here.' The youngster put his work down obediently and hobbled over.

Vratu kept watching the spot where Ilan last showed. He reappeared through a gap in the trees, still moving at a speed that suggested something was out of order. Vratu stood in full view and waved his arms. Ilan saw him and waved back reassuringly, then disappeared again behind the trees at the foot of the hill. A short time later he arrived at the top, puffing heavily.

'What is it?' Vratu asked.

Ilan took a moment to suck in a few breaths. 'How many canoes were on the riverbank when you left the village this morning?'

'Did you go all the way to the river?'

'I ran.'

Vratu made a face, unimpressed. 'Not many.'

'They cover the riverbank now,' Ilan gasped. 'There was smoke in the forest beside and people moving about like ants.'

Vratu thought about this. 'Did you see anyone this side of the river?'

'No, but I saw canoes going both ways.'

Vratu moved to the ledge and looked out over the forest as it paled in the gathering dark. 'He is coming.'

'Good.' Ilan sounded enthusiastic. 'Let us finish this. We will take the boy there tomorrow, then leave these hills and head for home.'

Vratu turned back around. 'While you were gone dark thoughts came to me,' he said. 'There are strangers coming, as we will be to them. Trust will not be easy to trade and we will be on our own. When this boy speaks he will have much to say.'

'By then we will be gone, as you said,' Ilan reminded. 'We don't go there to feast and make friends. We give him to his father and turn our backs. Run like the wind if we have to.'

'But who is his father? Do we walk into a trap?'

'You wanted it like this,' Ilan huffed. 'There is nothing we can do about that.'

'True,' Vratu said, and pointed to the boy. 'But he can.'

Thirty-six

Not a ripple lapped the shore, not a leaf stirred in the trees, and not a bird showed wing. Above its orange belly, the dawn sky was shading into a healthy blue.

Segros splashed his face, filled his cheeks with water and spat it back into the river. If trouble was imminent, he thought, one might expect the gods to make the signs obvious. More to the purpose, make them early enough to give their faithful subjects time to prepare. But it never seemed to happen that way. Not to him, at least. Perhaps this was because there were no gods. He stood and walked up the bank.

A few men worked in the fields, trying to maintain some semblance of normality. On any other day streams of people would be crossing paths by now, bustling about and chatting. But all the children and most of the women had quietly fled the night before. Only a few women remained to cater for the masses that had come.

A door opened and Segros saw one of Usonoli's clansmen emerge and take in the village grounds from the doorway. His gaze moved past Segros and stopped. His shoulders lifted, his chin came up and a frown appeared on his face.

Segros followed his gaze. At the Banquet-shed a woman was setting jugs of barley water on the tables. A man keeping her company lifted his head and his voice stopped. The smile slid from his face as he glared at Usonoli's clansman unflinchingly.

Segros watched the exchange with amusement. They reminded him of two bison about to butt heads.

Usonoli's clansman stepped from the door. His upper lip curled in a show of contempt as he made his way to the river. The eyes of the man at the Banquet-shed blazed after him.

Let them crush each other's skulls, Segros thought. None of this was his affair. So far Kulej had done well keeping the feuding clans apart, sending them in different directions as soon as they arrived and filling their stomachs straight afterwards. Even those too suspicious for a roof over their heads had agreed to camp on opposite sides of the village and stay out of trouble. Tempers had been soothed with a single promise – the boy was coming. But as a stalling tactic it couldn't last long. It was only a matter of time before a careless remark found the wrong ear, and a fray was only a knife-edge away. The only thing that stopped it happening already was a code of honour that forbade a man from bringing his fight into another man's village.

It made things interesting, but this was not the real reason Segros had come. He had not come to pay his respects to his sick father-in-law. He cared as much for the return of missing boys as he did for the harmony it might bring. But he was interested, very interested, in something else.

Much had he learned these last few days – about Vratu's stay the winter past, the extent to which these people had cared for him, whose roof he had slept under. The rest he had pieced together; stupidity was not amongst his vices.

He very much wanted to meet this man Vratu. And so he too would wait.

It was long before they had planned to meet, not yet midday, and she was there already. There could only one reason for this. And that reason meant he would be heading home with Ilan before the day's end.

For some time Vratu watched her from behind the trees. She was a peaceful thing, sitting with her head down and hands neatly crossed on her lap. Occasionally she looked up and her hopeful face turned each way, then it sank down again.

In a way he'd hoped she wouldn't be there. Better for them both if he turned away now, he knew. He should go on to the village and see this business through to its end. By the time she gave up waiting he would be on his way home with Ilan. She would cry for a while but this was inevitable. It served no purpose prolonging the pain.

But it was only a hunch that the boy's father had arrived. If not, they still had time together; time for swimming in waterholes and lying in each other's arms. In which case going on to the village was pointless. He should check with her first, find out the latest developments.

As soon as he stepped from the trees, the look on her face when she saw him told him his hunch was correct. She sprung to her feet and rushed over.

'Ye Vratu, much happen,' she cried, falling into his arms and clinging onto him like an upset child.

He took a step back and looked into her red-rimmed eyes. 'Is your father well?'

'Much worse. No talk, no move.'

'I will see him,' he promised, worried it might be too late already. He held her close and let guilt punish him.

'All men here,' she said quickly. 'They come for you.'

'The Ubren?'

'Yes, and more. Men we never see. People scared.'

Though he knew this might be their last embrace, the last moments they shared alone, he pushed her back gently and let his hands fall away.

'Listen to me. I have to finish this; I have to see these men. Go back to the village now and I will be there soon.' She tried to pull him back. 'Go now,' he urged, keeping her at arm's length.

Wolf-dogs often tried to creep after a hunting party, desperate to follow, and only a harsh tongue and threatening gesture stopped them. It always disturbed him to see the hurt in their eyes, the incomprehension on their pitifully loyal faces.

The look she gave him was the same.

He approached the village stealthily and stopped at the perimeter. The village was swollen with men, spaced in little groups everywhere. An abundance of canoes along the shore and lanky trails of smoke rising from the surrounding forest suggested many more afoot. Tables covered with bowls and jugs had been set up around the Banqet-shed and several women attended to the men gathered around. He could sense the potency of something about to happen, palpable enough to turn his stomach. Before his nerve could abandon him he stepped into the open.

At first no one noticed him. Then a man carrying a basket saw him and stopped dumb. '*Yehu*, Vratu!' he cried, dropping his basket and spilling leftovers all over the ground. 'Hesi nu, hesi, hesi . . .' he repeated, motioning frantically with his hands to follow.

Head after head now turned his way. Men seated at the Banquet-shed leapt to their feet and before he could take another step he heard his name bouncing away to the furthest corners of the village. Doors swung open and people poured out of houses. Cattle spooked in the stalls, crashing against fencing and bumping into each other. He recognised Horgeszba and Nruvag leading the brisk flow of strangers scattering the pigs in their way. A familiar voice called his name and he turned to see Kulej hurrying over.

'Vratu!' the Henghai repeated as he came up. 'You ask, they come,' he said sombrely. 'All of them.'

Vratu always thought of Kulej as a calm man. To see him flustered like this had him instantly on guard. 'How is Hrad-Uik?'

'Not good.'

He had no hope of getting to Hrad-Uik's house now. It was as if a snare had been sprung, catching him within and sending the whole village into upheaval. A wall of people pushed forward, forming a circle around him and blocking his path. There were the stern, perceptive expressions of what had to be leaders of men, and their fighting brawn standing tall and heavy beside: men with tattooed limbs and scarified chests, knotted biceps and broad shoulders, and not one of them was short of some form of weapon. Ethnic divisions dissolved quickly as they merged closer; everyone shared a common interest now.

He saw Abinyor standing beside her brother, her face flushed with worry. Nearby were several men he recognised as having native blood, though the look on their faces warned him this meant nothing. He averted his eyes and found his voice. 'Is the father of the boy here?'

'Yes,' Kulej answered.

Several grim and unpleasant looking men pushed their way through the crowd. A hulking man with a battered face and bottomless eyes stopped in front of Vratu.

'Does he talk?' he asked, to no one in particular. His voice was hard and deep, the voice of a man made to be heard.

'This is Romoyr of Usonoli,' Kulej said to Vratu. 'Father of the boy.'

Vratu pored over his face, looking for treachery in every contour. This man bore no paternal resemblance to Kubul. But as he looked closer he saw a faint mark on the man's neck similar in design to the boy's. Not that this was conclusive, for all he knew it could have been made the night before.

He returned the Ubren's steady glare. 'Come with me now, just you.'

'You are of the Brothers?' Romoyr asked.

Vratu had listened more to the intonations in the man's voice than the actual words. The trace of an Ubren accent had been undeniable. 'Come,' he said again.

Romoyr took a step forward. Someone put a hand on his shoulder to stop him and angry voices started up again. Romoyr held up his hand and silenced everyone with a loud command. Then he motioned for Vratu to lead.

After taking a few steps, Vratu checked behind and saw more than half the gathering following. 'Enough of this.' He stopped and spoke calmly. 'We go nowhere if we are followed.'

'Vratu,' Nruvag said patiently, 'this man has enemies.'

'The boy has enemies. No one follows us.'

'Where do you take him?'

'We do this as I say,' Vratu ordered, forcing command into his voice. 'Me and him. No one else.'

Still there was dissent. While Romoyr held out his hand to quieten his men, Vratu leaned on the fencing of the cattle enclosures to wait. Not far away stood his friend the bull calf, undecided as to who or what he should be snorting at. Vratu smiled at the thought.

The talk settled down. Romoyr asked him, 'Where do you take me?'

'I have your son.'

The headman's eyes sparkled hopefully and the frown faded. His chest inflated and he spoke deeply. 'I am waiting.'

'As is he,' Vratu replied curtly.

Romoyr's face softened further. He stilled his men with another gruff order and gestured impatiently for Vratu to lead.

As Vratu turned to go a sudden impulse stopped him. The words that followed were not planned. They sprung from another source; even his voice sounded different. And yet they flowed out of him with the smoothness of the air leaving his lungs.

'Before we go,' he said, 'in front of all these men, you must give your word. That when your boy is returned, it all ends. There will be peace.'

Romoyr stiffened. The hardness of the look he gave Vratu suggested that for all else, when honour was called upon, honour would be forthcoming. 'There will be peace,' he promised.

To his side, Kulej drew back. Vratu saw a turn of expression on his face that might have been surprise, might have been deep respect.

'You come too,' Vratu decided on the spur of the moment.

They walked toward the forest looming dark and secretive ahead. The golden canopy closed over them, a gust of wind shook the denuded branches and leaves floated down from above. Squirrels shot up trees and peered down, whiskers twitching. No one spoke. At a fork on the trail Vratu stopped and took out a short strip of leather. He checked behind one last time to see they hadn't been followed and held the strip out to Romoyr.

'Put this over your eyes.'

'Vratu . . .' Kulej began.

'This is the last I ask of him.'

To Vratu's surprise a trusting grin broke from Romoyr's otherwise surly face. He put a hand on Vratu's shoulder and gave it a friendly shake. 'I will play your game,' he said, taking the leather and blindfolding himself.

With that, Vratu's confidence lifted. This had to be the father of Konli of Usonoli. Should Kubul not be the man's son, Vratu had his hand-axe and knife at the ready.

'Wait here,' he instructed Kulej. He took Romoyr's thick arm and led him off the path a few steps. Ahead of them lay a jumble of boulders in the dappled light. Vratu put a hand on the man's shoulder. 'Stop.'

From behind the boulders stepped Ilan, an arrow fitted to his bow. At a nod from Vratu he motioned with his hand toward his hiding spot.

Out came Kubul. His eyes fell on Vratu and the blindfolded man. No one moved.

They all waited. The child looked at Vratu, then at Romoyr. A look of intense mental concentration appeared on the boy's face – a strange, foreign look startled out of hiding. His eyes narrowed, his back stiffened and he took an uncertain step forward, then another. Colour drained from his face, leaving it white with shock.

'Dudduh?'

Romoyr ripped the blindfold away. He stood aghast for a moment, then his voice roared out like thunder. 'Konli! My son!'

'Dudduh!'

They connected midway and the Ubren headman was on his knees, his hulking frame completely engulfing the small boy, and then he was sobbing, mumbling in a voice muffled by his son's shoulder. They crouched beneath the roof of swaying limbs and branches for a long time, while a long flow of words, soft as breeze, escaped the boy's mouth.

Ilan went over to Vratu. 'I am in awe,' he said. 'He *can* speak.'

'He will have much to talk about now,' Vratu said soberly. He couldn't take his eyes off Romoyr; this colossus reduced to tears.

Kulej joined the two young men. 'Your friend?' he asked.

'Ilan, here is Kulej.' Vratu gave a superficial flick of his hand. Ilan nodded out of courtesy, Kulej did the same.

'You and him only?' the Henghai asked sceptically.

'Yes,' Vratu said. Kulej chuckled and shook his head in astonishment. Romoyr began marching off to the village with his son in his arms.

'Come,' Kulej said, and when Vratu made to follow Ilan laid a hand on his shoulder to stop him.

'We need to leave, as you said,' he reminded him quietly.

'There is one more thing I have to do,' Vratu replied. 'It won't take long.'

Close to a hundred men had been waiting at the edge of the village, formed in tight groups and armed to the teeth, trading hostile glances until the emergence of Romoyr with his son in his arms put an end to the strange ceremony.

The Ubren headman lifted his son proudly above his head and shook him fiercely, lovingly, shouting out at the top of his lungs: 'See my son! My shining son! He lives! He will always live!'

As one the crowd burst into a deafening cheer. Within moments father and son were surrounded by a mass of men hailing the boy as if he'd risen from the dead, competing with each other to show their affections in any way possible. Expression showed on the boy's face in a way it hadn't appeared in months.

Barely a head turned toward the two Illawann as they followed Romoyr and Kulej through the crowd. Ilan fell behind, jerking his head in all directions, his fingers firmly fixed on the hand-axe at his belt. Abinyor weaved her way through the throng and Vratu was moved by the look of sweet inquisitiveness on her face.

'This friend?' she asked when she came up.

'Ilan,' Vratu said, 'here is Abinyor.'

With an effort, Ilan diverted his attention. His hand lifted off his weapon, his breathing slowed and a trace of interest showed on his face, but he disguised any approval with a surly grunt.

The swarm slid toward the house of Ivnisi. In the centre Romoyr still carried his son above his head, giving him an occasional shake. Kulej spotted Vratu and walked over.

'Come,' he said cheerfully. 'We celebrate now. Everyone is happy, runners leave for the east to spread the news.' He prodded Vratu's elbow. 'Come.'

Above the line of bobbing heads and spears thrust skywards Vratu saw Konli watching them, a tiny smile brightening his face. The boy's hand lifted and Vratu knew it was a gesture intended for him. As he raised a hand in response he was overcome by a sensation of emptiness. There was nothing left for him to do. He should have felt relieved, yet now he felt an unexpected sadness growing inside him. There was a jostle and Konli was lowered out of sight.

'Vratu?' Kulej prodded him again.

'I will come later,' Vratu answered. 'I want to see Hrad-Uik.'

Kulej nodded and disappeared into the crowd. While men filed into Ivnisi's house, Vratu and Ilan veered away unnoticed to follow Abinyor.

Several men stood outside Hrad-Uik's house. With long faces they watched Vratu and Ilan follow Abinyor inside. The three young adults walked past several teary-eyed women seated around the main table and entered the headman's room.

The old man had deteriorated since his last visit. Skin clung to his frame in shrivelled folds, so thin on his face that the finer curves of his skull showed through. The air smelled of decay. Vratu had seen death in all its guises, could feel its authority whenever it hovered like mist over a dying body, and there was no mistaking its presence there now.

Nankyi, sitting beside her husband, smiled at Vratu sadly. Abinyor leaned down and touched her father's head. 'Papa, Vratu tusi.'

The old man's eyelids flickered open and the corner of a cracked lip lifted. 'Ah . . . Vratu,' he wheezed, straining air into his lungs. His forehead contracted, as if he were having trouble focussing. Something was wrong with his eyes; his pupils were dilated and the colour of his irises had faded. His hand lifted weakly and fell back to bed. Nankyi clutched it quickly and he closed his eyes again.

Vratu kneeled down beside him. He moved a bit closer, put a hand on the old man's shoulder and said to Abinyor, 'I want you to tell him something for me.'

Abinyor nodded.

'Hrad-Uik old man,' Vratu said. *'Thank you* . . . for keeping me amongst the living.'

He looked up at Abinyor. Her eyes watered over as she spoke the matching words.

Hrad-Uik opened his eyes. He let go of Nankyi's hand and motioned for the native to come closer still. When their faces were level Hrad-Uik's parched lips moved feebly and Vratu leaned closer until his ear was a whisker away.

'Abinyor,' the old man rasped.

Vratu drew back. Deep in the dying man's eyes he saw the twinkle of a shared secret.

'What did Papa say?' Abinyor asked.

Vratu stared at her, his mind blank.

'Come,' Ilan elbowed him, 'it is done.'

In a daze, Vratu stood and walked out. Past the women in the main room with their sullen faces, through the stables and out the front door. Past bustling activity without looking. He had almost reached the riverbank when Abinyor called from behind.

'Vratu?'

Then he remembered their canoe was upriver and veered that way, increasing his pace without regard to whether Ilan kept up.

'Vratu?' she called again, louder and more urgent.

Once concealed by the trees he broke into a run, not stopping until he reached the canoe. They pushed it into the river and took up their paddles. He never looked back.

They reached the far side and hugged the shallows. Vratu sat in the front, hacking into the river with the paddle as if it were the enemy.

The timing of his stroke was out, the dugout rocked badly, but his companion kept quiet.

The sun was well into its descent and the fork with Heavy-Fish a long way off when Vratu stopped paddling.

'Why do you stop?' Ilan asked.

'Go to the bank.'

The canoe bumped onto bottom-sand. Vratu disembarked and Ilan dragged it ashore unassisted. Vratu clasped his hands behind his head and faced the river. 'Can you feel it?'

Ilan said nothing. All he could feel was a coming argument.

'I can feel it,' Vratu said, turning around. 'I think you do too. It has followed us this far and it will follow us home. I think our headmen and elders felt it too, long before we left, though no one ever spoke of it. And when we get back it will be worse. It is not a nice feeling to have.'

'Your mind needs medicine.'

'It is *fear*,' Vratu said. 'See what it makes of us.'

Ilan's features froze. 'What are you saying?'

'I cannot leave like this. Not again.'

'But you are being funny, yes?'

'There is more to do over there.'

'No!' Ilan disagreed vehemently. 'We did what you wanted to do. It is all behind us now.'

'Is it? Tell me good friend, for I have thought long on this matter.'

'You gave your word.'

'If we leave like this now, what will they think? All they will know about us, all they will hear will come from a boy with good reason to fear us. Is this what we want?'

'Vratu, by now there are men in that village who *know*.' Ilan slowed his voice, desperate to reason. 'They will be sitting there, talking about ways to avenge their people.' He pointed his finger accusingly. 'You were part of it, remember? All that is missing is who we are and where we can be found. What they cannot get from the boy, they will want to get from you. And you want to go *back* there?'

'To run from them shows we have something to hide.'

'Yes!' Ilan shouted now. '*We do!*'

'Do you want to live like this?' Vratu asked sharply. 'Always in fear, wondering when they will come for us? I am tired; tired of the fear, tired of this hiding. When I get home I want to sleep at night knowing the sounds I hear outside are not men creeping forward in the dark. I want to know the lands I hunt are free of angry men with spears and maces looking for the Illawann. I cannot leave now, not when I know I can stop it.'

'This is talk for another time.'

'When is there a better time?' Vratu cried, throwing his hands up in the air. 'Everyone is there! You saw what is happening!'

'It *is* her, yes?'

'What?'

'How long were you going to keep it from me?'

They glared at each other for a long moment. Vratu had to look away. 'I see. I did not mean to keep it from you – I should have told you sooner. But it is not for Abinyor that I go back.'

'You can fool yourself, do not try to fool me,' Ilan said harshly.

Vratu felt anger getting the better of him. He went over to the canoe and reached inside.

'Leave the girl!' Ilan's voice had the pitch of fright. 'Leave her! You don't belong over there.'

'Are you well?' Vratu asked over his shoulder as he removed Ilan's backpack and dropped it on shore. 'You whine like a child.'

'I whine because I see the sense you cannot. This woman took it from you.'

'Sense is not what this is about. This is about doing what is right.'

Ilan swore and retrieved his backpack. 'I see,' he said, throwing it back into the canoe. 'We will go and tell these men we came to do what is right. They will say that they also must do what is right, and they will laugh as they cut off our arms and legs.'

It only occurred to Vratu then that Ilan intended to go back with him. 'No,' he responded, humbled again by his friend's loyalty. 'Keep a fire going here so I can see you. It will be dark when I return.' He didn't want to hint that he partly agreed with him. There was nothing to gain by risking both their lives.

'They will feed you to the fish.'

'No. Hrad-Uik is my friend.'

'Your friend is staring at his gods.'

Vratu tried to ignore him as he emptied the canoe.

'What have they done to you?' Ilan asked softly. 'I knew a different man to the one I see now. I remember days when he and I woke in the morning and talked about how many fish we would bring home. We sat awake at night and he told me about a girl he was fond of. This man went on his Walk and was gone so long that everyone thought he perished in the snow.' He stared at Vratu without blinking. 'I think they were right. Another man came back in his place.'

'No,' Vratu corrected. 'His eyes were just opened.'

He checked over the contents of the small craft one last time. All that remained inside were his bow and arrows. 'And it is true that I do not belong over there,' he pointed downstream, 'but I am here now because I was pushed. By my own people. And now that I am here, I will be their voice. The voice of the Illawann.' He turned to look Ilan in the eye. 'The Walk goes on, my friend.'

'I see,' Ilan mumbled brokenly. 'Then I must do what I must do. I will wait, but not for you. I will light a fire and pray for the return of the friend I used to know.'

Vratu pushed the canoe into the water. As he stepped inside he turned around and saw Ilan walking away, hunched over. And he almost called out to him then, for the words that teetered on his lips were strong in his heart, and they needed to be said.

But his friend disappeared over the bank before he could say anything.

Thirty-seven

The light was fading when he returned to the village. He hauled his canoe ashore and walked up the bank tasting food in the air. Women set tables and men stood around in small groups holding mugs and talking. No one gave him as much as a second glance. Had they known the consequences of what he had set in motion, or that he was the last of his kind most of them would ever meet, or how often they would hear his name mentioned in the years ahead, they might have paid him more attention.

But they had no way of knowing these things. The men of the east had got what they came for and the villagers were simply grateful they could mourn their friend and get back to the harvest.

He walked unimpeded to Hrad-Uik's house and through to the main room. There the women waited, along with Hrad-Uik's sons and kinsmen sitting around the table sipping ale and drawing comfort from those bound by grief. There were the faces Hrad-Uik had introduced him to on that icy day an aeon ago, and it troubled him now that he'd made so little effort to get to know them.

When Borchek saw him come in he stood and motioned for him to wait. He called his sister's name and a moment later she appeared from the sleeping quarters, her face puffed and her eyes sparkling with tears.

'Is your father still with us?' Vratu asked her.

'He took *Huvsoi*. No more wake up.'

Vratu gave her a confused look, and Abinyor responded with a few mumbles that made him think further questioning was irrelevant. Borchek said something he felt was directed at him.

'Men ask where you go,' she told him.

There was a shuffle behind and Vratu saw Kulej come into the room. 'Vratu!' the Henghai greeted him with relief. 'We wait for you, not know where you go. New men have come, want to talk to you.'

'Who?'

'Big men. Come.'

Resigned to his fate, he followed Kulej and Borchek outside. They entered Ivnisi's longhouse and Kulej led them into the main room. A large group of men were seated at the table. All heads turned, their bodies tensed and Vratu felt himself measured.

Kulej pointed each man out. 'Vratu, here is Henghai Szujud and Henghai Hugba, here is Vurnud, Ordkicz, and Draavi from the Clan of Usonoli . . .'

One by one he went through the introductions. Here and there someone nodded when introduced, but most men returned a guarded look. Vratu acknowledged each in turn until Segros was pointed out, and then his eyes stopped there. His first impression was of a reptilian slant to the man's face, a thin mouth and tapered slits for eyes.

'This man is Kalisij,' Kulej pointed reverently to two men seated at the far end of the table, 'and this is his father, Unatks Vahichiwa.'

The Unatks watched him with shiny eyes. Age had sunk his frame and shrivelled his face, and yet there was an awareness about him that could only have come from a strong heart. Vratu was reminded of Voi and felt instantly drawn to the old man.

Kulej pointed to the head of the table, the only free space. 'Sit.'

'I prefer to stand.'

'Sit,' Kulej repeated sternly. 'Trust me, first time.'

Vratu hitched his leggings and slid onto the bench. Kulej sat down beside him. A wooden flask was passed down the table and a mug thrust under his chin. Kulej poured it full.

Vratu picked up the mug and baulked at the vapour. He forced it to his lips and tasted sour elderberry juice. It was rich and smooth in his mouth, and surprisingly not at all unpleasant. Briefly he wondered who had made it and where it came from.

'Where do you go now?' Kulej asked.

'Back to my people.'

'Uh, your people.' Kulej scratched his cheek. 'I ask again – who are

377

your people?' It was in his speech, heavy with insinuation. The boy
had spoken, all had been revealed.

'I am Illawann,' Vratu declared proudly.

There was a long silence, which Nruvag broke. 'We know of the
Illawann; they lived here once. Do you know what happened to
them?'

'I hear rumours.'

'From men who do not know how to use their eyes. You could be
amongst them, and not know it. You would expect to find them in
their old hunting grounds, or by rivers they once fished, living in the
same homes, wearing the same colours. And when they were
nowhere to be found you would think they had perished, and go
home to tell your people this is so.'

Vratu held the man's glare. 'What do you ask of me?'

Horgeszba interrupted. 'We ask why you stain your weapons with
the blood of our women and children.'

Vratu looked down at his mug, worried his fear was showing
through. 'That is not for me to answer.'

'You are wrong,' Horgeszba said. 'This question you alone can
answer.'

Vratu looked up in time to catch Kulej make a short, dismissive
hand signal clearly intended for Horgeszba. The sting faded from the
angry man's glare and with a show of reluctance he eased back into
his chair.

'Someone is here to see you,' the Henghai said. There were a few
whispers and Romoyr stood and left the room.

Vratu clasped his hands together to stop them from trembling.
The air felt humid, perspiration seeped from his forehead. 'I wish to
pay homage to Hrad-Uik,' he told Kulej.

At the mention of his father's name, Borchek swivelled his head.
Vratu felt as if a bear was hooking into him with its claws.

'Soon,' Kulej said. 'If it is not too late already.'

The door reopened and there stood Romoyr with Konli at his side.
There was a cheerier edge to the boy's face and the glow of youth
was back, but his eyelids drooped slightly and the smile that

appeared on his face stopped well short of broad.

Vratu left his seat and stepped nearer to the only presence in the place he felt truly comfortable with. '*Buno*, little man.'

Konli stood there shyly. They had changed his dress. There were emblems on his shirt and a beaded necklace Vratu had never seen before. The golden amulet was there, shining like sun on his tiny chest.

Romoyr said, 'Bring gift for you.'

At a gentle prompt from his father, Konli held up a bundle folded in leather. Vratu approached and took it from his outstretched hand. What he saw inside made him smile.

'Axe,' Konli croaked.

It was elbow-hafted ash, set with a beautiful obsidian blade. Vratu felt the gloominess in the dank room lift.

The side of Romoyr's mouth lifted, threatening to break into a smile. Konli tugged at his father's arm, pulling him down to whisper into his ear. Romoyr's mouth finally gave in, cracking into a broad grin as he straightened. 'Ask if you come back with us,' he said.

Vratu eyed the boy regretfully. 'I have taken him as far as I can.'

The smile slid from Romoyr's face and he returned to his seat leading his son by the hand. 'I fear an impossible debt,' he mumbled.

'I have a fine axe. We are even.'

'The life of my boy is worth more than an axe.'

The headman pulled his son onto his lap. Vratu held his gleaming eyes, trying to decipher if his last remark was one of insult or jest. This, his instincts had warned, was a dangerous man; a man too easily provoked. A man best avoided.

'Go with them,' Kulej said. 'Go and meet his people, see what has become of yours.'

Vratu raised his chin and spoke in a clear voice. 'You do not understand. I am an Illawann hunter. I came here only to return a boy to his father and give him back the life that was his.'

'And in doing so have achieved more than any of us,' a deep voice answered.

Vratu turned his head and saw Vahichiwa with his mug raised.

'Breon,' the Unatks resumed. 'It comes from Breon, a gift from a man named Abudu. Now it is a gift to you.' He put the mug down and continued in a smooth, lightly accented voice. 'The sweetest you will ever taste, Vratu of the Illawann.'

Vratu felt obliged to return to his seat. They all watched him sit down and pick up his mug. He took another sip, slurping unintentionally in a room made silent by the authority of its head.

'Do you know who I am?' Vahichiwa asked.

'I have heard.'

'Do you know what I have seen?'

Vratu shook his head no.

'I am old, my friend. I have seen things you could not have seen, been to places you could not know. I have met many tribes, many people, but until today I had heard only whispers of the people called the Illawann. Now I am here drinking with one.'

The old man leaned forward. 'I have seen much of your kind. You keep your distance, and you must feel so alone. When others come you respond the only way you know, with fear and anger, and when all is done and nothing has changed, you must wonder why you fight so hard to keep it that way, when what shrinks the distance between us is our want for the same thing.

'I can tell you of places where people live as thick as bees in a hive. People with skin as dark as the night sky, living beyond stretches of water that meet with the sky, beyond mountains as high as the sun. There is movement out there; movement that will see our children live in places you and I cannot begin to imagine.'

He settled back and a warm smile spread across his face. 'Men like you and I have sat like this before; will sit like this many times more. And for all we are, and all we may become, where are we headed if we do not?'

There was a long pause. Vratu looked down into his drink, the colour of Abinyor's lips.

'I feel an age approaching,' the Unatks said.

The sound of children's laughter drifted in through the windows, blending with the crackle of the hearth. Vratu looked up relieved. He would live longer yet.

Huge fires and regularly spaced lamps lit up the village precincts for the feast. Out of respect to Hrad-Uik the visitors did their best to keep their manner abstemious, but something momentous had passed, promising times were ahead, and the occasion needed a fitting entry into history. They even had the legendary Unatks Vahichiwa there as witness to the achievement. They slaughtered a young bull for the main course, when this wasn't nearly enough they haggled some more and another was slaughtered.

Not long into the evening Vratu decided to pay his respects to Hrad-Uik and speak with Abinyor. But as he passed through the main room headed for the sleeping section Borchek stood up from the table and moved quickly to block his path. A tense silence followed as they faced each other – Borchek with a threatening look, Vratu wondering what he had done to earn it. More confused than offended, Vratu left Hrad-Uik's family to themselves.

By his standards a curious night followed. Everywhere he saw men enjoying themselves while out of sight in a dark room people were grieving. Men with solicitous frowns filed in and out of the house of Hrad-Uik to fulfil obligations before returning to their places to appease appetites for food and drink. The few men present with a vague notion of Vratu's tongue would wave him over, and he would sit down amongst them and respond as best as he could to various well-meaning remarks before finding a reason to excuse himself. Much later, having completed his rounds, he settled down amongst a group of friendly faces where he could keep an eye on the house of Hrad-Uik.

At last he saw Abinyor emerge. Vratu stood. He had only taken a few steps when he saw Segros heading her way. Vratu stopped and watched him go up to Abinyor and put his hands on her shoulders in a kind manner. Abinyor bowed her head, then Segros noticed Vratu watching and a triumphant sneer appeared on his face. They held each other's gaze until Vratu felt silly and turned away. With nowhere else in mind to go he joined his bovine friends over at the enclosures.

A moving shadow caught his attention and he found himself in the company of Kulej.

'I know your trouble, I think,' the Henghai said.

Vratu looked him over, reminded of the man's perception. 'If these were my people,' he told him, 'we would be singing mourning songs.'

Kulej gazed at him solidly. 'Why did you come back?'

Vratu didn't know if Kulej meant that evening, or with the boy days ago. The safer reply was the latter. 'To give the boy back to – '

'No,' Kulej cut him off, waving his finger. 'Why ask Romoyr for his word for peace? Why not turn and go, be on your way long ago?'

Vratu stayed quiet.

'I tell you why,' Kulej said seriously. 'You a part of this now. You know what to do, have known all along. Same for many here. You . . . me . . .' He shrugged indifferently. 'Abinyor.'

Vratu's spine stiffened. Perhaps the Henghai knew. Perhaps everyone knew. And if they cared either way they would have done something about it. 'He breaks her spirit.'

'There is work for them, yes,' Kulej conceded. 'It will pass. She grows still, will learn to be happy with him. All girls the same.'

'No,' Vratu disagreed. 'Abinyor is not the same.'

A bull gave a series of loud groans and Kulej waited until it stopped. 'You ask me once how I speak your tongue,' he said. 'I learn in village of his people. My father and his father were friends and I know Segros for a long, long time. He has hard life, has many wounds. Why give him more?'

Vratu turned longingly toward the house of Hrad-Uik. Kulej saw where he looked. 'There has been too much fighting,' he said. 'Too much blood. Way now is forward. Come and talk, you will see.' He put a hand on Vratu's shoulder as he left.

Vratu returned to his brooding. A damp chill rolled in, the beasts dropped their heads and the village became quiet. One by one groups broke up and guests settled down to sleep beneath the moonlit autumn sky. He pushed himself off the fence and decided to try Hrad-Uik's house one last time.

In the main room he found Borchek and Yanukz slumped over the table snoring softly. By the corner of the forward wall Nuridj lay curled beneath a bearskin, and through the walkway came a faint glow from the far end of the sleeping quarters. As Vratu stepped toward it a voice from behind stopped him.

'Only the man's family dare enter that room.'

Vratu turned around. In a dark corner sat Segros, mug in hand. 'Why are you here, Illawann man?' he slurred.

Vratu returned his unfriendly glare and said nothing.

'I have been watching you.' Segros' voice contained only the mildest trace of an accent. 'You have a reason for being here.'

'These are my friends.'

'Hah!' Segros cackled. 'I beg to know why someone like you chooses to use that word so freely here.'

Vratu was quick to make the connection between his mug and his behaviour. He watched and waited.

Segros moved forward a fraction into the light and Vratu saw an insulted look on his face. 'You think these people are your friends? I thought so once. Prepare to receive them, for they will follow you wherever you go. When they come into your land it will never feel the same again. When you go home, look at your people. See their skin, see their faces. Cherish it. For you will share that with them as well, until it too is gone.'

Vratu had met madmen before. Now he thought he'd met another.

'I know your kind, Illawann man. Krul . . . Ukmaar . . . Ubnakar.' Segros took satisfaction at seeing Vratu's eyes narrow with suspicion. 'And other men soon to disappear from memory.'

Vratu regarded him warily. 'Why do you tell me this?'

'They asked if you want to see what became of your people. You won't find them. These people have swallowed them up.' He clamped his jaws together in a biting action. 'Those who lived here once are long gone. Your people, my people. I hear you have made some powerful friends. Heed this warning, you will remember it in the years to come.' He waved a finger at him. 'They will use you for their own purposes. They do this to my family and they will do it to you. What makes it so tragic is you give them the means.'

'I see before me a man who has lived his life with a full belly,' Vratu said. 'Why do you complain?'

'Uh! Very good. I see I talk to a clever man!' Segros raised his mug to him. 'We live off their fat and it makes us slow and lazy. You will be the same. You will hold out your hand and they will trick you into keeping it there. When you sit at their table feasting, making your body weak and your mind slow, ask them if they know the names of those who were buried here long before they came. Tell them about your lost beliefs and forgotten gods.'

He eased himself back into his corner. 'You hide in your forests, but you are already cursed. Their dead will have their vengeance, you will see. If there are gods, they will forsake your people as they have forsaken mine. So go home, Illawann man, while you still have one. There is nothing for you here.'

So this was the husband of Abinyor, Vratu thought. A man who made the shadows of his corner the darkest in the room.

Borchek stirred in his sleep. The breath caught in his throat briefly, then he shifted and resettled. After glancing over Yanukz and Nuridj to check they were still sleeping, Vratu faced the glow coming from the far end of the house.

Only the man's family dare enter that room.

A few steps away lay a man who had opened his arms wide when he had returned. Had taken him into his own home, treated him more like a son than a guest. In this house without sound he could almost hear his voice. His feet moved forward of their own accord.

Inside Hrad-Uik's dimly lit room, his wife and three daughters were seated on the bed. A gurgle sounded from the lungs of the man dying beside them and saliva dripped from his lips. The only other sign of life was the slow rising and falling of his chest.

Nankyi looked up and beckoned Vratu in with a sad smile and a nod. He moved forward, leaned over the old man and put a hand on his forehead.

'This is your last fight,' he whispered, 'and it will be over soon. I will sit with you because you are scared. I am Vratu, take heart knowing that I am your friend.'

In the deep of night, in that drawn out phase between midnight and dawn, Barak Hrad-Uik quietly passed away. His lungs deflated one last time, his rattled breathing ceased and he sank a little deeper into his bed. The women bowed their heads and moaned as a fresh spurt of tears rolled down their cheeks. Abinyor kneeled by the bed and rested her forehead against her father's. Nankyi sat down beside him and picked up his limp hand, the look on her face as lifeless as his.

Vratu respectfully left them then. In the main room Borchek looked up at him with tired eyes, and understood. He rose and nudged Yanukz awake, then went over to Nuridj in the corner and prodded him with his foot. In the shadows Segros stirred, gathered himself up and followed the sons of Hrad-Uik into the sleeping quarters. Vratu watched them go. The crying coming from the deathroom was quiet, the condolences were whispered. It was over.

The maple tree he had slept beneath on a cold winter's night long ago stood dark and silent on the village fringe. He headed over. Something in the foliage above rustled as he lay down on his back. Sleep seemed far away.

The sky was clear and the three-quarter moon shone so brightly it hurt his eyes. For some time he gazed at the heavens, thinking about the suffering he had seen and the mark it had left on him. The vastness of space scattered his worries and filled him with a profound sense of peace, and perhaps it was this sense of peace, like that moment just before one's mind passed into sleep, that made possible what came next. For like a ray of light through his murky thoughts his true purpose in all of this was revealed, and it surprised him that he hadn't seen it before.

He knew what he had to do now. It was bold, it was dangerous, it would have consequences, and it was consistent with everything he had done so far. Step by step he had been pushed – by his shaman, the blizzard, the wolves and the savagery – to this village, to this one night. The signs were there all along. Only now could he see them, as clear and reassuring as the moon and stars above.

'See me now, friend,' he said to the heavens, 'because I can see you more clearly now. I have been far and I am returned, and now I must be true to what you have made of me.'

His Walk led here, had always led here. There was one thing left to do.

Borchek laid a hand on Abinyor's shoulder. 'Leave him now,' he said, fighting the choking sensation in his throat.

She sat on the bed next to Nankyi. Everyone else had left. Hrad-Uik lay at peace on his back. They had cleaned his face and tidied his hair. He looked as if he were sleeping.

'Soon,' she replied. Borchek looked her over and decided to let her be.

Fatigue overwhelmed him as he walked away. As eldest son he had much to do now, and much more lay ahead, and the thought made him wearier still. He lay down on his bed and before he knew it had succumbed to the mercy of sleep.

It seemed he had scarcely closed his eyes when a hand rocked him awake.

'Borchek! Wake up! Wake up!'

He lifted himself up on his elbows and saw Yanukz's worried face behind a lamp. 'Hurry!' his brother pleaded softly, motioning with his hands. 'Come quickly.'

'What's wrong?'

'It's Abinyor.'

Borchek sat fully upright. 'What?'

'You need to speak to her.'

'What is it?'

'Come outside and see.'

As they left the room Yanukz put a finger to his lips to hush him, indicating at the same time the glow coming from his father's room where Nanyki silently grieved.

The village grounds were flooded with light from the moon, clear-edged against the cloudless night sky, lighting up their breath and illuminating clumps of sleeping bodies. Embers glowed from spent fires and smoke tainted the sweet-smelling air.

Weaving his way past prostrate guests, Borchek followed Yanukz down to the river. There in the moonlight he recognised Abinyor, Nuridj, and the native man Vratu, and heard the raised pitch of his sister and brother arguing. The river shimmered behind a small canoe wallowing at the water's edge.

Abinyor saw them coming and raised her hand aggressively. 'Go away!' she warned. 'I knew I shouldn't have told anyone.'

'He needs to know,' Yanukz said.

'He would have known,' she answered heatedly. 'Later.'

Borchek asked, 'Will someone tell me what is happening?'

'She is leaving,' Yanukz answered.

In the silence that followed Borchek gathered his wits fast. 'Are you going somewhere, little sister?' he asked carefully.

'You know I have to.'

'What is this?'

'Just . . . wish me well.'

Borchek looked past her, to Vratu. 'Are you going with *him*?'

'Yes.'

'To where?'

'I didn't ask.'

He moved forward and looked inside the small dugout. A few bulky bags and loose clothing lay inside. 'Why would you want to do that?'

'Because I cannot go back.'

'But this is madness.'

Yanukz said, 'That's what we tried to tell her.'

'Listen to me,' Borchek said kindly. 'We know what is happening between you and Segros. But stay and we will see to it, you and me. Don't go just to spite him.'

She kneeled down to fidget with something in the canoe. Borchek looked at Vratu standing to the side, wisely silent. All at once, like a smack on the head, it hit him.

'Oh no,' Borchek lamented. 'Sister . . .' He laughed then, hoping this would impress on her the folly of it. 'Have you taken to a savage?'

She didn't answer.

'Sister . . . little sister,' Borchek repeated, pleading with his hands. 'Are you sure? The moment passes and you'll be back to where you started and a long way from home.'

'Then I would be no worse off than before.'

Borchek stopped laughing. He turned to the native and gave him a menacing look. Still Vratu said nothing.

'Abinyor,' Borchek groaned. 'You can't go like this. Don't let Segros do this to you. Give yourself time. This needs to be thought through.'

'No!' Abinyor retorted, straightening up to face him with her hands clenched by her sides. 'If I did, I wouldn't dare go! And go I must, for all our sakes.' She lowered her voice. 'If I stay you will kill him.'

Never before had Borchek seen her more determined. In times past, when the time came for arguing, he had always got his way. Now he sensed his run was over.

'You're right,' she said. 'I do need time, but far from here. Perhaps then I'll come home. I can't say when and I don't want to make promises. I know this could be a mistake, but I don't care. It has been too long since I have been given a choice, and this is what I want. What *I* want!' she repeated, thumping her chest. 'He has given me so much hope, in so short a time. Surely that means something?'

'When did you decide this?'

'Until he talked to me just now I never thought about it. And now that he has asked me to go it would be easier to lie down and die than say no.'

'But would you be happy?'

She raised her hands and laughed for the first time. 'Why would I not be?'

'What about Papa?'

'I know,' she said. 'But it's over now and there's nothing more I can do for him.'

Borchek looked over his brothers. 'How many people have you

told?'

'Only who is here. I didn't want to tell anyone. You need to look Segros in the eye and tell him you knew nothing.'

'Oh sister,' Borchek said with a chuckle. 'All that tempts me is the look on his face when I tell him you left with our blessing.'

She wiped her eyes and the moonlight shone on her teeth when she smiled. 'You and Vratu are the same, do you know that?'

'Is that a good thing or bad?'

She sniffled again, this time though with amusement, and he felt his resistance buckling. 'People will want to know why you left without saying anything,' he said feebly.

'If I don't leave now I never will.'

They all waited. There was no one left to convince; it was all up to their new family head. A more difficult induction to his new authority he could not have imagined. He looked out over the shining river for a long time.

'All right,' he said at last, shaking his head resignedly. 'Why not?'

Yanukz said, 'There will be trouble.'

Borchek scoffed, then bowed his head. 'Go if you must, sister. Go and be happy. But tell this man of yours,' he sharpened his voice and looked up at her, 'the same as I said to Segros. If he does anything bad to you, or doesn't look after you, I'll kick him so hard up the crack it will take – '

'Borchek.'

' – at least three men to remove my – '

'Borchek!' She put a hand on his shoulder. *'Enough.'*

Borchek chortled softly. 'Go then. Go before I change my mind and fight you all over again.'

She took him in her arms and held him tightly. 'Please say goodbye to everyone for me,' she said. 'Especially Nankyi and Szanaj-kik and Tivikeh. Tell them I am sorry it has to be like this. I will see them again in happier times.'

'They will want to know why you didn't tell them yourself.'

'I don't want to argue with more people than I have to.'

Borchek took a step back, holding her at arm's length. 'Would you really have gone without telling me?' he asked, adding a note of hurt to his voice.

'I thought of it.'

'Why didn't you?'

Abinyor pointed to Vratu. 'He wanted you to know.'

The native had been standing there watching quietly the whole time. Borchek disengaged his sister and took a step toward him. His features were hard to see in the dark, but his hawklike poise was as crisp as the chill. 'You have a strange way of coming and going, friend.'

Then Vratu spoke, in that distinctive, guttural voice of his kind Borchek had never warmed to. He turned to his sister. 'What did he say?'

She leaned over the canoe and pushed a few items aside to make space for a seat. 'He sees you as his brother now,' she said without looking up.

The moonlit river flickered with the ripples they made pushing the canoe into the water. The sons of Hrad-Uik watched quietly as their sister disappeared from sight.

Borchek lay on his bed staring up at the dark ceiling, hands beneath his head, elbows out. Many thoughts went through his mind. His sister walking away from her marriage would do more than just set a few tongues wagging. Yanukz was right. There may well be trouble, but he had not been entirely joking with his comment about it being worth the look on Segros' face when he told him she had gone.

Occasionally he questioned the wisdom of letting her leave, which brought him back to the native. He felt a much deeper respect for the man now. And not because he had, at considerable personal risk, saved the life of a boy and averted a racial bloodbath. What impressed Borchek the most was that instead of taking Abinyor away without anyone being the wiser, Vratu had virtually *asked* for his permission. To a man whose family meant everything, the gesture of respect surpassed anything his own people had ever given him. Yes, he thought, he could grow to like this savage.

He imagined his sister paddling away. A tired arm would not slow her now. She would be in the front, following the gleam of the river and not talking, for much would be going through her mind. Just like him.

Already he missed her. Sometimes a memory made him grin in the dark, and he held on to the distraction as long as he could, trying not to think about his father lying cold and dead on a bed only a whisper away, for then the great weight of grief would descend, and the path of his future looked lonelier than ever.

The night was the longest of his life. Every so often his eyelids flickered rapidly and he felt sleep not far away, but he couldn't go that final distance. The straw matting beneath his furs crunched loudly as he tossed and turned.

Eventually he gave up. Moonlight streaming through the windows guided him out of the house.

The silver orb had sunk considerably. Shadows stretched further over the village grounds but everything else looked the same. The cold made him shiver as he walked over to the stalls where the cattle slept. As of tomorrow night, he decided, he would take them inside out of the cold.

Mo-ah's outline showed sharply and his hide glistened with a coat of moonlit dew. On seeing Borchek approach he took to his feet and gave his characteristic snort.

Borchek walked to the front of the pen, slid the top plank off its support and leaned it against a post. The bull-calf scuffed at the furthest end and grunted ungraciously. Borchek removed the lower plank and waited. The beast went calm and Borchek felt a curious communion between them as they watched each other through the dark.

Keeping to his side of the fence, Borchek paced back and forth waving his hands and clapping, but the stupid brute just stood there snorting and moaning.

'Oh, by the . . .'

At last the bull-calf trotted out the open end. Picking up pace he ran out over the fields, kicking up sparkling moisture and leaving a dark swathe through the stubble.

Borchek watched until the dark shape melted into the night. Then he went inside to join Nankyi sitting by his father's bed, waiting for dawn.

Epilogue

Konli of Usonoli opened his eyes.

Whenever he woke of late it took a while before he could remember where he was. Strange, he thought, this time it felt like he had returned from somewhere a lifetime ago. Noises outside were weak but he knew this was just a measure of his bad hearing.

Vaguely he became aware of a presence in the room. He rolled over and saw a boy standing near the entrance.

'Unatks Konli-Uik?' the boy said again.

'Yes?' he answered, wondering why everyone still used this title.

'They are ready.'

'Yes . . . yes.'

The boy left. Konli eased his protesting body off the bed and dressed. Tonight, he chose brightly coloured textiles and jewellery of origins lost from his memory. His house seemed to echo the creak of his old bones as he limped past the wall-lamps, muttering the language of a man tempting senility.

At the village centre he found the young men and boys who had come to hear him speak already seated. Konli of Usonoli took pride in his reputation as a master storyteller, and tonight they would listen to a story he told to perfection. He sat down on a large, grooved chair, and the gathering fell into silence.

'Strange . . . how the destiny of an entire people can be shaped more by the deeds of the few than its masses.' His voice was clear and strong, as if the very substance of the tale he was about to tell unleashed a power of its own.

'If you are a man of good heart, then you will cry more for what you lose than what you have never owned. If you are a man of honour, then you will wish to right your own wrongs before seeking vengeance on others. If you are a man of your people, expect those

393

closest to your heart to bring you the most pain. And if you are as blind as all men, the day will come when you will shun the man who would do you good, you will doubt his word when he speaks nothing but truth, and if you do not know him at the time, you will surely know him when he is gone, if for no other reason than the hole he will leave in your heart.

'Tonight, I shall tell you the story of the man who taught me these things without ever knowing. A man of whom you hear many truths and untruths. But you will hear the truth from those who called him a wise man, a good man, for his story is our story, and his Walk is our Walk. I have heard him called many things. I have heard him called Uru, Unatks, spirit man, wandering man. Most of you knew him as the Shaman of Uryak. It is true, he went by many titles. But I knew him,' he spoke softer now, 'when he was Vratu of the Illawann.'

Men who had heard the story over and again stepped forward to better hear. Konli of Usonoli had a way of speaking that ensured the story lost none of its appeal with each telling.

'We never see his kind any more. Alas, they have taken their secrets with them. Were it not for him you may never have known they were there at all, for they leave little sign of their passing, and he came to us at a time of instability and fear, when a stranger's face was not to be trusted, when war cries filled the air and songs of mourning drifted like mists through broken villages.'

Immersed in his memories, he lowered his head and closed his eyes. This story brought as much sadness as joy and was not that easy to tell. He needed to ease himself into it.

When he looked up he did not see an audience of young men and boys. In their place he saw a gathered mass of humanity the like of which he had never seen before or since, and felt a will like a strong wind in the powerful silence, while before him kneeled a man of tired muscle and brooding visage, head lifted high as he swore an oath, and beside him, a woman's face shining with pride and love. And he had closed his eyes to sear the image into his head, lest he ever confuse it with a dream.

The scene faded and the faces of fertile youth came back to him, as eager as those in his image.

'It is clear to me now,' he continued. 'This is where it starts. I will tell you his story and correct all that has been said and slandered, and then you can tell those who come after you, to keep him in our hearts and minds forever.'

A smile freed itself from deep inside. Of all his achievements in life his last came down to this, and simple though it was, he felt a great honour that it fell upon him to deliver.

And death he no longer feared, for he knew that only then, soon now, would he see his friend again.

Ric Szabo

Made in the USA
Middletown, DE
14 April 2020